Big Witch Energy

MOLLY HARPER

sourcebooks
casablanca

Published by Sourcebooks Casablanca, an imprint of Sourcebooks
P.O. Box 4410, Naperville, Illinois 60567-4410
(630) 961-3900
sourcebooks.com

Originally published in 2023 as an audiobook by Audible Originals.

Cataloging-in-Publication Data is on file with the Library of Congress.

Printed and bound in Canada.
MBP 10 9 8 7 6 5 4 3 2 1

For the friends who always listen—no matter how weird or random the problem—I am so grateful for you.

Chapter 1
Caroline

TRUDGING HOME THROUGH SNOW FROM her first felony, covered in a crust of fake blueberry pie filling, was not the way that Caroline Wilton planned on spending her one night off. But life as one of Starfall Point's resident witches-slash-ghost wranglers had a way of happening when Caroline planned to just sit at home, trying to read.

Her crime spree had started off innocently enough. Early Friday, Caroline had been inhaling her usual absurdly large post-double-shift coffee at Starfall Grounds when she heard Willard Tremont complaining that he'd been having pest problems at Tremont's Treasures. While not quite as grand as some of the other shops on the island, Willard's shop catered to tourists' thirst to take a little piece of the island's ambience home with them.

"I'm telling you. I've been open for thirty years and I've never had problems like this," Willard grumbled to Petra Gilinsky, the coffee shop's owner and operator. Starfall Grounds—just across the street from Tremont's—was a modern oasis in the middle of traditional Main Square shops, all bright copper and deep-blue calm.

A display case running the length of the store featured sumptuous pastries, fresh-baked by Petra and her twin brother, Iggy.

"I keep hearing weird noises, like something scratching all along the floorboards," Willard continued. "I never can figure out where it's coming from, and it's all hours of the day, doesn't matter whether I've got someone in the shop or not. Sometimes, I swear, it sounds like whispers."

Caroline damn near choked at that. Faint whispers from all corners of a room? Scratching noises? From her experiences at Shaddow House, the island's haunted epicenter, Caroline knew those were classics sign of ghost activity.

"Sorry," Caroline said hoarsely, pounding on her chest as Willard and Petra turned toward her. "Went down the wrong way. Good cinnamon roll, Petra."

Willard gave Caroline a confused look but continued, "It's gotta be mice or rats or something, but I'm not finding chew marks on any of the furniture. And I'm not finding droppings."

"Yes, please mention rats and droppings a little louder while leaning against my bakery counter, Willard," Petra deadpanned, waving airily at the empty coffee shop. "You're lucky it's a slow morning, or you'd lose your rugalach privileges."

"Sorry, Petra," Willard said, flushing red under his more-salt-than-pepper hair. Willard was approaching seventy and a creature of habit. Petra's cherry rugalach was a major component of his morning routine. "I've gone all distracted with this thing. I could lose customers if I don't get rid of...whatever this is before the summer season starts up."

"I told you not to buy that stuff from Sally Fairlight's

niece-in-law," Petra snorted, shaking her head. "Lindsay was way too excited about clearing all of Sally's stuff out of her new 'summer home.' She didn't even wait a week before 'de-Sallying' the place. There's gotta be some bad karma that comes with that."

"It was just a few things," Willard huffed. "But Sally *was* awfully house-proud. Maybe I should have just turned her away, let Lindsay have a yard sale."

"Eh, Sally would have hated that," Petra conceded, topping off Willard's tall black coffee. "Strangers picking through her stuff and haggling down to the nickel."

"I only bought the lot because I thought her collection of old cake stands was perfect for the store," Willard sighed. "My own ma had one of them when I was a kid. Pressed glass. A wedding present from her family back in Raleigh. I even put some of those pie-shaped air freshener things from Nell Heslop's candle shop in them, like a demo? They smell like real blueberry. I thought it would give the customer an idea of what they could do with it."

Willard just looked so upset, so bewildered, that Caroline decided then and there that she and her coven would do what they could to get whatever was troubling Tremont's—even if it was just rats. But Caroline was pretty sure it wasn't rats. Also, the fake blueberry air freshener pies at Starfall Wicks were disgusting— small, thin wax pie-shaped molds filled with a loose, gelatinous air freshener goo that jiggled inside the shell when tilted back and forth.

And they smelled like Barbie's rejected Dream Home air freshener, so really, they were doing Willard two favors.

Caroline wasn't sure exactly when they started thinking of

themselves as a coven, but that's what they were, a group of witches working magic together, depending on each other. They were family, a word that was particularly vital to three people who'd had a hard time finding one that worked for them.

Plus, it was a better word than "trio." Trio made them sound like a jazz band that played at corporate events.

Getting into Willard's closed shop had been easy enough. It was well known to locals that Willard kept the key to the back door under a plaster frog. It wasn't exactly a secure vault.

"I don't feel right about this," Alice Seastairs had whispered in the midnight darkness, holding the flashlight as Caroline unlocked the door. As always, Alice was dressed appropriately for a spot of light breaking and entering—black sweater, black jeans, black ski cap pulled over her shock of penny-bright copper hair. "Breaking and entering Mr. Tremont's shop. He's always been so kind to me, even if we are competitors."

"We're not breaking... We're just entering." Riley Denton-Everett had selected a "plausible deniability outfit" of jeans, snow boots, and a periwinkle hoodie that made her gray eyes appear bluer. Her plan was, if they were caught, to just pretend she was taking a nighttime walk in northern Michigan's early spring snow.

Caroline supposed that she and Alice were meant to be running away while Riley was lying her ass off. She thought maybe Riley was depending on the general curiosity about her—the newest local on the island—to carry her over the "potential criminal activity" conversational bumps. Riley was resourceful enough to make little annoyances like that work for her.

"It's not my fault that Elliot's been hiding his shop key in the same place for twenty years," Caroline muttered. They all relaxed ever so slightly when the door popped open without a sound.

Tremont's was a homier alternative to Alice's shop, Superior Antiques, where her unfriendly grandparents reigned with an iron fist. Tremont's had the *smell* of a proper antique shop, all lemon furniture polish and dust and—Caroline guessed—long-forgotten dreams. Huge stained-glass panels, harvested from old churches off-island, cast rainbow splashes of light from the front display windows. Old-school tricycles hung suspended from the ceiling by piano wire. Mismatched glass cabinets displayed silver candelabras, porcelain figurines, overblown costume jewelry, tin windup toys, anything and everything that might catch a shopper's attention if they could fight through the sensory overload long enough to focus on one item.

Caroline didn't even want to think about how many items in this place were "attachment objects"—something that meant so much to the dead in life or its significance in the person's death, that their spirit stayed connected to that item. Riley lived in a house full of them, with more than a thousand ghostly roommates. Caroline didn't know *how* she did it.

"You know, I'm concerned that, from the outside, a bunch of flashlights bobbing around a darkened shop might attract unwanted attention," she said, glancing around at the charming chaos of the interior. "Somebody sees that through the window, it's a pretty broad hint that this place is being burgled."

"Actually, I was thinking we might use this as an opportunity to practice some of our more 'basic witch' non-ghost-related magic skills, light a few of the candles in this place?" Riley grinned, gesturing to the displayed flammables. "If anybody sees candles glowing through the windows, they'll just think Willard is adding a little romantic ambience to the store."

Riley had seemed fixated on lighting candles with her mind ever since she'd gained her magic. Caroline was a little concerned.

"Do we really have time for that?" Caroline asked. "Isn't time of the essence when you're committing a minor felony?"

"Is there such a thing as a minor felony?" Alice wondered aloud. "If it's a question of lighters, Riley, I think Willard keeps one under the register. Also, why does Willard have so many candles in a shop full of flammable items?"

"He thinks it adds ambience," Caroline told her. "Even if they're unlit most of the time."

"Come on, I think it will be good for us, practicing a basic magical skill under duress," Riley implored. "It's not like the more hostile ghosts give us 'try again' chances while we're working with them, and that's with skills that we're actually pretty good at."

"Does 'haven't gotten us seriously injured yet' qualify as 'pretty good'?" Alice asked.

"You are *grumpy* when you're asked to stay up past midnight," Riley marveled.

"I get up at five thirty every morning to open the store," Alice countered.

Caroline frowned. "But you don't open until eleven."

"Yes, but my grandparents call the landline at six thirty, and if I'm not there, they pitch a fit that can be heard all the way from Boca Raton," Alice sighed. "It's easier just to get up early, even if it means keeping old-lady hours."

"We have got to get you a new job, sweetie," Caroline told her.

"Maybe Willard is hiring," Alice snorted. "Meanwhile, we've spent more time talking about me than it probably would have taken to light the candles with magical means or otherwise."

"I already did one!" Riley said, doing a happy little dance as she gestured to the flickering flame of a nearby hurricane lamp. Her cap of dark-blond Denton hair bounced around her elfin face as she enjoyed her moment of victory. Magic had come to them all late in life, and to Riley, every successful spell that did not result in loss of limb or eyebrow was a moment to be savored. "I did what Aunt Nora's books said, pictured the bright light of the candle, and I could feel it growing in my chest, like the flame started near my heart! And *boom*, fire! Well, not *boom*. Fortunately, there was no *boom*, but still, I have made fire! With magic!"

"While we were talking? That's cheating!" Alice gasped, just a little too loudly.

"Could we not yell while committing the minor felony?" Caroline asked, glancing toward the front windows of the shop. It was supremely unhelpful that the stained glass kept her from being able to see people approaching from the outside. But she could *hear* something, scratching noises from the far corner of the room, near a particularly creepy display of ventriloquism dummies. It was like her brain couldn't quite catch up to the noise, but she suspected the horrors of unsecured puppets had something to do with that.

"Still not sure that's a thing," Riley said, still smirking. "And just think of how many candles we could light if we did it *together*."

"We could burn down the entire shop, which is a *big* felony," Caroline noted.

"That's a good point," Riley admitted, chewing her lip. "But you still want to try it, don't you?"

"Well, yes, *clearly*, I do," Caroline shot back, laughing despite herself. She joined hands with Riley and Alice, her coven, the sisters she chose, even if the magic had chosen for her first. The familiar sizzle of that unearthly force zipped up her arm, straight to her heart. It made it so much easier for Caroline to imagine the warm glow of a flame building inside of her, wanting to burn, wanting to *be*. They giggled together, nervous about trying one of the more practical areas of magic that seemed to elude them, for some reason. She closed her eyes and felt the warmth growing, just as Riley described. It spread to the air around them and when Caroline opened her eyes, the room was bathed in golden light from dozens of flames—in lanterns, in candles, even a little Marilyn-Monroe-in-the-fluted-white-dress votive whose taste level Caroline found seriously lacking.

"Look at that!" Caroline laughed, clapping her hands over her mouth. Alice rolled her eyes, but she was laughing too.

"You have to admit, that's pretty cool," Riley said, her gray eyes glowing in triumph.

Caroline heard it again, the scratching that wasn't quite scratching. It *did* sound like whispering, and not particularly happy whispering. It sounded irritable, like the mutterings of someone who didn't think they'd be heard.

"It is *very* cool, and we don't appear to be in danger of committing arson, so let's get down to business, shall we?" Alice suggested brightly. She placed her hand on the nearest display counter.

The whispering got louder.

"OK, everybody else hears that, right?" Riley said quietly, glancing around the now well-lit room.

"Sounds like my grandmother after a couple of martinis," Alice said, tugging at her ear gently like she was trying to pop it.

"I'll have you know that I have never been drunk a day in my life!" a cranky voice rasped to their right.

Caroline should have known better. One of the weirder parts of Caroline's new magical gifts was being able to detect which objects were attached to a ghost. Or vice versa, really. While several items in the antique shop gave her nerves a small ping, the four cake stands—elevated cake plates with clear domes meant to display baked goods—to her left were sending psychic shivers down her spine. It just happened to be the counter where Alice was resting her hand.

As Willard had promised, each stand contained a wax replica blueberry pie air freshener. Caroline was very grateful the smell was contained under glass. The cake stands weren't the prettiest thing in the shop—but they exuded a certain power. These glass pieces—the largest fancy handblown glass, the others cheaper pressed pieces—were significant, especially to Sally Fairlight, who appeared behind them, looking *very* annoyed. And Alice's hand was resting right on top of the largest cake stand in the center of the counter. Of course, Alice's expert eye would be attracted to the *good* one—the favorite in Sally's collection, based on her reaction.

"Don't touch that!" Sally's ghost yanked the glass stand back, out of Alice's hands. Sally had been a "forceful" woman in life. She certainly hadn't gotten *weaker* after death. The lid tumbled off its plinth in the struggle, rolling on its rounded side. A wave of synthetic fruit smell struck Caroline in the face, knocking her back a step.

Sally's translucent fingers wrapped around the round glass knob on top of the cake stand, pulling it back. A wax pie had fallen into the lid in the struggle. Its weirdly fragile wax shell broke, and the unnatural berry filling oozed out. The ghost peered down at the mess. And then she grinned as if she'd just granted a gift and an idea all at once.

"Oh, no," Riley whispered.

A ghost could only physically interact with its own attachment object. And Sally had just figured out that she could use her cake stand lids to sling those horrendous-smelling blueberry bombs at the humans.

This was a problem.

"Mrs. Fairlight, you don't want to do that," Caroline said, holding her hands up and using her most soothing "addressing the drunk customer" voice as Sally swung the lid toward them, splattering the case behind them with fake fruit gel. "You don't want to make a mess of Willard's nice, clean shop."

"*She* called me a drunk," the old woman snarled, pointing a long, bony finger at Alice. Somehow, she was moving multiple cake stands. She was only supposed to have one attachment object. How was that possible?

"No, I didn't," said Alice. "I was talking about my own grandmother. I didn't mean anything by it, Mrs. Fairlight, I promise."

"Also, just how many of these stands are you attached to?" Riley cried. "You are *not* following the ghost rules!"

"This *whole collection* is mine!" Sally roared back. "And I don't want it here at Willard's! No one asked me!"

Sometimes, Caroline forgot how fast Alice was on her feet. When Sally picked up a stand to throw another wax pie, Alice managed to dance out of the way, dodging, while Riley's feet were doused in cobalt goo.

"Oh, come on!" Riley cried as her feet squelched through the mess. "These are my *good* snow boots!"

"Young people used to have more respect," Sally huffed.

"Well, really, we're not all that young!" Alice replied in an attempt to placate Sally, who was having none of it. How many of those air freshener things had Willard loaded into the cake stands, anyway?

Alice danced left to right as another wax pie vaulted off a stand and splattered against Caroline's stomach, covering her entire torso in cerulean glaze. All three of the living women froze.

"Aw, honey," Riley tsked, her tone sympathetic. "And that was your favorite early spring coat."

"Caroline, I'm so sorry!" Alice gasped as one more pie launched off a nearby stand and smacked Alice in the chest.

"All right, that is *enough*!" Alice hissed. "Ma'am, you will stop throwing these vile pie things at us *right now* and listen to what we have to say."

"So much for the whole, 'trying to stay quiet during the commission of a minor felony' thing," Caroline muttered.

"Still not a thing!" Alice cried, pointing at Caroline without looking at her, making Caroline snicker. Riley couldn't help but follow suit. And soon, as she always did, Alice was laughing too, but she managed to hide it by biting her lips.

"Fine," Sally harrumphed. "I'm all out of pies anyway. And I'll have you know, I never touched a drop in my life. My grandmother worked with the temperance movement!."

"Yes, Mrs. Fairlight, you mentioned it a couple of times,"

Caroline said carefully. "And I'm sure Alice didn't mean anything by it. She didn't realize it was you."

"I didn't," Alice assured her. "I'm very sorry."

"Not that you would know anything about me anyway," Sally sniffed. "Your grandparents never saw fit to let you close to anybody around here. The Proctors, all high-and-mighty. Thought they were too good for island folks—not that we wanted them around, thank you very much."

Riley glanced at Alice, who shrugged. "It's not as if she's *wrong*."

"I don't know this one," Sally said, chin-pointing at Riley. "You'd be Nora Denton's niece, then? Never got around to visiting little old me, I suppose."

"Sorry, I kinda had my hands full," Riley told her.

"Well, I'm sure Nora left you a pretty big job with Shaddow House," Sally conceded. "I've felt the tug of it, ever since my heart stopped. Useless thing hasn't done what it's supposed to for the last twenty years."

"You feel the house 'tugging' at you?" Caroline asked.

"That's something we haven't heard before," Riley said, frowning.

"Maybe the locks are getting more powerful since we started, well, fiddling with them?" Alice suggested.

Trust Alice to deem the attempted destruction of malevolent magical objects that trapped ghosts in place as "fiddling."

"Focus," Riley reminded Caroline quietly. "Miss Sally, would you be willing to separate from your cake stand collection? Move on to the afterlife? Because you're upsetting poor Willard, and you might scare off his customers. You don't want to close his shop."

Sally opened her mouth to protest, and Riley added quickly, "I know you don't mean to, but by their very nature, ghosts have a way of unsettling the living, just by being in the same room."

"Well, I don't know about any of this ghost business, but I'm not about to let go of my glassware just yet," Sally said. "I can't believe the nerve of my nephew's rotten wife. Some of these belonged to my *mother*; she brought them all the way up from Virginia when she followed my father here. And I added to her collection along the way. She used these all my life, at every special occasion, just to let us know how important our birthdays were, our graduations, our baby showers. The collection was supposed to go to *family*. I told Harmon that, so many times. And he just let that Lindsay just throw them away like they were nothing. I have to stay close to them, to make sure whoever ends up with them *appreciates* them."

Ghost problems were generally a lot like living people problems—resentments, old hurts, and regrets that festered and kept people from moving on to whatever spiritual resting place they were destined for after death. For the past year, the three of them had been slowly working through the more benign cases contained in the house, helping the ghosts move along to the next plane of existence, giving them peace. Or occasionally, like tonight, they would hear about a haunting on the island that had the potential to hurt people and seek it out.

Working with the dead was a lot less work when the dead person cooperated, which was a sentence Caroline never thought would enter her mind.

Riley mused. "So, if you're not willing to part with them,

would you be willing to, say, change venues, to Shaddow House? You could stay there, knowing that your cake stands are being stored with some of the most carefully guarded antiques on the planet."

Caroline pursed her lips. She supposed that was true. Antiques that were attached to potentially harmful spirits tended to be closely supervised.

"We could take you there tonight," Riley offered.

"Wait, what?" Caroline turned to Riley. "We don't have to steal the cake stands. Why not just come back and buy them tomorrow?"

"We can't leave the collection here," Riley said. "Sally could use her new skills to toss a heavy glass object at somebody and hit them in the head! No offense, Sally, but you don't seem to have a close grip on your temper."

Sally shrugged. "No offense taken, I suppose. I did throw all that mess at you."

"Or worse, someone else could buy it before we get back," Riley added. "We need to take it back to Shaddow House for safekeeping until Sally feels ready to move on."

"Are you saying I'll get to finally see the inside of Shaddow House?" Sally asked.

Like most people on Starfall, Sally had grown up on the island and never been allowed inside the mysterious semi-Victorian mansion with its ever-evolving mass of additions and façades. The house was a mystery most Starfall Point residents never solved, and every time Caroline got to see the inside, she felt the privilege of it.

"Well, that's not a bad deal," Sally said, sticking out her hand for a shake. Riley reached out to take it and barely blinked at the pins-and-needles discomfort of touching a spirit.

"But I can't steal from another antique shop!" Alice protested.

"It's not like there's antique shop owners' code," Riley told her. "And we're lucky that no one has heard the ruckus or seen the lights. We need to move along."

"There's a Michigan legal code," Caroline reminded her. "And it frowns upon theft. Generally speaking."

"All right, what is with all the legal talk? Are you doing that thing where you just sit back and make 'funny' comments without helping, like you're Jane Goodall studying a social grouping of idiots?" Riley asked.

"Little bit." Caroline jerked her shoulders. "I just like to be the voice of reason that reminds you that there are real-world consequences to the otherworldly things we do."

"Well, that's reasonable, I suppose," Riley conceded.

"Ladies, we've talked about how these conversations are not helpful in high-stress ghost situations," Alice reminded them.

Caroline considered that. "Yes, but we've also talked about the fact that I find the faces Riley makes when I make unhelpful jokes in those moments to be very funny."

Alice snorted, none too delicately. This was what Caroline treasured about her "ghost moments" with her coven. They were doing something very serious, and even dangerous, but they could still find ways to tease each other, to laugh.

"Caroline is right, stealing antiques is illegal," Riley conceded. "But we're leaving an antique behind that's worth twice what the cake stands are worth!!"

Riley held up a bag that contained a porcelain music box that had once been haunted by a ghost named Helena. It played *Three Blind Mice*, but because the little metal comb that created the notes was warped, that meant a too-slow, discordant rendition of the nursery rhyme echoing through Shaddow House. Riley maintained a very strict "creepy music boxes that play independently go into the trash compactor" policy. But because Helena was so sweet, Riley kept Helena's object until she moved on to the next plane.

"Did you seriously bring a haunted music box to a burglary?" Caroline asked.

"A *previously* haunted music box, and Alice was able to repair it in her shop, so it's not even creepy anymore," Riley said. "I thought we might need an unhaunted object to exchange for a haunted one—and I was right! And yes, I know how insane that sounded."

"But switching out a music box for glassware is going to throw his whole inventory system off!" Alice insisted.

"You mean that pile of notebooks that date back to…1982?" Riley asked, nodding at the haphazardly piled steno books leaning against Willard's massive metal cash register.

"I didn't say it was a perfect system," Alice said primly.

"I've known Willard a long time," Caroline told her. "If the creepy whispering stops—sorry, Sally, but it's true—he'll probably forget the cake stands exist by Monday. He's a nice man, but… unfocused. Speaking of, Riley, what are you staring at?"

"That's weird," Riley said, squinting at an etching framed on a nearby walnut sideboard. She crossed to pick it up. It was ink on paper, the iron ink so old and faded, it looked almost purple-blue behind the old glass. It looked vaguely familiar, like pieces she'd seen in childhood explorations of the attic at the family tavern, The Wilted Rose.

"Huh, I think my mom sold them to him, to be honest," Caroline said. "Willard went through a framing phase in the nineties. He asked people to bring in whatever historical documents they could find in their attics and started framing them in the acid-free preservation stuff. Mom found a bunch of these sketches at the Rose. She's not the sentimental type. Also, they're not particularly well-done."

"They're not that bad," Alice insisted. Caroline arched her brows, making Alice concede. "They're not great."

Riley peered down at the glass. "That's Shaddow House."

"No, it's not," Caroline scoffed. "The architecture's all wrong."

"Yeah, it's a different façade, but look at the windows," Riley insisted. "That weird sort of bay window that seems to hang off the east wing for no reason?"

Caroline blinked at the rough sketch. There were some similarities to the basic structure of Shaddow House, but it just didn't look like the house she'd been looking at her entire life.

"The house has been changed so many times over the years, we could be looking at the original design," Alice said.

"Who knows how many times it was designed and redesigned? Maybe this is something the original architect suggested?" Caroline asked.

"Or maybe an architect who got chewed up and spit out along the way," Riley observed. "There's a signature at the bottom, sort of."

She pointed to the bottom right of the sketch. It looked

like four tiny squares arranged into a cube. The date was obscured by some sort of damage to the paper. It looked like seventeen-eighty-something.

"If I was going to hide a mystical doodad, that's where I would put it—under the doorway. Doorways have magical significance," Riley said. "See, this is where it would be helpful if Plover could come along on these little field trips. He could tell us whether this is a legit theory or two-a.m. ramblings."

"So you'll take the cake stands, but not the framed pieces?" Alice asked.

"The cake stands are haunted, the framed pieces aren't," Riley said. "My moral fiber is flexible, not *absent*."

"Wait, you're going to come back to a store the day after you rob it?" Caroline asked.

Riley nodded. "Technically, this is burglary, and yeah, it'll throw Celia off my trail. Who comes to a store the day after they steal from it?"

"So, you admit that you're committing a *major* felony," Caroline said just as Alice asked, "You've never seen a single episode of a police procedural, have you?"

"OK, then it's settled," Riley said, clapping her hands. "I'll take these two. That leaves one for each of you."

"I don't think you're picking up on my tone," Caroline said as Riley carried two of the heavier cake stands to the door. "Also, should we trust the clumsiest person in the coven with two of the cake stands on an icy sidewalk? Including Sally's favorite?"

"I'm not the clumsiest," Riley began to protest. When Caroline and Alice turned to stare at her, she pouted briefly. "Fine."

"I'll take this one," Caroline said, wrangling the handblown lid out of Riley's hand. "Give the base to Alice."

"She's right. That is my favorite," Sally told them. She eyed Riley speculatively. "How clumsy are you?"

"It was one extremely old, expensive Moorcroft vase. *One*. And it wasn't even haunted!" Riley grumbled, before handing the base to Alice. "It was Plover's favorite, though."

"I think the two of us have a better chance of carrying one and a half cake stands each, than you have with the one in your hands," Caroline retorted, as they headed toward the door.

"Uh, ladies, the candles," Alice noted, gesturing to the remarkably well-lit shop. She pointed to the floor, where the foul blue gel was puddling at their feet. "And the mess."

Riley bit her lip as she surveyed the fake-fruit-scented lake forming around their feet. "Yeah, that's gonna take a while."

It did take a while to scrape the blue splatter from the floor and their feet, but fortunately the unnatural-scented gel seemed to want to be removed. Like it was sentient.

Caroline was never buying another scented candle, ever. Also, Willard was going to have to air out the shop for days.

After they left the shop, Caroline dragged a push broom behind them, obscuring their footprints as they walked toward the square. The snow on the main sidewalk was so thoroughly marked with boot prints that no one would be able to determine what belonged to them. She dragged her late brother's old baseball cap out of her coat pocket and slapped it over her chin-length dark hair. She wasn't about to suffer the indignity of a cold on top of smelling like the discount-store version of Strawberry Shortcake.

Sally floated over the surface of the snow, almost passively, as they walked through the dark, silent Main Square of Starfall. In the distance, the icy wind howled over Lake Huron's black waves with all the petulant force of an angry ex, but here, protected by the attached line of little shops, it was eerily silent. Caroline loved seeing their little town at night, like a slightly spooky Christmas card, no people or noise to disrupt the loveliness of the island under snow. Of course, it also meant an absence of the luscious melting sugar and chocolate smell that drew tourists to the island's fudge shops every spring, but one couldn't have everything.

Riley giggled as her feet slipped in the snow. They bobbled the cake stands but never lost their grip on them. It was like a haunted episode of *The Three Stooges*. Even as Sally yelled for them to watch themselves, Caroline only rolled her eyes.

They'd become a coven almost by accident. The magic had chosen Alice and Caroline to be Riley's partners in this venture— helpmates to assist the last of the Dentons to carry the burden of Shaddow House and all its craziness. And despite the unease of now seeing ghosts in places she'd previously considered "safe," Caroline found she didn't mind. They'd managed to get through their encounter with an undead "client" unscathed, and with a relatively peaceable solution.

"Remind me again why your family had to build this place on a hill?" Alice grumped as they hefted the stands up the road to Shaddow House, careful to avoid shops and houses they knew to have security cameras.

"Almost there," Sally sighed, staring up at Shaddow House. What had started off in the late 1700s as an isolated and stately family home on the hill had sort of mutated over decades of renovation to a semi-Victorian monster with a turret tower and rather melodramatic, gingerbreaded front porch with a variety of chimneys and additions that didn't make any sense. The robin's-egg blue siding contrasted sharply with the pale grays of the other houses, including—nope, nope, not time to think about *that* now.

Better to focus on the ghostly menagerie Caroline was about to walk into. It was never a good idea to walk into Shaddow House unguarded. There were hundreds of ghosts within its walls, attached to unlabeled objects all over the house. Literally anything in the house could be haunted, from the furniture to the dishes to Plover's beloved silver mail tray.

"You know I enjoy our outreach work with the undead community, but shouldn't we be focusing our energy on the search for the Welling locks?" Alice asked as they made the final climb to Shaddow House's gate. "Particularly during the slow season."

"What, are you afraid that our search for vital magical ritual objects won't fit into your tight schedule?" Caroline teased.

A year ago, it would have ended the conversation and Alice would have crossed the street to avoid Caroline for weeks. But now, Alice only rolled her eyes and said, "You know what I mean. The sooner we find the ghost locks and eliminate the threat, the better."

Caroline shivered. While she still didn't fully understand why a rival magical family would enchant a bunch of magical copper paperweights to enthrall the dead, it didn't sound like something she wanted in the hands of people who had proven themselves to be untrustworthy and sort of murdery.

Riley huffed. "Right now, the greatest threat is all of us sticking to the sidewalk in a film of frozen fruit-scented blue glop. Let's move."

"Caroline?"

Caroline froze in her tracks. She knew that voice. She'd spent every waking hour of her teenage years mesmerized by that voice. No. No. *Nonononono*.

She could feel every crinkle of faux blueberry-scented gel on her skin as she turned around.

Dr. Ben Hoult, her high school sweetheart, was standing on his parents' porch in all his way-too-fit-to-be-approaching-middle-age glory. Somehow, she'd mentally blocked that his childhood home was right next door to Shaddow House. He'd moved away years ago, so seeing him there again... It was like she'd been electrocuted, every muscle frozen, unable to move an inch. Or maybe Riley's dire warnings about sticking to the sidewalk had come true.

His face—how was it possible he was still so damned handsome?—was illuminated by his phone. His eyes were still that impossible shade of hazel that looked green in some lights and golden-brown in others. His hair—yep, he still had all of it, despite her more gleeful imaginings—was still dark molten gold, save for the slight feathering of silver at the temples. He'd grown a short, but impressive, beard, something he'd always wanted to do when they were kids, but had never managed to pull off because, you know, hormones are mean.

He was altogether beautiful, damn her eyes.

And Caroline and her friends were holding technically stolen furnishings on their way into a haunted house that no one on the island had been allowed into since they were kids. And they'd been none-too-quietly discussing magic and ghosts while covered in blueberry-scented goo. Again, while carrying stolen bric-a-brac.

Of all the weird things Ben had seen her do in their teenage years… This was still pretty bad.

Chapter 2
Ben

BEN WAS REALLY HOPING THAT moving to a remote island near Michigan's Upper Peninsula would mean that his kids' cell phone signal would be so weak, he wouldn't have to compete for their attention with a dozen social apps he didn't fully understand. But no such luck. Signal strength here on Starfall was just strong enough to send Mina and Josh running for their rooms to complain to all their friends back in Arizona about their boring and *groooooooss* new home.

How he felt the depth of disappointment and disdain communicated by all those extra teenager O's.

"Dad!" Mina yelled from upstairs. "Josh took the *good* bedroom! He was supposed to take the last one on the right! He is in direct violation of a verbal agreement painstakingly negotiated while driving between Iowa and Ohio."

"The Iowa-Ohio Housing Agreement is rendered null and void by the fact that one party negotiated while unaware that the last bedroom on the right is painted pink with *lace* curtains!" Josh hollered back almost immediately after. "I'm all for fluidity in gender norms, but add to that the fact that the windows face east, meaning I will take a direct shot to the eye from the morning sun, the totality of disadvantages outweighs the goodwill earned by honoring the agreement! Besides, Mina sleeps like the dead. If she's stabbed in the eye by the solar system, she won't even feel it. I will!"

"It's not about the wall color or your fragile sleep cycle. Sleeping in the smaller bedroom on the left puts me at the disadvantage of having access to two electrical outlets, instead of four, which is why I negotiated for the blue bedroom in the first place! I have way more electronics than you, when you consider my hair-care routine, and therefore, I need more outlets! And the bookshelves, which will be of no use to you!" Mina screeched. "Your lack of foresight does not invalidate the agreement!"

From the safety of the dark, cold porch, Ben sighed and pinched the bridge of his nose. Why was it that his kids used *bigger* words when they were cranky and tired? They sounded like underage college professors. He blamed private schools.

"Besides, more windows mean more sunlight, which means your corner of this icy hellscape will be warmer!" Mina cried.

Oh, Ben did not have it in him to explain that—unlike back in Arizona where sunlight turned any room into a pleasant greenhouse—windows did not make for a warmer room in Michigan. Windows only gave the cold air more places to creep in and make sleeping in three layers of clothing necessary.

"Guys, I told you there would be little problems like this when we moved into a house built in 1924," Ben called back. "Just live with it tonight and we'll fix it tomorrow when I can get it straightened out."

"Fine!" they yelled back in a unified tone that shouldn't have been possible, given the bickering.

Shivering into the coat he wasn't quite used to needing again, Ben shook his head. He should have known better than to think that the long drive and the excitement of an extremely bumpy boat ride over the newly thawed lake would tire them out enough to keep them from arguing as they moved into his parents' home, Gray Fern Cottage—a name that had always confused Ben. It wasn't as if there were many ferns in the yard. Most of those grew on the state-protected land on the other side of the island. But the Hoults had always been a proud, competitive bunch. He supposed the earlier Hoults thought that if their nearest neighbors, the Shaddows, had a house with a fancy-sounding name, they should, too. He figured the "cottage" bit was sort of self-deprecating, considering that the Hoult's shroud-gray house—while respectably spacious by most standards—was dwarfed by the enormity of Shaddow House.

"Dad, do I *really* have to share a bathroom with Josh?" Mina yelled from upstairs. "This is cruel and unusual!"

Sighing, Ben opened his favored shopping app and searched for power strips. And scotch. And then he remembered that shipping to Starfall Point was complicated by the fact that the island was only accessible by boat. There was no such thing as two-day shipping when you lived on Starfall. He would have to go to the hardware store the next day and hope for the best.

Even if Mina did deem sleeping on bedding used by the rental guests to also be *grooooooss*, Ben supposed it helped that they didn't really have to unpack or set up the house that night. The permanent move to Starfall wasn't going as he'd hoped, but somehow, exactly as he'd expected. His kids didn't know this place, the quirks of the island, the people, the house. The island was its own ecosystem with its own calendar and economy. And his kids were completely unprepared to negotiate any of it.

That was Ben's own fault. He'd let his ex-wife talk him into avoiding the island altogether after the kids were born. Isabelle hated sleeping in his parents' guest room when there was a perfectly good five-star hotel right there on the island. She hated the way locals treated Ben just like everybody else, good old Ben that they'd known since forever, and not "Dr. Benjamin Hoult." They didn't get the best tables in the island's restaurants. She couldn't throw his name around at the island's clubs because the island didn't have any. The best he could get for her on Starfall was a discount on fudge from as many shops as she wanted. Which she did not, because she was usually doing some low-carb thing. His now-late parents had retired to Florida and began renting the house out using a local property management company about ten years before, when Isabelle declared that they would just pay to fly the elder Hoults to visit *them* in Arizona.

"It's not like we can't afford it," she would huff, and Ben would just go along with it because it was easier than arguing. "Easier than arguing" had defined the last few years of his marriage, and Ben wasn't particularly proud of it.

So, if the kids were a little cranky settling into the house this first night, he was going to allow them all the squabbling room they needed. Even if it required scotch.

He was so caught up in his online search for liquid comfort—was the Starfall Party Store still open after all these years?—he almost didn't register the sound of boots crunching through the snow to his right.

Three women, bundled up against the cold, were carrying what looked like glass party trays up the sidewalk to Shaddow House. He couldn't quite make out what they were saying, but he definitely recognized the voice of the shorter woman in the Great Lakes Loons baseball cap. Then he heard the taller redhead say something about ghost locks. Maybe she was talking about a video game? Josh was always playing something called "Ghost Airlock IV" or "Blood Meerkat: The Revenge" or some such thing.

Caroline Wilton had never played so much as Super Mario Brothers in all the years he'd known and loved her. Then again, he hadn't spoken to her in almost twenty of those years, so what the hell did he know?

He had to handle this carefully. Caroline was known for her temper, and even though they'd parted in an expected, amicable way, that didn't mean she knew he was coming back to the island or she wanted to see him. Hell, he wasn't sure he wanted to see her right now, when he was tired as hell, smelled like a three-day road trip, and his teenagers could yell embarrassing nonsense from upstairs at any moment.

And yet, for some reason, his asshole brain chose this moment to break loose from his careful hold, and he blurted out, "Caroline?"

Dammit, Brain. You got me through residency, but you fail me now?

His brain had no excuses, only silence.

She was still stunning, Ben mused, all flyaway dark curls and moon-pale skin. He hadn't expected anything else really, even as he'd checked Starfall locals' social media many times over the years to catch a glimpse of her. She didn't seem to have any public accounts of her own, but he'd secretly hoped to see her in other people's photos. Now, he was glad he'd spared himself the torture. His eyes roamed over her figure, which had always been lush and curvy; her eyes, like smoked whiskey; her mouth with its distinct cupid's bow. Her mouth was something he'd always admired about her. Caroline Wilton had confidence.

"Ben!" she yelped, turning toward him, her eyes wide. She did not look happy to see him. In fact, she looked scared, as her eyes darted to a blond woman he didn't recognize and...was that Alice Seastairs? How were they out here, together, late at night, moving glassware and talking about video games? Why would Caroline be scared of him? And why did the air suddenly smell overwhelmingly like rancid blueberries? What was going *on*?

And Ben's stupid brain, for some reason, communicated to his left hand that it was a good idea to lift up and wave awkwardly.

"What are you doing here?" Caroline asked, her shoulders relaxing ever so slightly when Alice—*Alice*, who was Caroline's polar opposite back in high school and wasn't remotely connected to her social orbit—jostled the glass she was carrying and stroked Caroline's arm.

"I'm, uh, moving back," he said. "Dr. Toller interviewed me for the open spot at the clinic about a month ago."

"Since when?" Caroline said, frowning. "How did I not hear about that?"

"It's probably not something Dr. Toller wanted to get around before everything was settled," Ben said. "Didn't want to get everybody's hopes up about getting a second doctor."

"Yeah, but the Rose is the hub of most information on the island," Caroline mused. "Am I missing out on the important news bulletins?"

"We have had other things going on," the blond lady murmured. Caroline grumbled under her breath.

Ben blinked at her. Why were he and Caroline talking about the intricacies of small-town life when they were seeing each other for the first time in twenty years? Why was she so unreadable? And why was she spending time with Alice Seastairs, who had never had time for anybody when they were kids?

"So, you're still working at the Rose?" Ben asked.

"What else do you think I would be doing?" Her eyes narrowed. There was a bitter edge to her voice, and he supposed he deserved it. He knew her circumstances. She'd always insisted she couldn't leave the island. And what else was she supposed to do on the island besides work at her family's bar?

"If you're OK, we'll just take this up to the house," the blond woman said quietly. "Don't want the, uh, squirrels to get antsy."

Ben frowned. That was a weird thing to say. The island's squirrels were tucked away in their little nests at this time of year. He didn't remember meeting this woman in his years on the island, and she was giving off strong "recent transplant" vibes. Maybe she wasn't aware of the winter sleeping habits of tiny Northern tree-bound mammals?

"Oh, uh, sorry." Caroline cleared her throat. "Ben, you remember Alice. And Riley, uh, this is Ben Hoult. Ben, Riley is your new neighbor at Shaddow House."

"Nora let you move in? You must be family," Ben marveled.

"She was," Riley said, her pleasant smile never wavering.

Oh, shit, Riley's aunt was dead.

Dammit, exhaustion brain.

In that moment, he felt a pang of loss for Nora Denton. She'd been an aloof neighbor, but not an unkind one. His mother, like most people on Starfall, had spent years trying to coax Nora into the island's social circles—i.e., the Nana Grapevine, a grassroots social network of the island's elderly ladies. Hell, Mom had even insisted there was some distant family connection, a great-great-great-grandmother who had married a Denton cousin or something.

While Nora was gracious, and thanked people sincerely for the Bundt cakes and the offers for coffee, she never reciprocated. She never invited people into the cavernous confines of Shaddow House. Ben's mother had theorized that Nora didn't have permission from her employers, the Shaddow family, to have guests in *their* home, with what the entire island population assumed was a hoard of valuable antiques collected during their world travels "being robber barons or what-have-you." The Dentons had served as Stewards, caretakers to the Shaddows' property for as long as anyone on Starfall could remember. If Nora had passed, Ben supposed that Riley had inherited the position.

The only relative Nora had, to Ben's knowledge, was her sister, Ellen, who had broken family tradition and moved off-island the moment she turned eighteen. Maybe Riley was Ellen's daughter? She had her aunt's dark-gold hair and gray eyes.

Ben shook off his distraction. *Man,* it had been a long day. "I'm sorry for your loss," he said. "My own parents passed a few years ago, so I'm not updated on the island news."

"It's all right," Riley assured him. "I didn't meet her while she was alive, myself. Wait, *Ben? The* Ben? Oh, dang." Riley cast a wide-eyed and guilty look at Caroline. "Well, I'll just, um, go…that way. Far from this conversational awkwardness."

"Real smooth," Caroline muttered, smirking as Riley and Alice carted the glass pieces through the Shaddow gate. She turned her attention back to Ben. "Sorry if that was…weird. I wasn't expecting to see you, obviously."

"I can imagine. I wasn't expecting to see you tonight, either. I thought I would have time to adjust, I guess."

"Adjust, right, because you're going to be living here." Caroline blinked at him. "Long-term. Again. Great."

"So, uh, how have you been?" Ben said, rubbing at the back of his neck. He didn't know what else to say. *I'm sorry? I know we said we wouldn't talk, but it feels like I failed you by* not *talking? I missed you? My life hasn't turned out the way I hoped, and I suspect it's the absence of you that was the root of it?*

That was a reasonable amount of baggage to lay at someone's feet after twenty years, right?

"Dad, there's no internet!" Josh hollered from upstairs. "Mina, did you kill the internet on purpose?"

Ben's head dropped toward his chest. Of course, his children would decide to pipe up in this exact moment.

"There *is* internet, Josh, but it's unsecured Wi-Fi meant for the rental guests," Ben called back.

"Ew," Josh yelped. "I'm going to pretend you didn't say that!"

Caroline snorted but managed to cover it with a cough. That was kind of her. He and his spawn probably didn't deserve that.

"I have a technician coming to replace the system on Tuesday," Ben yelled.

"What are we supposed to do until then?" Mina demanded.

"Read a book?" Ben suggested.

"Ew!" Josh cried again, sounding truly offended.

"I accept your suggestion," Mina replied. "Particularly when laundry becomes an issue. You will wash your own smelly socks while I read."

Caroline burst out laughing now. And Ben's whole heart felt like it was going to a gooey caramel mush. He'd missed that sound so much, the music of it, the way she had dozens of different laughs, one for every occasion. Her whole face still lit up when she let any of them loose. That much hadn't changed.

"So." He jammed his hands into his pockets to keep from reaching out to touch her. He didn't have the right to do that. He jerked his head toward the house. "Those are my kids' disembodied voices."

Caroline snickered. "I'm sure they're charming when they've had some sleep and they haven't been hauled across the country."

"It will be an adjustment," he agreed.

"I'm just gonna…follow my friends," she said, jerking her head toward the front door of Shaddow House. He was struck with the bizarre urge to follow her, not to slake his lifelong curiosity about the house next door, but to keep this connection with Caroline. Seeing her again was like a balm to a wound he'd ignored for years: soothing, calm, comforting. He wasn't sure he deserved it, but he wanted it, selfishly, all the same.

But the kids were inside, and responsible parents did not abandon their children in the middle of the night on the same day that they moved into a strange house in a new place. His kids had been through enough.

Despite the frigid temperatures, the door was standing open. Ben could swear he could see the silhouette of a tall, thin man against the lights of Shaddow House, but it didn't look quite right... almost opaque?

Yeah, he needed to get some sleep.

———————

Clark Graves's office was all subtle masculine dominance, dignified navy and beige, dark polished wood, classic lines—the office of a covert douche-nozzle.

Ben didn't want to be sitting in the "cozy" environs of Tanner, Moscovitz, and Graves, one of the island's few law firms. He didn't like Clark or his office or his face. The man oozed smarmy self-satisfaction, even in the emails they'd exchanged over the last few months, like he was assured that he was better, smarter, than anyone *born* on the tiny island. Like he was doing them all a favor by deigning to live there.

If he'd learned anything over his medical career, it was that better education didn't necessarily mean smarter. Look at Caroline. She'd never been able to leave the island for, well, family reasons, so college was never an option for her. And her mind moved with a swiftness that scared the hell out of Ben, even when they were kids.

Caroline.

He'd hoped to slowly reintroduce her into his system, thoughtfully and with great preparation—not that awkward, rushed "hi there" kick to the gut the night before. But what was done was done, what was kicked was kicked. And all Ben could think of was his next opportunity to see her.

None of these thoughts were helpful, he noted, and would not settle the business that he and Clark were meeting to discuss. And he wanted this meeting to be over as quickly as possible—and not just because of Clark. He was more nervous about leaving his kids unattended on the island than he had been in Arizona—and there had been *rattlesnakes* in Arizona. And scorpions.

"I'm sorry that we had to meet like this, Ben, but as you said in your last email, interactions between yourself and my client have broken down to the degree that unmediated communication no longer seems productive or advisable," Clark said, smiling that toothy grin meant to put Ben at ease. They were just a couple of guys sitting around, shooting the breeze. "Which is a lot of lawyer-speak for 'I'm here to make sure everybody plays nice from here on out.'"

Ben gritted his own teeth at Clark's tone, like he was too dumb to understand that "unmediated communication" meant sorting out the total breakdown of Ben's relationship with the property management company that rented out Gray Fern Cottage. Martin Property Management was a sort of cadet branch of Martin & Martin Realtors, run by a nephew the family didn't trust with home sales.

"Your interactions with my client have devolved," Clark admitted. "Because of a series of misunderstandings. Perhaps Mr. Martin was a little…overzealous in his efforts to protect your property, which if you think about it, is a *positive* trait in someone who is renting your historic family home to strangers. If you would just put yourself in his place—"

"That's the problem. My place. Clifford Martin's not supposed to protect the property *from me*," Ben told him. "He doesn't have the right to tell me when I can occupy my own family home. Look, I'm not interested in a prolonged discussion. I just want to sever the relationship with the company as quickly and cleanly as possible."

"Well, you have to admit that will be somewhat complicated by the fact that you have moved into the home in question," Clark noted.

And that was the point of contention between Ben and Clifford Martin. Using Clifford's services had made sense when Ben's parents put the house up for vacation rentals. Clifford collected rent on time, kept the house clean, even arranged for repairs that time a frat bro tried to ride a Jet Ski down the stairs. But over the years, it seemed that Clifford felt more ownership of the house, establishing increasingly stringent usage rules for renters and making them uncomfortable, resulting in poor online reviews. Rentals declined to the point where the house was empty on July Fourth weekend the previous summer. That had never happened in all the years since Ben's parents had moved.

When Ben saw the house sat unused on the island's busiest weekend of the summer, he'd asked himself, what was the point of renting it out? And then he wondered, what was the point of paying a mortgage on an expensive home in Arizona when he had a perfectly comfortable house on Starfall Point? Why not move his kids somewhere they could live a quieter, calmer life, and maybe even thrive? The idea took hold, and Ben started preparations to take his family home.

He had expected his ex-wife to be the one who made the move

difficult, but while she barely raised an objection, it was Clifford who responded with a list of reasons why Ben should just stay in Arizona. While Clifford railed about the house's potential profitability and his own longtime dedication to it, Ben realized the objections boiled down to Gray Fern Cottage being the jewel of Martin & Martin's "rental crown." Clifford didn't want to lose bragging rights to that gem, to the point that when Ben informed him of the family's move-in date, Clifford yelled that Ben he had "no claim" to the house and hung up on him. From there, Ben was done.

So why was Clark pushing for Ben to stay in this unhealthy dynamic?

"There's no home 'in question,'" Ben replied, his voice level. "I own the home, legally, free and clear. There's no question about it."

"A home that you have under contract with Martin Property Management until the end of the month," Clark reminded him.

"I used the company website to book all dates between our move-in and the end of the month, which is allowed by that contract," Ben replied, smiling. Clifford hadn't liked Ben using that particular loophole.

"And there's nothing we can do to persuade you to renew?" Clark asked. "After all, you may need Clifford's services again."

"That's not a consideration for me," Ben said. "Beside the fact that my children and I have become permanent residents of Starfall Point, I make it a policy not to recommit to untenable situations."

"That's funny, that's not what I'd been told." Clark's smile was banal, but there was a curdling edge to it, like he knew he was poking at an emotional bruise.

One of the better things about moving away from Starfall had been the anonymity. If Ben so much as sneezed at the grocery store as a kid, his mother asked about him having a cold by the time he walked home. Out in the world, no one knew anything about his life that he didn't want them to know, and that included the slow, painful disintegration of his marriage.

Ben should have seen it, the way Isabelle talked about him and his med-school plans, the way she'd planned his career path for him. The way the kids seemed more like accessories than children, accessories meant to cement their marriage when he'd started to wonder if they'd made a mistake. He'd never had reason to doubt her story about "accidentally" conceiving far before they'd originally planned to have their first child, but then she'd insisted on naming their daughter "Benjamina," just in case he had any inclination to leave. Things tilted toward the absurd years later when Josh was born. Isabella had actually suggested changing Mina's name to Belinda, after Ben's mother, so they might make their son a "junior."

That was how she saw the kids, and Ben himself. Impassive art pieces in the gallery of her life, without their own feelings about how she placed them.

Also, Ben was pretty sure that had been a joke on *The Office*, and he wasn't about to "Nard-Dog" his own child.

In the end, Isabelle had loved being a polished, presentable doctor's wife a lot more than she loved the not-quite-polished doctor himself. It was what kept their marriage on its legs long after the kids couldn't do it anymore, after the comfortable life they enjoyed couldn't do it. He might have attributed these thoughts—which he only uttered to himself alone, in the dark of night, with a bellyful of scotch—as the mental meanderings of a bitter divorcé, if not for the fact that she'd left him for the chief of surgery at another hospital, who also happened to be the heir to an old-school timber empire.

Ben supposed Isabelle had done him a favor, leaving him, and not dragging the kids along with her to her new life in Denver—giving him the excuse to move the family back to his hometown. Apparently, her *new* doctor didn't like the idea of having teenagers around that he wasn't directly obligated to like. It hurt the kids, at first, but Ben supposed that his ex had done them a favor, too, making her allegiances clear. It wasn't easy for a woman in her forties to catch a man like Tom Winthrop the Third, after all. Isabelle wasn't going to do anything to jeopardize this chance at "real happiness." She'd told Ben so multiple times when she'd signed primary custody over to him.

Did Clark actually know about any of this, or was he simply inferring? As an officer of the court, he would have access to records detailing Ben's divorce, but why would he bother digging them up? It seemed like overkill for what was supposed to be a routine business meeting. Maybe Clark was just plain nosy?

Given the way Clark was smirking at him...yeah, he knew something.

"It's easy to say you're moving back in the spring," Clark said. "You'll be back in Arizona when your kids have decided they don't want to live through a second winter here. They'd miss their mother, I would think. Kids need their mother, after all. And single fatherhood... I don't know if that's something someone with your low stress tolerance is cut out for."

Ben's left hand flexed at his side.

Nope, nope. Punching a lawyer was the very essence of stupid, and he was trying to serve as a non-stupid example to his children.

In the next room, Ben heard Norma Oviette gasp in indignation. Good. Her employer had said something shitty, and Ben hoped it got reported to the Nana Grapevine. There was no justice swifter than justice imposed by the Nana Grapevine.

"If it's a question of buying myself out of the remaining three weeks, I'm willing to do that," Ben said calmly. "But since we're being a stickler about contracts, I can't help but notice there's no provision for that, if there are no rentals pending."

Clark's smile faltered a bit. "No, there's not."

"So, I'll just present you with this letter, written by my own attorney at Wendlin, Archer, and Smith, officially severing my relationship with Martin Property Management and asking that any final deposits of funds be delivered within sixty days. After that, any contact should be directed through my attorney, even contact from you." Never mind that Ben's attorney was a former college roommate he'd called "Smitty," who'd been known for setting his own farts aflame. Smitty had grown quite a bit since then.

"So, you're requesting that I don't contact you, either?" Clark asked.

"Not in connection to anything to do with Martin Property Management or Clifford," Ben replied.

The unspoken "I'm OK with you not contacting me at all" hung between them like a fog of gingivitis breath.

"Have a nice day," Ben told him, before getting up from the chair and walking out.

"I was really sorry to hear you and your wife split up," Norma said quietly as he passed her desk. Norma had always been a kind lady, who pickled cucumbers she planted in her own yard, then shared them all winter. "But I think your youngsters are going to be happy here. Belinda always wanted them to come see her at the cottage."

"Thanks, Mrs. Oviette," Ben said, swallowing heavily at the mention of his mother.

"Oh, I think you can call me 'Norma,'" she assured him.

He thought of Belinda Hoult, and what she would have thought of him calling a woman in her early sixties by her first name. "No, I don't think can."

Norma snorted, her deep-brown skin crinkling at the corners of her eyes. "You're a good boy."

Ben laughed, and as he moved toward the door, he glanced back into Clark's office. The façade of the casually confident attorney about town was gone, and there was a reptilian anger glittering in Clark's eyes—icy and calculating. For a moment, Ben wondered whether he'd just made a mistake, provoking Clark Graves.

Opening the front door, Ben sucked in a breath as the frigid air enveloped him. And then he lost it all over again when he realized that Caroline was only a few feet away, walking toward the Main Square. She had a dark-blue knit hat pulled over her ears, and her cheeks were pinked by the wind, making her eyes sparkle like amber. His heart gave a little lurch of nostalgia mixed with longing. He was really going to have to get that under control.

Maybe he should just stay still? Like she wouldn't see him if he just didn't move.

It was really a bad sign when you started treating an ex-girlfriend like a T. rex, particularly when she'd done little to deserve dinosaur treatment.

Oh, no, she'd noticed him. And he was just standing still like an idiot involved in his own personal mannequin challenge.

And she was still looking at him.

"Um, Caroline, hi," he said.

She gave him a smile that was sort of shaky, like she wasn't sure how it was supposed to fit across her face. "Hey, Ben."

"Sorry about the awkward reintroduction last night, with the screaming kids and the confused friends and the…again, the screaming kids. That's just not how I thought that moment would go, seeing you after all these years. I always pictured me being alone with you…" He paused, his head dropping almost to his chest. "And when *this* moment played out in my head, I thought it would sound a lot less creepy."

She snorted, but she didn't say anything. And that wasn't good because the cruel part of his brain that felt the compulsion to fill awkward silence made him continue babbling. "I guess we're going to have to get used to this again, bumping into each other."

Her dark brows quirked up. "It's a small island, Ben. I can handle it if you can."

He held up his gloved hands. "Of course, of course. It's just that I got used to…not seeing you."

Her bowed mouth quirked downward. Because that was an incredibly stupid way for him to put it. Why would he want to not see her? He wanted to see her as much as possible. He wanted to talk to her, to find out what had happened in her life over the last two decades because the life he'd built hadn't allowed him that sort of indulgence.

"Not that it's a bad thing, to see you. It's a good thing," he insisted. "I'm just getting used to the idea that I could run into you at any moment."

Her expression shifted into vaguely offended. "Because you think I'm going to be following you around or something?"

Ben shook his head. "No, no, I just meant…"

The phone in his pocket rang. Mina's number was scrolling across the screen when he took it out. "It's my daughter. Hold on just one second."

"That's fine. I need to get to work," she said, giving him a discomfited little wave.

As his phone continued to ring, he watched her carefully walk the icy sidewalk toward the public library. He swiped a hand over his face. He had faced down actual medical inquisitions and hadn't been this shaken up.

Across the street, he saw a dark shadowy figure in a long cloak step behind the Starfall Community Theater building. As cold as it got in the winter here, he'd never seen someone wear an actual cloak. Maybe it was part of some production at the theater?

But the theater only did summer shows.

Weird.

Chapter 3
Caroline

WHEN CAROLINE WAS AGITATED, she cleaned.

It was a habit she'd picked up in childhood, being left alone with her brothers, who seemed to leave a sticky film of spilled *something* on everything that they touched—even the two that were older than her. Things had been different then. Her father, Denny, had been the one running the Rose, with the cheerful confidence of someone who had never suffered a soul-shattering tragedy. And her mom had run knitting classes at fiber shop when she felt like it. The Wilted Rose had always provided enough of a living that Gert Wilton could decide when and how she would work. Then Caroline's brother, Chris, died, and Denny collapsed in on himself. Caroline had to move her cleaning habits to the Rose.

"She's panic-cleaning," Alice muttered out of the side of her mouth. "I've never seen her do this."

"Well, there was that time that she organized all the teas in my pantry by brand and then type. But that was when that antique dealer in Modesto shipped us a box full of—"

"Squirrels!" Alice chimed in.

Riley cleared her throat. "Yes, 'squirrels.' The noise alone was enough to drive her to alphabetize."

"They weren't that bad," Alice insisted.

"They were carrying their own heads around the house, and those heads were yelling—in French—until we managed to bind them inside that creepy basket," Riley reminded her. "I felt really bad moving them to the previously unknown secret supervillain basement level so we wouldn't have to hear them. Also, what sort of person wants to *buy* an executioner's basket from the French Revolution? Can't really blame the squirrels for being emotionally attached to the last thing they saw before they were guillotined."

"We really need to do some sort of mass email to let your aunt's old contacts know to slow down the 'squirrel donation' mailings," Alice said, sipping her coffee. From the corner of her eye, Caroline could see her trying not to grimace. Coffee served from the Rose's twenty-year-old coffee machine had a distinct bitter burned taste that the older locals appreciated. Alice was used to making her own coffee in her little single-serve coffeepot at Superior Antiques, which she cleaned and descaled religiously. Riley, however, had worked in so many weird office complexes over the years that she was immune to bad coffee.

"Shaddow House is the only safe place they know to send them," Riley said, shrugging. "It's more difficult than you would think to off-load squirrels from your home or business."

"You two know I can hear you, right?" Caroline said, turning to them. "And that means customers can probably hear you. Also, our rodent code word for ghosts probably isn't nearly as clever as we think it is."

Caroline waved a hand around the bar's wood-paneled interior, which was lit with an array of neon beer signs that coordinated with racks of taps from the beers served over the years. Particular attention was paid to classic Guinness ads, which had been a favorite of Caroline's great-uncle Louis.

In the afternoons, the Rose was definitely more of a restaurant than a bar, where a lunch crowd gathered when they couldn't find room at one the more tourist-oriented Main Square bistros. Over the years, Gert had mastered the art of dressing up canned soups and basic sandwiches with a few flashy ingredients so they could charge fourteen ninety-five for a tuna melt. Caroline didn't have the heart to tell people who praised her mother's chicken chowder that it was basically watered-down cream of celery with chopped rotisserie chicken and green onion chiffonade. She considered this an abuse of the Food Network's teachings. Sometimes, Caroline thought it was the pretense that exhausted her mother, pretending she was the woman who could handle it all.

"I concede your point," Riley noted. "But I think perhaps you're a little more stressed out by the return of a certain someone than our too-loud discussion of squirrel matters."

"It only makes people think we're a little off," Alice told Caroline. "People have thought I'm a little off for years. But I agree that it's the awkward interaction from last night that has you all atwitter."

"You mean Sally?" Caroline replied blithely.

"Yes, clearly, I mean Sally," Riley deadpanned.

"When does your contractor get here for your meeting?" Caroline asked pointedly. Riley only chuckled into her coffee.

"If you don't want to talk about Ben, we don't have to talk

about him," Alice told Caroline. "But maybe it would help you process your emotions a little bit before you scrub the finish off of this very old bar."

Caroline glanced down at the scarred old oak bar top, shiny with steaming-hot water from Caroline's third wipe down of the morning. Caroline tossed her cleaning rag into the nearby bar sink.

"It's normal to be upset, seeing someone that used to mean a lot to you, after a long separation," Riley told her quietly.

"I'm not upset, exactly, it just brings up a lot of feelings that I thought were settled," Caroline said. "Ben and I were high school sweethearts, childhood sweethearts, really. And it was before..."

Before she'd accepted that her college plans were never going to happen, that she would spend her entire life on this tiny patch of land because...well, the Wiltons had never really understood why. They just called it "the curse." Any Wilton who stepped off the island for more than a day—exactly twenty-four hours—would suffer some violent, often humiliating death. The number of relatives Caroline had lost to being hit by a mainland taxi was just not mathematically feasible. Great-uncle Louis who hung all the Guinness posters in the bar? He'd died when Caroline was five, having left the island to finally see his beloved Tigers play. He managed to make it thirty whole hours before he missed the boarding ramp for the ferry, bumped his head, and drowned on the return trip. Caroline herself was almost hit by a campus bus when she'd dared to travel to Lansing for an admissions interview, ending her college aspirations very quickly.

"I realized we were never going to work long-term," Caroline said. "He was so smart, he actually graduated high school almost two years early, working at his own pace at the island school. He had all these scholarships... He had his big life plans, and I wanted him to have that. I wanted him to be happy, to have the whole world out there as an option. I tried to be all stoic and selfless about it, but yeah, it hurt that he was able to go out and live his life so easily. He came back those first few years, every holiday, but seeing each other was just too hard, you know? So, he stopped, and...I moved along to my casual but discreet dalliances with tourists."

It wasn't a pattern of behavior she was ashamed of, and it had helped her cope. She'd *told* Ben he needed to go away to school. But a tiny part of her that she didn't want to admit existed hoped that he would find a way not to leave her. On one hand, she couldn't blame Ben for abandoning her. It wasn't like there was a college on Starfall. On the other, knowing that he was out there in the world, living his life, it hurt. She'd avoided social media because she didn't want to see his life. She knew he'd gotten married young, had kids. Oh, the idea of seeing him happy was chilling to her, and that probably made her selfish; she was willing to accept that. And so, she'd replaced him with a series of men that didn't matter, because when she pushed them away, it didn't hurt.

"They're not nearly as discreet as you think they are," Caroline's mother told her as she passed by with a tray full of turkey melts— fancied up with sweet potato fries and a canned cheese sauce Gert doctored with five-spice powder and candied jalapeños.

Gert's creped arms bulged under the heavy burden. Her iron-gray hair was swept back from a face that was pale and drawn into tired lines. Dark circles stood out under her wide brown eyes.

Thin lips that Gert had once carefully enhanced with carmine-red Elizabeth Arden lipstick were chapped and bitten.

Sadness and fear gripped Caroline's heart with twin fists. She had the most unsettling feeling that she was looking into her own future, working herself to the bone for a family that couldn't stir itself to recognize her effort. The inevitably of it all, the weight of it, seemed to chase Caroline through her dreams at night, leaving her more exhausted when she woke.

She shook off the useless woolgathering and ran around the bar after her mother. "Let me take that, Mom."

"No, no, I've got it," Gert sighed. Caroline could smell cigarette smoke on her breath, a sign that her mom was having a worse day than usual. "But if you could find time in your busy chatting schedule to go check on the fryer before the fries burn, I'd appreciate it."

Oof, score one for Mom in the Great Maternal Passive-Aggressive Comment Roundup, in which "Gert Wilton" was permanently inscribed on the Eternal and Universal Grand Champion Cup.

Feeling like a chastised teenager, Caroline shot Riley and Alice an apologetic look before she backed into the tiny kitchen, retrofitted for commercial service in the ancient building. The food smelled good, and the space would pass a health inspection, but Caroline cringed internally at the dingy cutting boards, crumby counters, and general disarray. She was grateful that the swinging kitchen doors kept her friends and customers from seeing the mess.

She watched the bubbling fryer as instructed, but also eyeballed the employee roster near the back door. As she suspected, her brother, Will—yes, really, Will Wilton—was scheduled to work the lunch shift that day, but simply hadn't shown up. After all, it was Tuesday, and Will couldn't be expected to sacrifice his Tuesday—or Wednesday or Thursday or most days ending in Y—to something as inconvenient as showing up to work. After all, his twin brother, Wally—yes, again, really—only showed up for every other shift on his own schedule. Why should Will have to do more than that?

"Thanks for not setting the place on fire, I suppose," Gert muttered as she carried the empty tray into the kitchen. "I heard you out there, talking about the Hoult boy."

"He's, like, forty," Caroline noted. "And a doctor. Hardly a boy."

"But, either way, out of your league," Gert told her. "He's got a job and two kids to take care of, and he doesn't need you and your 'casual dalliances' making things messier for him."

"Thanks, Mom," Caroline said, smiling with a sweetness she didn't feel.

"I'm just saying, even if Ben is…comfortable…for you"—Gert said carefully as she dipped another basket of sweet potato fries into the bubbling oil—"you're not at a place in your life where you could be a good influence on those kids."

Hurt had her changing the subject. Caroline didn't need her mother's dissertation on what she was and wasn't capable of. And right now, she didn't know what to do in terms of Ben. Conversations with him seemed to derail themselves before they even started, and Ben seemed to be by turns uncomfortable around and suspicious of her. Did he really think she was going to just follow him around the island, waiting for the chance to talk to him? She wasn't some desperate stalker.

Or maybe she was. She did spend an inordinate amount of time thinking about someone who would never truly be part of her life again. It was pointless, and she didn't want to waste her life on pointless things. So, when her eye landed on a Harp tap on the far counter, she was happy to seize on the chance to change the subject.

"When did we decide to serve Harp?" Caroline asked.

Her mother jerked her shoulders. "The Harp distributor offered me a better deal."

"Wait, we're going to serve Harp *instead* of Guinness?" Caroline replied. Harp was a fine product, but they had some pretty hard-core Guinness drinkers in their clientele, and she doubted they would be very happy about switching brands. Hell, Guinness was a key part of the bar's décor, if it could be called that. "When did we decide to do that?"

Her mother sniffed. "Well, you know, maybe if you spent less time at Shaddow House with that Denton girl, you would know more about how we run things around here."

Caroline stared at her mother, mouth agape, as the older woman moved efficiently about the kitchen. Gert had no real room to complain, and Caroline knew that. Caroline still worked her shifts (plus extra) and did her job to the best of her ability, but the bar wasn't her whole life anymore. Did her mom resent that?

Gert hissed as the fryer oil popped and her hand got hit by a rather sizable splash. Caroline moved quickly toward the freezer to grab the medical ice pack they kept there for just such an occasion. She wrapped it against Gert's skin with a dish towel and took over the fryer. "Mom, you can't serve and do the paperwork for this week *and* cover the kitchen for Will. Why don't you just call him in?"

"Will has other things going on today, and if he needs help, we help. That's what family does for each other," Gert said.

"It's not like he's donating bone marrow, Mom. I'm pretty sure he's playing video games in his underwear," Caroline shot back.

Gert shook her head. "You don't know that."

Caroline pulled out her phone and checked Will's favorite social media app. She showed the screen to Gert, whose face registered disappointment as soon as she recognized Will's shirtless couch selfie.

"'Just a chill day ahead, killing beers and shooting zombies,'" Caroline read aloud, her eyebrows arched. "'Hashtag, Me Time.'"

"Your brother helps in his own way," Gert insisted. "You know how he is."

"Unreliable? Feckless?" Caroline suggested.

"That's not fair," Gert said, her cheeks flushing red. Caroline was grateful, she supposed, to have at least put some color on her face, even if it was from anger.

"You're right, he wouldn't be much more useful if he actually showed up for work," Caroline muttered. "Could you at least call Wally in?"

"Oh, I don't want to bother him," her mother said dismissively as she waved Caroline away from the fryer. "It's easier if I just do it myself. I can handle it."

Caroline knew better than to suggest her father come in. Denny had barely stepped out of the house since Chris died ten years before, another Wilton curse statistic. He'd just dropped the bar into Gert's hands and retreated into his easy chair.

"Mom, you're getting older," Caroline said.

"I beg your pardon?" her mother gasped, turning around and

wielding her spatula like a sword. Caroline reminded herself that half of bravery was doing something stupid, and the other half was knowing it was stupid and doing it anyway.

"You're not going to be able to keep this pace up forever, and you'll have even less time if you keep pushing yourself like this," Caroline told her. "I can help you, but that help only goes so far because I stubbornly insist on having a life. Ask for *help*. From the *boys*."

"The boys help in their own ways," Gert insisted.

"What ways exactly?" Caroline demanded. "Challenging your ability to improvise because they ditch work? Keeping the account books balanced by promptly cashing their checks?"

"Caroline, stop it," Gert hissed. "If you're so worried about me, *you* could help out more. You know how to work the griddle."

"Right, because that's obviously the more reasonable solution, so much better than asking your employees to, you know, be employed," Caroline shot back. "Would you at least consider hiring outside help who might actually show up for their shifts?"

"Someone outside the family?" Her mother scoffed. "Where are we supposed to get the money for that?"

"Well, we might be able to take in more money if customers know they have an above-average chance of getting their food," Caroline muttered, backing out of the kitchen. Her own cheeks flushed red when she saw the expressions on Alice and Riley's faces. While the other customers were blithely munching on their lunches, it was clear her friends had overheard everything.

"Sorry," Caroline muttered.

"I think we've both established that our own dysfunctional family backgrounds leave us uniquely qualified to understand,"

Alice replied quietly as Riley reached across the bar to squeeze Caroline's hand. Alice balanced it out, placing her hand on top of theirs. Instantly, Caroline felt settled as their magic wrapped around her own and soothed Caroline's nerves. She smiled at them and reluctantly pulled her hands from theirs before her mom could come out and see that particularly demonstrative waste of time.

"Where is that contractor to distract you from my mortification?" Caroline whispered, searching the bar for an unfamiliar face.

"Yeah, sorry to use your workplace as my conference room, but the fewer potential breaches of Shaddow House, the better," Riley replied.

"Eh, I've met Cole Bishop a few times, when he did the kitchen remodel for your Aunt Nora," Caroline said. "He's nice, easy on the eyes. Doesn't say much."

"It was before Natalie's time, so she can't help much there," Riley said.

"I still don't get how construction is going to work, letting a civilian in the house," Caroline noted.

Riley shrugged. "The ghosts have to choose to show themselves, for non-witches to see them. Plover has practice, keeping the other ghosts under control because of previous construction projects. As for Cole, Plover only said that he was 'less annoying than Mr. Edison.' Unfortunately, he said that in front of Edison, which started a whole new thread of conversation, and I had to play mediator between my boyfriend and my British...squirrel father. And Cole has considerable experience working with historical buildings, which is its own construction specialty. Aunt Nora's journal describes Cole as 'reliable and unremarkable,' which makes him invaluable."

"Which means he may be of use to me," Caroline said, pursing her lips and waggling her eyes with a speculative sass she didn't quite feel.

"Don't use my contractor to release your unresolved high school sweetheart tension," Riley gasped, though she was laughing. "I need him to stay on task."

"I may also need him to stay on task!" Caroline retorted.

"Seriously, I have to get some sort of project started, no matter what Plover says about it being 'ill-timed and ill-advised,'" Riley replied. "There hasn't been any sort of construction in the house since Aunt Nora died. The spirits are getting...bold."

Caroline grimaced. When she was a kid, construction at Shaddow House *never* seemed to stop, but the locals didn't know that wasn't a demand by the mercurial (and fictional) owners, the Shaddow family—but an effort by the Dentons to keep the dead occupants confused.

"Creeping up near your bedroom?" Alice guessed.

"I woke up to that clown ghost standing in the hallway, staring at us while we slept, which is the *last* time I leave the bedroom door open," Riley said, pursing her lips. "Really, gotta figure out which object Jingles is attached to, because he has gotten *too* comfortable."

Caroline shuddered. While there were times Caroline envied Riley living in the legendary house, she liked knowing she could go back to her little cottage near her parents' family home, where sleeping didn't require special runes to keep her bedroom clown ghost–free. Heavy was the head that wore the crown of Steward of Shaddow House. It was a burden that Riley's mother had tried to spare her, keeping her away from Starfall until the previous year.

"So, your brothers didn't show up for work again?" Riley asked quietly as Caroline moved to pull refill pints for the table of four in the corner.

When Caroline returned from serving them, she said, "Mom refuses to *force* the boys into coming to work if they don't want to—which was a luxury I was never afforded. Instead, she runs us both into the ground because that's easier, I guess?"

"Are we talking misogynistic undertones to the family dynamic or is she just unable to physically force them off their couches?" Alice asked.

"Little bit of both maybe?" Caroline guessed. "Mom was harder on them when we were little, but then we lost Chris, and she just can't bear to do anything that will upset them. And I guess both boys sort of settled into taking the easy route. That was always their nature, and Mom just let them lean into it. But I was always able to sort of work through it. Mom can, too, so now I guess we're both supposed to."

"Chris passed a few years ago, right?" Riley asked.

Caroline swallowed heavily. It wasn't exactly a secret. Everybody on the island knew what happened. But even sharing magic, even knowing about Riley's unresolved feelings about losing her own mother, talking about Chris with someone Caroline cared about somehow made it real. It was something Caroline had to work up to. The loss was still simply too much.

"Passed is a very gentle way of saying my brother fell from a footbridge," Caroline said, squeezing Riley's hand. "He was in Grand Rapids, meeting a girl he'd been talking to online. Jenna. She's a sweetheart. We kept in touch…afterward. Chris was trying to be romantic, meeting her at the bridge, like something out of an old movie. But he slipped on the ice and *somehow* managed to fall right over the railing, into the water. It took days to find his body."

"Look, I know you don't really like talking about it, but is there an origin story for the curse?" Riley asked quietly. "Like you built the bar on land stolen from another Starfall family or one of you pissed off a fairy queen or something?"

"No," Caroline said, shaking her head. "And I'm not even sure 'curse' is the right word for it. It was just a pattern that some auntie a few generations back put together. And the family just sort of accepted it, as more and more of us died off."

"Isn't that, in itself, sort of weird?" Alice suggested. "I mean, everything on Starfall has a story. The mailbox on Third Street has a little historical plaque on it because JFK dropped a postcard in it."

Riley's dark-gold brows winged up. "Really? That's kind of cool."

Alice nodded. "He and Jackie visited before he was elected. There was a big debate over whether the Duchess should be renamed 'The Presidential Hotel.' The historical committee almost imploded. Mrs. Martin and Mrs. Oviette still don't talk over it."

"Why all the interest in my family...problem?" Caroline asked as her mother hefted a tray of sandwiches out of the kitchen and across the room to a table of Perkinses. The family ran several ferries in the tourist season, but when the lake was too, well, *frozen* for boat traffic, they spent their days overhauling boat engines.

Riley took a sip of her coffee, lowering her voice so it was barely audible to Caroline from behind the mug. "Well, I'm wondering if it has anything to do with the little old lady in purple, glaring at you from behind the jukebox?"

Caroline tried to be subtle when she turned, moving to pour Alice more coffee. There was indeed a lady in a very formal purple brocade dress, the sort of thing one saw in historical paintings from the late 1700s, early 1800s. The rich shiny material—a sort of robe that closed over a long, loose white gown—seemed like the kind of thing you would wear before bed. It barely moved when the ghost shuffled backward into the shadows of the basement entrance. The ghost seemed to be staring up, over the bar, where some of the family artifacts were arranged—old photos, a landscape of the island that had hung there since before her father could remember, framed newspaper articles, softball trophies.

Caroline had never seen this specific ghost in the Rose before she had magic, but she'd learned that was normal. Since her magical "awakening," Caroline spotted ghosts in places all over the island that she'd never suspected of being haunted. Magic simply changed one's perception. And it had been a while since the three of them had been in the Rose at the same time. Maybe the ghost sensed the three of them up here and decided to creep out and see for herself?

"Does it seem to you like there's something off about her?" Riley asked.

"Other than that fabric being so out of place here, I want to yell at her to stay still before she gets ketchup on her skirt?" Caroline asked dryly.

Caroline noticed her mother was standing less than five feet from the dead lady and didn't seem affected at all. So, Caroline supposed that the part of her that was recognized, chosen by Riley's magic, didn't come from Gert's side.

"No, it's as if she's trying to trick us," Alice said, her brow furrowing. "Hunching herself over, moving as if walking hurts. I don't think she's as old as she's making herself out to be."

"I think she's from a different era though," Caroline observed. "That part seems real. I don't think she's wearing a Halloween costume or anything."

"It's just something 'not right,'" Riley said, shrugging. "But I mean, it is a dead person backlit by a neon moose beer sign, so... Oh, I think she heard that. Didn't like it."

The ghost glared at the three of them, which somehow seemed more sinister from the shadowy corner, and faded from sight.

"Well, that's not good," Caroline mused.

"At least she's not tossing beers across the room at us?" Riley suggested with a false brightness that sounded brittle.

"Don't give her ideas," Caroline told Riley.

Just then, the front door opened, and a gargantuan dark-haired man had to actually duck his head to walk through it. His piercing blue eyes scanned the room until they landed on Riley. He grinned, showing perfect, even white teeth through a beard lightly salted with silver. The cold spring wind cut through the room like a knife, making Eric Perkins yell, "Shut the door!"

"Oof," Caroline said. "I don't remember Cole looking that good last time he was here."

"I think that's your sexual frustration talking," Alice said.

"I will not be shamed," Caroline informed her as she went to the bar to fetch Cole a mug of coffee. She left Riley to her meeting and went about her lunchtime business. Every few minutes, she glanced up to the corner to see if the lady ghost returned. Caroline wasn't sure if she was relieved or disappointed when she didn't.

Later that night, Riley summoned Alice and Caroline to Shaddow House with the promise that she had "something cool" to show them.

Caroline was curious what it was, but she still wasn't sure if she wanted to go, and might not have if Riley hadn't promised her that Cole was long gone. The big man might have been attractive, but he'd annoyed Caroline by noting several "possible structural problems" with the bar, including a watermark on the ceiling that Caroline had never noticed before. In Michigan, a leaking ceiling was a major problem, particularly if it was winter. Ice jams, pestilence, and chaos were sure to follow.

She knew Cole was probably right; the building was a sort of Frankenstein's monster with an ancient foundation, plus additions made and torn down and remade over the years. It would shock her if there *weren't* plumbing issues, roof leaks, and an eventual implosion of the HVAC system. But honestly, Caroline didn't have the time or the patience to deal with a remodel. And adding one more straw to her mom's burden? Caroline wasn't going to do that.

She carefully walked up the icy steps to Shaddow House. As neither Riley nor Edison had grown up in the snowbound north, they hadn't quite mastered the art of salting. It made reaching their door an exercise in potential injuries.

Once she was safely on the sweeping front porch, she approached the door with its ornate bronze doorknob. She was careful not to put her thumb near the rounded depression on top of the lock, which was molded with an outline of a house with an S shape in the middle. When Riley unlocked the door for the first time, that insignia had extracted blood from her thumb before it would allow her inside the house—sealing a magical blood pact that bound Riley to Shaddow House for the rest of her life. Caroline hadn't trusted the door since—though she supposed a magical blood pact wouldn't make much difference for her.

Caroline had grown up looking up at Shaddow House like some sort of unapproachable museum, and now she practically had her own key. Occasionally, the door would even open to her without anyone touching it, like it did this evening.

Caroline paused, pursing her lips. "Still haven't figured out how you can do that."

The house wasn't supposed to be sentient, but it seemed to have...opinions. Caroline could feel them as she moved from room to room. Caroline was just glad that (as a member of Riley's coven) the house's opinion of her was positive. It was a bizarre new reality in her previously unremarkable life that she hadn't quite accepted yet.

"I'm here!" she called. Magic sang across her nerve endings as she crossed the threshold, sending a pleasant little hum up her spine. The inside of the house was a combination of a wizard's den and a kooky Victorian mansion. It was elegant and immaculately constructed of polished wood, burnished brass, and a rainbow of paint and enamel, but also chock-full of antiques from every era and weird touches like staircases that rose directly into ceilings and windows that opened to coat closets—little idiosyncrasies added to confuse the ghosts. There were so many details, it almost hurt the human eye to take it all in.

The Dentons had originally worked as mediums in London, helping people communicate with lost loved ones and evicting the more malicious specters to the next plane. The clients moved along untroubled, and the Dentons either stored the still-haunted items or sold the objects that were no longer attached. Over the years, those sales built into a considerable fortune, which the Dentons invested wisely. By the time they reached the New World, they'd also amassed a huge collection of haunted items they sought to store in a safe place. The family chose Starfall because of its energy, whether it was from ley lines or copper deposits under its surface, no one really knew. The Dentons just knew it felt *right* to build their home there.

Caroline knew the feeling. She'd felt at home in other buildings, but this was one of the few places she felt *accepted*. Riley and Alice didn't judge. They didn't make her feel guilty for every little missed gesture or failing to read someone's mind. They just wanted her to be OK.

Caroline grinned at Alice, who was curled on the end of the sofa in the cavernous but somehow cozy family room, sipping tea and reading one of Nora Denton's old journals. Riley's aunt had left them a treasure trove of magical education materials, as no member of either of their families had ever practiced magic—to their knowledge.

Caroline had been calling Alice's grandmother a witch for years, but under a different context.

In the last year, they'd learned as much as they could about the Dentons' magic system of charmed herbs and salt, combined with runes the family had created—drawn on the air with one's hands. (Riley was still disappointed that there was no wand involved.) So far, the laws of magic seemed like a complicated set of instructions that the three of them never saw in their entirety. She could see ghosts on her own and talk to them, but for any sort of spell work, Caroline needed Alice and Riley.

It seemed that each of them served a particular purpose within the group. Caroline's own magical gift seemed to focus on communication with ghosts, which sort of went along with her day job—bartending. People wanted to talk to her, tell her their problems, and when you were trying to figure out the unfinished business that was keeping a spirit bound to earth, that was an essential skill. Sometimes, they needed something simple, like a phone call allowing them to hear a beloved dog. Other ghosts required more. Riley seemed to specialize in finding that something more, not to mention moving haunted objects around without touching them. The "finding something more" made sense, given Riley's rich and colorful work history, which gave her a knack for interpreting subtle clues and solving intricate mysteries. The telekinesis bit was probably related to her being Denton witch by blood, rather than magical selection.

Alice's special gift hadn't become quite clear yet, but Caroline was sure they would figure it out. Alice was too competent in the other areas of her life to not have one.

A roaring fire burned merrily in the wide stone hearth. It still rattled Riley that she needed a fire in the spring. But even without the cold, it was expected when one of the house's ghosts was attached to a brass match cloche and enjoyed "making things cheery" for the girls. (A ghost child being the one to start fires was really not ideal.)

The unidentified "ceiling ghost" that oozed like an oily mass overhead (and occasionally dropped chandeliers on Kyle, the previously heretofore unknown nemeses)? Not as cheery. Even if that chandelier drop had ultimately been helpful and the ceiling ghost hadn't shown itself since, it creeped the three of them out, knowing that particular spirit was somewhere in the house, lurking. Neither Riley nor Edison had been able to find any mention of it in Nora's journals or "ceiling hauntings" in the house's massive library. So for now, they did what they had to do and kept their eyes up. Caroline was happy to do that *in the library*. A voracious reader, she still couldn't believe her luck, finding a treasure trove of obscure, beautiful books she could borrow any time she wanted—provided they weren't haunted.

Her life wasn't like other people's lives.

"Good evening, Miss," Plover greeted her from the foot of the stately hand-carved stairs, all translucent silver mist and gaunt features. Bowing at the waist in his dark pin-striped suit, as elegant as it was opaque, he smiled at her—well as close as Plover got to smiling.

"How's the new arrival?" Caroline asked, nodding to the cake stands, which she could see displayed on the kitchen counter through the open galley door.

"Quiet, contemplative," Plover said, with a note of approval in his voice. "I don't think Mrs. Fairlight was quite prepared for the reality of Shaddow House's interior. But as you know, newcomers are rarely prepared for it."

"Wait, you didn't put her next to Charlie's silver box, right?" Caroline asked, referring to the histrionic Regency-era gentleman attached to his murderous wife's silver service. "That's just mean."

"I did not," Plover said. "I thought it prudent to give her a few days to adjust before that particular trial by fire."

Caroline snorted. "How's Riley holding up?"

"Miss Riley is tired," he said. "She's overextending herself. Miss Alice is trying to help, but Miss Riley has the typical Denton stubbornness. She doesn't want to burden the two of you with the search for the remaining Welling locks."

Caroline frowned. The locks were ritual items that a rival magical family, the Wellings, had hidden in the footprint of Shaddow House after befriending the Dentons centuries before. The palm-sized copper pieces looked like industrial on-trend objets d'art —three loops attached together around empty space.

The Wellings claimed they wanted to help the Dentons in planning a "ghostly communication center" to assist people in contacting departed loved ones. But the Wellings secretly planned to use these locks combined with the location's energy to steal ghosts' wills, allowing the magic user to control them—most likely to murderous ends. The Dentons eventually uncovered the plot and drove the Wellings away, but the locks still remained hidden in the house like supernatural time bombs.

The Dentons had spent generations trying to find and remove the locks hidden throughout the house, to prevent the Wellings from taking them back. They'd only managed to find one before Riley arrived. Kyle had found two more with the help of information from the Wellings, which the coven promptly reclaimed after his death, along with another they found behind the fireplace—giving them a total of four locks. So, most winter nights were either spent reading the previous Dentons' journals or exploring the secret basement level that Plover had shown them—only accessible with a coin key Riley wore around her neck. So far, that had only revealed a spiraling cavern full of red metal doors and the increasingly scary-sounding spirits contained within. There was no secret drawer anywhere in the house labeled *there's totally not an evil object hidden here.*

Which would have been super helpful.

Plover was staring into the kitchen, where another ghost, Natalie, was chatting with Riley as she heated up Caroline's favorite cider with cinnamon sticks. In life, the smartly dressed brunette had been employed by a dating app designer, where she'd become so attached to the dry-erase board she'd used for team meetings that she'd stayed with it, even after she was struck by a food truck. Natalie was still an introvert who preferred to stay in the kitchen near her board, but it made Caroline feel better, knowing that Riley had someone her own age, living—so to speak—so close.

"Well, that's just stupid," Caroline murmured. "That's what we're here for, to share the burden."

"I told her so as well," Plover replied quietly. "Without calling her stupid, of course. I would never do that."

"Of course, you wouldn't," Caroline snorted, prompting Plover to quirk his lips. Plover was fervent in his devotion to the Dentons, though none of them knew whether that was the root cause or the result of his logic-defying romance with Riley's Aunt Nora. Riley still wasn't ready to ask questions about that, and Caroline didn't blame her. The mental images alone…

"So, on that note, Riley says you're not thrilled with the renovations she has planned. Is it because you're worried about Cole? Do *I* need to worry about Cole? Because he's tall enough that I'm going to have to recruit some people if we're going to take him out," Caroline said.

Plover held up his hands in a sort of calming gesture. "No,

Mr. Bishop seems like a perfectly reasonable choice for the construction. It's just the project she has planned. I'm sure there are
more worthy projects she could devote the Denton resources to—a
memorial to her aunt, perhaps, or bolstering the Gothic folly her
great-great-grandfather had in mind. This library renovation... It
seems unnecessary."

"Because it's going to benefit Edison?" Caroline guessed.

"It just seems so indulgent," Plover sniffed. "He's only just
'moved in,' and we don't know whether that's going to be a long-
term situation. After all, he hasn't bothered to propose marriage to
the lady of the house."

Caroline wished she could pat Plover on the shoulder, but he
didn't really have one. Clearly, Plover was still adjusting to the idea
of another man living in Shaddow House after so many years, sharing his territory, sharing Riley's attention. It would be sort of cute,
if there weren't such high stakes involved.

"Engagement is a bit of a touchy subject for Edison, given what
happened to his late fiancée," Caroline reminded Plover gently.
"Right in front of him."

"In my time, it wouldn't have been acceptable for a man to
simply move into a woman's home and make himself comfortable,"
Plover griped. "And for all his earlier helpfulness, I don't know if
he's a fit partner for a Denton. I find him...wanting."

For Plover, there was no harsher criticism he was willing to
voice. Ultimately, Caroline doubted it had anything to do with
Edison himself. Ghosts just hated change. That was part of the
reason for the constant, somewhat ill-planned construction projects.
Stairways leading into the ceiling. Bricked-over closets. Windows

opening onto solid walls. Ghosts were used to moving about the human world as they'd known it. Time moved differently for them, and when walls or even furniture were changed, they tended to focus on that rather than aiming their energy at nearby humans. Caroline had never heard of a ghost being so fully invested in human relationships, but Plover was sort of singular.

"What does Riley have to say to your objections?" Caroline asked.

"She says that if I quote 'keep it up,' she'll 'put in a Pilates studio, complete with a water feature and aerial-silks hanging from the ceiling.'"

"And you...don't want that?" Caroline guessed.

"No, I do not," Plover said, shaking his head. "A library is much preferred."

"Riley does have a way of ending an argument," Caroline replied.

Plover looked wistful for a moment. "Much like her aunt."

Having been trapped on Starfall Point for her entire life, Aunt Nora had chosen to move on to the afterlife immediately after her death. Plover, however, had unfinished business, wishing to see Shaddow House well-maintained and protected, so he stayed. The choices of both had always struck Caroline as particularly sad, but given her own situation, she couldn't say she would choose differently.

These maudlin thoughts were interrupted by Riley bustling into the parlor, steaming mug in hand. She bussed Caroline's cheek, casual affection Caroline was still adjusting to, but appreciated. Riley turned and made a rather grand gesture toward the three framed pieces she'd arranged on the mantel, next to Lilah's match cloche.

"I bought the etching, just like I promised," Riley said proudly. "And two more, just in case there was some sort of karmic imbalance for stealing the cake stands."

Alice frowned, adjusting her reading glasses on her nose. "Is this the 'cool thing' you brought us over to see? Multiple pieces of bad art?"

Riley nodded. "I don't know if it's bad. I kind of like it. And when I asked Willard what was new, he didn't even bring up the pilfered glassware. I'm kind of wondering if he noticed it was gone. Isn't that great? We're off the hook."

"I'm just not sure this qualifies as a 'fun surprise,'" Alice said.

Caroline nodded. "When I hear 'fun surprise,' I expect there to be glitter or frosting involved. Balloons, at minimum."

"Next time I'll set more appropriate expectations," Riley said dryly as Caroline took her mug over to the mantel to study the framed sketches.

"I still think the placement of the door means something," Riley continued, nodding at the drawing of Shaddow House. "Doorways have a lot of magical significance. It's the transition point between two worlds, inside the home and out."

"If I was going to hide a mystical hoo-ha, that's where I would put it," Caroline said, tilting her head as she looked at the landscape sketch, placed next to Riley's clear favorite. It showed a cliff overlooking turbulent water. And one particular rock formation in the foreground caught her eye, five conical stones that had somehow formed a sort of tiara-shaped fence line close to the cliff.

"That looks like Vixen's Fall," Caroline said, picking up the framed piece.

Alice tilted her head back and forth, frowning thoughtfully. "I wouldn't know; I never had the nerve to go out there myself."

"Why not?" Riley asked.

"One of those things that circulate among the teenager types," Caroline said. "The story goes that a woman, a sneaky temptress out to show her ankles to any man willing to look, died...somehow at the cliff. There are several different versions of how it happened, depending on who you ask. She was pushed off. She fell off in some sort of rompy mishap. She jumped off, knowing that she would never have the heart of the man she wanted. The bottom line is that she was found dead in the water under what came to be called Vixen's Fall. And because she was an unrepentant ankle-barer—"

"I'm picking up on a certain editorial tone," Alice noted.

"Well, as you get older you realize that some of the cautionary stories you hear as a young person are aimed at keeping you— particularly female 'you'—in your place," Caroline said, frowning. "Because of her supposedly wanton character, the woman in question wasn't buried in our little churchyard. No one really seems to know where she was buried. But the story goes that if you walk too close to the Fall on a full moon—and you're an unmarried young man or a married woman—the Vixen will reach up over the edge, grab you by the ankles, and pull you over."

"Good grief." Riley shuddered. "That's so creepy. And a weird set of stipulations."

"Well, obviously, we don't know anyone that's actually happened to," Caroline said. "It's probably one of those urban legends, 'friend of a friend' story elements tacked on to a real event that morphed over time into an evil, ankle-grabbing demon lady."

"Who hates married women and unattached men," Riley noted.

"Why do I always walk into the room during these moments in conversation?" a deeper male voice asked behind them. Tall, dark-haired, and dapper, Edison Held stood in the foyer, looking concerned. Riley crossed the room and kissed him lightly, taking his coat and scarf.

"Nothing to worry about," she promised him. "Your ankles are safe."

"Of all the pieces for sale in Willard's antiques shop, your girlfriend chose a sketch of one of the more notorious haunted locations on Starfall," Caroline told Edison as he handed her a mystery novel she'd wanted to borrow from the public library. Close friendship with the head librarian had to have *some* privileges.

"Well, of course, she did," Edison replied.

"But rest assured, we are not going out to this spot to investigate an urban legend," Riley told him. "We have enough on our plate with the library renovation and the lock search and all the ghosts we are currently dealing with."

"Have we settled on the library renovation, Miss?" Plover asked, wrinkling his nose.

"Pilates studio, Plover," Riley reminded him.

Plover let out a put-upon sigh. "Yes, Miss."

Chapter 4
Ben

LIVING IN A STORM SYSTEM carrying rabid badgers that could blow through your house at any moment, carrying turmoil in its wake. Such a badger-nado was currently turmoiling through his kitchen, slinging toaster pastry crumbs and insults at an alarming rate.

"I was *saving* those Pop-Pies as a special treat," Mina was shouting, her chestnut hair falling over her face.

Though two years older, sixteen-year-old Mina's forehead barely reached her lanky blond brother's shoulder, something Mina resented deeply. She'd always been tall for her age, with an older sibling's confidence in permanent superiority. And then Josh hit his freshman-year growth spurt, with all its shin pain and thoughtless snacking…and everything else was chaos.

"The grocery here doesn't have them, and I don't know how long it's gonna be before I can get more of them out on the Ice Planet Hellhole!" Mina yelled.

"The grocery has Pop-Pies," Josh countered, rolling his eyes. That had always been Josh's response to Mina's moods—indifference, quiet, calm…because he knew it got under her skin.

Being so much bigger than other kids in his class, and knowing how any physical response from him might be seen as scary, Ben's youngest child had learned to master the strategic long game of emotional warfare. "They just don't have Banana Berry Beignet."

"So *why* did you stuff *my* Banana Berry Beignet Pop-Pies in *your* giant mouth?" Mina shrieked at a decibel only teenage girls could create. She was wearing flannel pajamas in an eye-gouging shade of yellow, printed with dancing fried eggs. Mina rarely wore anything but bright colors, her own form of cheerful rebellion.

"Honey, I'll take you by Starfall Grounds and get you a pastry for breakfast, OK? I hear that Petra's doing amazing things with rugalach," Ben said, keeping his tone soothing and even, his palms in the air—as one did when one approached an angry badger storm.

"It's not the same," Mina insisted. "And Josh needs to be held accountable for this clear violation of the Phoenix Breakfast Food Streaming Service Peace Accords!"

Ben pinched the bridge of his nose. Back home, the Breakfast Food Streaming Service Peace Accords had taken weeks of negotiation after an unfortunate incident involving Josh eating the last gluten-free salted caramel Cronut from Mina's favorite local bakery. Mina retaliated by child-locking all of Josh's streaming service preferences to classic children's television programs like the Teletubbies.

"You can just go by Starfall Grounds on the way to Starfall Pages in a Starfall pedal cab," Josh replied, a sly smile breaking out over the long-lined, even features that reminded Ben so much of his own late father, sometimes it hurt to watch Josh laugh. "And then we can stop at one of fifteen Starfall fudge shops. Why is everything on the island named Starfall Something?" Josh frowned. "Don't you guys find it confusing?"

"It can be," Ben acknowledged. "And I think people just want you to know how proud they are to live here."

"Well, I'm not proud of living here," Mina whispered, her hazel eyes seeming three times as large through the shimmer of tears collecting on them. "I'm just trying to get through it so I can go to college and get out of here. And Josh, I would be careful about using your toothbrush for the next twelve to fourteen days."

"What does that mean?" Josh asked, frowning. "And why are you being so specific?"

With one last narrowing of her eyes, Mina sniffed, stomping up the stairs and making sure Ben felt every single step. Josh turned to him, his own eyes widening with growing panic. "Why is she being so specific?"

Ben stood and poured them both a cup of coffee. He asked quietly, "So what's going on with your sister?"

He tried not to cringe as his son dumped three heaping tablespoons of sugar and a quarter cup of creamer into his mug. It wasn't as if it would stunt Josh's growth. The kid was three inches taller than Ben. "Look, we survived saying goodbye to your friends, the move, hauling all of our stuff to the house using pedal wagons, and the fact that the movers lost *two* boxes of Mina's books without a Mina explosion," Ben said.

"They weren't her particularly old and dusty books, which worked in our favor," Josh said.

"Is something else bothering your sister, or is it an accumulation

of all of the very natural and expected anxiety she's feeling over...
everything I just mentioned?" Ben asked.

Josh looked sad, but amused. Josh was more observant than the
average teenager, certainly more observant than people gave him
credit for. And as much as Ben hated to use his child as an informant,
parents had to use whatever resources they had at their disposal.

"It's nothing personal," Josh told him. "I think she's just strug-
gling with the move, which is, I remind you, preventing her from
graduating with her friends next year. And this environment is the
exact opposite of what we're used to, weatherwise. And people act
like they know us, just because they know you. You know how she
hates it when people assume...anything."

"Do you think a job would help?" Ben asked. "Something to
keep her occupied?"

"As long as you make it seem like her idea, yeah," Josh said.
"If you suggest something, she'll just quote a bunch of child labor
laws at you."

"Smart. She does like to memorize things out of spite," Ben
said, nodding. "What about you? There's not exactly a music con-
servatory for you to join up with here. Or a school basketball team.
We've got to find something for you, too."

Josh shook his head. "I don't know, Dad, I think I'm OK with
giving the violin a rest for a while. That was always more of Mom's
thing. I think I'm looking forward to having a break. And maybe
I can find some pickup games with some of the guys around here.
There are *some* kids my age at school, just not enough to form an
official team."

Ben placed a comforting hand on his son's shoulder. Josh had shown an interest in the violin, and a moderate talent for it, at age ten. His mother had pushed him to practice, hours upon hours, until the joy had been completely sucked out of music for him. And yet, he was still expected to practice. Nothing Ben said to her could convince Isabelle that she was ruining any chance they had of Josh pursuing the violin long-term. Not even when Josh threatened to *run away* if she made him quit the basketball team to protect his hands, all for an instrument he only showed *some* interest in. Isabelle had insisted that she was only trying to bolster Josh's future college applications, but Ben suspected her vehemence was based on classical music being a "more refined" interest compared to basketball. The women on her charity boards wouldn't be impressed with basketball.

And poor Mina, whose talents were less quantifiable, didn't get used for clout at all—which was somehow worse. When Mina fought back with her neon clothes and gleeful sarcasm, Isabelle only tried to restrain Mina's personality further, admonishing her to "be practical" and "take life seriously." The silent implication was that there was nothing special about Mina, so she was going to have to work harder to make it in the world. Mina's rebellions were maliciously rainbow-infused, and Ben admired her all the more for it.

"So, what's *really* going on with your sister?" Ben asked.

Josh peered up at his father, sipping his coffee. "Remember how we were supposed to be visiting Mom in Colorado this summer?"

Ben nodded.

"Mom texted," Josh told him. "She said that Tom isn't comfortable with the idea of hosting us in his house so soon after the wedding, and with the bonus room remodel…"

"Wait, what do you mean so soon after the wedding?" Ben exclaimed. Glancing up toward the stairs, he lowered his voice. "Your mom's wedding is supposed to be sometime this fall!"

"Apparently, they decided to move it up...to last week," Josh said, pursing his lips and nodding.

Ben felt an awful pressure in his chest as he watched Josh try to fight back the hurt, the absolute insult of his mother making such a huge step without a thought to Josh or Mina's feelings. "Your mom got married without you guys?"

Josh nodded, staring down into his coffee. "She said the venue had an opening and Tom just happened to have room in his schedule. Tom's family was in town for Easter and with the spring flowers coming into bloom, they just couldn't waste the opportunity."

Ben raised his hands, bewildered. "And she said all this *by text?*"

Josh nodded. Ben raised his hand to the back of Josh's neck and pulled him close. Josh was trying not to sniff, but he was a fourteen-year-old boy, and his mom was the one behaving like an inconsiderate kid. And she'd hurt Mina, which was a particular hot-button issue for Josh. They might occasionally bicker and stage elaborate negotiations-slash-retributions over petty pastry squabbles, but the pair of them were tightly bonded because they had, in essence, served in a bad parental marriage foxhole together.

Ben swallowed the lump building in his throat. "It's OK to be upset, to be hurt. You don't have to pretend you're not because it's your mom, or because you don't want to worry me."

Josh's head moved up and down against Ben's shoulder.

"And maybe we need to get in touch with the therapist back in Arizona?" Ben suggested.

Josh squeezed Ben's arm. "Yep."

"You know you can't use your toothbrush until we get a replacement, right?" Ben asked.

Josh nodded. "Yep."

"Also, you might want to hide the replacement where she can't find it," Ben added.

Josh sighed. "My floss, too."

It had required both chocolate rugalach and raspberry rugalach to mollify Mina's pastry-based indignity. She'd threatened to steal Josh's chocolate rugalach, but then he'd held it up over her head, out of her reach no matter how high she'd hopped. While she protested mightily, it always made her laugh. And, thus, a delicate peace was restored with their world.

Ben trusted that his children would return to the house and not reduce the island to rubble within the next few hours while he worked at the Starfall Point Community Clinic. That was new for him, knowing that his kids were somewhere, unsupervised, and he told himself that this was part of the reason he'd moved them all "home." For all its shortcomings in grocery availability and extra-curricular activities, the island felt safer than the busy city environment the kids had grown up in. Given that cars weren't allowed in the more historic areas of the island, including their neighborhood, they didn't even have traffic on Starfall. Ben's commute to work was a seven-minute walk.

Ben stood in the supply closet that had been converted into an office for him. The clinic had been designed for one primary care provider at a time, and the clinic's other physician, Dr. Toller, had been flying solo for more than ten years. He was very much looking forward to sharing the workload. Ben wasn't quite up to seeing patients yet, but he was moving into his office, becoming familiar with the filing system, reviewing the cases of longtime patients, so he could be prepared for the inevitable illnesses and emergencies.

Life as the doctor of a small island clinic was a never-ending cycle of back injuries in adults and children with colds and flu. And in the summer, the tourists would come with their sunburns and fishhook injuries. The strange accidental death of a boy named Kyle Ashmark over the winter was one of the few emergencies of its kind in years.

"I know you're not going to have a lot of room, but the good news is all of the files are kept into another room...now," said his new nurse practitioner, Samantha Vermeer. Samantha was a newcomer to the island, a Milwaukee native who was looking for a break from the bustle of the city. Personally, Ben thought she'd overshot it a bit.

Ben paused to put his hand on the newly hung wallpaper—a strange khaki color with maroon and navy-blue pinstripes. He was pretty sure it was left over from when the clinic was originally built in the 1940s. It gave the room a sort of Norman Rockwell sepia-toned quality, as opposed to the antiseptic white of most medical offices. What hadn't changed was the constant ringing of the phone. It never stopped ringing, which didn't seem to perturb Samantha at all, as she leaned her tall frame against the door.

"Between me and you, Dr. Toller's just tired," Samantha admitted. "He's been doing this alone for so long. That's a lot of weight to have on his shoulders. He doesn't get sick days, himself. He doesn't get vacation days. And sometimes, it can get frustrating, dealing with people who don't listen to advice and are surprised when they have the same problems over and over."

"Well, that's why I'm here," Ben chuckled, closing the digital patient portal on his new desktop computer. Knowing his patients for decades...well, it was going to present its own set of challenges, in terms of awkwardness, but he knew things about them personally that would help him serve their interests. For instance, he knew that—no matter how he might protest that he was sticking to his diet—Mr. Qualls hid behind his garage every night so his wife wouldn't see him enjoying a bowl full of ice cream, even in January.

Samantha asked. "How are the kids settling in?"

Ben paused. "Well, I don't hear screams or sirens...but the island only has the one ambulance...so..."

"I'm sure they're fine," Samantha said with a laugh.

"I'm gonna go get lunch and then go check on them," Ben said. "First full day tomorrow."

"I'm going to warn you now, it's going to be a big one," Samantha told him. "The phone's ringing off the hook, and you're booked out for appointments for the next five months."

"That's what that is?" Ben cried as the phone jangled to life in the background.

"Oh, yeah, we normally get maybe ten calls a day," Samantha said, nodding. "It was part of the reason I took this job, Dr. Hoult."

"Sorry, Samantha," Ben said, running his hand through his sandy hair. "And you might as well call me 'Ben' if I'm causing you this sort of stress."

"Well, I was going to eventually anyway," Samantha told him. "I was just trying to be First-Day Polite. And it's OK, it just reminds

me of why I quit working in a big-city ER. And technically, the clinic
is closed today, so I'm just letting most of them go to our voicemail."

"Can I grab you a sandwich or something, for your emotional
distress?" Ben asked.

"Oh, for the amount of calls coming in, you're going to have
to pony up something from Petra's," she retorted, leveling a pair
of dark-brown eyes at him. "Possibly a whole tray of something."

"Understood," Ben said, sliding into his jacket. He texted the
kids, telling them they could join him for lunch. By the time he made
it to Main Square, they hadn't responded, which was troubling.

Ben pulled his hood up to protect his head from the light snow-
rain mix pelting the sidewalk. There was a certain fluid energy he
enjoyed about summer on the island, thousands of feet on the cob-
blestone streets of the historic district, the smell of melting butter
and sugar wafting out of the fudge shops. But this quiet, windblown
solitude had its charms.

Isabelle had always insisted she got this sort of "meditative
space" from those yoga retreats in the desert...but Ben had never
seen the appeal. The desert could be beautiful, but it was so...unwel-
coming. Any time he'd tried to hike on the paths near their gated
community, his thoughts were on a loop of *That might be a rattle-
snake. That might be a scorpion. Am I drinking enough water? Why
does everything here want to kill me, including the sun?*

He preferred snow and wind, the way every winter seemed to
have its own personality. Ice could kill you, but it followed rules.
Desert creatures didn't care about rules.

His feet crunched through the slush as he passed a number of
restaurants and shops closed for the season. It just wasn't feasible for

the owners to stay open without the huge summer crowds. Petra's bakery, the bookstore, the general store—they were included in the handful of year-round exceptions.

So much seemed the same about Starfall, and yet, so much had changed. He wasn't sure if that conflicted with his expectations or not. It wasn't as if he'd never come back to the island after he left. Cell phones had only just come into common use when he'd left for school, and even then, texting and social media hadn't developed into what would have given him a constant window into what was happening back on Starfall. He'd come home, those first few Thanksgivings, but he'd mostly stayed in the house with his parents.

And if he had happened to see Caroline, she'd acted like she barely knew him. She'd stared past him, barely spoke to him, actively looked for someone else nearby to talk to. After his sophomore year, he'd studiously avoided seeing Caroline at all. It hadn't been hard since she was always busy, running the Rose. That was Caroline, always working. She complained about the strain of it, but she could never just sit still—unless she was reading. There were times he wondered if her brain developed her reading interest as some secret coping mechanism to give her body a break.

Even when they were young, Caroline knew how much her parents depended on her to keep the bar going. Her brothers might show up for their shifts, but they spent more time jawing with their friends than they did serving beers. Caroline was always the shoulder to take on the burden. But if one pointed that out to any of the Wiltons, they would have protested mightily, insisting that the boys helped in "other ways."

Almost without thinking, Ben had turned toward The Wilted

Rose. He hadn't been able to talk to Caroline at any length, and he wasn't sure he was ready. He wanted to see her so badly, he didn't think he could trust himself to behave like a rational man. And yet, there he was, standing in front of the battered wooden exterior.

The Wilton family had changed the sign back in the 1970s, all dull gold lettering and overtly curled script looping around a drooping red rose. People were still talking about it. As he walked into the bar, Ben was struck by the familiar smell of spilled beer and savory home cooking. He hadn't spent much time there when he was young. It was too awkward, being served by Caroline's family. They knew what he was doing with their daughter on the beach. Everything was as he remembered, though, just older, more worn. And the same was true for Caroline's mother, whose small shoulders seemed more stooped, her hair almost entirely gray, while it had been a shiny sable when he'd left for school.

Gert moved through the dining room crowded with locals, warming up coffees, grabbing empty plates on her way past tables. As she bustled back into the kitchen and returned a few minutes later with a tray crowded with soup bowls, Ben wondered where Caroline's brothers were. Even as kids, the Wilton kids had helped out in the bar, doing whatever chores minors were allowed to do by the state—basically anything that didn't involve touching alcohol.

Behind Gert, Caroline was moving about the bar with a brisk efficiency and a teasing smile. But when she saw Ben, it just sort of slid right off her face. That hurt. He certainly hadn't expected to be a delight to her, but he didn't want to steal her joy. Maybe he should just leave?

"Ben! It's so good to see you!" Gert cried with an affection that startled him. Gert was not a warm woman. Instead of hugging him, she patted him on the shoulders with both hands, an old, strange habit, but Ben found some comfort in it. "We were all so glad to hear that you were moving back. Why don't you sit in my section, so we can catch up?"

Gert led him to a worn wooden table for four, and he felt guilty for occupying it as one person. Maybe he should text the kids again so they could join him? He eyed the menu Gert handed over and saw that it seemed that the burgers and smoked whitefish dip of his youth were still on offer with some expensive-sounding additions—candied this and sun-dried that.

Weird.

Ben ordered the turkey artichoke melt and tried not to feel like a creeper as he watched Caroline work. When she didn't look at him, she was relaxed, at ease, comfortable. And again, he had to wonder, how could she still be so beautiful after so many years? Every time he looked in the mirror, he seemed to see an older and more exhausted man staring back at him. He'd thought time was to blame, but given that Caroline barely seemed to have aged, he was starting to wonder if it was his two adolescent roommates. Or maybe the desert sun...or Mina insisting on learning how to ride a moped.

He needed to find something else to focus on.

He checked his phone and found a text from Josh:

No 🕐 for 🪨. Mina found 📕 about creepy 🏠 next door on grandpa's shelf. Fallen down reading 🐰 hole. Won't see her for 📅 .

Why did his son insist on communicating in tiny pictograms? Was it really easier than spelling? At this point, Ben supposed he should be grateful for punctuation. Between phone hieroglyphics and the legalistic international treaty language during arguments... no, he definitely preferred the treaty thing, even if it did leave him feel incredibly stupid compared to his own children.

Mina would probably toss the book aside earlier than Josh anticipated, which could lead to trouble. There wasn't much real information about Shaddow House available, even in the books written by locals. Ben was pretty sure his father only kept them around for renters who didn't know any better. The Shaddow family wouldn't even allow photographers inside the house, so all of the pictures were exterior shots. There were theories, of course, among the locals about why the Shaddow family never came to the island anymore, why they never allowed locals inside the house, whether the Dentons were somehow secretly related to their employers through some scandalous love-child situation.

And of course, with any old house with a mysterious past, there were rumors that it was haunted. If he wasn't a man of science, he might even be tempted to believe them. Living next door, Ben had seen things as a kid, shadows moving in windows—the shape of which seemed too tall to be old Miss Denton. He'd heard noises, laughing, screaming, the sound of a veritable crowd of people when Miss Denton was always alone. His parents had always dismissed his reports as imagination and told Ben to leave nice (though distant) Miss Denton alone.

Maybe it was better just to watch Caroline than to think about these things.

Over the course of the lunch rush, Caroline seemed to get distracted. Her eyes kept darting across the room, to the little hallway entrance to the cellar. He couldn't see what she was looking at. That corner was a rare, shadowed area of the dining room...though it did seem darker, somehow, than it should be in a room mostly lit by neon. Whatever Caroline saw, it was putting a little frown line between her brows.

A series of pops overhead drew his attention to the ceiling. Outside, the weather seemed to pick up, the wind moving wispy clouds across the sky like a bad comedian getting the hook. The ceiling seemed to be creaking...a lot. He supposed that was normal. His own house never seemed to stop groaning and popping. It took a lot of getting used to after living in new construction for so many years. The good news was the kids would never be able to sneak out of the house. Every step would be loudly announced by squeaky floorboards.

He could only hope.

"Caroline, dear, how are you?" Margaret Flanders asked as Caroline brought her table iced tea refills. It was the veritable council of Starfall social cornerstones. Margaret, who had run the children's section at the public library for as long as anyone could remember, was holding court over several core members of the Nana Grapevine. Judith Kim was the island's longest-serving postmistress. Regina Clemmons opened her ice cream store, Starfall Scoops, right before Ben left for school. Norma Oviette seemed to single-handedly run Clark's law office, which only proved the woman had the patience of a saint...or she was going for some sort of long-con revenge situation to destroy Clark's business, which Ben wholeheartedly supported.

"And how is your little friend, Riley?" Margaret asked.

Caroline, still preoccupied by whatever was happening near the cellar door, turned to Margaret as Margaret continued, "She hasn't had much to say to me since the winter. I'm afraid she's a little skittish around me since I fibbed to her about Eddie leaving. I was just trying to help the two of them get over their little fight. They're so sweet together."

"Oh, Riley's not a grudge-holder," Norma assured Margaret. "She's just had a lot on her plate since she moved here. It can't be easy, running that house on her own. Hell, it was a job for her aunt, and she'd done it all her life."

"She could have help, if she opened the house to the public, like Eddie wanted," Margaret sniffed. "But I suppose he's dropped that since he's been able to move into the house himself."

"Interesting way to go about research." Judith chuckled.

"Riley's never gonna break tradition beyond that," Regina said. "She may not have known Nora, but you can tell she respects her memory."

"When have you had time to learn so much about Riley?" Margaret asked, her gray brows arched.

Regina shrugged. "You give people ice cream, they tell you things."

"Ladies, enjoy your lunch," Caroline said, stepping away from their table and turning to Ben. For a moment, it was like she'd forgotten he was the one sitting at the table and the customer service smile fell from her face to a much more reserved, blank expression.

That was not becoming more fun with repetition.

"Ben, how are you settling in?" Caroline asked.

"Oh, there's always a million things you forget you're going to need for a new place. You know how it goes," Ben said, nodding.

"Not really," Caroline said, just one octave short of a verbal eye roll.

Ben wanted to slap his hand over his face. He was an idiot. Caroline had never moved into any new home—just an older house inherited from family. He sighed.

"Look, Caroline, I'm not trying to make things uncomfortable between us. I know we're probably not going to be best friends, but I don't think we have to be this…awkward? I thought we left things on a pretty decent note."

"Yes, and then we didn't talk for almost twenty years," Caroline said. "That was not an accident. At least, on my part. You had your own life, and I was happy for you."

"And you've had your own life too—" Ben said.

"Not like you have, and *you know why*. I told you about it when we were kids. And now is not the time for this conversation," Caroline replied, glancing over at Margaret's table. Then her eyes darted upward as the ceiling groaned.

"I can't believe we're having this conversation at all," he said, lowering his voice so the members of the Nana Grapevine within earshot couldn't hear him say, "Talking about curses like they're a real thing that exist."

"I thought you understood," Caroline whispered. "It wasn't personal. It wasn't that I didn't want to be with you. Do you think it was easy? Knowing you were out there in the world? While I'm stuck here? You know what's happened to my family. Hell, you went to a couple of the funerals."

She looked so upset. And he wanted to turn the tide of this conversation. He hadn't been able to talk to her in forever, and he was messing it up. "I understand that you believe the curse is real, and I'm not going to insult you by trying to change your mind."

"Don't patronize me," she said. "I don't care if you think it's real or not. I do, and I'm the one whose neck is on the line."

"Caroline, please. This isn't how I wanted this to go," he pleaded. "I've been trying to tell you how much I missed you—down to the marrow in my bones—since I got back on the island, but I keep messing it up."

"Well, it's not exactly how I pictured this conversation going," she huffed. "At this point, I can't even fake the dignity of pretending I haven't rehearsed what I was going to say to you...over and over in my head, when I couldn't sleep. And in those imaginings, I didn't picture the words 'curse' or 'funeral' coming up."

"Let's start over, please. I don't care why we split years ago. It still hurts, but I don't want it to keep us from—" He sighed. "So much has happened since then, and I'm so afraid that I'm going to mess this up this time around. And I might miss out on connecting with you again, on hearing how you've been, what you've been doing. I just don't want to lose out on the chance to know who you are now."

"Oh, sure, I'm a whole new person," Caroline said, smiling and shaking her head. "Living in the same place, working the same job, in the same building. It's the sort of huge change that spurs personal development."

"Technically, we're both different people, on a cellular level," Ben told her, making her laugh. "You're body regenerates cells every minute you're alive. I'm a doctor. I know things."

Oh, how he'd missed that laugh.

"So, I'm new Ben, better than New Coke, I promise," he said, reaching out to her. He saw the hesitation cross her face, as if for a moment, she considered letting the business of the bar distract her and let her dash away. But she took a deep breath and extended her hand.

"OK, new Ben," Caroline sighed. "Nice to meet you."

His fingers closed around hers, warm and familiar, and it was like his homecoming was complete. For just one second, everything was right.

And then, overhead, it sounded like the fist of God was knocking on the roof.

"What the?" Caroline looked up, blinking as plaster dust sprinkled down on her face like snow. Ben stood, a sour, heavy feeling settling into his gut as the other customers slowed their movements, looking up at the ceiling with their forks halfway to their mouths.

Ben started to say, "Caroline, I think we need to—"

The building shook and the room went dark as wood and debris cascaded over the windows facing the water. Ben launched himself and pulled Caroline under the table with him as the floor trembled. In the distance, he could hear screams as he tucked his chin over Caroline's head.

She fit against him as she always did, like she was made for him. But he didn't want to admit to himself how happy he was to have her in his arms again, when her world seemed to be collapsing around them.

Chapter 5
Caroline

THE WORLD HAD GONE NOISY and white, like it was snowing inside the bar—which, well, after the year she'd had seemed unlikely, but not impossible.

Caroline could sense that Ben was holding her. She could register the warmth of his chest against her cheek. And while it was welcome, all Caroline could really concern herself with was panic for her mother, for her customers, for the Rose itself. It felt like a family member was dying right in front of her, and there was nothing she could do about it. And yes, that was a little bit of a hot-button issue for her.

Her fingers tangled in Ben's flannel shirt and the smell of pine and spice filled her nose. It brought her back to herself, to stolen moments in Ben's old room, after she'd climbed up the trellis at Gray Fern Cottage. He hadn't changed his cologne in all these years.

These were truly inconvenient thoughts to have when a building was trying to smack you around.

The noise finally stopped, and the floor wasn't shaking anymore. Ben squeezed her even tighter and then released her, and while everything in her screamed for her to get up, to check on everybody—she couldn't budge as Ben crouched over her, checking for injuries. He was so close she could reach out and brush her fingertips across his lips like she used to, after all this time. How many days had passed with her pretending she didn't miss him? How many other names had she whispered trying to balm the wound? And now, he was looking at her like he loved her and all it did was hurt more.

"You OK?" he said, cupping his hands around her cheeks. "Does anything hurt? Did you bump your head?"

Caroline blinked at him. Was she OK? *Had* she bumped her head? Because her thought patterns did *not* seem healthy. Maybe she was just post-crisis randy? It had happened before with particularly dangerous ghost cases.

Ghosts.

Death.

Family.

"Mom?" Caroline scrambled up, practically throwing Ben off of her. He stood, helping her to her feet. Her mom was standing in the middle of the room, staring back at where Caroline had been tucked under Ben's body. "Mom!"

Caroline hurtled across the room, throwing her arms around her mother, who seemed healthy and whole—mostly annoyed. Gert's arms tightened briefly around Caroline before pulling away.

"You're all right," her mother said, almost to herself as much as to Caroline. "You're all right."

"Does anybody need medical assistance?" Ben yelled behind them.

"What the hell happened?" Caroline cried, surveying the confusion. While there was a lot of white plaster dust floating through the air, it didn't seem like anyone was bleeding or clutching broken limbs. Customers were mostly coughing and waving their hands in front of their faces to chase off the dust. Caroline didn't want to think about what they could be breathing in. Tables and chairs were overturned across the floor, like a giant, angry child had a tea-party tantrum. Dishes lay broken on the scarred wooden floor, but that seemed to be the result of people scrambling away from the porch... the porch that was just sort of hanging off the main section of the building like a loose tooth, teetering toward the edge of the hill.

"Does it matter?" Gert scoffed. "Call Celia and tell her we're gonna need emergency services."

Caroline blinked at her, too distracted by the sight of what the family called "the keeper's quarters" upstairs now collapsed in the outdoor dining area her father had added only ten years before. She could see the sky through the ceiling. That was bad.

But, obviously, no one was dining al fresco with snow still on the tables, so fortunately, the debris had landed away from the crowd. At least no one was hurt.

When Caroline didn't immediately pull her phone out of her pocket, Gert rolled her eyes and used her own phone to call. Caroline glanced up. The bedroom above was now visible through the open wound in the ceiling...right where Cole had noted the watermark only days before. It had been such a small thing, about the size of a Frisbee, and now...how had it gotten so much worse, so fast?

Ben moved methodically around the room, checking people over. Cole's massive frame appeared at her left, his hand on her shoulder, as if he wanted to keep her from walking closer to the fractured ceiling.

"Uh, it looks like your ceiling had a heart attack," he said, frowning.

Caroline nodded. Now that it seemed there were no injuries in the crowd, that this wasn't some escalation of her family's spiritual fuckery, she felt her body slowly relax. She felt very tired, which was probably the result of her adrenaline ebbing. "Is that a technical term?"

Cole shook his head. "Nope. I'll take a look, see if I can figure out the problem and how extensive the damage is."

A pained smile stretched across her face. "Thanks, Cole."

Outside, she could hear shouting as the front door of the bar was yanked open. Alice and Riley were standing there, panting, coats hanging off their shoulders, boots half-tied, as if they'd run out half-dressed. Which they probably did.

"Don't come in!" Cole shouted. "It might not be safe!"

"Quiet, you," Alice barked at him, throwing her arms around Caroline. Her exhaustion was still there, but with Riley and Alice's magic nearby, it didn't seem as severe. Riley put her arms around the both of them, and the chaos raging inside Caroline quieted. They were here. She was safe.

Alice told her. "It's just a building. We can figure everything else out."

"We felt you," Riley said. "It was like a full-body shriek."

"I scared Mitt Sherzinger pretty badly on my way over," Alice confessed. "I also may have knocked him right off his bike tires as I tore down the sidewalk. It's possible I owe Mitt an apology."

Caroline nodded. She turned her head toward the bar, where most of the family's pictures and mementos had shaken loose from their places on the high shelf—all but one, the old landscape that had hung there for as long as Caroline could remember. It hung steadfast, despite the weight of the frame and the dodgy craftsmanship that held it in place. Caroline frowned, her eyes traveling down to the area behind the bar, near the kitchen door. The ghost in the purple dress had moved there, in the shadows behind the ice machine, glaring at everybody as if she was annoyed that they were being so noisy. At the same time, she looked...satisfied? Like the family had this coming?

"You guys see her, right?" Caroline asked.

"Yep," both of them chorused.

"That can't be good," Caroline muttered.

Riley shook her head. "Nope."

In the aftermath of the "ceiling heart attack," a crowd gathered outside the Rose while Trooper Celia Tyree strung yellow CAUTION tape across the entrance. Cole inspected the damage as Iggy Gilinsky and his brother-in-law, Jeff Flanders, climbed onto the roof, nailing a tarp over the external damage. This didn't strike Caroline as particularly safe, but she wasn't in the habit of trying to tell Iggy what to do. Judith and Regina were in the Wiltons' garage taping together boxes to store what supplies they could salvage. Norma and Margaret stood in the snow, creating carefully organized labels. Samantha arrived to help Ben clear each and every person who had been inside, to make sure they hadn't suffered any injuries that needed to be reported to the Wiltons' insurance company.

Petra had set up a table with thermoses of coffee and tea for those who were helping, and even those who weren't. Rugalach was reserved for people who were helping, though. Petra had standards.

While it had been an absolute bastard of a day, it warmed Caroline's heart to see her community coming together to help her family. And yes, it was a little embarrassing, especially when some of the people helping them should—by all rights—be at home recovering from their near miss with the ceiling. But this was what Starfall did. When Judith's husband, Steven, had a heart attack, Gert had organized the meal train. When Norma's grandson needed help with chemistry, Caroline tutored him. Islanders helped islanders. It was simply the Wiltons' turn.

Denny Wilton had arrived on the scene just a few minutes before, but unlike Caroline's mother, he hadn't approached the entrance. He just stood there, in his parka, staring at the building and looking defeated. Will and Wally had arrived too, but were largely useless, only picking up exactly what Gert directed them to and putting it down in the exact location she specified. So her progress was actually slowed down by their presence.

Caroline suspected the boys had only come to help clear away the items that could be salvaged because they knew it would look terrible that everybody else on the island showed up to help and they didn't.

Cole joined the three ladies outside, wearing an honest-to-goodness Bishop Reconstruction hard hat. On another day, the sight of a big, bearded virile man in construction gear might have done it for Caroline, but all she could see was the destruction, and Ben, gently caring for the people whose close brush with serious injury made Caroline want to weep.

"OK, I'm pretty sure this was the result of a slow leak in the roof," Cole told her. "Over time moisture wicked in and everything deteriorated on that side of the building until that section just couldn't hold its own weight. Particularly, when you take into account the uh, hasty construction on the outdoor dining area? Whoever built it was supposed to use bracing. Without it, the porch put extra, unsupported weight on the existing exterior walls. Like putting a ten-pound earring on your ear, eventually, that earlobe is going to have some real problems."

While Alice and Riley shuddered, Caroline swallowed heavily. Her father had been little over half-finished with the project when Chris died. He was too paralyzed by grief to even think about proper bracing and had trusted her brothers to finish the porch for him. He'd refused all offers of help from Iggy and Jeff, wanting to keep other people out of their suffocating bubble of misery. They had done—to no one's surprise—a hasty job by the barest definition of the word. And her mother didn't have the will or the energy to tell them so. Caroline also suspected Sven, who happened to be the county inspector-slash-property-assessor, felt bad for her parents when he certified the finished product. That combined with the obligation he'd felt, knowing Gert had taken care of his family when he was ill, was probably enough to get a "it's probably fine" certification.

Riley gave a decisive nod. "OK, well, Cole, I think you're going to have to start work here immediately. Caroline's family depends on the Rose. It's a big part of the community. We can't just leave it open to the elements. Can you imagine if this would have happened during football season?"

"It's possible you've lived on this island a little too long," Alice noted.

"I don't usually take on last-minute projects on the fly," Cole protested, his dark eyes going wide. "This seems like a bad idea."

"I don't like to throw around the words 'unlimited resources,'" Riley told him. "So, I won't do it lightly. All repairs to the Rose will be covered by the Shaddow Foundation Trust."

"You can't do that," Caroline cried.

"I can and I will," Riley insisted. "Consider it a historical preservation project, which is right up the Shaddow Foundation Trust's alley, and I have complete discretion about the sort of projects the foundation supports."

Riley usually played down her fortune, referring to the Shaddow Foundation Trust, when it was basically just her checkbook. Inheriting a family mansion and more than enough financial assets to keep it running had its benefits, which she really hadn't adjusted to after a lifetime of paycheck-to-paycheck.

"But I had plans for your library all drawn out," Cole protested.

"It's the family's responsibility to take care of what's important to the island," Riley said. "Particularly, when you consider how certain factors involving the Shaddow family may have contributed to the condition of the building."

"Uh, what does that mean?" Cole asked, his dark brows furrowing.

"The Shaddows were partners in the original construction of The Wilted Rose and insisted on certain specifications. If they hadn't meddled so much, maybe the building would have lasted longer," Riley lied smoothly. It concerned Caroline, that she was able to do that so easily.

Caroline objected. "I know my mom. Family pride won't allow anything else."

"OK, OK," Cole said, writing some notes on a yellow legal pad with his enormous, long-fingered hands. "But what about your library renovation, Miss Denton?"

"It's Riley," she said. "And it can wait until Caroline's work-place is safe."

"I don't like this," Caroline told her. "We have an emergency fund, just for situations like this. You have to when you own a prac-tically ancient building. I insist on paying half."

"This is a rough guess, of course, but this is the neighborhood of what you're looking at," Cole said, holding out his pad.

Caroline eyed the piece of paper, where he'd scribbled a rough estimate of what it would cost to fix the ceiling, the upstairs bed-room, the outside dining area, the porch—a big, old six-figure esti-mate. "My family will cover *a quarter* of the repairs."

And they were going to have to borrow money to cover *that*. The emergency fund had just been completely blown out of the water. Or maybe into the water. She didn't know. It had been a long fucking day.

"Done," Riley said, shaking Caroline's hand. "Cole, draw up a work contract with a formal estimate and let's get started. Any chance of the Rose being open for the tourist season?"

"Not for Memorial Day, but maybe by the end of the summer," Cole said, pursing his lips. "I've never had a job pitch go this way."

Snow was peppering his dark beard with white flecks, giving him a sort of grumpy wizard appearance. Riley patted him on his shoulder, or at least, what she could reach of his shoulder. Riley wasn't much taller than Caroline. "Welcome to Starfall Point."

"Well, I guess it works," he grumbled. "Celia asked me to inspect the building for the state's oversight offices anyway. I'll make some phone calls, come up with supply lists, formalize the estimate."

He stalked off, muttering under his breath.

"Is it possible that you've become a little too accustomed to throwing your financial weight around?" Alice asked gently.

"I've been told where and how I'm going to live for the rest of my life," Riley said. "One of the benefits of this gig is having money to throw at problems. I've never had that before. Also, it sort of solves some problems for me. Plover is still pitching a fit about the renovations. Poor Edison basically has a disapproving live-in father-in-law...except not living."

"So really, this is to help you, not me," Caroline mused.

"Eh," Riley waggled her hand back and forth.

"What was all that about the Shaddow family contributing to the deterioration of the Rose?" Alice asked.

"A little bit of improvised motivation. We don't know that the ghost lady in the barroom *didn't* contribute to the cave-in," Riley insisted. "For all we know, the temperature variations that come along with hauntings, changes in air pressure, humidity—that can all mess with the integrity of construction materials."

"I'm not sure about that," Caroline said, pulling her jacket tighter against the wind.

"In particular, I don't think that humidity thing is correct," Alice added.

"I'm grasping at straws here," Riley admitted. "But I can't let you face this on your own, particularly when I think the ghost lady contributed to the bar falling apart, somehow. Even if the bar isn't her attachment object and she can't physically interact with it. Something... something was off about the look on her face, right now, watching the aftermath of everything fall apart around you. I don't trust her."

Caroline turned toward the building and its gaping wounds, through which she could see the purple-dress ghost pacing back and forth, an unsettling grin on her face as she prowled the inside of the bar like a shark tracking injured prey.

"That seems reasonable," Caroline said.

"And you've never seen her before the other day?" Alice asked.

Caroline shook her head. "Not once, but you know, the ghosts only show themselves to us when they want us to see them. I mean, she would have to be connected to my family somehow, right, to be showing up around the Rose? Maybe she was trying to warn us of what was coming?"

"So, it was a warning smirk?" Riley asked, arching her brows at Caroline.

"OK, probably not," Caroline said.

Caroline scanned the crowd again. Ben was pulling a sizable splinter out of Iggy's hand. Her dad had changed positions, far away from the crowd, his coat collar pulled up around his ears. Her brothers, predictably, had set up camp near the rugalach.

"I'm gonna go check on my dad," Caroline told them. "Can you make sure my mom doesn't wear herself out?"

Alice and Riley nodded solemnly.

Denny was staring at the second floor, his expression haunted. He'd been a tall, heavyset man once, but time and heartache had whittled him down. Caroline had gotten her eyes from him, but now Denny's were shadowed and framed by deep lines.

"Maybe we should just let it fall apart and slide into the water," Denny rumbled, though Caroline wasn't sure whether he was talking to himself or to her. "Maybe we should just burn what's left."

"Well, that's one plan," Caroline acknowledged. "But we kind of depend on the income to buy food and stuff."

"I'm sorry, baby," he sighed. "I'm sorry you kids are stuck with this, stuck in this place. I wish things were different for you."

"Dad," she sighed. "Don't start that again. It's not your fault."

"But it is," her father insisted. "I brought this on you."

"No one brought this—"

Her phone rang, and it was their insurance agent, distracting Caroline with blessed minutiae—and her brain leaped for the chance to deal with something she might be able to control. She was still working out whether their coverage included "roof heart attack" when her brothers approached.

Caroline ended the call. It was not looking good, in terms of roof-heart-attack coverage.

"Hey, uh, it looks like you guys have all this under control," Will said, rubbing his hand over the back of his neck. People rarely believed that the boys were twins. Will was bald as an egg, thin and angular, while Wally was rounded, with their dad's thick dark hair and a cherubic face that had always gotten him out of trouble when they were kids. They were fraternal in appearance but identical in their ability to avoid responsibility. It would have been impressive if it wasn't so damned irritating..

"There's really not much we can do here," Wally continued. "So, I think we're just going to head home."

Caroline's jaw dropped open. Dozens of people were milling around the site, trying to find a way to help. But Wally and Will were just gonna casually wander away?

"And it's pretty cold out," Will said. "I've got a cough already, and I don't want to make Tabby sick."

Caroline rolled her eyes. Will's live-in girlfriend, Tabby, was a desk clerk at the Duchess Hotel, a job she'd secured after Caroline removed her from her position at the Rose. Physically. Despite Gert's "family only" policy, Will had insisted he "couldn't" work without Tabby there—not that the difference in effort was noticeable in Tabby's presence. But in the end, Tabby spent more time on her phone than she'd spent waiting tables, plus she had a terrible habit of leaving that phone in random places. One unfortunate model had ended up in the kitchen's grease trap.

"Fine," she sighed.

"Uh, I don't suppose that Mom got any of the food out of the kitchen?" Wally asked. "Maybe a turkey melt or two?"

"What?" Caroline gaped at him.

"Well, you don't want it to go to waste," Wally insisted, his voice getting louder.

"And I'm sure Tabby would appreciate it if I brought home dinner for her," Will added, matching Wally's volume. "You know how hard she works."

Caroline resisted a second eye roll. She supposed that ultimately, the family should be thanking Tabby. Without her, Will would probably still be living with their parents. He had moved Tabby into the Wilton house a few years before, but she couldn't stand how "sad" the atmosphere was and seemed to think it was her job to cheer things up—by moving things around, throwing things out—including Chris's things.

Frankly, Tabby was lucky Gert hadn't removed her from the planet.

"I'm pretty sure all the food is contaminated with ceiling dust," Caroline told them.

"Could you check?" Will asked.

"No," Caroline huffed. "If you're not going to be helpful, go home."

"Fine, but there's no reason to be rude," Wally told her. "We're not the ones who let the roof cave in."

"What the—" Caroline turned to her dad, looking for him to defend her, or at least, remind the boys that no one "let" the roof cave in. But her father had already turned away, walking back home.

Nearly a week later, Caroline and Gert walked down the sidewalk, trying to keep the brisk wind from blowing the financial papers out of their hands. The gray skies definitely reflected their mood. They'd spent the afternoon at the island's lone bank branch, trying to secure funding for the renovations at the Rose. It had been disheartening, seeing how little the bank really seemed to value the bar, in terms of collateral, or as a viable business. The branch manager, Georgie Farthing, assured her that the family was highly regarded, but the bar's "potential projections" made them a risky investment.

The rising temperatures had mostly cleared the snow slush from the sidewalks. They weren't quite dry yet, but it definitely meant less strain on the tarps covering the roof at the Rose.

She could feel the frustration coming off her mother in waves. Gert had protested the idea of taking Riley's money at all, when Caroline had told her of the offer, but at this rate, they might have to rely more heavily on the "Shaddow Foundation Trust" than they'd originally planned.

"Borrowing money," Gert huffed. "The Wiltons have never borrowed money in our lives."

"Well, times change," Caroline said.

"I just don't like the idea," her mother griped.

Frustration rose in Caroline's belly. Not liking the idea of borrowing money didn't change the fact that the place needed to be repaired. "Well, what else am I going to do, Mom? The boys don't have the credit score we need to secure the financing. Hell, *you and Dad* barely have the credit score we need."

"I know," Gert said. "It just pains a parent, to make a child responsible for their burdens."

"Well, get over it," Caroline replied bluntly. "We don't have any other options."

Rather than comment on Caroline's saltiness, her mother changed the subject. "What do you think of this Cole character?"

It mattered that her mom was asking her opinion. She rarely did that.

"Well, he has a lot of experience with historical properties, which we need. We only want to do this once. Dad, I guess, didn't know what he was doing. And it was finished quickly, after Chris…"

Her mother nodded, blinking away the moisture gathering in her eyes. Caroline immediately regretted saying her brother's name so casually. "I suppose we're lucky it held together for so long."

As they stepped off the curb to cross the street toward the Rose, Caroline heard a noise to her left. She glanced up Waterfront Street, toward Shaddow House. A teenage girl was riding a dark-purple moped toward them at breakneck speed. In that weird, absent way only possible when panic makes time slow down, Caroline thought, *I think that's Ben's daughter.*

The girl had carried herself with a lot of bravado when Caroline had seen her in Starfall Grounds with Ben, wearing jeans in "emergency-vest orange" and a lime-green sweater, but she didn't have that bluster now. Her eyes were wide with panic as the moped seemed to be streaking out from under her. She wasn't in control of the bike, that much was clear. And the wet streets didn't seem to be helping as her hands wrenched the brakes.

Caroline grabbed her mother's shoulder and jerked her back, flinging Gert against the sidewalk. Caroline was turned away from the moped when it felt like she'd been punched in the side by a fist made of glass shards and nails.

Caroline was tossed onto the ground, rolling across the cobblestones like a tumbleweed. She couldn't breathe. Everything hurt. *Everything* felt like it was on fire, from the top of her head to the tips of her toes. It was like her body went into reset mode and she couldn't grasp onto any single sensation or thought. She forced herself to take in air.

No. No. Mistake. Air made her insides burn, too.

"Mina!" Ben was running toward them, pelting down the sidewalk, carrying a blue medical bag. Caroline wanted to tell him to slow down, to stop running, or he could trip. But again, her insides were on fire, burning the wires connecting her brain to her mouth.

Caroline's eyes rolled up to the gray skies overhead, the wisps of white rolling by. The next thing she knew, Ben's face was hovering over hers. He was barking out orders at the people around them. She could see Cole kneeling next to him.

Cole seemed more confused than afraid, which was a weird thing to stick in her brain, but it did. Ben, on the other hand, was completely panicked. But somehow, he was still able to examine her with a clinical tenderness that made her heart hurt. Dammit, that was the one thing that didn't hurt.

Gert was so still, her eyes blank and glassy with terror. Riley was there, too, holding Caroline's hand. She could hear Alice yelling in the distance.

Aw, so many people I love, right here. This is nice. And the more Riley squeezed her hand, the less Caroline hurt. That was nice, too. Oh, wait, no, she remembered reading somewhere that it was bad when you stopped hurting. It meant you were going into shock.

Was she going to die? No, no. She was safe here, on the island. She should be safe here. Why wasn't she safe here? Her eye landed on Alice, holding Mina, shushing her gently as the girl sobbed into Alice's shoulder.

That was good. Caroline didn't want Mina to feel bad about this. She didn't mean to hurt Caroline. Kids did stupid things sometimes. None of them had ever figured out how Chris had set the shower curtain on fire. While he was in the shower.

Chris.

Was this how Chris felt before he died? Scared and fading from everything around him? Was she going to see him again now? Part of her almost longed for it, as much as she wanted to live. Chris had been the one she could trust, the closest to her in age, the other "dependable" one.

Ever since she'd met Plover and all the others, she'd wondered. Was her brother a ghost out there somewhere? What would he have been attached to? His laptop? His guitar? Her parents hadn't been able to bear changing anything in his room, even all these years later. No, she would have sensed it, if Chris's spirit was still somewhere nearby. But she wished he was nearby. She missed her brother so much.

"Caroline," Ben panted, checking her eyes. "Sweetheart, please, stay awake, OK? Please."

"Caroline, look at me, OK?" Riley commanded her. "I need you to focus on me. Listen to my voice and keep your eyes open. Caroline!"

Riley squeezed her hand, and Caroline felt better. The fire inside her middle was almost entirely out now. But her head felt fuzzy, like she couldn't grab on to her thoughts...

Oh, Riley. How was Caroline going to help Riley with the ghosts if she died? She wasn't about to become a ghost, haunting Starfall. If she saw a light, she was running toward it. She'd been stuck on this island her whole life; she wasn't about to be stuck here after death.

And then, Caroline remembered, Riley's mom had died in a car accident. She didn't want Riley watching this happen.

"Go," Caroline whispered.

But also, holy hell, producing that one word had hurt so much.

"No, I'm staying," Riley whispered back and held her hand impossibly tighter.

Caroline looked beyond her, to the Rose, where she could sort of see the blue tarps flapping on the roof. The woman in the purple dress was standing in front of the entrance, staring at Caroline's body like she was a specimen in a jar. And she looked annoyed again, which was a weird response.

All of the pain and the cold felt like it was leaching out of her body and into the ground.

She could hear Ben calling out to her as her eyes fluttered shut. "No, Caroline, don't close your eyes. Caroline!"

She didn't drift off to sleep so much as plummet.

Chapter 6
Caroline

CAROLINE WALKED THROUGH THE SILENCE without fear. The moon was bright over her shoulders, blue-white and full of promise. Starfall has served its purpose, but now she was done with it, with its people. She had a whole life ahead of her, waiting for her like an open door, and she was ready to run out of it.

As her body—which was not her body—moved down a worn dirt path, Caroline heard these thoughts in her head, knowing they were not her own. These words in her head were an echo of someone else's feelings—the joy was muted, like a particularly good story she'd been told before. They weren't the thoughts of someone she knew, and yet somehow, they felt familiar. This woman was happy, hopeful, like Caroline used to feel as a kid on Christmas morning, the torturous ticking of time before decadent wonder.

The surroundings were familiar enough, In the place where Caroline could feel her own thoughts. This was Vixen's Fall—the craggy cliff face dropping into the strange little crescent moon–shaped inlet filled with sharp, fang-like rocks. Why would anyone want to visit this place at night? It filled Caroline's stomach with dull electric dread, but this woman didn't seem to share that apprehension.

Emmett was coming. They would leave this place. Their new life was starting. No more waiting. No more backbreaking work for people who looked down on her.

She heard a noise behind her, a branch snapping.

"Emmett?"

The trees that grew close to the cliff's edge, the same trees that had cradled her and her lover during stolen midnight hours and sheltered them from discovery as they laughed together, seemed so sinister now. They created deep shadows that suddenly made her afraid.

Within those shadows, she heard leaves moving. *"Emmett, come out. This isn't funny and we need to leave."*

No answer. Caroline could feel the annoyance building in her (host's?) head, crowding out the fear. That was good. The body, whoever was carrying Caroline like a passenger, wasn't used to fear. She worked better with annoyance. She moved closer to the trees, to the shadows. *"Emmett, the boat—"*

White hands, soft hands that had never known a true day's work, shot out of the shadows and closed around her shoulders. They were *strong*, so much stronger than this body had expected. Those hands drove her back, toward the cliff, moving her feet over the dirt like useless rag-doll legs. How were they so strong? They'd all been fooled. The cliff face was getting closer. Caroline could feel the wind against her back, hear the waves crashing beneath her as she was shoved farther and farther away from safety.

She felt the world give way from beneath her feet, and she was falling. The cliff's edge grew smaller and smaller, giving her the upside-down sense of floating as the crash of the waves grew louder. And all Caroline could seem to focus on were the soft, white hands backlit by the moon.

And as the darkness swallowed her, one thought echoed through her mind, the person she regretted leaving behind. The person who would never know what had just happened to her.

Emmett.

Caroline gasped—a hoarse, labored sound even to her own ears—as she broke the surface of the dream like water.

Everything in her body hurt, from the crown of her skull to the tips of her toes. But it was an indistinct pain, muted somehow, like the emotions in her dream. Her brain felt slow, like the last time she'd decided, in a fit of overconfidence, to taste test several new brands of bourbon. Her eyes didn't want to open. She could smell Ben's cologne, in a distant haze that was still comforting. That made sense since she seemed to be lying in a bed at Ben's clinic. The pillow beneath her head wrinkled with a papery crunch. Beside her, a monitor was beeping in the most annoying pitch possible.

When her eyes finally opened, she could make out the familiar shape of Ben, standing beside her, scribbling on a clipboard. And she couldn't seem to move one of her feet.

"The fuck?" she whispered, pulling absently at the plastic tubes taped to her wrists.

"Caroline!" Ben dropped the clipboard and rushed to hover at the edge of her bed. His hands were warm and gentle as he cradled her jaw, and yet, he was obviously being scientifically objective as he tested her eyes, pointed a penlight at her pupils—measuring and judging and drawing conclusions. He adjusted the angle of the light and made her wince.

"Ow. If I wasn't on what I suspect to be a very high caliber of pain meds, I would be very annoyed by this," she muttered, shying away from the light. It felt like he was stabbing her in the back of her skull. "Nope, still annoyed."

"Well, the next time I get run down by a moped, you can drug *me* and put *me* through concussion protocols," he replied.

"Deal." She laughed, or at least, she tried to, but even that slight motion sent waves of knife-sharp agony in a burning line from her chest to her left knee. How could a tiny attempt to move her midsection hurt her *knee*?

There was a moment when Caroline could almost see the doctor part of Ben's brain shut off and he was just a man who was frightened. He dropped down, kissing her feather-soft, and even though the muscles in her right arm screamed in protest, she reached up, grabbed the front of his T-shirt, and urged him closer. She had missed his mouth, his kiss, the way he tasted like cinnamon, that pine and spice smell.

For a moment, she didn't hurt. She didn't worry. All she could feel was the warmth and peace of being held by Ben. And she was happy. She wanted to wallow in that happiness, make it last, make it theirs, but all too soon, he was pulling his mouth away from hers to gently lean his forehead against hers.

And the selfish, post-near-death-experience-hormonally-fused part of her brain screamed for her to demand more kisses, maybe even nudity.

"You scared me," he breathed against her lips. "I almost lost you, Caroline. It happened right in front of me, and I couldn't stop it. Please don't ever—I almost *lost* you. *Again.*"

The agony in his voice was so profound, Caroline couldn't help but think of the woman on the cliff, the bewildered grief as she fell into nothing and knew she would never see her Emmett again. What Caroline had seen was that woman's memory, not a dream. Caroline knew that now. She just didn't know what to make of it. But she would do whatever it took to not feel that loss, to keep Ben from feeling that way, even if it meant facing down whatever the hell was happening in her life at the moment.

He kissed her again, pressing a tiny bit more of his weight down on her and she grunted in pain. It seemed to startle him, and he pulled away from her. The doctor mask fell into place again, and he was all business. He sat back, looking her over.

"All things considered, you're doing pretty well," Ben told her. "Nasty bump to the head from where you fell back against the sidewalk. The moped clipped your ribs pretty good. Couple of them are cracked and a few are broken. That's going to require you to wrap them every day until they heal up. You've got a sprained ankle, a wrist that's not quite sprained but definitely *strained*, and a heck of a road rash, with which you will become familiar over the next couple of days. That and a veritable rainbow of bruising."

"That all tracks," she said, nodding and regretting it deeply. *Ow.*

Being so close to him *twice* during a crisis while he showed her nothing but how much he cared about her, wanted her safe—well, it helped break down those awkward walls that remained between them. It was hard to keep someone at a distance once he'd seen her "rainbow of bruising."

Ben sighed. "Now comes the awkward part. My daughter is the one who hit you. Considering our, uh, history, and the fact that it was my minor child that hit you, I wouldn't blame you if you asked to have your care transferred to another doctor—while you and your lawyer prepare for the inevitable lawsuit. Between the injuries and me kissing you while you're my patient, I wouldn't blame you."

She scoffed—again, fucking *ow*. "How exactly are you going to transfer my care to another doctor? Dr. Toller is the only other doctor on the island, and he just announced that he's on vacation for the next week."

"You know about that, huh?" Ben asked.

"He was very enthusiastic about announcing *that* the other night at the bar—The bar! My mom!" Caroline exclaimed. Out of instinct, she tried to sit up so she could get to her mother, but that fire returned, burning her whole body with agony. She shrieked.

"Take it easy," Ben told her, helping her settle back on the bed while she breathed through the pain.

"That was a mistake," she wheezed.

"It's going to be a while before your brain adjusts to the reality of what your body has been through. And I don't know, I could pay a friend to come stay and treat you while you recover." Ben said, scrubbing a hand over his face. "And your mom is fine. She's actually sitting with my kids at the moment, convincing Mina that her life isn't over and she won't be blacklisted from colleges for being a murderous criminal."

"You left your child with my mom, with the goal of encouraging said child?" She laughed, and the pain shooting down from her ribs to her legs stole her breath all over again. Dammit, she had to stop doing that. After a few moments, she was able to concentrate enough to speak, and said, "Please assure Mina that I'm not dead, so she's at least not a murderer. And I'm not suing you, either. Your kid made a mistake. It happens. And I saw the look on her face right before she ran me down. I think she's scared herself so badly, you're not even going to have to yell that loud."

"Too late," he said, looking faintly chagrined. "Already did it. She wasn't supposed to be driving the damned moped at all, much less near Main Square. She was just so excited when our moving pods finally came over on the ferry. And she's hardheaded when it comes to learning new things, like driving on wet, worn stones."

"Wonder where she gets that?" Caroline snorted.

"It's a mystery," Ben told her. "Anyway, Mina shouldn't have been riding somewhere unfamiliar, and she definitely shouldn't have been riding toward people. She won't be driving anything with a motor in the near future."

"Don't be too hard on her," Caroline told him.

"Well, either way, I'll make sure all your medical care is covered, even if I'm not the one providing it," he assured her. "And you will have everything you need at home, and at the bar, until you're back on your feet."

Her brows rose, and it was the first physical reaction she'd had all night that didn't burn like poison. "What does that mean?"

"Hey Caroline, good to see you conscious." Samantha Vermeer poked her head through the door, her stethoscope swinging around her neck in time with her long dark bob.

"Samantha, sorry, I can't wave," Caroline said, grinning at her.

"Well, since this one can't see other patients today, your state of emergency is turning my day an interesting shade of anarchy," Samantha told her. "And you're gonna want to let the family in before they take the waiting room apart."

"Oh...no," Caroline breathed. "My family."

"Do you want to let them in?" Ben asked.

"I guess so," Caroline sighed. To her surprise, when the door opened, it wasn't her parents or loud-ass brothers, it was Riley, Edison, and Alice. Her family. She smiled happily as Alice and Riley flung themselves through the door.

"Gentle!" Ben cautioned them as they tried to slip through the maze of medical equipment for something like a hug.

"We understand, Doctor," Alice assured him, even as she cradled her cheek against Caroline's shoulder. Riley was quiet, pressing Caroline's uninjured hand against her face and her forehead against Caroline's collarbone.

Caroline could only imagine the panic that Riley felt, seeing the aftermath of another loved one's serious automotive accident. "I'm sorry," Caroline whispered.

"Nope, she who is struck by a motor vehicle does not apologize," Riley told her.

"It was hardly a motor *vehicle*," Caroline said.

"And yet, we're still going to count it," Edison said, carefully sliding in for his own half hug, pressing his shoulder to her less-injured side.

Caroline absently patted his arm. "Aw, we hug now?"

"Three near-death experiences and you get a hug for free," Edison told her.

When she frowned, he added, "I'm counting the thing with the ceiling"—he paused and glanced up at Ben—"squirrel."

Caroline pursed her lips. "Fair."

"You have fifteen minutes." Ben leveled a stern look at Riley and Alice. "Try not to wear her out too much."

"Plover is beside himself. He really resents that he can't come visit too. And he sends these." Riley placed a vase of pansies in a rainbow of colors on the little hospital table. And a box of chamomile tea.

"We have our own tea here," Ben noted as he checked the IV bag hanging over Caroline's head. He made some adjustment, and Caroline swore she could *feel* the warmth of something being released into the space near the line in her arm.

"Yes, but pansies mean 'You occupy my thoughts,'" Riley said, sniffing.

"And chamomile means 'energy in adversity,' which is Plover's way of saying 'Don't let the bastards get you down.'" Caroline added, grinning loopily. Yep, something had definitely been released into her arm.

"Yeah, Starfall Blooms did not stock fresh chamomile flowers for emergency one-hour deliveries," Riley said, her face finally relaxing enough to smile. "Weird. Plover wanted me to add eucalyptus for protection, but I thought that would be a little smell-forward for an enclosed medical space."

"Thank you, that was considerate," Ben said, nodding.

But apparently, Caroline's mouth wasn't empty yet, because she was still talking. "Even though Plover would never curse and neither one of us would ever want to imply that Mina is a bastard. She's a nice kid."

Everybody seemed to be staring at her.

"Have I mentioned I'm on drugs?" Caroline asked.

Ben had a confused look on his face. Oh, no, did she not say what she thought she did? His lips twitched slightly as he wrote something on his clipboard. "Got it."

She smiled. "Tell Plover thank you for me."

"I will," Riley said, nodding toward a large arrangement of sunflowers Edison placed on the table beside the pansies. She didn't sound super pleased about it, to be honest. "Margaret came by earlier and left you those."

"Twelve minutes," Ben told them, his tone serious as he closed the door behind him.

For one of those minutes, the three visitors just sat there quietly. Caroline realized the depth of how badly she'd scared her friends and was struck with a wave of guilt, knowing the strain she'd put on them, and then, no small amount of gratitude that she had people in her life to worry about her like that.

Outside her door, she heard Ben ask someone, "Who's Plover? I've lived on this island my entire life and I've never met a Plover."

There was a note of jealousy in his voice, and Caroline didn't want to process the shame she felt at being happy about that.

Finally, Riley said, "I had to force your mom out of here, to take care of poor Mina. It got…very loud. I was sort of shocked it didn't wake you from your mini-coma."

Caroline winced. Margaret had been right about Riley being skittish around her, but not for the reasons Edison's assistant suspected. With all the issues with her own mother, Riley didn't have a lot of room in her life for warm, friendly grandmotherly types.

It reminded Riley of everything she didn't have, and wouldn't ever have, now that Ellen Denton had definitively moved on to the next plane. Riley was much more comfortable with no-nonsense, with-holding women like Gert Wilton. It was, by some cruel trick of fate, Riley's wheelhouse.

"Sorry about that. And it was more than a mini-coma. I had... I think it was a vision. I was another woman. I don't know her name or who she was, but I was standing at the top of Vixen's Fall. And someone ran out of the shadows and shoved me into the water. I think she knew who pushed her, but I didn't see who it was. And I died. I don't know if I drowned or died from the impact with the water or even a rock, maybe, but I was dead. And I died with a lot of regret."

"Do you think it was a ghost reaching out to you?" Riley asked, frowning. "Seems sort of weird, attacking you with a moped to do it."

Caroline shook her head. "She felt a lot older than the moped, so I doubt it was attached to it."

"Are you sure it's not just some dream you had because you spent the better part of an hour staring at my sketch of Vixen's Fall?" Riley asked, frowning. "Your brain's way of processing the trauma?"

Caroline considered that for as long as the drugs would allow. "It could be the head injury talking, but it didn't feel like a dream."

"Maybe it's connected to the purple lady in the bar?" Alice suggested.

"It feels...like it's connected to me," Caroline said. "And I know that sounds weirdly conceited, but it just does."

"Well, you were the one hit with the moped," Edison noted.

"It just feels important, all of it," Caroline said, yawning. "And maybe the purple lady...maybe it's about her, too."

While she blinked off to sleep, Caroline stared at the flowers at her bedside. Sunflowers, while cheerful, meant "false riches." Caroline wondered what Plover would have made of that.

It had taken many promises from Riley, Alice, and Caroline herself to keep Caroline away from the Rose before Ben would allow her to go home. Both women agreed to sleep over at Caroline's tidy little bungalow down the hill from the Wiltons' larger house, Caroline's great-grandparents' answer to a mother-in-law suite. Riley would have gladly taken Caroline to Shaddow House for full supervision—something Plover almost demanded—but with Caroline's ankle, there were just too many stairs for her to stay there.

The two of them checked on her and fed her regularly. They'd agreed to help her with the daily ritual of unwrapping the bandages around her ribs for her shower. This morning's episode had been colorful both in language and in contusions, but she was comfortable—at ease on the sage-green couch she'd specifically chosen for its squishiness and "reading position back support."

Even when Ben stopped by with his kids in tow, to relieve her friends from duty and prevent her from trying to join her mother in the Rose cleanup effort, she stayed calm. When Josh handed her roses with hands that looked *exactly* like his father's, she'd shrugged it off. But then Mina, who was basically Ben reborn with his big hazel eyes and fine-boned features, started to cry, and Caroline lost her composure.

Mina looked just as pasty pale as she had at the scene of the accident, her remorse obviously genuine as she whispered, "I'm so sorry. I'm so sorry for hitting you. I'm so sorry this is how we're meeting. The bike just got away from me—the roads are *never* this slick in Phoenix—and I couldn't control it, and the next thing I knew, you were standing in front of me and everything seemed to get so loud all at once and I swear I saw—"

"It's OK," Caroline reached out with her untethered hand and wrapped it around Mina's cold fingers. A warm electric sizzle ran up Caroline's arm, to her chest, and in her addled state, her first thought was that it was a blood clot or a cardiac incident with offbeat comic timing. But then she remembered the flavor of this particular sensation—strange and alien, yes, but not scary. It was the feeling of coming home. She'd felt it when she'd touched Riley's shoulder that first time, the same moment that Alice had touched her hand. The three of them touching physically had cemented their magic, something they hadn't realized until weeks later.

Did this mean Mina had magic, too? What did this mean for Riley and Alice? Ugh, her head hurt too much to try to figure this out on her own. Josh sort of lurked in the background, observing the scene with a solemn expression. Caroline respected that. She'd learned more eavesdropping at the bar than she had in all her years of school.

For her part, Mina only looked confused at the zap. Caroline understood the desire to write this feeling off as static electricity or nerves.

"You didn't mean to do it, and I'm going to bet that you will be the most careful driver on the island for years to come," Caroline told her, as Mina nodded tearfully.

"I don't think that I'm going to drive again, ever," Mina swore.

"Well, then you moved to the right place," Caroline replied, making Josh snicker. Mina glared at her brother, but the tension in her narrow shoulders relaxed ever so slightly.

Ben eased Mina away so he could do the super-rude penlight stuff to her eyes again. And to Caroline's shock, Josh went to her sink and began putting away the breakfast dishes Riley had left on the drying rack.

"Um, the tall one is putting away my dishes," Caroline noted as Ben checked the swelling on her ankle. "Why is the tall one putting away my dishes?"

"Because he's the only one who can reach the high cabinets?" Mina suggested, a smile quirking the corner of her mouth for the first time since she'd entered the house. "And you have a splint on your wrist."

"And because for the next several weeks, my kids are going to be your arms and legs, so to speak," Ben told her.

"It's an appropriately ironic punishment for Mina," Josh told her cheerfully. Mina looked like she wanted to hiss at him but hid her face behind her curtain of dark hair. "And I'm coming along because when I'm left unsupervised for too long…bad things happen."

"But that's—What about school?" Caroline spluttered.

"We're registered for in-person for the fall. But it's sort of too late for us to join classes this year, so we're wrapping up the spring online," Josh said. "Mina actually prefers it."

Mina waggled her head back and forth. "I'm a self-starter."

Caroline asked, "But what about when I go back to work?"

"Um, that's not going to be a consideration for several weeks,"

Ben insisted. "I doubt you'll be back on your feet before the repairs to the Rose are completed. We went over this when you were released. With your ribs, you can't lift anything heavier than a cup of coffee. You can't put weight on your ankle. You can't bend. You can't move too fast. Hell, if I could, I would forbid you from sneezing too hard."

"Not sure how she would prevent that, Dad," Josh said, pressing the Brew button on her coffeepot. A few seconds later, the smell of percolating water hitting grounds filled her kitchen.

"What the useful and tall brewer of life-giving coffee said." Caroline pointed at Josh. He grinned at her.

"I didn't say it was a rational direction," Ben admitted. "So, for now, my kids are going to help you around the house. And when it reopens, around the bar. Mina in particular will work until she repays the approximate cost of what you would have been charged if you had to pay for medical treatment as a result of the accident."

"And she's agreed to this?" Caroline asked.

"I don't *love* it, but there's a certain karmic balance to it," Mina grumbled.

"This feels weirdly unethical… Isn't this how that fake pilot in *Seinfeld* started?" Caroline asked.

"I just need adult supervision while Dad's working—because again, bad things—and besides, hanging around a bar can only help my new-kid street cred," Josh told her.

"No," Ben said, shaking his head.

"What's *Seinfeld*?" Mina asked.

"Oh my god!" Caroline yelped. "What have you been teaching this child?"

"I'm not a child. What's *Seinfeld*?" Mina asked again, the rosy color slowly returning to her face.

Ben scrubbed his hand over his face, but behind his fingers, Caroline could see the beginnings of a smile. "You know, out of everything that's happened today, this is the most mortifying."

"Well, clearly, my first task is pop culture education," Caroline gasped. "Ben, how could you?"

Both kids looked a little uncomfortable at Caroline's raised voice, so she decided to dial it back a notch, even if she was just joking. It wouldn't do to make the kids uneasy when she was apparently going to be supervising them for the foreseeable future.

Wait, did she just agree to be Ben's nanny?

"Mina likes to *read*," Josh told Caroline. "She didn't make her Netflix profile until we moved to the island."

"I will make you a watch list," Caroline told Mina. "And a booklist, because I see how you're eying my shelves there, girly."

"There's just so many of them," Mina said, making subtle grabby hands toward the sage-green floor-to-ceiling bookshelves that Caroline had installed herself.

Caroline laughed and then regretted it. "My mom's always said that if this half of the island slides into the lake, it'll be from the weight of my books."

It was as if speaking her mom's name had summoned her. Gert bustled into the house, holding a covered dish with her right hand because her left arm was in a sling. Will and Wally trailed in behind her, empty-handed. Ben's brows arched as she crossed into the kitchen and preheated the oven.

"Mom, what happened to your arm?" Caroline cried. "Why did I not notice the sling before?"

"Uh, she may have hurt her shoulder when you yanked her out of imminent danger and threw her on the ground," Mina said, chewing her lip.

"It's not a big deal," Gert insisted from the stove. "It's just a mild sprain."

Caroline looked to Ben, and he shook his head.

"Should you even be carrying a hot dish around?" Caroline asked, trying to sit up and wincing at the pain radiating up her middle. When was *that* going to stop?

Gert waved her good arm. "It's fine."

"You couldn't have carried the dish?" Caroline glared at Will, who flopped into an oversized cream-colored armchair while Wally nudged at Caroline's feet.

"Budge up, will ya?" Wally said, tapping at her uninjured foot.

"Um, no?" Ben said, frowning at him. "She needs to keep that ankle elevated."

Wally just blinked at Ben, as if he didn't understand the words coming out of Ben's mouth.

"Your dad said he'll be by in a few days," Gert said, sliding the casserole in the oven.

"A few days?" Mina said, frowning.

"He just can't see you this way," Gert told Caroline, ignoring Mina. "Once the bruises heal up a bit, he'll be ready."

"I could be back at work by then," Caroline mused.

"No, you won't," Ben told her, making Caroline roll her eyes.

"Yeah, this really isn't a great time for you to be laid up," Will said, yawning. "With so much going on at the bar, we could really use you."

"Well, if it happens again, I'll try to be run down by a moped at a more convenient time," Caroline snapped. Mina deflated a little at her side, prompting Caroline to pat her shoulder. That same electric sizzle ran up her arm. Mina blinked at her but said nothing.

"That would help," Will sighed, completely obtuse.

"Look, guys, you're just gonna have to maybe pitch in a little more at the bar while I'm out," Caroline told them. She heard her mother moving around the kitchen, not really accomplishing much, but also not engaging in the conversation. "Especially if Mom's not at one hundred percent."

"Hey, I've got stuff going on at home," Will objected.

"Like what?" Caroline asked.

"Tabby's been working extra shifts at the hotel," Will said. "Something about the manager freaking out because the owner is coming in for an inspection soon. And that means I have to do the cooking for us at home!"

"You're a *cook at the bar*," she reminded him.

Will shrugged. "Yeah, well it's different at home, and I have to do the laundry."

"Yes, these are things that most adult people manage to do to take care of themselves while also working. Figure it out," Caroline said.

She looked to her mother, who was still busy in the kitchen, as if she was in a one-woman show about a kitchen-cleaning mime.

"Ugh, why do you make things so hard?" Will groaned, pushing himself out of his chair. He practically flounced out of the house.

Wally, who had never managed to figure out where to sit, shrugged at Caroline and followed his twin out.

Her mom walked over to the couch and smoothed Caroline's hair back from the patch of road rash on her forehead. "You know how stubborn Will is. You're just so good at taking care of these things."

"Yes, but I physically can't. I am literally under doctor's orders. And really, you shouldn't be doing much either," Caroline said. "You're just going to have to ask Will or Wally to do it."

"She's right," Ben added. "I'm willing to give you a print version of the doctor's orders. In great big font."

"They're not going to be happy about it," Gert sighed.

Caroline waved her good arm. "And yet, here we are. Ow."

Gert patted Caroline's shoulder. "Get some rest, Caroline."

Her mother ambled out of the cottage, leaving Caroline to stew in embarrassed silence until Mina observed, "Your family kind of sucks."

"Mina!" Ben barked.

"It's OK," Caroline sighed as Ben pulled a fluffy green blanket—a gift from Edison—over her legs.

"Don't tell us that they mean well," Josh told Caroline, carrying her favorite *I could be reading, but you keep talking* mug to her. How had he known that was her favorite? "That's something that we learned in therapy—that making excuses for people doesn't make them better. Or make you feel better. It just lets the sucky situation go on longer."

"The tall bearer of coffee makes sense," Caroline said, smiling despite herself.

Josh held up his hands. "I usually do, and everybody's always surprised when it happens."

Chapter 7
Ben

IT WASN'T THAT HE DIDN'T trust Caroline's family, it was that he *knew* Caroline's family. He knew that as soon as a few days passed, the scare of almost losing Caroline would wear off—and they would be more willing to return to the status quo than to fill the void of tasks Caroline usually performed. The Wiltons would make it sound perfectly reasonable for her to "just sit" at the bar while they cleaned, and then within hours, they would make it sound even more reasonable for her to help them move something or hand them something, and by the end of the day, she would be rebuilding the roof herself.

He'd tried to give her a few days of space. He got regular reports from his kids, who spent pretty much every day at Caroline's house, helping her. Riley had given him her cell number and texted him pretty consistently, updating Ben on Caroline's swelling and the bruises. It probably wasn't the most responsible thing to do, as a doctor, but she was probably more comfortable with her friends wrapping her ribs than him anyway.

But now, it was Dr. Toller's first day back from vacation and

Ben had to do a follow-up. His gut told him she would be at the Rose. He only hoped he wouldn't see whoever this "Plover" person was. Ben knew that Caroline wouldn't stay single after he left Starfall. Hell, he'd married a whole other person and had children, but the fondness in her voice when she talked about this Plover, it wasn't a "casual friend" fondness. What kind of name was Plover, anyway? Wasn't a plover a kind of bird? This person was important to Caroline. And that made his heart hurt, even though he knew he didn't have the right to that.

He wanted Caroline to be happy. She deserved that, but he didn't know if he could sit back and watch that happen with someone else. And he knew that made him sad and small, but he wasn't sure he was good enough to put his own feelings aside. He didn't know if he loved her enough to let her go a second time. And he did love her. He'd known that all those years ago when he left Starfall, he would never stop.

And yet…the idea of her making a life here on the island with someone else…

He stood at his kitchen door, checking his medical bag for supplies, sighing. "Get your shit together, Hoult. Be a grown-up. She's gone through enough. Let her be happy."

He steeled his spine and walked outside, fully prepared to march over to the Rose and tell her family off for pushing her too far, too early…only to see Caroline through one of the side windows of Shaddow House—one of the huge glass panels of the atrium only visible from his side porch—lounging on a chaise with a blanket around her shoulders, staring down intently as if she was reading.

Clearly, his gut was an idiot.

Ben blinked as his brain tried to keep up with what he was seeing. "Huh."

She was resting. Following doctor's orders. *Not working*. He would get to know this woman, Riley, and learn her ways.

So if Caroline was in Shaddow House…wait, where were his kids? Were his kids *inside Shaddow House*? A sudden sense of dread and yet, acute jealousy, struck him right in the middle. He'd wanted to get in that place for years—even though he sensed there was something not quite right about it—and it had only taken his kids a couple of days? Also, he was a terrible father.

Ben dashed down the steps of his cottage and through the gate of Shaddow House. He felt a mounting sense of something important and potentially dangerous building at the base of his brain stem. It sounded like an awful lot of talking inside that ornate front door, especially for a house that was only supposed to be home to two people. It struck him as odd that such a large house didn't have at least one security camera pointed at the door. But if there were cameras keeping Shaddow House safe, he couldn't see them.

He knocked on the door and the talking seemed to soften, like Ben had walked into a party with toilet paper on his shoe. He could hear whispered conversation from the general direction of the atrium and then heard footsteps. Riley answered, looking confused. "Hi, Ben."

"Hi, I was going to go check on Caroline at the Rose, but…she's not there? She's here, which I'm very confused about. Also, are my kids in your house?" Ben asked.

"Welp, Caroline's mom damn near talked her into going into work today," Riley shouted over her shoulder in a very pointed fashion that Ben thought was probably for Caroline's benefit. "And your kids—rightly so—called me and ratted her out. So, I talked her into coming here, and now that the building has been cleared, your kids went over to the Rose to help with the cleanup. Caroline's mom is supervising them, and since you told them they were going to be responsible for helping Caroline there, too, we thought that would be OK?"

Relief and a little bit of disappointment filled Ben. He'd hoped that the kids would keep him updated on this sort of thing. But living here on Starfall was supposed to give them more freedom, he reminded himself...and at least they were doing something productive? "No, no, it's fine. I'm just, uh, adjusting to the idea of loosening the parental reins a little bit."

Riley beamed at him. "It's nice that you worry. It means you care."

"And the kids were right to rat you out, Caroline!" Ben called into the house, making Riley snicker. "I'm very proud of my network of informants—who inform everybody but me."

"I guess you need to come in to examine Caroline, huh?" Riley said.

"Well, being within ten feet of the patient is an essential part of the in-person examination process," Ben said, nodding. Riley glanced around, and almost looked like she was asking for permission, before she finally nodded and opened the door wider for him.

He felt an odd electric buzz up his spine as he entered the house. The interior lived up to all of his expectations, between the opulent, colorful décor, the strange antiques—a huge grandfather clock, a suit of actual armor, a...bronze stork playing a saxophone? None of it seemed to match, but it all belonged together. Except for the stork, that was just freaking weird.

Caroline was seated in an airy light-filled room lined with glass. The space—and its ferns and seating—seemed to be oriented around a stone fountain of a woman in a flower crown kissing a skull. He could see why someone living on Starfall would want to have a room like this to prevent winter blues. Sometimes, being cooped up within four walls for months on end could get sort of…intense.

Caroline was surrounded by books and notebooks with three framed sketches lined up against the base of the fountain nearby. She seemed to be comfortable, seated and warm, with a steaming mug of tea at her elbow and an adorable pair of black-framed glasses perched on her nose. She was staring down at a large copper bowl on the table to her right, frowning. That was sort of strange given that the bowl was half-full of bits of rose quartz?

It was the same expression Mina had when doing trigonometry homework. Wait, was Caroline doing homework? About rose quartz? Oh, no. Riley seemed nice, but he hoped she wasn't trying to "heal" Caroline's ankle with woo-woo stuff she found online.

Caroline smiled up at him through those adorable glasses and his heart did a familiar beat-skip-beat. "Your kids are working their butts off right now, helping my mom box up the unbroken glassware and plates—which is especially important, since she only has the one working shoulder—so be prepared for some grumbling when you get home," Caroline told him. "Mina has sent me 'fire emoji,' 'squid emoji,' and 'foot emoji.' I don't know what that means, but it can't be good."

"Mina is texting you?" Ben asked.

"Yeah, Josh sent 'burrito emoji,' 'snowflake emoji,' and what looked like a face made out of dotted lines," Caroline said, holding up her phone to show him. "But I think at this point, they might just be messing with me. Is this really how kids communicate?"

"Honestly, I don't know," Ben told her. "It is possible they're just messing with you."

Both of his kids were texting Caroline. (And calling Riley, apparently.) He didn't know how to feel about that. It was good that they had adults they trusted, and that *he* trusted, that they could talk to—but wasn't it also adding more complications to all of their lives?

"As you can see, I am sitting, with my foot elevated, not lifting anything heavier than these books," she told him.

"Under duress," Edison Held commented as he came down the steps. He smiled at Ben as if it wasn't strange for other people to be under Riley's roof, but there was a note of discomfort in his eyes as he shook Ben's hand. "A lot of duress. I had to bring her some titles from special collections that I'm not technically allowed to remove from the public library to get her to sit still."

"The *betrayal*," Caroline gasped. "You're supposed to be on my side."

Edison shrugged. "Well, being a literary outlaw, I am going to go back to the library to hide out. I'm going to pack up more boxes of books to make way for when Cole...eventually gets here."

"Sorry, Edison," Caroline groaned. "I know you were looking forward to your own office here at the house."

"Eh, this just means I get to spend more time cataloguing the books before they're reshelved," Edison said. "And you know I love that."

"When you eventually go back to work, can you take that empty Tupperware back to Margaret? I left it by the front door, next to Plover's tray," Caroline said. "It's clean and everything. Tell her I said thank you for the soup."

Plover. There was that name again. And he had his own *tray* at Shaddow House? What did that mean? Did Plover live here?

"You said the soup tasted like sneeze and kale," Riley noted.

"Don't mention that part," Caroline told Edison.

"I will tell her it was an unforgettable taste experience," Edison agreed, nodding to Ben. He kissed Riley goodbye. "Be careful."

Interesting.

After Edison left, Riley turned to Ben. "If this is an official medical visit, why don't you two go into my office, where you'll have a little more privacy? Caroline doesn't need to strip in a glass room."

"No such thing as privacy in this house," Caroline muttered as Riley helped her hobble into the office. He noted that Riley shoved several papers and books into her large ornate wooden desk and then locked the drawers, which seemed...excessive. What exactly was it that Riley did for a living again?

Riley seated Caroline on a not-exactly-comfortable-looking blue leather sofa across from an intricately carved white marble fireplace. A fire was already burning merrily in the grate, which would help because the room felt colder than it should. It was the nature of living in one of these drafty historical houses, Ben told himself. Gray Fern felt like living in a wind tunnel sometimes.

Ben knelt in front of the couch as he examined Caroline as clinically as he could manage. Considering her mishap, she was in pretty spectacular shape. The contusions were in the right stage of reduction. Her road rash was healing. Her ankle was roughly ankle-sized. The bruises were in the yellow-green "dying grass" color phase, which was a good sign.

"The bruising kind of looks like a Monet painting," Caroline said as he helped her sit up and slip back into her shirt. "I don't hate it."

"Just keep doing what you're doing, the not working and the sitting part," he told her. "Over-the-counter pain meds as needed. Don't let your brothers talk you into moving furniture or deep-cleaning their houses or something."

"I would say that's silly, but you've met them," Caroline nodded. "And does that end the doctoring part of this appointment?"

"Sure," Ben said, nodding.

"Good," she huffed, grabbing his shirt with her good hand and pulling him closer. He sort of squeaked—in a manly fashion, obviously—as she dragged him from his kneeling position and practically into her lap. Her mouth closed over his, and she seemed to inhale him. Ben's hands planted themselves on either side of her hips, and somehow, they slipped under her butt. It was a terrible and immature thing to think…but it felt just the same.

Oh, he was going to hell, if for nothing else than this massive violation of…all of the doctor oaths.

He moaned at the taste of her—Earl Grey tea and some sweet pastry—as her tongue flicked across his lips. Her good leg wrapped around his waist, pulling him even closer. Her fingers slid down the front of his jeans, and his whole body screamed *yes* as he went aching and hard under her hand. His hips bucked as she tugged at his zipper. Her grin was downright intimidating as his weight shifted against her, pinning her against the couch. She squealed and it was *not* a good sound.

"Sorry!" he cried. "Sorry!"

He leaned his forehead against hers. "Oh, man, I'm so sorry. Believe me, but we can't. I can't," Ben said, pressing his lips to her cheek as he nuzzled against her. "It's too fast, too much, too soon."

She nodded as he pulled away, and he prayed he wouldn't see hurt on her face, but instead it was…fear? Oh, no, was she afraid of him now? He shouldn't have kissed her, but she was just so close and she smelled so good and she felt just like she used to and he never stopped lov— *What the hell was she looking at?*

He turned his head to see a black, oily shape sliding along the office ceiling like a larger-than-life amoeba. Caroline was shaking and her hands wrapped around Ben's shoulders as she tried to force him behind her.

The oil sort of oozed down from the ceiling directly above them, almost to eye level with Caroline when Riley came running in with a silver bowl. "Caroline!"

Caroline's arm darted to a side table and grabbed a dish full of rose petals and…salt? In unison, they threw salt at the black oily mass. Riley made a hand gesture that looked like drawing a closed hand across her heart and then mimed shoving the mass away. Caroline could only manage the shoving motion.

The salt sizzled against the surface of the…apparition? It let loose an animal shriek and withdrew into the ceiling, and—thank God—away from them. Ben whimpered, his head whipping back and forth, trying to figure out what just happened. His knees seemed to go out, and he sank to the floor.

"I told you keeping salty potpourri dishes around was a good idea," Riley panted as if this was a completely normal thing to happen in the middle of the morning. "It doesn't bind them or enclose them anywhere, but the hostile ones certainly get the point. No trespassing, you ceiling-crawling dick!"

"Oh, I'm glad you're here because I don't think I would have been able to pull off that hand gesture," Caroline huffed, flopping back on the couch. "Ow."

"Not strong enough to get rid of the bastard, but I don't think he—or she, let's be progressive here—is gonna try to get that close again," Riley said. "Oh, jeez, Ben. You OK?"

Ben was not OK. His eyes kept darting back and forth between Riley and Caroline, and then back at the ceiling because, what if that thing came back? Also his pants were partially unzipped, and that was a problem.

Caroline patted Ben's chest. "Ben?"

All of the blood and air seemed to return to the sensible parts of Ben's body, and he screeched, "WHAT THE FUCK?!"

"If it makes you feel any better, I said exactly the same thing the first time I met Plover," Riley told Ben as she served him a mug of chamomile tea. They'd moved back into the atrium because the office and the possibility of whatever the hell that thing was returning made Ben incredibly uncomfortable.

Alice had arrived while Ben was sitting there, waiting for his world to make sense again. Apparently, she'd *felt* Caroline and Riley's distress in dealing with the ceiling thing—something Ben would process later. Alice had simply given him a reassuring pat on the shoulder and a sympathetic smile. Caroline was back on her chaise, blankets intact, drinking more tea. Edison, who had returned from the public library on Riley's frantic call for help to get Ben off the floor, poured Ben a rather large glass of whiskey. He was hovering, waiting for Ben to spill either of his beverages.

Ben's life was madness. He let out a slow breath. "So ghosts are real?"

"Yep," Caroline said. "Usually, they're a little better at hiding than that. But the ceiling ghost is less predictable than the others."

Ben gestured the hand occupied by a whiskey glass. "Ghosts."

"Mm-hmm." Caroline nodded. "Also, we're witches. Our magic helps us communicate with the ghosts. And occasionally, send them running when they violate personal space."

"OK... Sure. Have you always been a witch? Like when we were dating?" Ben asked.

"Oh, no, I'm a late-in-life magical bloomer." She paused to nod toward the copper bowl full of rose quartz pebbles. "I was actually practicing when you came in. Riley can full-on levitate antique furnishings, but I can't seem to lift a rock—which is discouraging."

"You were trying to lift a rock...with magic?" Ben asked.

"I told you, lifting stuff is my special magical talent, we just haven't found yours yet," Riley told her gently, apparently ignoring Ben's question.

"Story of my life," Caroline grumbled. "Oh, and the Shaddows don't exist."

"Wait, what?!" Ben exclaimed.

Alice topped off Ben's whiskey glass. "The Dentons made them up so people wouldn't ask questions about why they never let people in the house. They wanted to be able to do their work while they sort of faded into the background. It only took a few generations for everybody to forget that they'd never really met the Shaddows."

"I feel so betrayed...and a little gullible," Ben said, sipping the tea and then the whiskey. Both burned. "I can't believe we didn't question it. I mean, I guess we did. Everybody on the island has their own 'Shaddow theory.' But I don't think anybody guessed they were being Keyser Söze'd."

The others snorted and he said, "Oh, man, it's nice to be around people old enough to get that reference...but really, *ghosts*?"

Riley looked faintly embarrassed. "I'm so sorry, Ben, that was the worst possible ghost for you to meet for the first time. Most ghosts are actually really nice. They're people, just like you and me. They're just, let's say, corporeally challenged. Um, Plover, would you please show yourself to Dr. Hoult to prove it?"

Nothing happened.

"Plover, please? If you would be so kind," Riley asked in a very intentionally sweet tone. "OK, this is embarrassing, and I'm going to have Eloise do it if you don't cooperate. Or worse, the clown ghost, and that would be humiliating and terrifying for the both of us."

"Plover?" Ben's face lit up. "Plover's a ghost?"

A thin, distinguished-looking man in an old-fashioned suit materialized to his right like smoke unfurling. He inclined his head respectfully. "Doctor."

"Plover is a ghost." Ben repeated, not bothering to hide his grin of absolute delight. Plover wasn't competition for Caroline, he was a *ghost*. And it made sense that Caroline said his name with such affection. He looked like something straight out of one of her BBC movies.

"Yes," Plover intoned. "In this house, I am *the* ghost."

"That's pretty much true." Caroline nodded. "He's Riley's right-hand man. And my personal favorite."

A burbling noise sounded from the fountain, and frankly, sounded like insulted burbling.

Caroline winced. "I'm sorry, Eloise. You know I love you too."

Plover smirked and bowed to Caroline. And then Ben wondered if maybe he underestimated the potential of ghost competition for Caroline's affection.

"And there are ghosts all throughout the house?" Ben said.

"The majority of us have elected not to show ourselves to avoid overwhelming you," Plover said.

"Thanks, I appreciate that. I like you a lot more than the ceiling ghost," Ben muttered into the whiskey. "He's replaced Clark as my least favorite person-and-or-thing on the island."

"Oh, no, Clark is the worst," Riley said. "Edison found proof at this kid Kyle's house that Clark was paying Kyle to terrorize us. And then, uh, the ceiling ghost dropped a chandelier on Kyle when he broke into the house to steal some ghostly objects."

Ben blinked at her. So *that* was how the Ashmark boy died?

"It was a whole thing," Caroline said.

"Anyway," Riley continued. "We found out Clark was behind it, so we're thinking of blackmailing him if he becomes more of a problem."

"I still don't like that plan," Edison told her.

Ben took a moment, trying to process everything Riley had just told him. So Clark was involved in a break-in at Shaddow House? Was that the reason he'd been so tolerant of the poor management of Gray Fern? Keeping the house empty of renters would allow Clark to watch Shaddow House from Ben's own windows? No wonder Clark had been so persistent about trying to get Ben to renew his contract with Martin Property Management. Hell, Clark had written Ben three emails in the last two weeks asking him to reconsider.

"That was a lot," Caroline told Riley. "For a first-timer."

"Well, I've never had to explain this to a new guy before. It takes a little more to summarize than I thought it would," Riley said, jerking her shoulders. "Besides, he knows about the ghosts. And you trust him. Plover…is tolerating him."

"I am undecided on Dr. Hoult," Plover sniffed. "Of the blackmail? I approve."

"He's never liked Clark, either," Edison assured Ben. "Plover also didn't like the security cameras Riley and I installed all around the perimeter of the first floor to try to prevent future break-ins. And he was none too subtle about his gloating when the ghosts' energy shorted them out in less than twelve hours."

"It was only a small fire, sir," Plover said, smirking.

"Well, everybody likes to be proven right, even if they don't have a pulse—wait, Edison, why are you going through things at Kyle's house?" Ben asked. "Did you break into *his* house?"

"I was the only one Kyle was close to, so I'm the executor of his estate," Edison said. "I think he left the receipts behind as some sort of fail-safe."

"You're the executor of the will of a guy who broke into your girlfriend's house?" Ben asked.

"It's complicated," Edison sighed. "But this is kind of nice, really, to talk to someone about it."

"Right?" Riley exclaimed.

"OK, I have seen this with my own eyes, so I'm just going to believe everything you're saying," Ben said, draining his glass.

"See, the ceiling ghost was actually helpful," Caroline noted.

Riley scoffed. "Yeah, but not on purpose."

Ben nodded to the books strewn around them, the framed art propped against the fountain. "So, what are you reading here when not trying to levitate rocks?"

"Latest ghost investigation. I've been seeing this ghost lately, around the bar. And then when your daughter knocked me unconscious, I had a vision of the cliffs at Vixen's Fall." She paused to chin-point to the framed sketch. "And a woman being shoved off of them."

"Oh, do you think it's the ghost that grabs people's ankles?" Ben gasped. "That story has freaked me out since I was a kid."

"I don't know," Caroline said, grabbing for one of the very old books Edison had apparently stolen from the library. "In the vision, it felt like this girl seemed hopeful, innocent. Well, OK, a little resentful, but she just wanted to meet some boy she loved—um, Emmett; *her* Emmett—and get away from the island. And I think the story we heard when we were kids was that she was sort of a man-eater?"

"I'd always heard that a rejected lover threw her off the cliff when she accepted some richer man's proposal," Ben said.

"I heard she jumped off because her groom left her at the altar," Alice said. "Why do so many ghost stories involve brides?"

"Folklore has a tendency to be rewritten with each generation," Edison said. "The truth is probably some really mundane version where she ticked off her sister or something. Also, a wedding day is always fraught with terror-slash-poignancy."

"Well, on that note." Caroline flipped the book open to a page. "I was doing a little light reading. This is the journal of the Mrs. Reverend Elias Lettston. Only, it's not so much a journal as a one-woman, unpublished gossip column. Maybe she thought it didn't count as gossip if she didn't say it aloud? And she doesn't name names, which is really frustrating. Again, I suspect she thought it made her somehow more virtuous, or something. Anyway, she has the tea on everybody on the island—who's sleeping with who, who's cheating who in land deals, who has scurvy. Which I guess was a little more scandalous back then. I keep finding references to a 'Rose.' I'm having a little trouble following ye old script here thanks to aging paper, fading ink and, well, horrific handwriting—like, worse than Riley's."

"Hey!" Riley griped.

Caroline shrugged and continued, "It sounds like there was a nurse working for my family back when we ran the bar as an inn. Back then, a nurse could mean a nanny or even someone who tended to an older family member. Mrs. Lettston calls this nurse an old maid, kind of vindictively, to be honest. And she implies in not-so-subtle backhanded language that this nurse wanted the innkeeper for herself. She was 'wilted' by time, bitterness, and lack of manly attentions, and thought she could take my great-great-great-however-many-great ancestor's place for her-self. Or maybe she succeeded, and the evil nurse *is* my great-great-great-however-many-great ancestor. I don't know yet because Mrs. Lettston literally tracked every daily movement on the island, and she left about ten years' worth of journals to get through. But man, I hope not, because that could mean I'm related to a murderer."

"So you think maybe that's where The Wilted Rose got its name?" Ben asked. "Like a warning?"

"Could be," Caroline said. "Could be that I'm seeing the vision from this Rose's perspective, meaning she was punished by the angry wife. Or I'm seeing the fall from the doomed wife's perspective and Rose got her way."

"Sure," Riley said. "Or maybe it's entirely unrelated and we're dealing with a ghost that has nothing to do with your family. Or maybe, you just hit your head really hard because you were run over by a moped—sorry, Ben—and the vision doesn't mean anything. It's unprocessed angst over the historical fiction you were reading last."

"But maybe, just maybe, this ghost chose to reveal herself to me because she has something to do with my family," Caroline insisted. "Maybe if we help her, or hell, banish her, if necessary, I can break the curse or spell or whatever. And me or any member of my family could leave the island for a day without worrying about being run down by an ice cream truck."

"I don't want to be a downer, but that's a pretty large intuitive leap," Edison said.

"I'm aware. But if there's even a remote chance," Caroline said, waggling her head.

Ben's jaw dropped. "Oh, Caroline."

Caroline's brows rose. "Yeah?"

All the blood seemed to drain out of Ben's face. He was cold, everywhere. He'd doubted her. He'd never thought of Caroline as "crazy," per se. But he'd thought she'd used the "curse" or bad luck or whatever as an excuse not to leave her demanding family, like it took away her agency, kept her from having to claim her choices. He'd blamed her for his having to make a life without her. And yet she'd only been responsible, sensible even, to stay on the island when leaving meant certain death.

"We're just going to go…" Riley said, gently leading Edison out of the atrium.

Plover stayed by the fountain, glaring at Ben. "I don't know what you did, but I can tell you, sir, that I doubt very much that you deserve the affections of Miss Caroline—"

"Plover!" Riley called from the next room. Plover mimed pointing at his own eyes and then pointing at Ben.

Ben wrapped his arms around Caroline. "I'm so sorry. I didn't believe you. But you were telling the truth the whole time, weren't you?"

She shrugged. "Well, I don't have magical confirmation, but—"

"But if magic and ghosts are real, why not curses?" he said. She nodded. "I'm sorry that I took all that time away from us."

"You needed that time away," Caroline said. "You needed to make your life, fulfill your purpose. And I needed to stay here and let Riley find me so I could fulfill mine."

"You're a *witch*," Ben marveled. "I mean, Gina Mursky used to say that about you in high school all the time, but to see it for myself."

"It takes some getting used to," she admitted. "But I'm still the same me."

"Still have superstrong hands," he noted. "And a really great ass."

"Don't you forget it." She laid her head on his shoulder as he laughed. "You know, it's sort of funny… In Plover's flower language, ferns represent magic. Secrets. Maybe your ancestors knew all about what was happening in Shaddow House, when they named your place?"

"Let's just tackle one huge magical family mystery at a time, OK?" Ben said.

Chapter 8
Caroline

CAROLINE HADN'T MEANT TO END up at the bar. Really. And she couldn't even do much but sit on a stool and help her mom sort through the financials for the month—a task made even harder by the big red number sitting where their profits should have been.

And yet, here she was, picking food and liquor receipts out of customer receipts because Will and Wally could never be bothered to save those separately. The customer receipts stack was a lot shorter than the provisioning stack, and that was a scary prospect. Shutting down the bar was going to hurt, even with the emergency fund and Riley's help.

And Caroline wasn't sleeping. The vision she'd had after the accident, that poor woman being shoved from the cliff—she kept seeing it in her sleep, night after night, sending her screaming into consciousness every few hours. Despite the stress of it all, financial juggling was still more welcome in her headspace than her thoughts of Ben.

Every spare moment she replayed their kisses in her mind, reliving every moment. He'd rejected her. In her head, she understood that it was most likely due to her debilitating injuries and the intrusion of a Peeping Tom ghost, but in the darker moments, when she was alone with her thoughts, she wondered—was it because she was older? She knew she didn't have the dewy youth of her teenage years, but she wasn't exactly a troll. Or maybe it was just typical post-divorce wobbles? She didn't think Ben was still hung up on his ex. He rarely mentioned her...but maybe that meant that he *was* hung up on her.

Argh.

Caroline didn't know how to process this. She'd never taken rejection like this personally. She was used to doing the rejecting. And if she was rejected, it was by someone she didn't care about, so it barely stung. But from Ben? It stung, it burned, it cut.

Being at the bar was a welcome distraction.

Maybe it hadn't been a good idea, having Mina, a daily reminder of her dad, working in the Rose. But she kept showing up, day after day, early according to her mother's reports. Josh usually tagged along. The compulsive need to prove he could lift more heavy objects than his sister—for no other reason than knowing that it bugged her—made for a productive competition. That meant that Gert was accomplishing more than she expected on a daily basis—something that was honestly unprecedented in the Wilton family.

"Dad texted me, says it's time for your midmorning meds," Mina said, holding up her sparkly blue cell phone. It went with her T-shirt and the bandana tied around her hair, both a shade of shocking arctic blue. "And then he said that if you're on your feet at all, I'm supposed to 'throw you in the nearest wheelbarrow and push you over to the clinic' so he can yell at you. Does my dad think there are just wheelbarrows sitting unattended around on the island?"

"Your dad's a man who enjoys a nice hyperbolic metaphor," Caroline said, pulling her meds out of her purse and demonstrating that she was taking them.

Caroline was a little ashamed that she'd expected a couple of doctor's kids to be soft, spoiled, unwilling to work—maybe years of dealing with her brothers had left her jaded. And she was mentally retracting those words. Both Hoult kids worked hard, and even if it was to spite each other, it was welcome. The area underneath the bar had been scrubbed and cleared for dismantling. The deep freeze had been defrosted and the frozen mozzarella sticks restacked by reverse expiration date. The keg lines had been untangled and removed. Josh had identified several kegs in the tap room that were well past their prime and put them in a "disposal" pile, most likely saving her family from a food poisoning–based lawsuit.

Mina snickered. "Thank you, Caroline."

"For taking my meds without a wheelbarrow intervention?" Caroline asked.

"For talking to me like I'm a person," Mina said, shrugging. "Despite the fact that I'm responsible for you being on those meds."

"Well, you are a person," Caroline noted. "But I'm not worried about you reinjuring me. I'm way more afraid that you will somehow detect everything I secretly hate about myself and throw it in my face."

Mina marveled, "Wow."

"Teenagers are terrifying," Caroline replied.

"Only when provoked," Mina insisted. "Look, Dad thinks he's

taking care of us, and that's great. We appreciate it. But we worry about him. He doesn't seem to understand that."

Caroline's head reared back at the sudden shift in conversation. Was this what it was like inside a teenager's head?

Mina was still talking. "I can see that you like my dad. And I think my role in this whole dynamic is that I'm supposed to be a snotty jerk who yells in your face that you'll never be my mom, but really, Josh and I just want our dad to be happy. We want him to have something, *someone* really, for himself. It would be nice if you were that something or someone. He likes you. I can tell."

"I don't know if this is appropriate," Caroline said, shaking her head. "Your dad and I have a history that I don't think I should talk about with you. There are rules about this sort of thing, I'm sure."

"I respect rules," Mina said, nodding. When Caroline pulled a doubtful face, she barked, "Hey! In the interest of setting those parameters, I think I should inform you, formally, that if you do anything to hurt my dad—or Josh, who also falls under my umbrella of protection, no matter what he thinks—I will destroy you."

"Understood." Caroline nodded. "Will I receive confirmation of this threat in writing?"

"No, I wouldn't leave a paper trail," Mina scoffed. "I'll make it look like an accident...if anyone happens to find your body, which is unlikely."

"I believe that you are capable of that," Caroline said as Mina flounced off to follow whatever direction Cole gave her.

Gert returned from the office with a stack of invoices. "Mina made you take your meds?"

"Under threat of a wheelbarrow," Caroline grumped while Gert sat next to her. Gert just sort of stared at Caroline. She'd never been one for jokes in the workplace.

"I don't think we can save that one, Ma," Wally huffed, pointing to the booth in the far rear corner of the barroom. It hadn't been touched by the collapse. From her vantage point, Caroline couldn't even see dust on the table. Will knew that between the two of them, Wally had a higher success rate of wheedling grace out of their mom, so he was sort of hovering in the periphery, not really doing anything, but appearing to be busy wiping down chairs. *Appearing* to be busy was his superpower.

"Are you saying that because you don't want to have to carry it across the street to the salvage container, and the Dumpster is closer?" Caroline asked.

"No!" Wally cried. "I just think we should scrap it and get something nicer."

Gert's tone was much gentler. "Honey, new booths cost money, and we're trying to save as much as possible. Please take the booth to the salvage container."

"Can Caroline at least help?" Wally groaned. "These things are heavy!"

Caroline lifted her crutch from the floor and waved it at him, to remind him of her injured ankle. She winced at the strain that put on her ribs, but it proved her point. How was it that Wally was three years older than her and yet, he still sounded like a toddler?

"What about them?" Wally whined, chin-pointing to where Mina was standing on a stepladder dismantling the display of family memorabilia behind the bar and carefully taping it in bubble wrap. Cole was right next to her, measuring the space behind the bar. She only hoped Cole didn't add to their misfortunes by knocking Mina off her ladder or something.

That wasn't fair. Cole had been a sunny and steady presence in the barroom during the stressful cleanup process. He also had the uncanny ability to manage to find a single vision for the renovation through the cacophony of four battling Wilton voices. And he was easy on the eyes, which Caroline appreciated—all burly, bearded charm and big blue eyes. And while he might have fit her "not a local" requirement, it just didn't feel right, picking up the big, old flirty signals Cole had been laying down since they'd met.

"Cole is busy," Caroline's mother reminded them. "And remember *we're* handling the furniture removal because it reduces Cole's bill."

"Well, what about the kids?" Wally asked, nodding toward Mina.

"The kids are already pulling their weight," Caroline said through clenched teeth. "You might watch them and pick up some pointers."

"Caroline," her mother chastised her softly. She noted that Gert didn't correct her.

Mina turned around and pulled out her earbud, having that teenager's preternatural ability to know when someone was talking about her. "Everything OK?"

"It's fine, sweetie, just keep doing what you're doing," Caroline said, smiling at her. As soon as Mina returned to her task, Caroline turned back to her brother and growled. "Pull your weight or catch a foot up the ass."

Wally took a step back. Behind him, Mina went back to carefully taking down the landscape painting that had hung behind the bar since Caroline's childhood.

"Caroline!" Gert huffed, even as Will and Wally hustled to take the rear booth out. "You don't have to talk to them that way."

"Thanks, Ma," Will grumbled.

"Because that's my job." Gert turned on Will. "Your sister's right, Will, it's damned embarrassing that my grown sons are being outdone by a couple of high school kids in my own bar. Stop looking to everybody else for empty hands and start getting your own dirty."

Caroline's eyes went wide, but she was no more shocked than Will and Wally, who hadn't been on the receiving end of their mother's lecture voice for years. Her mother had not only expressed disapproval for her brothers' actions, but had told them to do *more*. Caroline was afraid to move for fear of breaking this unprecedented stream of motherly correction.

"Jeez, Ma, don't get so worked up!" Wally gasped. "We're going."

"Don't we get credit for showing up?" Will grumbled as they wandered away.

"No!" Caroline and her mother called after them.

Caroline gently nudged her mother with her shoulder. "Thanks, Mom."

"Don't you start," Gert said, her voice tight with discomfort as the boys hauled the table out the door, grunting and complaining the whole span of the floor. "I know, I've let them…get too comfortable with the way things are. I just don't know how to get them to *try* again. And I'm so tired all the time, and it just feels like it's too big of a fight to take on today, and then tomorrow, and then the next day, and you've always been so dependable…and…"

"I get tired too, Mom," Caroline said quietly.

"I know," her mother said. She breathed quickly through her nose and nodded to the Hoult kids. "Now, those two, they know how to work."

"Yes, they do," Caroline said, watching a smile curve her mother's lips. "They're like Ben, in that way."

Outside, Caroline could hear a scuffle and a crash of wood against stone. It sounded like her brothers were arguing over "who dropped it." Gert rolled her eyes. "I'll take care of it."

As Gert hustled out the door, Caroline saw Mina's shoulders stiffen. She was standing on top of the ladder, staring toward the basement entrance. Her expression was familiar. Was Mina seeing something? Caroline wondered.

Kids saw ghosts more easily than adults did, and teenagers were a little closer to their childlike perceptions. Maybe Mina could see the ghosts consistently without the benefit of magic?

Josh turned around, staring at the basement door, his face pale as parchment. He pulled at his ear, as if it itched. Mina climbed down the ladder, walking toward the door with that same apprehension. It was a feeling Caroline was familiar with by now, waiting to see that awful woman's face peering out at her from around the corner. Josh walked outside, still tugging at his earlobe.

As Mina passed her worktable, Caroline said quietly, "Mina. On the day you hit me…"

"Thanks for phrasing it like that," Mina shot back dryly.

"On the day your moped collided with my torso," Caroline amended. "You said you 'swear you thought you saw'…something. What did you see?"

"It's stupid," Mina said, shaking her head.

"I promise you, it's not," Caroline said.

"I thought I saw a woman wearing an old-fashioned dress, like something off of *Gilded Age*?" Mina said, waiting for Caroline to nod. "Her hair was up in this sort of puffy updo, and she was carrying a *parasol*, just walking around outside the theater."

Caroline chewed her lip. The ghost lady from the Duchess occasionally wandered to the Main Square, seeking out the location of Waterstones, a sweetshop that dated back to 1880. Caroline could hardly blame the ghostly dame. If Caroline couldn't eat anymore, she'd hover wistfully outside of a truffle display, too.

"She was probably just a historical reenactor or something," Mina insisted. "There seem to be a lot of those around here."

"Have you been seeing a lot of them since you moved here?" Caroline asked. As they spoke, the purple-dress ghost materialized in the shadows, watching them. Josh had already hauled a box full of dishes out the front door, and Caroline wondered if he was finding a reason not to stay in the room. Could he feel the miasma of cold discomfort this woman's spirit seemed to spread through the very air around her?

"Feels like it." Mina's mouth opened, as if she was going to add something, but she pinched her lips shut. Caroline reached out to take her wrist, and an electrical crackle of energy sparked between their hands. Across the room, the purple-dress ghost grinned, the wild edge of it sending a shiver down Caroline's spine. The blood drained out of Mina's face.

The woman's mouth wasn't moving, but a rasping voice practically scraped across the surface of Caroline's brain like steel wool. *"Poor, sweet girl. Look at them, making you work your fingers to the bone. You're too young to be toiling away. If you were my own daughter, I would make sure you had the time to enjoy yourself. They're stealing your life from you..."*

It felt...wrong, like she was listening to a radio skipping across the channels. Caroline didn't think she was supposed to be hearing it, even if it did feel awfully personalized toward Caroline.

"Sometimes, we see things that don't make sense, and sometimes we hear things that make even less sense," Caroline said carefully.

The purple-dress ghost's head snapped toward Caroline. Her grin had turned to something calmer and scarier. Determined. She faded back into the shadows.

"I've been hearing things since I first walked into the bar," Mina blurted out, not loud enough for Cole to hear, but clear to Caroline. "Josh, too, but I don't think he wants to admit it. He keeps talking about someone leaving a TV on upstairs here, hearing the voices. But why would you leave a TV on upstairs in rooms that have been wrecked?"

"OK," Caroline said, nodding and trying her best to sound nonjudgmental and calm.

Mina's voice was low. "It's like a whisper, like two different voices at once. I think she's trying to sound nice, sweet, but there's something else, just *mean*, underneath it. It's like that fairy-tale grandma you know you can't trust because the minute you take the candy from her hand, she's gonna throw you in an oven. I don't want her around Josh if she's going to whisper like that. She's trying to trick us, and I don't know why."

"OK," Caroline said, taking Mina's hand. "It's going to be all right, I promise."

A crashing sound from behind the bar caught their attention. Cole was looking back at them, a mortified expression turning his face bright red. The framed landscape of Starfall Point, the one that Nora Denton used to sit at the bar and stare at on her rare visits, was broken between his massive hands.

"Damn, I'm sorry," Cole said, sounding absolutely contrite. "I'm usually a little quicker on my feet than that. Or...with my hands, I guess. Knocked it right off the shelf trying to get it down without a ladder, because I tried to be a smart-ass."

"It's OK, the whole family hates that painting," Caroline assured him. Mina followed close at her heels as she approached the bar. "We just didn't have the heart to toss it because some ancient, untalented Wilton painted what this part of the island looked like before the bar was built."

"Huh, will you look at this," Cole mused, peeling the broken frame away from the backing. A second layer of canvas was poking out from under the landscape. Cole set the painting on the bar and pulled a series of tiny nails from the backing—which, in itself, seemed impressive in terms of hand strength. "There's another painting under this one."

The three of them worked together to remove the nails. The fragile canvas flaked old paint onto the floor as they worked. "Maybe we should wait for Edison or someone who knows what they're doing," Caroline mused. "For all we know, this is some priceless piece of Starfall history."

"I don't think there's a Van Gogh under here, Caroline," Mina told her, regaining some of her "Mina-ness." When they pulled the landscape canvas away from the second layer, they revealed a face that almost made Caroline shriek. Mina recoiled, grabbing at Caroline's hands.

"Whoa," Cole marveled, swallowing heavily.

This was considerably better art than what Riley bought from Willard's place. It wasn't a wedding portrait, even though the gown the woman was wearing was made from a luxuriant cream silk. One could tell by the way the light was painted over the soft folds of the skirt. The lady was sitting rigidly in a chair so spindly and impractical, it had to be expensive. The subject was the purple-dress ghost, but younger. Not necessarily softer or happier, but younger. There was no hint of a smile curving her thin lips, or warmth in her hydrangea-blue eyes. She was holding her head at such an angle that she was looking down her long nose at the viewer no matter where they were standing. It was like one of those creepy funhouse pictures, but way more judgmental.

It was at this moment that Caroline remembered that in Plover's flower language, hydrangeas meant "heartlessness."

This was a painting that was meant to be displayed over a mantel, to frown down at future generations and let them know they were not living up to standards. But something was off about it. It was…trying too hard? It was as if the woman's head had been old-timey Photoshopped onto a grand lady's body. Her features were too rough, too boxy, for the delicacy the silk gown implied. Maybe the subject had borrowed a dress for the occasion, to prove that she could afford to wear a white gown when most people bought clothes for their durability and resistance to stains?

It didn't matter, really. Caroline was just trying to find a way to avoid mentally processing the dread this painting transmuted in her belly. Was this the nurse described in Mrs. Lettston's journal, the one that tried to usurp her employer? The famous Wilted Rose? The portrait would be an expensive tribute to an employee, particularly given the fancy dress, but maybe, if she'd actually managed to marry the Wilton husband she'd been targeting, it was possible.

There was something altogether strange about it. Not just the mendacious appearance but the magical vibrations coming off the canvas. Caroline got the feeling that this wasn't an attachment object, but it was definitely important to someone…not nice.

"Obviously, I can fix the frame, free of charge, off the clock," Cole said. "It's my responsibility, for breaking it."

He could, but she didn't want Cole taking potentially haunted debris to his house and muddying the ghost waters.

She used to think like a normal person. What happened?

"For now, let's put it with the other display items and store," Caroline said. "We've got too much other stuff to worry about for you to be exhausting yourself on side carpentry projects."

Cole shrugged. "All right then."

The phone in Caroline's pocket buzzed. She muttered, "Speaking of which."

She prayed it wasn't a text from her mother asking her to break up whatever fight between Will and Wally was *still* happening outside. The text was from Riley.

Big development. Get here ASAP.

Now Riley was using the emojis.
Shit.

It had taken considerable time to explain to Cole, Mina, and her family why she suddenly had to head home. And then, she'd had to convince Mina to leave immediately because she didn't want to leave a vulnerable teenager unattended with an aggressive (and honestly, passive-aggressive) ghost. And then, she'd had to sneak the not-quite-a-wedding-portrait into a tote bag and get it out of the bar. And *then*, she'd had to limp home on her crutches, or at least, she would have, if Riley hadn't sent Mitt Sherzinger to fetch her in one of his pedal cabs.

"Riley's started a tab for you," Mitt told her, his shorts bunching around the legendary thigh muscles required to haul tourists all over the island on his pedal-powered machines. "You are not to try to crutch your way home under any circumstances. You call me, and I'll come get you."

Caroline started to say, "But—"

"You were hit by a small motor vehicle last week," Mitt reminded her.

Caroline shook her head. "But you—"

"You were hit by a small motor vehicle *last week*," Mitt said again.

"Fine," Caroline sighed, slumping back into the seat, even as it made her ribs scream. And yeah, she was secretly sort of pleased that Riley had thought to take care of her. It was one of the things she was still getting used to, as part of being in a coven.

Just a few minutes later, Mitt rolled up to the gate of Shaddow House, and Caroline realized the wisdom in driving her there. There was no way she would have made it up that hill on her own.

"Thanks, Mitt," she said, carefully climbing out of the cab. Riley was waiting at the gate to help her up the stairs.

"Hey, Caroline," Mitt whispered, handing over her crutches. "What's it like in there?"

"You wouldn't believe me if I told you," Caroline said, winking at him.

"I knew it," Mitt sighed.

Alice was fluffing pillows on the parlor couch when Caroline walked in—something that apparently required Plover's supervision. Caroline had been careful to leave her tote bag outside the front door. Even if she wasn't sure the painting was an attachment object, she was not about to bring it into the house and trap an unpleasant ghost inside with people she cared about—living or dead.

"Miss Caroline!" Plover called, rushing to meet her. "So glad to see you."

"Someone got used to having you around during your convalescence," Riley observed as they helped Caroline get settled.

"All I'm missing is a shawl and a lace cap," Caroline muttered.

"Enough of your grumpery, because we have cause for celebration," Riley said, emptying a linen bag onto the coffee table. "We found another lock!"

"What? When did that happen?" Caroline exclaimed. "I feel weirdly excluded!"

"I was at work, so I missed out on it, too," Alice told her. "And to be fair, we have jobs, but Shaddow House is Riley's full-time job. We can't expect her to wait until we have time to search."

"Thank you for your understanding. I found it in the secret

basement level Plover only revealed to us recently," Riley said, her tone pointed.

Caroline shuddered. The "secret level" only accessible through the cellar felt like an express subway route into hell. A spiral mineshaft leftover from early copper mining efforts on the island, it was lined with locked metal cells that reminded Caroline of submarine doors. Each door seemed to contain its own variation of ghostly screaming. So…basically, it was a basement full of nightmare spirits. Considering the ghosts allowed to have free range upstairs, Caroline could only imagine what was lurking downstairs.

"I did apologize for that, Miss," Plover reminded her. "And I was only trying to ease you into the ways of Shaddow House. You must admit, the horror show in the basement is a bit much."

"True. I suppose you're forgiven. Anyway, do you remember my idea about the original location for the entrance?" Riley said, pointing to the sketch she'd bought from Willard's shop. "The lock was buried in an area of the secret-lair level, under where the door would have been. I'm guessing the Wellings didn't know it was a secret basement. They just knew there was a handy spot where they could hide it between two load-bearing stones, near where they thought the door would be."

"Just to review, you didn't *move* the load-bearing stones, did you?" Edison asked.

"No," Riley promised. "I dug around them."

"I'm not sure that's better," Alice said.

"Can we just celebrate the fact that we found another one?" Riley demanded.

"I found one of the good bottles of champagne your Aunt Nora stashed in the pantry!" Natalie the dry-erase board ghost yelled from the kitchen. "I would get it for you, but I can't move it!"

"Thank you, Natalie! That is the kind of enthusiasm I was hoping for!" Riley cried. "Also, good job shouting!"

"We don't mean to bring you down after your hard-earned success," Alice assured her. "It's just that, the more of these locks we locate, the more logistical issues we have. For instance, is it smart to store all of the locks in one place, from a strategic point of view? We can't move them from the house, obviously, because that's a terrible idea, but should we hide them in different locations so if someone manages to get inside, they won't grab all of them in one swoop?"

"That's a good point," Riley conceded. "Though I'm not sure re-hiding them is smart, either. We could lose them all over again."

"And how are we going to destroy these things?" Caroline asked. "We've tried spells. We tried dissolving the locks in acid. We even tried smelting one. All we did was leave some very interesting patterns in the stone in the atrium, which Plover took quite personally."

"Yeah, my sense of victory is definitely waning," Riley said, chewing her lip and flopping onto the couch. She pinched the bridge of her nose. "OK, I accept all of your points. My celebration was a little premature. I'm just...looking for a win, I guess, considering the relatively rough month we've had. Caroline nearly getting knocked inside out and all."

"I appreciate the effort to find a silver lining," Caroline assured her. "It's considerably more cheerful than my thought patterns about the locks lately."

Riley's brows arched. "Meaning?"

"Well, I've been wondering, do you really think that the Wellings are going to all this trouble just to control ghosts and get access to ghost assassins?" Caroline asked, shaking her head. "I mean, untraceable murder was probably super handy hundreds of years ago, but that sort of thing can be accomplished by drones nowadays. Why are they still trying so hard to get at them?"

"I think denying bad people access to ghost assassins is probably a good policy regardless," Alice noted.

"I'm just saying that it doesn't seem like a relevant goal nowadays," Caroline said. "Your magical ancestors didn't have the full story when they started building Shaddow House. Maybe your Aunt Nora didn't have the full story when she died. Maybe it's something more sinister?"

"Maybe we're looking at this the wrong way," Edison suggested. "Maybe instead of trying to destroy the locks, we should try to figure out what they're supposed to do. If we knew what the Wellings wanted to do with them, we could, I don't know, beat them to the punch. How do we know what they are and what they do anyway?"

"Because of my Aunt Nora's journals," Riley said. "She was pretty clear about the fact that locks both attract and bind the ghosts' power. And that the Wellings' whole plan was to weaponize that power against their enemies."

"And how did *she* know that?" Edison asked. "Because of what her family told her, from what they gleaned from clues the Wellings left behind? So, it's possible we don't really know what they do. Or at least, not everything that they do."

"She did write 'multiple loops for multiple magical uses question mark' in her journal," Riley said. "So, what, we conduct experiments to see what the locks can do? That seems…ill-advised."

"Everything we've done since you've stepped on the island is technically ill-advised," Alice reminded her. "By the standards of most average people."

"Fair," Riley sighed. "So how would we even start?"

Caroline's expression was half grin, half grimace. "It's funny you should ask."

Standing outside in the darkened yard of Shaddow House, Caroline felt a little guilty for disrupting the elegant peace of the property. While it wasn't exactly well-tended vegetationwise, there were multiple statues from various mythologies arranged in a sort of sundial formation around a recently painted white gazebo. Cozy benches lined the inside of each octagonal angle of the gazebo, creating a reading space Caroline envied on a soul level.

"None of these statues are haunted, right?" Edison asked. They'd chosen a corner of the garden relatively obscured by Gray Fern Cottage. The last thing they needed was nosy non-Hoult neighbors seeing their activities over the fence. Weirdly enough, it was the first time they'd really had to worry about such a thing at Shaddow House.

"Not to my knowledge," Riley said as Alice clipped the disturbing canvas to a display easel they frequently used to examine artifacts. It was sort of weird they had a designated easel for ghost artifacts, but Caroline had learned not to question this sort of thing. "I think one of the prewar Dentons wanted to give us a place to go without ghostly company—which was thoughtful of them. So, what do we have here, Caroline?"

Caroline adjusted her stance on her crutches to approach the easel. "So, before you yell at me about mistreating historical artifacts, Edison, I didn't know I was going to be handling this, so I did the best I could."

Edison looked affronted, his face shifting pale under the full summer moon. "I don't...yell. I talk...emphatically."

All three women gave him a bemused look. Edison added, "I talk emphatically...at a louder than average volume... OK, but it's just about this one thing!"

Riley burst out laughing and kissed him. Behind them, Plover made an aggravated huffing noise from the kitchen door. He and Natalie had to watch the proceedings from there, as the magic of Shaddow House kept them inside.

"OK, so this is a painting that we found hidden under another painting at the bar," Caroline said, waving toward the purple-dress ghost's stern younger visage. Riley, Edison, and Alice winced in unison.

"Yeah, she's a piece of work," Caroline agreed. "And even less pleasant in person. As far as I knew, the place wasn't haunted. But it's her portrait. The ghost is definitely the older version of her, but her whole persona feels faked somehow, like she's not as old as she looks, not as sad and sick. Her voice doesn't sound right. It's got layers to it, like some badly mixed demo tape. And since I started seeing her around the same time as the dreams started, I think the two issues are connected."

"What dreams?" Alice asked. "I thought you only had that dream once after the accident."

"Yeah…it's more a nightly show inside my head," Caroline admitted.

"Caroline!" Riley exclaimed. "We don't keep things like that from each other! That was the agreement!"

"I know, I know." Caroline nodded. "But I was still processing everything, and I felt like I was going crazy after the accident, and with Ben in town, and I've just been so scattered. And since the dreams weren't waking you up, too, I figured it was just a psychological thing. And I didn't want to bother you with it if it was all in my head."

Riley threw her arms around Caroline, quickly followed by Alice. Edison stood on the periphery, awkwardly patting Caroline's shoulder.

"You're never *bothering* us," Riley said. "That's the point of this whole thing. We're in it together, or it's dangerous and scary and it doesn't work. So, if something wakes you up in the middle of the night and you're scared, you call us."

"If you see a creepy ghost in a place you've never seen one before, you call us," Alice said.

"If you and Ben hook up again, you call us," Riley said. "Because we're going to need details."

"I would like to be left out of that call," Edison noted. "I do not need the details."

Laughing, the hug broke, and they separated to examine the painting. There was no artist's name scribbled on the back or the bottom corners, which seemed unusual. The painting was also lacking a date and the name of the subject—which would have been super helpful. Edison guessed from the style and the clothing that it was late 1700s to early 1800s, which told them relatively little as that was a big boom period for the island's colonization.

"So, um, can you make her talk to you?" Riley asked. "Because I'm not feeling a lot of 'ghost energy' coming off the painting, like I normally do with our, uh, guests. It's just sort of residue, like a dish that wasn't washed properly."

"That was one coffee cup and I said I was sorry," Edison sighed. Alice snorted.

Caroline shook her head. "She only seems to talk to me at the bar."

"Well, let's see if we can force the issue." Riley disappeared inside the house and came back moments later with a Welling lock. Plover and Riley both seemed to brace themselves as she walked out of the kitchen door.

"Plover, any change?" she asked over her shoulder.

Plover attempted to push his hand through the kitchen doorway but was blocked by an invisible magical wall. He shook his head.

"Feels normal to me!" Natalie told them.

"So...removing one of the locks from the house doesn't release a thousand-plus ghosts onto the island, good to know," Riley said.

"Is that one of those things that we should have tested on the fly?" Alice asked.

"Probably not," Riley admitted. "And we should probably do this as quickly as possible before some Welling heir senses a disturbance in the universal energy that only seems to be detected by dedicated assholes, or something."

"So what do we do?" Caroline asked. "Shake the lock at it until some demon face appears in the paint?"

Riley poured a careful line of salt in a near-perfect circle around the easel and the lock. "Well, I've been reading up, and I think the closest thing we could do would be a 'summoning.' Basically, we try to force the spirit to materialize in front of us, in the circle."

Riley spent a few minutes reviewing the hand gesture necessary to complete the ritual, a pinched position of the right hand, drawn toward the chest. If it had been a shadow puppet, their hands might have looked like a bird's head. The three of them took their places outside the circle and took some clearing breaths. They made the drawing gesture and...nothing.

They tried again. Caroline focused on listening to her sisters' breathing, on the cool wind on her cheeks, and the light shining down on them. They made the gesture again and the lock sort of jolted on the grass. But the ghost lady didn't materialize, and the painting was unaffected.

"Well, that's something," Alice said, frowning.

They repeated the drawing gesture and the lock rose from the ground, nearly to eye level. It seemed to glow, first red and then bright-yellow symbols stood out against the copper. The lock dropped to the ground and where it had levitated, a little pinhole light had formed.

"Oh," Caroline said, swallowing thickly. "What is that?"

The light expanded into a vortex the size of a grapefruit. Inside of it was...nothing. No light, no sound, no stars. It was a void, and it filled Caroline with a sense of dread so profound, she wanted to run from it, screaming. But she wouldn't leave Riley and Alice behind to deal with this.

Riley didn't seem concerned so much as repulsed. Alice was

staring into that nothingness with her head tilted to the side. "I think it's a doorway. There's something on the other side. I don't know what it is, but it's not…good. But it doesn't have to be bad, I suppose?"

"I am getting a very different feeling," Edison said.

Riley nodded. "It wants us in there. And I don't like it."

"We feel little to no effect, Miss," Plover called from the house, sounding very confused.

"What do we do with it?" Caroline asked.

"Shove all the leftover dryer socks into it?" Alice suggested. When the others gave her a confused look, she huffed, "I'm allowed a little bit of whimsy, every once in a while."

"How do we close it?" Caroline asked.

"Well, the opposite of a summoning," Riley said, making the same ritual gesture backward, drawing away from herself. They followed her motions and the grapefruit reduced to an orange and then to nothing. The lock cooled and returned to a normal color. They followed Nora's instructions for properly closing a circle and cleaned up the salt.

"Maybe this is what happens when you try to use the locks on unhaunted objects? Or objects that have little ghostly dish spots on them?" Caroline suggested as they collapsed onto the gazebo benches with a bottle of wine.

Caroline sighed. "Well, the purple-dress lady didn't show up, and I'm a little relieved. I'm not sure what I would have done with the painting if she was attached to it. Burning it seems appropriate but mean. But I wonder if the portal would have been stronger if we had used a real attachment object?"

"It's something I'm not too eager to test at the moment, but it sounds like a valid theory," Riley said. She was nestled into Edison's side, looking very tired. "And *I wonder* why the Wellings dragged my family into this whole mess, the construction of the house, any of it…"

"Money," Caroline said. "Money makes the world go round, and there doesn't seem to be a spell to create it. Alchemy seems to be a bust. Plus—if a haunted object makes the locks work harder—your family had the trove of haunted antiques they needed to power whatever they're planning to do with the locks."

"Maybe the whole thing was a setup," Riley said. "It seems like an awfully big coincidence that the Wellings just happened to be heading to this tiny island at the same time. The Dentons had to have a reputation in the ghost community, right? People knew they had cash. Maybe the Wellings targeted them."

"Also a valid theory, but not particularly helpful to have hindsight. A more pertinent question: What do you think this new development means about the ghost locks?" Alice asked. "What were they meant for?"

"Besides ghostly world domination?" Riley considered. "Thinning the veil between the two worlds. Making death itself not work anymore so we're all just stuck wandering the planet with no reprieve in sight?"

"Well, that's bleak," Caroline snorted as a light clicked on upstairs at Gray Fern Cottage. "Oh, um, something else I forgot to mention… Mina can see ghosts. And given that I feel the same sort of electric buzz around her that I felt around you two, I think maybe she could have magic, too. Maybe Josh; I'm not sure. Mostly, he seems to hear things."

"Oh, sure, that makes sense," Riley said, nodding absently. Suddenly, she sat up. "Wait, what?"

Chapter 9
Ben

AFTER AN EARLY EVENING DINNER, Ben left Mina and Josh at home to indulge in a bit of solitude as he walked out the door of Gray Fern Cottage. Yes, he'd done it at the suggestion of his daughter, but he was pretending that it was his idea. Because she was usually right about this sort of thing in a way that was preternaturally annoying.

Still, it was so pleasant out here at night, so quiet. No patients. No ringing phone. No anthill-style foot traffic. No teenagers—as much as he loved them to the very marrow of their bones—who argued viciously over snack foods. He could *think*, string a few thoughts together, even.

He pointed his feet toward the Wiltons' corner of the island. Caroline was supposed to be home—but given the upheaval at the Rose and her family's tendency to find work for her—who knew? He wanted a moment with her, just one moment uninterrupted by teenagers or rude customers or magic.

Magic.

Caroline was a witch. Magic was real. Ghosts were real. And in a weird way, it gave him more hope for the world. Because there was more out there for them than just hard, cold science. At the same time, there were much scarier things in the world than what even his careful series of parental lectures could prepare his kids for—scarier than Ben could even imagine. It was a double-edged nightmare.

He could hardly wrap his head around it. And because he rarely got to see Caroline alone—thanks to her schedule, his schedule, the kids' needs—he couldn't talk to her about it. He didn't want his kids to know just yet, if Caroline chose to share with them. He got the impression that her family didn't know, which seemed smart on her part.

He'd resented her for so long, blamed her for limiting herself, for being afraid to leave the island because there were a few unfortunate accidents in her family. And the whole time, she'd been under a very real threat. Every memory, every argument they'd had back then, every moment she'd seemed cold on his visits home, took on a different tone. She wasn't afraid, she was a hostage. And yeah, his feelings were still real, but if he'd only known…

Well, he wasn't sure it would have changed his response to finding his former flame being dropped into a wheelbarrow outside Shaddow House with her injured ankle propped up on some improvised pool-noodle contraption.

"I just want to say, for the record, that this is humiliating," Caroline was saying as they loaded her into a wheelbarrow.

"But we padded it," Edison replied.

"I knew I shouldn't have told you about Ben's threat," Caroline groused. "Somebody's gonna see me wheeled through town like a sack of potatoes."

Alice stuffed another pillow behind Caroline's back. "If we thought we could do this on one of Mitt's pedal cabs, we would."

"Plus, we would have to explain why we were going out there," Riley told her. "And that would be confusing for more people."

"Um, what are you doing?" Ben asked.

All of them startled, looking almost guilty when they turned around to find Ben staring at them. They were dressed in hiking clothes—even Caroline, whose hiking boot wasn't quite laced tight over her still-tender foot. But it was way too late in the day to be heading into the woods.

"Going for a walk?" Caroline suggested, her smile bright.

"You're in a wheelbarrow," Ben said, noting the rusty garden conveyance. "It's not even a new one."

"In our defense, you gave us this idea," Alice told him.

Seemingly eager to change the subject, Caroline asked, "Um, Ben, what are you doing here?"

Ben held up a small travel medical bag. Mina had handed it to him as she practically shoved him out of the house after dinner. "Mina suggested I go for a walk...and she knew I would eventually end up walking toward your house, because she's basically a criminal profiler given her TV-watching habits... Did she know you were going out here tonight?" When most of the group nodded, he gasped. "She tricked me. My own flesh and blood, the betrayal!"

"Aw, she's trying to *Parent Trap* you!" Riley said, grinning. "Wait, would *Parent Trapping* them involve a group activity?"

"Teenagers rarely do anything alone," Ben informed her. "Trust me, group gatherings are one of their better impulses."

"That was a pretty flimsy story," Edison noted.

"Yeah, I'm really gonna have to put more effort into questioning her," Ben muttered. "I've let my guard down since we moved to a relatively low-risk location."

"You live next door to one of the most haunted houses in the world," Riley noted.

"We moved from Arizona. Rattlesnakes and scorpions," Ben explained, shrugging. The others nodded as if they understood. That was comforting. This was nice, spending time with other adults. He didn't have time for a lot of socializing before. His coworkers wanted to talk about work, when he certainly got enough of that at the hospital. And his ex... She never seemed to like spending much time with him in general. And if these people wanted to talk about ghost stuff or whatever weird activity they had planned, well, his schedule was pretty open.

"So, is this secret Shaddow Society business or something?" he asked.

"Oh, that's an interesting title for our little group," Alice said, grinning at him. "The Shaddow Society."

"I still think 'Shaddow House Ghost and Friday Night Euchre Club' is a perfectly valid name," Riley said as they pushed the wheelbarrow along the path into the woods. Ben just...followed. They didn't object, so he supposed he was welcome.

"We don't even play euchre!" Caroline sighed as she settled back into the wheelbarrow, as if resigned to her fate.

"So, it will throw the Wellings off of our trail," Riley shot back, making Caroline laugh.

It took them relatively little time to cross the island, considering they had to push Caroline uphill in a few spots on the dirt path.

The sun had just set when they approached Vixen's Fall. The place wasn't as creepy as Ben remembered it. He'd only made the trek out here once as a kid, and that had been on a dare, proving his nerve by tempting the angry seductress ghost to grab at his ankles. He'd gotten within a foot of the cliff for about three seconds before dashing back to the "safe" spot of the Crown rock formation. He was lucky his idiot friends hadn't shoved him over the edge.

"This is not good for your ribs," Ben told her as Caroline hissed at a bump in the trail. He was pushing her, giving Edison a break for a while. Edison had dashed ahead, pointing out some ridge in the distance that served as an important lighthouse location a hundred years before.

"I'm fine," Caroline insisted. "And it's good for us to get out of the house every once in a while, as much as it might hurt Plover's feelings."

"Plover seems a little bossy for a dead guy," Ben observed.

"Eh, he was a patriarch in need of a family," Caroline said, smiling fondly up at Ben. "We're his ladies, and he worries about us, which seems reasonable. At least more reasonable than Charles."

"I'm almost afraid to ask," Ben said.

"Slightly histrionic Regency-era gentleman attached to the silverware of the beloved wife who poisoned him," Caroline replied. "He's sweet but a little high-strung."

Edison's enthusiastic footfalls slowed as they approached the cliff face. His shoulders stiffened, and Riley slipped her hand around his and squeezed. Vixen's Fall was sadder than he remembered, the shadows deeper.

"Is he OK?" Ben whispered.

"Um, Edison has a pretty severe fear of water," Caroline told him quietly. "He saw his fiancée die in a boating accident."

"But he lives on an island," Ben noted.

"Yeah, he knows," Caroline said. "It's OK as long as he doesn't look at the water."

Edison hung back as Alice and Riley got closer to the Crown, studying it. Ben pushed the wheelbarrow as close as he was comfortable and helped her stand.

"Um, what do I do?" Ben asked.

"You can stay back here with me," Edison offered from his position down the hill. Ben supposed it was easier not to see the water back there. The two of them watched the women stand in a circle, breathe, and work through some hand motions Ben didn't entirely understand.

"It can be sort of emasculating, not having magic, when you're in love with a witch," Edison observed. "The ladies put themselves at risk to protect the living, and we're sort of relegated to a sidekick position. But, it's still rewarding. And Riley is so happy. It makes it worth it."

"Well, Caroline and I aren't...it's complicated," Ben said, much to Edison's amusement, apparently, given the way the man was smirking at him.

Suddenly, Ben heard Caroline gasp and turned his attention to her. She was standing stiffly, with Riley and Alice gripping her wrists. Ben supposed that made him feel better, considering her proximity to a fifty-foot drop.

"What is happening to her?" Ben asked.

Edison didn't seem particularly upset, which Ben found some

comfort in. "Um, she's probably having a vision. Or maybe a ghost is possessing her. Either or, really."

Ben looked to Edison, aghast.

"It's probably fine," Edison assured him.

Ben inched closer. "I'm just gonna…yeah."

He raced up to Caroline's side, feeling only a little insulted when Alice and Riley moved protectively around her. Caroline's eyes were rolled back, so only the whites were visible. Her breathing was steady, but Alice and Riley wouldn't let him get close enough to take a pulse.

"Let's get her a little farther away from the edge," Riley murmured. Alice nodded and finally moved away so Ben could curl his hand around Caroline's wrist. The touch of her skin *seared*, a wretched sizzle against the palm of his hand. She gasped and turned her hand so she was holding *his* arm. He didn't know if this was magic or nerves or guilt, but it *burned*. Riley and Alice pulled their hands away, and Caroline threw her arms around Ben. He wasn't prepared for it, and their weight shifted back, falling to the ground in front of the Crown rocks.

"Ow," Caroline grunted into his chest. She was on top of him, glaring down at him with one eye while the other was clamped shut in pain. "I thought we were worried about my ribs."

"Are you OK?" he demanded, propping her against the center rock of the Crown.

She nodded slowly, but said, "No. Another Technicolor re-enactment of the mystery lady's death. I still don't know if it was the purple-dress ghost, but given the whole youthful hope thing the victim had going… I doubt it?"

"Did you hit your head?" Ben asked, eyeing the rock behind them.

"It's a long story," Alice told him as they helped Caroline up. Immediately, Ben missed the warm weight of her, but it seemed inappropriate to bring that up now. They maneuvered her back to the wheelbarrow.

"Anything new?" Riley asked.

Caroline shook her head. "I kind of thought if the purple-dress ghost was gonna, I don't know, reach out, now that she's talked to me, it would be here. But it was just more of the same. And even though I concentrated really hard on trying to see the face of whoever was pushing me off the cliff—that still really sucks, even when you know you're not going to die, by the way—they were wearing some dark-colored cloak with a hood over their face. It's kind of impressive, being able to commit murder with obscured line of sight."

As they began trundling Caroline home, Ben quietly asked Edison, "Eventually, this is all going to feel less weird, right?"

Edison pursed his lips. "No."

———————

To his credit, Edison tried to explain as much as he could to Ben on the walk back, the history between the Wellings and the Dentons, Riley discovering her magic, the locks.

As they approached Shaddow House, Ben noticed a large, fluffy, gray hound staring up at the house with its head cocked to the side. Caroline asked, "Do you think Mimi can see the ghosts? She seems to spend a lot of time staring at your house. Should we call Iggy?"

"Probably," Riley said, scratching behind Mimi's ears. "She's just angry my house is the one building on the island she hasn't been able to get into."

"Mimi will not be contained," Caroline said, nodding sagely. "Um, also...there seem to be a lot of lights on in the house."

"And there are people moving around inside," Alice said.

Riley groaned. "Aw, man, not again! How many times can my house get broken into?"

The whole group paused as a pop song suddenly blared out of Shaddow House. It was muffled, but Ben recognized the cheerful bubblegum tune from the many, many, *many* rotations on the cross-country road trip playlist. "Oh...no."

Ben raced up the steps to Shaddow House, and through the front door's glass, he saw his children standing inside, unsupervised. And Plover was standing there looking very proud of himself.

Oh, no.

The front door swung open...by itself. Ben would take time to process that later.

"Kids, what are you doing in here?" Ben asked.

He took the "parent minute" to count all of their limbs, fingers, and toes—and then checked their surroundings for broken valuables. Nope, all the extremities were there, and no antiquities appeared to have been damaged. There was, however, a slightly creepy little girl ghost in an old-fashioned nightgown staring at him from the stairs. A male ghost in a dark-blue cutaway Regency-era coat seemed to be pacing in front of the fireplace. And a ghost woman in a modern sweater set peered at them from the kitchen, ducking her head back in the door as soon as she realized Ben could see her.

His children were fine. In fact, they were smiling, but looking a little sheepish. And Plover appeared to be very pleased with himself.

Riley asked, "How did you get in?"

"Well, we thought we saw someone walking around in your house," Josh said. "And that didn't make sense, and we were worried. But then we thought, maybe it was that Clark guy—"

"Who I still don't like that much," Mina added. "Because Dad warned us about him being an enormous douchebag."

Josh added, "So we went into your backyard to see if we could get a closer look."

"Not to confront a burglar, Dad, we know better than that. We just wanted to see who it was before we called the cops, so we could give them a description," Mina said. "But when we got to the back door, it sort of unlocked itself and swung open."

"Which we found to be weird," Josh said. "Considering there was no one standing in the kitchen."

"They could have been hiding behind the door," Caroline noted. "Waiting to smack you over the head with something heavy."

The rest of the room's occupants turned to her, ghosts included, grimaces on display. Caroline added, "You try being a woman who comes home to an empty house at night and see what thoughts regularly occur to you."

"Oh, yeah, that's a good point," Mina said, frowning. "Before you get too mad, Dad, I would remind you that the parts of our brain that assess risk and consequences have not finished developing yet."

Ben groaned and pinched the bridge of his nose. That part of the lecture, they heard...of course.

"So we walked in—" Mina said.

"Because we just wanted to make sure everything was OK," Josh assured Riley.

"And Plover was there," Mina said.

"I disagreed with his decision to let himself be seen or allow them inside," the man in the blue coat clarified. "I'm sure they're lovely children, once you become acquainted with them. But they're so *loud* and a little excitable. But ultimately, the house seems to approve."

"Really, Charles?" Mina scoffed. "*We're* excitable?"

"I like them!" the lady ghost yelled from the kitchen.

"Thank you, Natalie!" Josh called over his shoulder. "You're pretty cool, too!"

"I wanted to simplify Miss Caroline's life, wherever possible," Plover said, smiling fondly at her.

"Not really sure that's what this accomplished..." Caroline said, shaking her head.

Plover continued as if she hadn't spoken. "As the staff, that is my job. Not having to hide her nature from the children would accomplish that, since Dr. Hoult is obviously going to be part of Miss Caroline's life. I knew neither Miss Riley nor Miss Caroline would violate their promise to protect Shaddow House's secrets, so I decided to take a more proactive approach."

"By letting strangers into the house?" Riley asked. "No offense, kids."

"None taken," Josh replied.

"Did I know that the young lady would also be a practitioner of the Denton magic? I had some inkling, but not entirely, no. However, it seems like a welcome and very convenient side effect," Plover said.

"Is it normal, that magic just shows up all of the sudden for a kid who has never even expressed interest in it?" Ben asked, his voice squeaking.

"As normal as it was for Caroline and me," Alice said. "It's one of those 'magic chooses the user' things that we probably won't ever fully understand. Riley needed helpers and so we received magic. Maybe the magic has decided she needs more help. Or maybe there's a family connection between the Hoults and the Dentons a couple of generations back that sort of smoothed the way, genetically speaking."

"Oh! That would be cool!" Mina said, her eyes bright with excitement. "I could call you 'Aunt Riley!'"

"I don't hate it," Riley said, shaking her head.

"I think we're supposed to be here," Josh said. "I've had this gut feeling since we got here that this is where our family belongs. Like...everything just makes more sense."

"I know what you mean," Mina said. "I've been feeling it, too. It's kind of like a special tingle I've never felt before."

"Ew, Mina!" said Josh.

"Not like that." Mina rolled her eyes, then raised her hand and a coaster flew off the nearby table. "Like that."

Riley blinked. "Um, I wasn't able to do that, not with that sort of control, until I'd been here a while. Wow."

"It only works on the haunted stuff, though," Mina observed, sounding annoyed.

"The coaster is haunted?" Ben asked, brow furrowing.

"By the ghost of a housewife who was extremely protective of her furniture," Mina said, nodding.

"I've been using it for months, putting my ciders on it," Caroline muttered. "Aw, now I feel bad."

Mina continued, "Josh doesn't seem to have 'direct' magic like I do, but his hearing is weirdly receptive. He could hear ghosts on the other side of the house that I couldn't, which seems fair. He's always been the listener, between the two of us."

"I wasn't sure of what I was hearing, but it's good to know I wasn't, you know, losing it," Josh said. "Plover and the gang are the first ones I've seen."

Ben recalled the voices he heard from Shaddow House as a teenager, the laughter, and he wondered whether this was something Josh inherited from him.

"It sort of makes sense, when you consider that—even with the male members of the family practicing and seeing ghosts in the past—the Denton magic seems to be matrilineal, or at least, female-focused," Alice said. "The house, the magic, is making up its own rules out of necessity."

"It's been a little scary," Josh confessed. "But I can block them out, if I concentrate hard enough."

"On his first *day*?" Riley gasped.

"In your defense, kids grow up faster these days," Caroline assured her.

Josh shrugged. "It's like music: when I don't like the sound of one part of a composition, I just don't see it or hear it. Drove my violin teachers nuts."

"Should I be offended that the kids seem better at this than I am?" Riley asked Plover. "Honestly, I'm a little bit offended."

"In my experience with the Dentons, younger practitioners

always have an easier time adjusting to their newfound abilities than those who found their magic later in life," Plover assured her.

"And now, how do you feel?" Riley asked kindly. "It can be a lot. And you two have already got the whole teenage angst thing going on."

"It's...better?" Mina said. "It's sort of comforting to know that everything *can't* be explained. Because that means everything is knowable, and I'd rather that not be true? I mean, I have magic. I can do stuff. I don't know what yet, but it's going to be *awesome*."

"And I'm OK with just the hearing stuff, because honestly, everything else seems like...a lot," Josh said. "Besides, you've always said you were just waiting to find that thing you were good at. Clearly, this is it."

"Not quite the thing I was picturing," Mina said. "Hard to put 'ghost whisperer and part-time witch' on a college application."

"Maybe with the *right* college," Josh told her, nodding solemnly.

Riley grinned and wrapped an arm around Mina. "Welcome to the Shaddow House Ghost and Friday Night Euchre Club, kiddo."

"Still not the name," Caroline told her.

Josh shrugged. "It's still not as weird as the hair I've got showing up in unexpected places, so...yeah it's fine."

"Ew, Josh!" Mina said, shaking her head at him.

Josh jerked his shoulders.

Riley glanced up at Ben. "As long as your parent and guardian approves of you joining said club, because I don't want to contribute to the delinquency of a minor."

"I-I, wha...?" Ben moved his hands helplessly as he managed to reach a heretofore unknown level of panic. "What does this mean?

I mean, the puberty era, I could handle, sort of. But this, I can't buy a book to help me explain this...or one that will explain it to me."

"Ew, Dad," Josh grumbled.

"That depends on which bookstore you go to," Mina added.

"I can't tell you that it's not dangerous," Caroline sighed. "After all, we're trying to protect the house from a rival magical family that's trying to steal secret artifacts so they can use the ghosts for their own ends."

Mina looked absolutely thrilled at the very idea of this sort of intrigue. "Really?"

"I think I like you," Alice murmured. "You're a little bit of chaos in a bottle, aren't you?"

Mina wriggled her eyebrows.

Oh, no. Mina had found like-minded souls. Ben knew this day would come.

"I can tell you that no member of my family, to my knowledge, has died from their interactions with ghosts," Riley said. "The Dentons died off from what seems like pervasive fear of commitment. Sorry, Plover."

"Your aunt made 'commitments' to me in every way she could," Plover said.

"Really?" Josh marveled. "Way to go, Plover."

Josh held his fist up for a bump. Plover just stared at him.

"I can't keep them from this, can I?" Ben asked.

Caroline shook her head and looked a little sad. "Probably not. But we won't teach them anything you're uncomfortable with. I can't leave the island, but your kids... I don't think the same rules apply. If you wanted to take them away from here, I wouldn't blame you. I just don't know what it would do to them, physically, emotionally. We didn't give them magic intentionally, I swear. The island, the magic, whatever it is, it's a wild card."

"It's still pretty cool to get picked," Mina said.

For a moment, Ben's heart caught. Mina's gifts were *finally* quantifiable. She couldn't necessarily use it to get the attention she deserved, but she was special. And she knew it. There were people who would recognize it and value her for it, but also simply because she was Mina—sassy mouth, Pop-Pie issues, bright colors, and all. She'd found like-minded souls...and Ben had been right to be terrified of this eventuality.

Ghosts. Freaking *ghosts*.

"Magic chooses the user," Riley said. "I'm not sure why it chose you, Mina. And I'm not sure why your hearing is so sensitive, Josh. But there has to be a reason. There's something you can do that the house or the universe or whatever bureau of ridiculousness that oversees these things has decided you need to do."

"You're making us sound terribly disorganized," Alice noted.

"If there's one thing the Shaddow House Ghost and Friday Night Euchre Club is, it's disorganized," Riley said.

"Still not the name," Caroline said.

"I kind of like it," Mina said.

Josh agreed. "Me, too."

"Do they get a vote?" Caroline asked.

The corners of Alice's mouth pulled back. "Yeah, I think the magic pretty much guarantees they do."

"We're also going to be in charge of music choices from here out," Mina informed Riley.

"Oh, no." Riley looked aghast. "Plover, what hath thou wrought?"

Plover shrugged. "It's not so bad, really."

Chapter 10
Caroline

GERT WILTON DROPPED HER CELL phone on the kitchen counter, narrowly missing the sink where Mina and Caroline were de-funking walk-in racks that probably hadn't been washed in years—which wasn't surprising, really, given Will's kitchen management.

"Well, for Pete's sake," her mother sighed.

"Which one was it now?" Caroline asked carefully. Mina picked up the racks and excused herself, carrying them to the supply closet to dry. Caroline smiled at her.

"Your cousin Gus fell off a ladder," her mother said, frowning. "The man's been a roofer here for fifteen years, and he fell off a ladder changing his porch light bulb. Gave himself a concussion. Your father says he's lucky he didn't fracture his skull."

One would think that Caroline would blame the upheaval on the magical landscape of Shaddow House. But no, over the last week, her great-aunt Myrtle had slipped on a freshly mopped floor, dislocating her hip. One of her uncles tripped down the stairs in front of his house and landed face-first in a birdbath. And now, cousin Gus nearly got taken out by a light bulb. All while they remained on Starfall Point.

Was the curse escalating because the coven had been trying to communicate with the ghost at Vixen's Fall? If anything, the purple lady ghost here at the Rose had gone quiet. Not so quiet that they felt comfortable with Mina working at the bar without Caroline around, but not trying to directly communicate with either of them. She just lurked in the shadows, glaring. If Mina tried to approach, she disappeared. It was sort of passive-aggressive, as far as ghosts went, but still effectively creepy. And if Caroline tried to approach, to talk about her unresolved business or whatever was making her creep around the bar, she just faded into the darkness.

Gert sank against the counter. "It just feels…wrong, all these accidents, on top of your moped incident. The island is supposed to be safe for us. I couldn't bear it if something happened to one of you."

Caroline wished she could tell her mother about what the coven was trying to do, looking into the curse, trying to resolve what had plagued their family for so long. But they'd already expanded their little circle of trust beyond what Caroline had ever imagined, thanks to Plover's impulsive decision-making skills. The idea of including her parents in that circle, which would include her brothers, because they were incapable of keeping secrets—that was just a bad idea.

"I don't know," Caroline said. "But none of them have suffered fatal injuries, right? And in terms of clumsiness, our family has always been a little above average."

Gert's smile was thin. "That's true."

"But I'm almost healed up," Caroline said, even as she winced at the soreness in her middle. "I'll be back on my foot, the other one, at least, before you know it."

"Good, because I really need the help around here," Gert sighed. "I can't believe how grimy we let the place get over the years. Will's gonna need to do a deep clean before we reopen."

Caroline decided that progress was the better part of valor and chose not to mention that Will was going to pitch an absolute *fit* when presented with the word "deep" combined with the word "clean." She pulled the last rack out of the sink, wincing at the pain in her ribs. Mina rushed out to grab it and take it from her.

"You all right?" Gert asked. Caroline nodded, even if it was a lie, and carried several racks into the storage closet at the back of the kitchen. It was right next to the office, or at least, the little cubby where they'd managed to shove a desk. She noticed as she passed that the box of memorabilia was on her mother's shelf, shoved between messy stacks of paperwork and bottles of whiskey. Caroline had decided to bring the canvas back here after they'd experimented at Shaddow House. They weren't sure if it was haunted and if it was, she didn't want to take a chance of somehow dragging the ghost into the house with Riley. But she'd left it sticking up out of the box, among the trophies and picture frames. It was gone, and so was the landscape that had been nailed over it.

"Did you move the painting of the purple-dress lady?" Caroline whispered.

Mina shook her head emphatically, glancing around, as if the ghost was listening. "No, that thing…gives me upsetting feelings. And Josh won't go near it…because I told him not to. It's really the first time he's actually jumped at the chance to do what I've asked."

Caroline snickered. "Mom, what happened to the painting?"

"What painting?" her mom asked. "The sad little landscape your father has always refused to throw away? I don't know."

Caroline walked through the kitchen to the barroom. Cole was finished with the upstairs repairs to the second level and bolstering the patio outside, which didn't require much beyond bracing with proper lumber. He had moved on to patching the hole in the ceiling. It was sort of nice, not being able to see through the floor upstairs.

"Hey, Cole?"

Cole turned on the ladder, plaster trowel in hand—and woo, a few months ago, she would have taken full advantage of the delectable derrière at her eye level. Cole was a treat that she would have gladly added to her no-guilt rotation. Well, maybe she would have waited until the renovation was done because she knew better than to mess around where she ate.

But now Ben was in the picture. Bright, beautiful Ben, who knew what could make her laugh and cry and scream with pleasure. Suddenly, the idea of taking Cole home for some enthusiastic and aerobically effective sex seemed a little hollow and sad. Dammit. She had gone and made progress to being a fully emotionally evolved adult.

In the corner, she saw the purple-lady ghost materialize. She was smirking, as if she was enjoying Caroline's butt-based bewilderment.

"Everything OK?" Cole asked.

"Yeah, that canvas, the one you offered to reframe?" Caroline said, jerking her thumb toward the kitchen. "Have you seen it?"

Cole grimaced. "Not since the day I broke the frame, like a jackass."

"It's fine," she assured him. "It's not like we found out it was an heirloom or anything. I just can't find it in the junk box."

"Huh." Cole climbed down from the ladder, wiping his hands on a bandana in his back pocket. "I haven't seen it."

While this was weird, Caroline wasn't sure that panic was in order just yet. The painting being missing didn't necessarily mean someone stole it. The purple-lady ghost could have moved it through sheer evil determination. Or hell, it was equally possible one of her brothers could have used it as scrap paper. She was frowning in the direction of the basement entrance when Cole spoke. "So I was thinking, there are other bars in this town, besides yours. And maybe we could go to one of them and have a drink? Consider it market research."

His smile was so warm and friendly. It was clear and definite, while everything with Ben was so murky and uncertain.

Caroline told him, "I appreciate the invitation, Cole, but I'm..."

She didn't know how to define it. Hopeful elsewhere? Desperately seeking closure? Horny and nostalgic? None of those sounded good. She had feelings for Ben, deep, resounding, complicated, messy feelings. And even that wasn't enough to scare her off.

"It's Ben, huh?" Cole asked kindly.

"Yes," she said, sounding more sure than she felt. "At least, I hope so?"

Cole shrugged. "Well, everybody talks about the two of you like you're the Romeo and Juliet of Starfall Point, with a slightly less tragic ending."

"Only slightly," Caroline said.

Cole's grin was one of good-natured disappointment, sending a little thrill of relief through her belly. "Well, good luck then. But if he messes up, give me a call."

She laughed. "Thanks."

"I can't even hate him because he's so nice," Cole huffed.

"He really is, isn't he?" she said, throwing her hands up.

"It's the worst," Cole said, laughing as Mina and Gert walked out of the kitchen. Gert's hand was on Mina's shoulder, a rare gesture from someone who didn't hand out affection easily.

"I think we've done all we can today," Gert announced. "Cole, you about done for the day?"

Cole glanced up at the drying ceiling. "Sure."

"I'm making olive burgers for dinner, if any of you are hungry," Gert said.

Cole seemed pleased by Gert's offer. "Oh, that's nice, thanks!"

"What the heck is an olive burger?" Mina asked, shuddering.

"You take ground beef, mix it with chopped olives, brine, and mayo. And then make burgers," Gert told her. "You don't have that back in Arizona?"

"No, why would you do that to an innocent hamburger?" Mina gasped, making Gert cackle.

"Thanks," Caroline told her. "But Mina and I have plans with Riley."

"You're heading up to Shaddow House?" Gert asked, frowning. "Again? What do you do up there?"

Caroline smirked. "Oh, play albums backward, try to summon the spirit of Jim Morrison."

Best to lean into the worst expectations and play them off like a joke, rather than make some lame excuse about board games and movie nights.

"Wait, who's Jim Morrison?" Mina asked, frowning at her.

"Your father has failed you," Caroline informed her.

"Well, there's no reason to be a smart-ass," Gert shot back.

"I hope that's not true," Caroline said, kissing her cheek. "I'll see you later. Bye, Cole!"

Cole waved them off while Gert helped him lock up. Mina helped Caroline walk toward home. "Your ankle is killing you, isn't it?"

"Yes, it is," Caroline admitted.

"And yet, you stood on it for hours, helping your mom clean. Has anyone every told you that you have a little bit of a martyr complex?"

Caroline nodded grimly. "Yes, they have."

"Also, we have plans with Riley?" Mina asked.

"Do you *want* to eat olive burgers?" Caroline asked.

Mina made a gagging face. "No, I do not."

They walked along, Caroline gritting her teeth with every step. She distracted herself, saying, "So you're taking this whole magic thing in stride, all things considered."

"When I touched your hand, that first time, in the clinic," Mina said. "I felt that weird electric zap. It was the same thing I felt when I stepped onto the island for the first time. Well, when we moved here. I don't know what it felt like when we visited when we were babies. You know, before, when my grandparents were alive? My mom hated it. Didn't like visiting when we couldn't even enjoy ourselves like tourists. Anyway, I guess that was magic, from the start. Weird."

"And you just accept it?" Caroline asked.

Mina gave her a look that was almost pitying. "My generation has dealt with the existence of the internet and the dwindling polar ice caps since birth. Why would magic be so out of the question?"

"Good point," Caroline conceded.

"It's different for Josh, and I'm worried about him," Mina said. "I don't think he likes being left behind. He likes being able to hear the ghosts, but it's hard for him, seeing me doing more. I don't want him to feel like he's alone, you know?"

"Well, that's what the coven is good for," Caroline told her. "You never feel alone."

"Have you heard anything from the purple-lady ghost lately?" Mina asked suddenly.

"No, she's just lurking in corners. It feels like she's sulking a little bit," Caroline said.

"Me, too. Weird," Mina mused.

"Most things are when it comes to ghosts," Caroline told her.

When they reached Shaddow House, Josh burst out of the front door and bounded down the stairs to help Caroline up.

"I'm all right. I'm all right," Caroline assured Josh as he hustled her up by her elbows.

"Yeah, but Dad's inside and if he sees you limping like that *and* walking up the steps, you're in for a forcible ice pack *and* a lecture," Josh replied.

Caroline nodded quickly. "Good call."

Ben was waiting inside, talking with Riley. While Riley seemed content, Plover was standing nearby, giving Ben a decided stink eye. Ben, however, seemed distracted, and a little agitated.

"Hi, Riley!" Mina called, coming into the house. She curtsied to the butler. "Mr. Plover."

Plover bowed. "Miss Mina."

"Everything OK?" Caroline asked.

"I was just explaining to Plover that while I respect the need for privacy and secrecy at Shaddow House, I am pretty firm on my plans to have a security camera pointing at your backyard," Ben told her.

"I'm actually pretty excited about this plan. It would have been super helpful last year," Riley said.

"I am still...unenthusiastic," Plover said, frowning.

"And I understand that," Ben replied. "But I have to put the needs of the living people I care about over the demands of the dead."

Plover pinched his lips closed, though he was staring at Mina, Caroline, and Riley. "All right, then."

"Good, then it's settled." Ben reached out to shake Plover's hand. Realizing that was corporeally impossible, he frowned. "Sorry."

"And while Mr. Plover and Dad were negotiating, I was just studying 'ghostly communication skills' with Riley," Josh said, slinging a backpack over his shoulder.

"No fair!" Mina huffed.

"Well, *I* didn't run a human being down with a small personal motor vehicle," Josh countered. "So, my work schedule is a little more flexible."

"Fiiiiine," she sighed, rolling her eyes. "Can I come over tomorrow, Riley? I have the day off."

Riley nodded. "Um, sure."

"And I better get these two home and fed, otherwise, people

in authority start making calls." Ben kissed Caroline quickly, with a casual air that made her heart quiver. Had they arrived there so quickly? These thoughtless gestures of affection?

And then he followed it up with a deeper, longer kiss that made her knees do this weird wobbly jelly thing. When she finally came up for air and managed to focus both eyes, she saw Mina and Josh exchange meaningful looks. But they didn't seem upset. Caroline chose to see that as a positive sign.

"Elevate that ankle and stay off of it," Ben told her as he hustled the kids out the door. "I saw you limping."

"Told you!" Josh crowed as he walked out.

"Spirited, but very polite young people," Plover announced with approval, smiling after them.

"Hi, everybody! I came as soon as I could close the shop." Alice came through the front door, all smiles until she took in Riley's unsettled expression. "Riley, are you OK?"

Riley's eyes were wide, and she was sinking onto the bottom step. "I don't know what to do. The kids are always at the house. They don't ever seem to want to leave. They're just *here*. All the time."

Alice looked to Plover, who shook his head. "Well, if they're annoying you, just send them back home to Ben. I'm sure he would understand. He's a loving father, but he's not one of those 'smiles beatifically while his children damage valuable items' fathers."

"Speaking from shop experience?" Caroline asked. Alice arched a brow and nodded.

Riley threw her hands up. "They're not being annoying. That's the thing. They're actually delightful company. They're smart.

They're helpful. They clean up after themselves, which I never expected. It's just…that they want to spend time with me."

Caroline gasped, all fake indignation. "Those little bastards." Plover's gasp was real, so she added, "Sorry, Plover. Just a joke. Look, this is normal, developmentally speaking. They're seeking you out as a cool older person."

"And that alone, I find suspect. I don't know how to handle it!" Riley exclaimed. "I was summarily rejected by pretty much every member of my family, including my mom and…in some instances, my dad, though that was more of a matter of indirect convenience because my half siblings refused to see him if I was around. I don't know how to handle people who seek my company intentionally. People who aren't you, Alice, Edison, or a bunch of dead people."

Caroline tilted her head, staring at Riley, prompting her to exclaim, "They're calling me 'Aunt Riley'!"

"I think that's very sweet," Caroline told her.

"OK, but what do I do? Everything I learned about intergenerational relationships comes from my extremely unhealthy repressed family dynamic or after-school specials!" Riley exclaimed.

"Riley, they're just people," Caroline told her. "Just talk to them like they're people. Terrifying and incredibly smart people, who will outlive us by about ten, twenty years. I mean, between the two of us, I should probably be more afraid of them. If things progress with Ben, they could just decide they don't want me around, which is a valid choice. Then, I lose the relationship with Ben *and* with them. And worse, if they do want me around, I could end up being a stepmom. Oh…oh, wait." Caroline swallowed heavily and suddenly, giving Riley an imploring look. "That's terrifying. What if I'm a bad one? Like in one of the fairy tales? I don't want to end up wearing red-hot iron shoes and dancing at Mina's wedding."

"It's possible you're getting ahead of yourself," Alice told her.

"You could also choose not to be an asshole to two innocent children," Riley added. "That is always an option."

"I don't know if people go into those relationships *planning* to be an asshole, and that's what so scary about it! What if my intentions are good and I still end up hurting them?" Caroline asked.

"Well, I'm still…undecided about the kids issue," Riley said. "And I feel unqualified to give you advice, but I guess the best thing I can tell you is that you're one of the most thoughtful, deliberate people I know. If you approach this relationship, reminding yourself of how much you love Ben and how much you don't want to hurt them, I think you'll manage it."

"It's not a bad thing, to gather people who like you, especially if you like them in return," Alice told them both. "Some people might even call that a *family*."

"Point taken." Riley's lips tilted, and she put her chin on Caroline's shoulder. Alice patted their shoulders. "Thanks, you two."

"It's what we do," Alice said.

"So, on to less fraught matters. What are our plans for the evening?" Alice asked.

"I think we should break into Clark Graves's office," Riley said, reaching into a nearby credenza and pulling out three gray woolen ski masks.

"Oh, sure, I don't have anything to do tonight," Caroline said, nodding. "Wait, what?"

They decided to be a little more methodical about their breaking and entering this time. They waited until dark, wore dark clothes, and carried gloves in their pockets. They had drinks at a McPartin's, a tourist-oriented Irish pub across the street from Clark's, watching the lights blink out of the windows one by one.

"Why are we doing this again?" Alice asked, sipping her bubbly water. She was pale and a little twitchy, but that seemed normal before one committed burglary for a second time in a few months. Fortunately, the locals had learned to accept slightly odd behavior from the three of them since they started spending time together. Caroline's heart was warmed, knowing that people seemed happy that Alice had found friends, but she found she didn't particularly like being written off as one of the town's many eccentrics.

Riley took a long drink from her cider. "Because Clark's been too quiet lately. And I don't trust that. I've thought about doing this for a while, plus there was something Ben said, when he was at the house earlier. About Clark approaching him to move out of Gray Fern and find some newer, fancier house on the island so the property management company can rent out Ben's place for the season. Why would he push that so hard, unless he was planning something, using Gray Fern as a base?"

"He's hassling Ben and the kids?" Caroline frowned. "Yep, gloves are coming off."

"Were the gloves ever on?" Alice asked. Caroline snorted.

"So you and Ben, huh?" Riley grinned.

"I wouldn't have thought it would happen *again* in a million years, but somehow... Maybe?" Caroline said, staring at the motion of the staff behind the bar—fluid and unhurried.

"It's driving you nuts, drinking at someone else's bar, isn't it?" Riley asked.

"Yeah, because it's better-run than ours," Caroline griped, watching the easy way the waitresses moved between tables, handing off much-needed items and cooperating in a way that the Wiltons never quite managed.

"Shouldn't we tell somebody?" Caroline asked. "Warn people that one of the few lawyers on the island is a criminal mastermind?"

"We've talked about this. What are we going to do?" Riley asked. "Go to the police and complain that Clark used his position as my lawyer to orchestrate a break-in at my house to steal my haunted tchotchkes?"

"I wouldn't lead with that," Alice murmured. "Also, your hypothetical calls to the authorities are becoming pointedly sarcastic."

Caroline asked, "Is there some sort of magic we can do to, I don't know, bind his actions? His intentions? Track his location like a magical 'Find My Friends'?"

"I think we're treading some pretty precarious magical waters here," Riley said. "We have to keep *our* intentions pure or they're going to bounce back on us times three."

"So. No giving him a magical rash, got it," Caroline grumbled.

The hours passed and the lights winked off across the street at Tanner, Moscovitz, and Graves. The ladies turned their heads away from the window as Clark stepped out of the front door and locked it behind him. They waited another hour to make sure that Clark wasn't going to come back for a forgotten file or something and then one by one left the table, taking different routes to end up behind the law office, at the back door. They each had already pulled on their ski masks, just in case Clark had security cameras they hadn't spotted so far.

Riley's "rich and colorful work history" career had led to a diverse array of skills, including lock picking. The back door offered her little challenge, which honestly made Caroline worry for Clark's clients. They listened for any noise in response to their entering, but nothing. They moved through the darkness, careful to stay away from the windows as they passed through the door marked *Clark Graves, Esq.*

There were a few "ghost pings" hitting Caroline's system from around the perfectly nice, if boring office done in navy and cream. They seemed to be attached to a few antiques on the desk, and the brass clothes horse in the corner. But the ghosts were distant, and sort of sad—as if they, too, were bored by hanging around Clark's office.

Alice hung back as Caroline and Riley quietly rifled through the contents of his desk. Riley knelt in front of the locked right-hand drawer, tools at the ready.

"This looks familiar," Caroline whispered, holding up a notepad with the firm's griffin logo on it. A piece of that logo had been included on a fragment of a note Kyle had left behind at Shaddow House after he'd broken in.

"Bingo," Riley whispered as the drawer gave way. Riley's fingers danced across the top of the files. She pulled one marked, "Gray Fern." Instead of boring paperwork involving rental agreements, Riley pulled out printed photos of Shaddow House clearly taken from the upper floors of Gray Fern Cottage. None of the photos included anything terribly interesting. Riley walking into the house. Edison walking out in the morning. Strange shadowy figures in the windows, but nothing exciting enough to post on the internet as *proof of the afterlife*!

"Why the hell is he printing copies?" Caroline scoffed. "What is he, seventy?"

"Digital fingerprints are harder to destroy?" Riley guessed.

"Well, the fact that he's surveilling Shaddow House shows this is about more than just a property management dispute over Gray Fern," said Alice, her ski mask still in place.

"He's got to be working for the Wellings," Riley wondered aloud. "I mean, why else would he be so interested in Shaddow House?"

Behind them, the light switch flicked on. Caroline froze.

Shit.

Clark was standing in the doorway, smirking. "Oh, girls, this is not going to look good when I call Celia at the precinct to report that the three of you broke into my office."

"Really? You're going to tell on us?" Riley pulled her mask up. She sat in Clark's desk chair, fluffing her mussed hair, as if this wasn't a terrifying turn of events. "We've been worrying about you potentially being this big bad supervillain, and your response is to *tattle*? I'm almost disappointed."

Caroline took her own mask off, because what was the point? Poor Alice stood frozen, her uncovered neck gone ghastly pale.

And yet, Riley still seemed bored with the whole thing. Caroline supposed this was what came with living with dead people; Clark didn't seem like much of a threat.

"No, wait, scratch that," Riley said. "I'm glad I have this opportunity because I want to tell you what an absolute *dick* you are—lying to my aunt like you did, trying to trick her, take advantage of her. And the only consolation I get from the whole thing is that she was *smarter* than you. She knew something was off about you. She never let you in the house. She never trusted you completely, so all your smarmy bullshit maneuvering didn't work. You were outwitted by a septuagenarian. Congratulations. You suck at life *and* being a supervillain."

"Oh, Riley." Clark's grin was sharp and smarmy. "I'm flattered you see me as that much of a hazard, but I'm just a small part of the bigger battle. I'm a contractor, the help. Oh, no, don't frown like that. I've never been too proud to admit it. I don't care about the living or the dead. I care about getting paid. You need to worry about that big picture because it's coming into focus, faster than you can even imagine. And I have a feeling you're not going to like what you see."

"Oh my god, this metaphor is getting labored," Riley muttered, managing to sound bored.

"You don't need to worry about me," Clark said. "You need to worry about that big picture. You need to worry about the inside threat, the rat in the silo, gnawing away at you. You're not going to know what hit you, and it's going to hurt."

Caroline swallowed heavily. What could Clark mean? Who could hurt them like that from the inside? One of their own family members? Her mother? One of her brothers? She couldn't think of anything they could know or do that would damage their efforts at Shaddow House. Though Caroline guessed that was the whole point of "not going to know what hit you."

Riley, though, didn't show a moment's doubt on her face, simply smiling at him. Which seemed to piss Clark off.

"Go ahead and grin," he hissed at her, pulling his phone out of his pocket. "You fucking witches, thinking you're all so smart. Your bitch aunt, lording it over me, thinking that I had to dance to her tune."

"Easy there, speaking ill of the dead," Riley told him blithely. "You say I should look at the big picture? You're missing a couple of things yourself."

She pointed upward, and Clark followed her hand motion, finally realizing that the letter opener—a pretty little pewter piece with a mother of pearl handle—was floating near his face. He blanched as he backed away. He didn't dare reach up to grab it as the point was aimed directly at his eye. He retreated until he fell back against a nearby chair, tumbling into the seat.

Riley rounded the desk and leaned closer. "For one thing, we're not the only ones who have something to lose here. We have proof, concrete proof, that you paid Kyle to break into my house for the sole purpose of stealing from me. Not like this little late-night visit that could be misconstrued as us having an urgent legal matter and not understanding your business hours."

"I thought the office had a *public* back entrance," Caroline said, her eyes wide and intentionally guileless. "How were we to know Clark wasn't here?"

"What?" Clark scoffed. "Kyle would never think to keep— what do you have?"

"Why would I tell you that?" Riley laughed. "I have enough to at the very least, get you disbarred."

"Oh, now Riley, play fair!" Clark exclaimed.

Riley brought her arm down, and the letter opener plummeted toward his chair. Clark's legs parted just in time for the blade to dig into the wood between his thighs. "The time for fair play and worrying about feelings is at an end. Am I clear?"

Clark swallowed thickly and nodded. "Crystal."

"We'll leave out the front," Riley said, smiling at him. She stopped to pull Alice gently toward the door.

"Did you really just reverse-Uno-card blackmail him?" Caroline said.

Riley frowned. "Not really sure. It was my first time blackmailing someone."

"Well, you did great," Caroline told her.

Alice was pale, her hands trembling as they pushed the door open.

"Hey, are you OK?" Caroline asked. "Clark was probably just talking out of his ass, trying to sow discord."

"It just got a little scary for a minute there, more physical than I expected. Good thing that letter opener was haunted," Alice whispered.

"We probably could have used some warning you were going to stab his chair," Caroline noted. "You scared the hell out of me."

Riley pouted slightly, muttering, "I wasn't aiming for his chair."

Chapter 11
Ben

DID IT COUNT AS A parent-teacher conference when your kids' magical mentor texted to ask you to come over "really quick" for a "talk"?

It still felt weird to walk into Shaddow House as a welcome guest when it had been a secretive fortress, shutting him out, his whole life. But his kids were inside—not just welcome, but *honored*, guests—and therefore, the doors were always open to him. Plover may not have been a fan, but he'd made that policy clear.

Part of Ben knew that the ladies were devoting so much time to helping the kids adjust because having untrained magic bouncing around the island wasn't just dangerous to others, but to the kids themselves. But still, it was a little weird to have this much time alone in his own house. He was able to keep up with his patients and update their files. Hell, his email inbox was clear. That hadn't happened since before Josh's kindergarten graduation.

And now…he just had time to sit around and think, which was never good. He wanted Caroline in his life—not just because he *wanted* her, but because life made so much more sense with her in it. The kids seemed to adore her, which was an unexpected gift he was sure he didn't deserve. He knew it wouldn't be easy, just to fold her back into his life like the last twenty years never happened, but he wanted whatever she had to offer. He hoped that offer included a place in *her* life, long-term.

And just when Ben was starting to feel happy and settled into that groove, his ex called, and everything got turned on its ass again.

Thank goodness Riley texted him to distract him from his emotions twisting themselves inside out. Her message only said, "please come over when convenient," and yet he raced up the stairs to Shaddow House, as if he could outrun his co-parenting problems. He found Josh and Riley sitting in her office, staring at a weird paperweight thing made from copper loops.

"Hi! Did Josh break something?" Ben asked, skidding to a stop in front of her huge desk. "How valuable was it?"

"No! Why do you always assume I broke something?" Josh exclaimed.

"Because of that time at Grandma's house," Ben said. "And that time at TechStop. And that time at the zoo."

Riley turned to Josh. "What happened at the zoo?"

"There was an incident. At the Polar Zone habitat," Josh mumbled. "All of the penguins were *fine*."

Snickering, Riley turned her gaze back to the lock on the desk. Ben could tell it wasn't a good thing. He didn't have to be a witch to feel that. It was angry, cold, hateful, and furious. It wanted to hurt anything it could reach, including his son. Ben wanted to throw the copper weight through the window, far away from his child...but it would just land in the atrium and that wouldn't make much of a difference. Also, the damn thing was magic, so it would probably just come back to him like an evil boomerang.

"I texted you because Josh had himself a ghost moment and his breathing got a little...intense. And I was afraid he was going to pass out," Riley paused to gesture between her shorter-than-average frame and Josh's much taller one. "If he ends up on the floor, I cannot pull him back up. The physics are stacked against me."

"Oh! Medical stuff. Something I can handle," Ben said, kneeling in front of his son to check Josh's pulse and pupils.

"Dad! Dad, I'm fine," Josh promised, fending him off.

"If I may, young sir, you did turn the approximate color of oatmeal," Plover said.

"Plover! Bro Code violation!" Josh gasped.

"I don't know what that means," Plover replied. "Does this Bro Code translate to 'ignoring potential medical crises to one's own detriment'?"

Josh pouted. "No."

The little self-care lecture sounded like something that had been repeated often enough that it was now rote. Ben would have to thank Plover later for that, even if he did violate some unspoken promise to protect Josh's anti-parental privacy.

"It's so much more fun watching him forcibly sensible-male-father-type-figure someone else," Riley sighed, smiling to herself.

That knocked Ben back a step. His kids hadn't had grandparents for years, not since his parents passed. And now they had a ghost grandpa? Weird.

"So, Josh, what has your heart rate spiked and your face oat-mealed?" Ben asked, earning an approving nod from Plover.

"It's fine," Josh said. "I just, um, heard some really loud whispers from the basement? And I thought, since I was down there, I might as well look for the entrance to the that secret basement thing that Aunt Riley was talking about?"

Ben arched a brow. Josh was posing everything as a question, something he only did when he knew his actions were, well, questionable.

"You probably shouldn't be wandering around in another person's house, like a burglar, especially when burglars have previously died in that house," Ben noted.

"You make a good point, but there was just a bunch of junk down there," Josh agreed. "Nothing dangerous or haunted. Just old Christmas decorations and furniture and a weird number of taxidermied animals. And then I heard this voice coming from behind the wall—the one near the back of the house? I think it's under the kitchen. There were all these scorch marks on the stones, like I don't know, somebody tried something magical they weren't supposed to. And the thing behind the wall was saying...not nice things—all sort of crap about my mom and how sad I must be that she couldn't be bothered to move here with us. It said I was accepted here, I could stay here forever. All I had to do was take the locks out of the house."

"Oh, no, honey," Riley said. "That's not true."

"Oh, please," Josh scoffed. "I'm a teenager who spends time on the internet. You don't think I know when I'm being lured by a predator?"

"I don't think that makes me feel *better*," Ben mused.

"Anyway, I figured anything trying that hard to trick me was worth digging up. I couldn't pull it through the wall like the one you talked about, so I grabbed a shovel and dug it out."

A sudden darkness above their heads pulled Ben's eyes toward the ceiling. That creepy oily figure was back, and it seemed... pissed? It was pacing around the room, moving erratically between Riley and Josh—as if it couldn't decide which one it wanted to hurt. It slithered along until it was hovering right over them. Ben stood with his arms out, like an idiot, as if he could shield them all from whatever the hell that was. Plover tried to grab at it, but it just darted out of the way. It stretched, viscous and angry, toward the lock on the desk. Riley seemed to realize how close it had gotten to her desk and snatched the lock from the surface. She hissed as her hand made contact with the metal and tucked it against her chest.

The ceiling ghost didn't have a face or form, just undulating negativity. It stretched toward Ben, and a mouthlike hole opened up in its surface and let loose the scream of a hundred men condemned. Ben fell back into his chair. Josh leaped up from his chair and tossed a dish of potpourri salt at it, and it shrunk back into the ceiling, into nothing.

"Freaking ceiling ghost," Riley huffed, dropping the lock back on the desk. "Dammit, those things are cold."

"Well, that thing didn't seem happy," Ben said.

"Maybe it's mad that *I* found a lock?" Josh wondered. "It didn't sound like the basement voice, if that makes you feel any better. Plover, can you communicate with that thing?"

"It doesn't seem to have a true voice. It doesn't feel quite right," Plover said. "I don't think it's the same sort of ghost as the rest of the residents of the house."

Josh asked, "What if it's a poltergeist?"

Riley turned to him. "What?"

Josh repeated, "Poltergeist. It's German for 'noisy ghost' or something."

"I know what it means…because Plover told me when I first got here," Riley admitted.

"OK, so poltergeists are usually associated with a teenager in the house going through the usual hormonal changes of puberty and the trauma of losing their childhood innocence," Josh said. "The theory is that changes in the kid's brain triggers psychic stuff that was already there. You combine that with the pissed-off will of your average teenager and next thing you know—pickle jars are exploding and shampoo bottles are flying all over the place."

"Really?" Ben frowned. "Those movies from the '80s made it seem like it was all evil preachers and pool skeletons."

"Total misunderstanding of the concept," Josh said. "There's no spirit involved in the haunting, but these things can develop personalities. Some of them even communicate with the family or whatever paranormal investigators they hire."

"Where did you learn all of this?" Ben asked.

"You guys really underestimate the educational value of screen time," Josh told him. "Anyway, the haunting usually goes away when the kid gets older. But sometimes, the psychic stuff is just so strong that it sticks around, even if the kid moves away. You said these Welling assholes—"

Before Ben could even correct him, Plover intoned, "Language, young sir."

And Josh actually looked ashamed! His cheeks had gone red and everything! Ben gaped at Plover. How was a ghost better at parenting his children than Ben was?

"Sorry, Mr. Plover," Josh said. "You said the Wellings were strong magic people themselves, that they were planning all this stuff behind your family's back. That's an awful lot of will concentrated in one place. And it just sort of got stuck here for hundreds of years. What if the creepy ceiling thing is like a poltergeist, but it's like an echo of what the Wellings wanted?"

Riley considered it. "That would explain why the ceiling creep doesn't follow the usual rules, except for the salt. Salt is sort of an elemental thing. Can't fight that."

"Mina is going to be so mad that she missed all this," Josh sighed. "Can we just not tell her?"

"That's not how we do things," Riley told him. "Hiding things only creates confusion and complications and sometimes, police involvement."

"OK." Josh considered that for a moment. "I think I like that better, anyway."

"So go home and get some rest and I will stash this with the rest of the locks," Riley said, giving Josh a hug. She winked at Ben. "And plenty of fluids."

"Does hydration help with magical stuff?" Ben asked.

"Couldn't hurt," Riley replied.

Josh and Ben shuffled out of the house after another failed fist bump attempt with Plover.

"Why don't we go by the Rose, pick up Mina, get some ice cream at Regina's?" Ben suggested as they turned their feet toward town.

"Sounds good," Josh said. "But I would just like to point out that you only take us out to ice cream when you have bad news."

"That's not true," Ben said.

Josh asked, "Want me to list them off?"

"I resent being so predictable," Ben muttered.

"Hit me with it, so I can process it before we have to tell Mina. That way, I can help *her* process it without bystanders getting hurt," Josh said.

Ben sighed. It wasn't his son's job to help his daughter process her feelings. It was Ben's job, but that also didn't change the fact that Josh was right. It was better for both of them to be there for Mina, instead of Ben alone.

"It's not that bad," Ben insisted.

Josh lifted a sandy-blond brow.

"Your mom texted me, asking why you haven't been in contact. Have you really not texted her in three weeks?" Ben asked.

Josh sort of blinked at him. "Oh, yeah, I guess so. Weird. We've just been so busy, I haven't thought about it. And she texted *you* instead of texting me about it?"

"I get that, as the parent, it's her job to contact you," Ben began.

Josh pinched the bridge of his nose, looking a little too much like Ben for his comfort. "But if I don't contact her, her feelings will get hurt and suddenly, this thing will happen where she *pretends* she wants to see us but makes excuses at the last minute so she doesn't have to. And she makes it all about her."

"I don't want to invalidate your feelings, but that's not a great way to talk about your mother," Ben said.

"It's true, Dad," Josh insisted. "She doesn't want to see us, but she hates the idea that we don't want to see her."

He put his arm around his son. "Something to talk about with our therapist?"

"Yeah, probably time for a video session." Josh nodded. "Oh, man, did Mom say anything about Mina? Or worse, *to* Mina?"

"Not if she didn't contact you," Ben said. "Also, most of the island is still standing, so…"

Josh thought about that for a long moment. "Do you think she's given up on Mina?"

Ben's chest ached at the very idea of giving up on his little girl. Mina, who was finding her footing in this strange, new place with her strange, new powers. Mina, who didn't seem to feel the need to dress in *all* of the eye-catching colors anymore because she'd found herself. There was nothing left to rebel against. He wasn't about to let that get derailed by Isabelle's selfish agenda.

"I hope not. I would hope that a parent never gives up on their child," Ben said, not sounding entirely sure of himself. "I'm sorry. This is a lot for you to deal with, buddy."

Josh shrugged. "It sort of sucks to have a passive ability when Mina gets to, you know, fling things around the room."

"I meant, about your mom," Ben said.

Josh shook his head. "Oh, yeah, but that's just more of the same, isn't it?"

"Well, both of these problems are completely outside of my experience," Ben told him. "But I'm here, if you want to talk."

"Sure," Josh said. "I'm going to run ahead, tell Mina to get her stuff together so we can get to Regina's before she runs out of Petoskey Stone."

Josh jogged ahead at double the speed Ben's old ass could have managed. While Josh seemed completely at ease with all the ghostly developments, Ben was...uneasy. The transition into working with the ladies had just been a little too smooth. What if the house is gauging them, sizing them up as the next possible Stewards of Shaddow House?

Riley was the last of the Dentons. If she decided not to have children, who would be there to take her place? Would his children never be able to leave Starfall? Or worse, would Mina, with her more powerful magic, be expected to stay on the island while Josh went off to make his way in the world? How could either of them be asked to take on the burden that Caroline had faced all her life?

These were thoughts too heavy to introduce over bad-news ice cream.

Chapter 12
Caroline

"ADULTS-ONLY MEETINGS" TOOK ON A whole new context in a small-town, multigenerational coven. That wasn't the weirdest thought that had ever crossed Caroline's mind, but it was definitely in the top ten.

The three senior coven members were sitting on the porch of Shaddow House, drinking "grown-up cider" late into the night, discussing the kids' dizzying magical development. Plover did not appreciate his exclusion from the discussion, so they propped the door open so he could participate.

They could already detect which random antiques were attachment objects and which ones weren't—though Mina scored more accurately. Riley had set up a whole test involving pieces from Alice's family shop mixed with attachment objects from the house. Between the two of them, they managed to pick out the creepy stork with a saxophone, a murdered kayaker's paddle, and Natalie's dry-erase board—from the next room! But then, Charles had an actual tantrum when he saw his dearest Edith's favorite soup spoon being used in such a "disrespectful display of charlatanry."

Riley had to write him a personal note of apology—and judiciously left out the bit where she explained that the test wasn't "charlatanry" if it involved genuine psychic powers.

While Josh definitely enjoyed his time with "Mr. Plover," Mina was pretty much a daily presence at Shaddow House. If she wasn't working at the Rose, she was working at Shaddow House. Caroline got the impression that Mina wanted female company. She understood. There were times, growing up with three brothers, that she felt completely overrun by testosterone. And Caroline at least had her mom to balance things out.

"It feels weird, meeting without the kids," Alice noted, sipping her cider. "Like we've formed a club within a club."

"I know, but I don't want to say any of this in front of them and make them nervous," Riley said. "I feel like their advisor or their den mother, or something. The thing is, they're pretty much lapping us, in terms of development. Mina is already doing spells it took us *months* to master. And I know Josh can only hear, but he seems to communicate better with the ghosts than I do now."

"I'm just glad they're on our side," Caroline muttered. "Can you imagine if they were working against us?"

"There's no shame for you in their 'promotion,' Miss," Plover assured Riley. "Frankly, the pair of them remind me of your mother and Miss Nora at that age."

"Is it because we're not progressing fast enough?" Alice asked. "Our magic decided we needed an A string, so to speak?"

"Oh, man, does that mean we're the B string?" Caroline gasped. "RUDE!"

"From what I understand, it's not a judgment of your work,"

Plover assured her. "Magic does what it will, to help maintain the balance of the house. Adding the young people to the effort is only meant to make you stronger, not replace you."

"Thanks, Plover," Riley said. "Though, I'm starting to feel like the youngest sibling on a family sitcom getting the 'your parents will still love you, even when the new baby comes' very special episode talk."

"I did not understand a single word of what you just uttered," Plover said.

Riley laughed. "So, change of subject to adult topics we should not and could not talk about with the kids around—how are things with Ben?"

"Oooh, yes!" Alice cried, clapping her hands together. "I've wanted to ask, but I didn't want to intrude. Also, I didn't want to emotionally traumatize the kids talking about their father's sex life in front of them."

"There's no sex life," Caroline objected. "Not yet."

Riley's jaw dropped. "Really?"

"I'm going to excuse myself," Plover mumbled, disappearing from the front door. "There are some things I do not need to overhear about my ladies."

"Not me!" Natalie called from inside the house. "I want to hear every word! I can't live, but I can live vicariously! Well, sort of!"

"I realize that I am not exactly tightfisted with my favors," Caroline said.

"Is that really how you want to phrase that?" Riley asked.

"Now that I've heard myself saying it out loud, no," Caroline amended. "And no, we haven't had sex yet. For one, we haven't had time or opportunity. There's Ben's schedule at the clinic. And then the kids. And I've been wrapped up like a bruised mummy for weeks. So, yeah, we're taking things slow. Which is…nice? I mean, there's still baggage there—and by that, I mean emotionally, because I would never refer to his children as baggage. That's wrong. I actually expected to have more issues getting to know the kids and them adjusting to the idea of their dad dating again, but that part has been surprisingly easy."

"Magic is the great leveler of playing fields," Alice intoned solemnly, even as her lips twitched into a smile.

"I think we're just sort of moving past all the really old stuff, what happened between us when we were kids ourselves, because we don't have the words or the time or the emotional energy to explore all that," Caroline said.

"That doesn't sound great," Riley said carefully. "That sounds like leaving an unchecked land mine in the middle of your relationship and hoping for the best."

"I'm not disagreeing with you," Caroline said. "I just don't know how to approach it."

"Both Edison and I have our own 'land mines,' and even when we do make the effort to talk about it, it can blow up in ways you don't expect," Riley told her. "And our past issues don't stem directly from each other."

"I know, I know," Caroline sighed. "I think we're just moving slow and waiting to see what develops naturally. Without too much pressure or heavy conversations."

"Well, I will not tell you 'I told you so' when the fight springs up out of nowhere," Riley assured her. "We will just be here to liquor you up and assure you that your point in the fight was absolutely correct and he was super wrong, even if he is objectively right."

Alice squeezed Caroline's hand. "We will pretend that logic and accountability do not exist, for your sake."

Caroline nodded, taking both of their hands. "You are really, really good friends."

Their laughter fell short as Mina exploded out of the side door of Gray Fern, stomping down the steps and into the street.

"Well, that's not good," Caroline said, watching Mina storming toward the Main Square, toward the Rose. She was practically leaving a steam trail in her wake.

"Yeah, um, we should go," Riley agreed, hopping up to lock the front door.

The three of them followed Mina as she half ran down the street. Caroline was able, to her surprise, to keep up with Riley and Alice, which she considered progress in her healing. But Mina was smaller and faster, not to mention younger. The three of them arrived at the bar just in time to see Mina tossing a rock at the front door.

"Um, Mina, I'm already pretty much capped out on my construction budget, so if we could *not* break the windows, that would be great," Caroline told her, bending at the waist and panting.

"Come on out here!" Mina yelled, tears streaming down her cheeks. "Come out here and answer for that bullshit, you hateful old..."

"Mina!" Riley cried. "What is going on?"

The purple ghost slipped through the front door, grinning at Mina like she was a favorite treat. She didn't speak, only glided closer to the teenager.

"Shut up," Mina cried. "You don't know what you're talking about!"

"What in the hell?" Riley huffed. "That's the ghost you two have been dealing with here?"

Alice shuddered. "She's terrifying. She reminds me of my grandmother."

"Ouch," Caroline muttered as Mina took a large box of kosher salt she'd carried from home and poured it as close to the ghost's feet as she could get. But the ghost wouldn't hold still, slipping away from Mina like a kid playing keep-away. Caroline could see the ghost laughing, but couldn't hear any sound, which was disconcerting.

"Just hold still and shut *up*," Mina cried.

"OK, I applaud the ingenuity, but that's really not how we do things," Riley said. "Let's just slow down."

Mina grunted and ripped the top of the salt box off, tossing the contents at the ghost, who just sort of sauntered back through the front door, as if Mina didn't matter at all. Mina fell to her knees, crying.

"Oh, honey, no," Riley cooed as they rushed to her. "You're gonna get salt all embedded in your kneecaps."

"I just want her to shut up," Mina sobbed. "I don't want her in my head, saying those awful things. It's like I'm not safe, even at home. She keeps sending me these nightmares."

"I thought you said she hadn't been talking to you," Caroline said, dropping to her own knees and hugging Mina tight. Riley was right. The salt crystals stung.

"I didn't want you to worry. You seemed so freaked out when I said I could see her. And she's tried to trick me," Mina sniffed.

"She tried to play mom, to make me see her as this poor, defenseless thing. But she's not; she's crafty. She's been telling me all this stuff about my mom and you and how no one is gonna love me and she's the only one who understands and it was some accident that I got magic. And soon enough, Riley's gonna take it back. It should have gone to Josh because he's the one who's sensitive and talented, not me."

"That's not true," Alice told her.

"She used to live here. She's so angry. And she says you don't really like me, that Wiltons don't know how to love, not really, but that you'll fool my dad and he'll forget all about me and Josh and—You're a lying old bitch!" Mina hollered, stomping toward the half-constructed entrance.

"Easy, killer," Riley said, catching Mina around the waist and preventing her from getting too close to the door.

Mina swiped at her cheeks. "She showed me all this stuff...and she's so *mean.*"

"OK, OK, but you don't need to talk to her alone anymore. OK?" Caroline told her. "You're basically all paid up, in terms of labor swap for medical expenses. So maybe you and Josh just shouldn't spend any more time here at the bar."

"No, no, don't send me away!" Mina squeaked, clinging tighter to Caroline.

"I'm not sending you away," Caroline promised, kissing her damp hair. "I will come to your house as much as you want. And you're welcome at Shaddow House any time."

She looked to Riley, who nodded. "Yep. Any time at all. If you're scared, you come over. If you're sad, you come over. If you're suddenly feeling like you're gonna storm through town in a blind rage and throw some rocks at a historical building...*maybe* call first."

Mina snorted. "OK."

They heard footsteps approaching. Josh and Ben were running up the hill, obviously winded.

"I need to work out more," Ben huffed, holding up a device in a glittery blue case. "Mina, if you're going to run out of the house like a bat out of hell, at least take your cell phone."

"Sorry, Dad," Mina sniffed as he hugged her. "I'm OK."

"Ghost stuff?" Ben asked Caroline, his chin balanced on Mina's head. She nodded. "Can we talk?"

"It's OK, Meanie," Josh said, putting his arm around her shoulders. "I'll make you that gross herbal tea you like. The kind that tastes like feet and social ostracism."

"We'll get them home," Alice told Ben. "Can you walk Caroline to her cottage?"

"Sure," Ben said. "I'll see you two back at the house. Lock up until I get there."

The two of them walked into the darkness, the moon lighting their path back to the Wiltons' property. Ben was oddly quiet, tucking his hand around Caroline's waist, though it felt like he was trying to carry her along without her realizing it. Which was weird.

Her big old family house loomed high on the hill, but she led him to the cottage, even as his feet wandered toward the porch where he'd kissed her goodnight so many times. He finally spoke when they reached her front door. "Look, are my kids safe?"

She opened her door, making a sweeping gesture to welcome him inside.

"I don't know if any kid is *safe*. This isn't a safe world. But I'll talk to Riley and Alice to figure out a way to protect both kids from ghosts messing with them in their sleep. Honestly, we should have thought of that before," she said, raking her hand through her hair as she sat on the couch. He walked over to the fridge to get her a glass of water. Of course, he knew where the glasses were. When they were young, this cottage was where they'd gone when they wanted to do…things, because his parents were light sleepers and eventually figured out how good Caroline was at climbing up his trellis. After her grandmother died, the cottage sat empty, and her parents were not nearly as careful with the keys as they should have been.

"Do you think the house is trying to turn the kids into the new Stewards?" Ben asked.

Caroline's mouth dropped open. She hadn't considered that, but honestly, she could see why Ben would be concerned. "I don't know."

"Should I be worried about that?"

She pursed her lips. "I don't know. Possibly?"

He flopped onto the couch, next to her. "Am I being insensitive, asking you this?"

"No," she assured him. "You're worried for your kids. It's a good thing. I am also worried for your kids, because I like them, very much."

"That makes me weirdly happy." He took her hand, lacing together their fingers. "This is nice, being together at the end of the day, even if that day was punctuated with ghost issues."

"Most of my days are punctuated with ghost issues," Caroline said.

"I just mean, I've never had this, talking about my kids with someone who really understood them," Ben told her, pulling her close.

Caroline frowned. "Um, what about their mom?"

"Isabelle... This is going to sound like 'sour grapes' ex talk, but I don't know if Isabelle understands either of the kids. That was... never really her goal? She worried about their futures, their grades, their extracurriculars, the college choices, their career paths. She didn't worry so much about their happiness," Ben said.

"Well, that's...no, it's a dynamic I'm painfully familiar with. I'm not going to lie," Caroline said.

"There are reasons we're not together anymore. That's just one of them," Ben said. "I know that nostalgia can do a lot to influence one's recall, but...nothing has been as easy or comfortable as being with you."

"I don't know if relationships are supposed to be easy or comfortable," Caroline said, studying their joined hands. It was a weird feeling, to *know* how his hand was going to feel against hers. The long fingers, the long road map lines across his palm, the square, neatly clipped nails and how they would gently scrape against the base of her thumb. How could someone's hands not change in more than fifteen years?

"Yeah, it probably doesn't speak well of me to look at it that way," he said, "but nearly every relationship since you has felt like wearing a pair of shoes that was two sizes two small, on the wrong feet."

"I'm not sure being a cozy old pair of shoes speaks very well of *me*," Caroline replied dryly.

"You know that's not what I mean," he scoffed, kissing her knuckles. "I mean, it pinches at you. Every step hurts to the point that you dread moving. Just when you get used to the old hurts, new ones pop up."

"OK, I think I understand the shoe metaphor a little better," she admitted.

"I think I married Isabelle because it felt like it pinched the least? Which again, sounds like a terrible reason to marry someone, particularly when the person who seemed so easygoing and encouraging turned out to not be who she was, at all," Ben said.

"Well, I can't say I was looking for something easy or difficult," Caroline said. "I think I was just…bored, looking to fill time and not feel so alone. Which I will also admit, is not a great look, in terms of grown-up interactions. But when your life is so defined—knowing that you're going to live your life in one place, that there are no other options, you stop seeing other big life steps for yourself— relationships, marriage, children," she said as he buried his face in her hair. "And after you, I wasn't sure I really wanted any of that long-term stuff. It hurt less, looking for something that also had a finite window. I felt like I was in control of it, when I controlled nothing else."

"Quite a pair, aren't we?" he mumbled into her neck.

"We were," she said, stroking his back. "As I recall, we were quite the pair, in this very room."

"We *are*. And I happen to recall the things that we used to do in this very room. I've gotten way better at those things," he promised, making her laugh.

"You weren't bad in the first place," she assured him.

He kissed her, and it felt different than those kisses in Riley's office. There was a giddy anticipation to it, because this was heading somewhere. Somewhere naked.

Ben pulled her into his lap, throwing her leg over his hips. He was so much bigger than she was, able to move her around easily. And while that could be intimidating with someone she didn't know—this was Ben.

Ben, who loved her. Ben, who would never hurt her. Ben, who was growing hard underneath her, dragging his hips against hers. His hand slipped carefully up her ribs, teasing along the sides of her breasts in that way that always made her ache—teasing but never quite touching where she wanted. He gently gripped the back of her neck, pulling her mouth to his.

She moaned into his mouth, chirping as he stood, carrying her back to what was her guest room. She took her lips from his, panting, "My room's at the end of the hall."

"Oh, right," he chuckled, nodding, turning into the primary bedroom. He didn't comment on the fact that it used to be her grandmother's bedroom, for which she was very grateful.

No, no, don't think about the potential ghosts of family members that could be watching you right now, her brain commanded. Thank goodness, her body obeyed, because she might have wept otherwise or finally unlocked Riley's upsetting telekinesis, powered by sexual frustration.

He set her on the bed with a tiny bounce, crawling carefully over her as she kicked off her shoes and then his. He dragged her jeans down her hips, dropping them to the floor. He bit gently at her hip bones, making her jerk up off the mattress. That had always been her secret weakness. And no one else had managed to find it unprompted.

"Unfair," she groaned.

"Never said I was," he said, grunting when she rolled onto him. Her ribs protested a little, but she ignored them for the sake of pressing his wrists down on the quilt while sucking on the pulse point at his throat. He whimpered, and that made her grin.

"Oh, that smile scares me so much," he whispered as she shimmied out of her shirt. While she was distracted, he tossed her back on the bed and dragged his lips between her breasts, down her stomach, until he reached her navel. He bit down gently on the skin of her belly as he reached between her thighs. He pushed her panties aside and found just the right place to touch, making her squeak.

"That's a new one," she murmured.

He grinned up at her. "You ain't seen nothing yet."

She rolled her eyes and yanked at his collar, pulling him to eye level with her while also removing his shirt. She felt his knee spreading her thighs, and she wrapped her legs around his waist. He kissed her and she tasted a memory—cinnamon toothpaste and summer nights and the sneaky thrill of stolen hours in a "misappropriated" bedroom.

With no little difficulty, she leveraged her way up on her elbows and rolled over him. She hissed at the pain rippling up her torso, but muffled the sound against his chest. He felt just like she remembered, sliding down his body until her hand wrapped around something that was also quite familiar. He groaned, the tail end of the sound just a little desperate. And when she wriggled her thumb in just the right spot, he shuddered as he always had.

It was good, knowing someone this well, knowing all the places and noises and scents. It was strange and yet not, even when he arched up, sliding inside her without the fumble and hesitation of their younger years. She rolled her hips, balanced on that edge of pleasure-pain, moving with him. His fingers clutched frantically at her hips to slow her down, something he used to do when he was afraid of finishing too quickly.

"Wait, wait, wait," he whimpered, making her giggle. "That's not nice."

Fueled by desire and delight, she canted her hips again until he made a little bleat of surrender. She leaned down, kissing him as they moved together, over and over. Teasing him was forgotten as the heat rose in her belly, making her dizzy. That sizzle of nerves seemed to spread through her entire body in a way that was entirely new. Was it magical? Or the sweetness of connecting with someone whose fingerprints were etched so deeply on her heart?

Ooof, reunion sex was making her weirdly poetic...and it wasn't particularly good poetry. But the sex...that was definitely good. Sweaty and satisfying and...when had Ben learned to do *that* with his thumb? It was almost too much, but...*oh*.

Caroline wasn't sure if she fell or she was pulled when she hit the mattress. But suddenly, Ben was splayed over her, and she could only hold on and wait while the stars building behind her eyes reached supernova.

She clutched at his shoulders, holding him close, listening to his heart thundering at this throat. He cupped her chin in his fingers, pulling her mouth up to meet his just before he cried out, hips stuttering, breath mingling with hers. She feathered her fingers through his damp hair, enjoying the expected spicy pine scent.

Ben collapsed, careful not to drop his entire body on top of Caroline's smaller frame. He pulled the sheet over them both as he leaned his forehead against hers. "I missed you."

She smiled. "I missed you, too."

Chapter 13
Ben

IN THE FAMILIAR DARK OF his room, Ben rolled over and found Caroline's side of the bed unoccupied.

He sat up, blinking, looking toward the bathroom. Nope. Dark. He paused, listened. He could hear Josh snuffle-snoring down the hall, and Mina's muted music—to deal with the snuffle-snoring. But he couldn't "feel" Caroline in his house. Her cheerful energy was conspicuously absent.

Until last night, she'd been so leery of staying over. She didn't want to give the kids the wrong impression, she'd told him. She didn't want to be a bad influence. And then Mina had thrown a spare toothbrush at her and told her to stop overthinking it.

Maybe she'd gotten up in the middle of the night to avoid an awkward breakfast scene? He was sure his kids wouldn't be the ones to put *Caroline* on the spot. They thought she was the most reasonable adult they'd ever met, which went a long way with both of them.

Or maybe Caroline's disappearance had nothing to do with him and the kids. Maybe she'd gotten a telepathic message from a member of her coven and she needed to rush over to help. But if that was the case, wouldn't she have told Ben first in case she ran into ghostly danger?

These were questions other single dads didn't have to answer.

On his nightstand, Ben's phone buzzed. His security-cam app showed notification after notification slipping up his screen. He opened the app and saw a clip of Caroline moving past his doorbell camera. She was limping, but there was a strange listlessness to how she was moving her upper body—none of Caroline's usual verve. Her arms were just sort of hanging at her sides, and even as she opened his front gate, she moved as if a puppet master was pulling her strings. And her feet were bare.

Caroline knew better than to walk around town in bare feet—broken bottles and who-knew-what sort of foot-piercing dangers lurked on the cobblestones.

"What is she doing?" he muttered. He slid his feet into his sneakers and grabbed their jackets. Caroline's shoes had been set neatly on the rack near the front door, right next to Josh's. He tucked them under his arm. Then, he tore out of the house, dashing back to lock the door for the kids' sake.

He ran toward the Main Square, his footsteps echoing across its eerily dark, silent stones. Caroline had already made it past the public library, still hobbling on her sore ankle. Had she woken up in the middle of the night and tried to sneak out before the kids realized she was there? And how had she managed to make it out so quietly? Every step in Gray Fern was an announcement of a foot on the squeaky floor.

"Caroline!" Ben cried, finally catching up to her as they neared the turn to the Rose. Was she really trying to go to the bar right now? He'd never known Caroline to sleepwalk. Had she developed some sort of sleep disorder while he was away?

He grabbed her shoulders, but she didn't protest. She didn't even make a sound, merely stared at him—well, no, she was staring *past* him, like he wasn't even there. She seemed to be staring at the moon, to be honest.

"Caroline, what are you *doing*?" he demanded. "Are you all right? Where are you going?"

She didn't answer. She simply began walking, bumping shoulders with him as she passed, as if he wasn't even there. He dashed around her.

"Caroline, sto—" He stopped, seeing himself reflect in the blank white glassiness of her eyes. "Oh, shit."

This wasn't a sleep disorder. This was something supernatural. And while everything in him screamed to take her back to his house *immediately* and get her somewhere safe, he knew that would only make Caroline's "work" more complicated and ultimately, more dangerous.

Sighing, he gently pushed her to a nearby bench, and docile as a doll, she let him slip on her shoes and glide her jacket over her arms. She might be possessed or whatever, but she would be warm.

Also, she would sock him in the eye if she ever heard him call her "docile," so he would keep that to himself.

She stood and shuffled along the street. To his surprise, she didn't turn toward the Rose but toward the path that led to the state park lands. That particular footpath continued all the way through the woods to the other side of the island.

There was only one thing she—or whatever was in control of her—could be interested in on that side of the island.

"Ohhhh, shit," Ben muttered, pulling his phone from his pocket. "Shit. Shit. Shit."

———————

It took far less time for the others to catch up with them than Ben expected, even in pajamas. Of course, neither Edison, Riley, nor Alice had an injured ankle to slow them down. Hell, Edison was carrying a to-go cup of coffee when they reached the footbridge leading to Vixen's Fall.

"You stopped to make coffee?" Ben asked, sipping the contents of the cup as Caroline crossed the bridge.

"Coffee-enthusiast ghost attached to one of those fancy one-man programmable barista machines, just recently acquired," Edison told him. "We always have coffee."

"Nice," Ben said.

"So, for future reference, yelling 'ghost emergency' into the phone and then hanging up is not what we would call 'helpful communication,'" Alice told him.

"I was pretty out of breath by the time I called you," Ben admitted. "Sorry."

"It's OK," Alice said, nodding to Riley, who was hovering near a still-mobile Caroline, looking stricken.

"Do we have any idea where she's going?" Edison asked.

"I think we know," Alice said as they climbed the hill that eventually led to Vixen's Fall. In the distance, the full moon glittered on waves that should have been impossible on a lake. Despite growing up on the island, Ben had only been this far out on the island a hand-ful of times, and never under such perilous circumstances. How was it possible that there was a surface of the island that stretched this far up? It seemed a different planet from the gently rolling hills in town. And the waves? How was it possible the lake was creating waves like that? The noise seemed to be boxing Ben's ears, unnaturally loud.

Alice jogged forward to join Riley and Caroline as they got closer to the edge of the cliff. The five rocks that formed the Crown came into view. Each of the women had a grip on Caroline's arm, to keep her from jumping off the rock's edge. The fear and dread burning at Ben's chest banked a little as Caroline dropped to her knees. Riley and Alice knelt beside her.

"Oh, ow," Alice said, wincing and blinking. "Caroline is having an extremely powerful vision. And I can see it over what I am currently seeing right now."

Riley nodded, keeping one eye shut. "It's like a double photo negative with a side of stabby migraine. Oh, this *sucks*."

"Is there anything we can do?" Ben asked.

"Prescription-strength ibuprofen?" Alice suggested, wincing.

"What are you seeing right now?" Edison asked gently.

Riley's voice took on a spooky, hollow note as she said, "We're the girl from Caroline's vision. Emily. Her name is *Emily*. And she's running to Vixen's Fall. She's thinking, Emmett anchored his boat nearby. It's risky and they're going to have to sail the long way around the island to get to the mainland, but it's the only way to leave without being seen."

Alice's voice took on that same eerie tenor. "Emmett's family doesn't want him to marry a servant. They have a wife in mind for him, a rich one. These dreams of being an artist are ridiculous, they say. And honestly, Emily sort of agrees with them, because his drawings aren't very good, but she loves that he wants to do something different with his life. She can't even trust the people she works for, because they have too many connections to Emmett's parents. But the moon is full and the water is high and they were going to sail together."

It was…well, downright creepy when all three women snapped their heads to the left in unison—as if they all heard something behind them. Together, they said, "Emmett?"

Ben and Edison had to turn around and look, because—yikes.

"Emmett, come out. This isn't funny, and we need to leave," the women chorused together. Their voices had taken on a sort of softened British accent. The hollow echo of it sent a shiver down Ben's spine.

"Emmett, the boat—"

Both Riley and Alice let out screams that were absolutely blood-curdling. They dropped to the ground, their eyes rolled back, showing only white. Caroline stayed on her knees, head tipped back, but her eyes were white now too.

Edison scrambled forward. "Riley!"

Before Ben could reach Alice, Caroline caught his arm—even with her head tilted back. Slowly, she tipped her head forward until her still-white eyes were level with Ben's. She reached up and cupped Ben's face. "Emmett."

"Who are you right now?"

Caroline shook her head and smiled as if he was being silly. With her eyes rolled upward, it was…really upsetting. "Emily."

"OK, Emily. Nice to meet you. Could you get out of my girl-friend?" Ben asked.

Caroline shook her head. "She *has* to see."

"What does she have to see?" Ben asked.

Rising to her feet, Caroline took his hand and led him behind the Vixen's Crown, close to the cliff's edge. Too close. She knelt in front of the middle stone and ran her fingers over its surface. She took Ben's hand and placed it on something sharpish carved into the rock. Even in the dark, it felt like four boxes stacked into a cube. It reminded him of something, but it escaped him.

"Our initials. Two E's turned toward each other, to make four squares," Caroline-Emily said. "He buried me here. They would have left me there, in the dirt by the churchyard. They gave so many reasons why I didn't deserve a decent burial with decent folk. But the real reason was her. They didn't want to cross *her*. So Emmett brought me here, in the dark, to our place, to bury me where I was loved." She smiled sadly. "And then he left, ran far away from his family. And he never came back."

The sense of loss in her voice was deep, so profound that he couldn't say anything besides, "I'm so sorry."

"He did his best for me, to keep me safe. But now, there's no one left to care. Except for Caroline. She came here, made contact with me—despite *her*. Caroline *cares*. Bury me, in a real grave, somewhere respectable. And I'll be able to rest," Emily spoke through Caroline.

"That's your unfinished business?" Ben asked.

"Wouldn't you say that's enough?" she asked dryly.

"That's a good point," Ben admitted. "Do you think you have an attachment object?"

Caroline-Emily seemed to think about that for a moment. "If not my bones, perhaps the buckles on my shoes? They were real silver, and I worked hard to earn them. They were buried with me, as I would have wanted."

Ben smiled gently. "That makes sense."

Caroline sagged against him, to where he had to hold her up by her elbows. That otherworldly Emily voice was still coming from her lips. "I can't hold this for long. I needed all three of them, together, here, to speak. But she's so much stronger. It's not right, her being this strong."

"Is it so hard for you, to talk to Caroline? Through her?" he asked. "Because of this other ghost?"

The Caroline-Emily hybrid nodded, almost frantically. "She's kept me away, from the day Caroline could see us. Had to reach out, in some way she wouldn't understand. It had to be about love. Your Caroline, she understands love, but not *her*. She's so powerful. Even in death. She had us all fooled."

"You keep saying 'she' and 'her,'" Ben said. "Who are you talking about?"

"The same woman who pushed me off the cliff. The same woman who kept me from being buried in the churchyard. R—"

A burst of green-gray light from his right nearly knocked Ben on his ass. A spectral, skeletal woman was screaming inches from Ben's face like a hurricane made of screeching. Caroline tumbled to her side. She rolled out of Ben's dazed grip. His breath caught, and he didn't have time to worry about the angry ghost lady—who was *not* Emily, he could just tell from the angry brow and the peeling, rotten skin—howling at him while he tried to wrestle Caroline's dead weight away from the precipice.

"Fuck. *Off!*" Ben hollered back.

Was he crazy, or did the dead harridan look almost offended?

"You heard him, fuck off!" Suddenly, Riley was sitting up and the ghost was hit with a face full of salt she threw from a small linen bag. With one last sneer, the ghost sizzled into nothing.

"Ow." Riley flopped back to the ground. "*Ow.* Fucking ow."

Caroline gasped into a conscious state. "Are we awake?"

"Yes, and it's terrible," Alice grumbled into the grass. "Why am I face-down?"

"Why are we awake?" Caroline demanded. "And why does it hurt so much? And why is Alice face down?"

"I'm so sorry, Alice!" Edison exclaimed, crawling over to her side to help her sit up. "Riley went down and I panicked."

"That's OK," Alice huffed as Edison helped her sit up. "I just need someone to pick the grass out of my teeth."

"Oh fuck, that hurts," Caroline groaned as Ben cradled her into his shoulder.

"What she said," Riley moaned, lifting an arm to flap in Caroline's direction.

"Why am I here?" Caroline asked. "Why are you all here? Is this going to be some very unfortunate *Wizard of Oz* situation? Or did I get slipped some party drugs in a nonparty context? Is that why I'm asking so many questions?"

"You sleepwalked," Ben told her. "You don't remember?"

Caroline shook her head. "I had the same dream, walking up to Vixen's Fall to meet Emmett. But then those hands pushed me, and everything went gray. It felt like I was underwater. I could feel Riley and Alice with me, but I couldn't reach out to them. I could hear your voice, but I couldn't talk back. I couldn't even hear what Emily was saying. And the barroom ghost yelled in my face. *Bitch*."

"It was awful. Let's not ever do that again," Alice sighed as Riley helped her to her feet.

"Agreed," Riley groaned as the rest helped Ben and Caroline up. "Also, is it just me, or was that the most aesthetically challenged ghost we've seen so far?"

"She was definitely in a later stage of decomposition," Ben said. "What ghosts I've seen at Shaddow House seem to be in a 'fresher' state."

Riley's lips twitched. "Is that an official medical opinion of ghosts?"

"Oh, the journal articles I could write…that would immediately get my license taken away and then get me committed," Ben sighed.

"So why the sudden change in 'freshness?'" Riley wondered as the five of them trudged back through the grass, toward town.

"Maybe that's her real state, spiritually speaking?" Edison suggested. "The purple-dress-lady guise at the bar was just a sort of… well, the fairy tales would call it a 'glamour,' to keep up appearances? To make people she allowed to see her drop their guard?"

"Well, who the hell has time for ghost vanity?" Riley griped.

Caroline suggested, "Ghosts, mostly?"

The house lights of Gray Fern were blazing when they returned, prompting Ben to run up the stairs much faster than Caroline could manage on her ankle.

The kids? Were the kids OK? Had the ghosts staged some sort

of distraction to get the adults away from his kids to use them somehow? He didn't know how that would work, but dad panic didn't
allow for logic in times like this.

Ben threw the front door open to find Josh and Mina standing
in front of the couch, arms crossed and disapproving expressions
securely in place.

"Where *have* you *been*?" Josh cried, in a downright rude imper-
sonation of Plover as Caroline walked through the door. "Do you
know how *worried* we were? What we thought happened to you?"

"Ooh, ease it back some, Josh," Mina said, her expression confused when Alice, Riley, and Edison followed through the door.
"Going a little too British and elderly."

"Do you have no compassion for my poor nerves?" Josh
demanded.

"Oh, no, you went full Austen. That's an overreach," Mina
murmured out of the corner of her mouth.

"Guys, we're sorry, we just had a little bit of a middle-of-the-
night sleepwalking encounter with some lady ghosts," Ben told
them, hugging Mina tight. "I should have left a note or a text or
something, but it was a quickly evolving situation."

"Really?" Mina sounded way too intrigued by that for Ben's
comfort. "Lucky!"

Josh snapped out of his melodramatic mien instantly. He put his
arm around Caroline, prompting a tired smile from her. "Oh, man,
we *felt* this horrible ghost scream a while ago. That's what woke us
up. And when we realized you were gone, we just thought you guys
just snuck off for some private...eh..."

"Naked fun time?" Mina suggested.

"What? No!" Josh hollered, giving his sister a fully horrified look.

"I never want to hear you say those words together again," Ben said solemnly, making Mina cackle. "Not even when you're eventually having...naked fun time yourself."

Josh shrieked indignantly, putting his hands over his ears. "Just stop talking!"

Ben added, "Fifty years from now. When I'm dead."

Mina's nose wrinkled as she waggled her head back and forth. "That seems like a late-in-life start, honestly."

Josh didn't respond, only sighed wearily.

"OK, OK, let's end the conversational trauma now and talk about dead people," Caroline suggested, clapping her hands and using a bright "camp counselor" voice.

"Sounds good," Josh said, pointing at her. "Who was it this time?"

"Emily. The Vixen's Fall ghost," Alice informed them. "Who was not so much of a vixen as a victim. She was actually very sweet and didn't make a single grab at our ankles."

Caroline winced as she settled her weight on the couch. Ben sat on the coffee table and elevated, then massaged her foot to counter-act the inevitable swelling as he explained what happened. Alice and Riley bustled around the kitchen, boiling water for tea, pouring the coffee the kids had already made. By the time they came back to the living room with cups, milk, and sugar, Ben had reached the point of the story where the angry decomposing ghost screeched in his face.

"Do the kids really need to know about all this?" Caroline asked. "It seems like too much for them. The inherent creepiness of full-body possession in my sleep."

"Um, yeah, because if we'd had the full picture about this Emily getting tossed off the cliff, I could have told you that Rose-the-creepy-barroom lady was the one who probably did it," Mina scoffed.

"I'm sorry, what?" Caroline asked, nearly spitting out her piping-hot coffee.

Mina shrugged. "Oh, she hated Emily. Rose hated everybody, honestly. But especially Emily."

"Pause," Caroline said patiently, raising her hands. "Explain."

"Remember when I called Rose a dirty bitch?" Mina asked.

"Vividly," Riley deadpanned. "But mentioning her name—might have been helpful."

"I'm not good with details, sometimes, when I'm mad…or hungry…or sleepy," Mina told them. "And right before I started yelling at her, I guess maybe I was particularly stressed out, or my third eye was pried open or something. But she treated me to a sort of video montage that I think was supposed to make her seem sympathetic, but it was really just middle-aged lady ravings all at once—like she was downloading a zip file into my head, but I don't think she knew what she was doing. It sucked because she was the actual worst. Sorry, Caroline, I know she was an ancestor of yours, but she was full-on, reality-star-exposed-on-YouTube brand of 'yikes'. And the funny thing is, I don't think she meant to do it. Because what she showed me…"

"Uh, we need less 'stream of Mina-consciousness' and more of a linear narration," Josh told her.

"The vocabulary lists are really paying off, Josh," she said. "OK, fine. So, what Rose was trying to show me was her life as a poor unappreciated housewife, sick, miserable as her family just sort of blithely ran the inn and ignored her. But the truth was, she ran that place with an iron fist, and she managed to do it from her sickbed upstairs. And she *loved it*. She controlled who the family bought ale from, who they bought their food supplies from, whose tab got extended, who got to pay their rent late. Did I mention that your family used to own a lot more than just the Rose? They owned cottages and farms all up and down the shoreline and made a pretty penny gouging people for living in them."

Caroline nodded. "So, my family managed to fritter a real estate empire away. Shocker. Wait, so Rose, as in 'the Rose?' I thought The Wilted Rose was supposed to be named after some angry spinster nursemaid, like a cautionary tale against trusting too easily."

"Well, it *is* a cautionary tale," Mina said, wrinkling her nose. "Her husband, Henry, might have been the public face of the inn, but it was Rose running the show. All while inviting the neighborhood ladies in her boudoir-slash-control-room for tea and sympathy. She fed them a steady flow of gossip she learned from eavesdropping on the very loud conversations happening in the bar. It gave her considerable influence and power in the community because no one wanted to cross her or be the one she was gossiping about. Her husband was also afraid of her. And so were her kids. I mean, 'afraid' isn't the right word. They lived in terror of her, like she was a monster in their closet, and she sort of loved that. She *loved* pulling the strings and watching them dance—I mean, she was subtle about it. She used the art of the veiled insult, the backhanded compliment, the threat of a cold shoulder, a well-timed coughing fit, or just falling into what I guess would be considered a coma—back before people realized how rare comas are—if she was even vaguely disappointed. Her family was just so terrified that she would turn her evil eye on them, or that they would be blamed if disappointment over their 'misbehavior' was what sent her over the edge and killed her. They were conditioned, like hostages or cult members or..."

"We get it, honey," Riley drawled. "She was the worst."

"Well, then, Emily came along, with her bright smile and her perky boobs," Mina said.

"Emily? My Emily?" Caroline gasped.

"Yep, Emily was supposed to be a sort of nanny to Rose's children. Even though she was supposed to be there for the kids, Rose found a way to dominate Emily's time, sending her into the barroom to fetch this, fetch that for her. She constantly sent Emily on errands and pointless little chores, just to remind her of who was in charge. Emily spent so much time taking care of Rose that a second nurse was hired for the kids, and Emily was in charge of Rose. The inn prospered, so it wasn't a huge problem, financially. Emily was beloved by Henry, the kids, and the people in the inn. Well, Rose didn't like that, or her children's preference for Emily. So Rose started to none-too-subtly imply, during those gossip visits with the neighbors, that Emily was a little too close to Henry. Suddenly, Emily is not as well liked, and people start seeing Rose as this brave, sad woman who needs more community support, more attention," Mina said.

"Oof, that is some advanced social engineering given the time," Riley marveled.

"Sounds like she was the original Nana Grapevine," Mina said.

"How do you know about the Nana Grapevine?" Edison asked.

"How would I *not* know about the Nana Grapevine?" Mina shot back, sounding insulted. "Do you realize how little gossip there is, for such a tiny town? Gossip is my lifeblood. Anyway, Rose sensed a disturbance in her spider's web of machinations. Emily had developed an interest in Emmett, the age-appropriate, *single* son of a local solicitor. The solicitor and his wife found out, thanks to Rose's intervention, and did *not* approve. They thought Emily was the one who was giving Emmett all these dangerous ideas about running away for some sort of *artistic career*. And Rose took the idea of Emily leaving the island really personally—like, weirdly personally. The insult of it, Rose wouldn't accept that."

"Rose started implying that she's getting weaker and thinks it's possible that Emily is poisoning her. Her health got worse and worse, or so she claimed. Mostly because she was taking a tiny dose of rat poison when she thought that nobody was taking her illnesses seriously—just enough to make her a little sick. She asked the local solicitor to write a will and asked the other ladies of the neighborhood to take care of her kids 'after she's gone.'"

"This is some ye olde true crime bullshit," Josh said. Ben cleared his throat. Josh just shrugged.

"Rose started to suspect that Emily was catching onto her fuckery," Mina noted.

"OK, the line is blurry, but it's still there!" Ben exclaimed. "The language!"

Mina merely chuckled. "Rose treated Emily worse and worse, and she could sense the desperation growing in Emily, so she pushed up the timeline. She had a few more 'sickly spells,' spread a little more gossip. She overheard Emily talking to Emmett at the inn and found out that she was supposed to meet him at the cliff at night to elope. But Rose got there first. She pretended to be taking to her bed for one of her 'early evenings' and snuck across the island. Nobody would ever believe it because it involved running. She got to the cliff before Emily, hid behind the Crown rocks—it was called Starfall Crown back then—and shoved her right off the cliff. No hesitation. No conscience. No regret, not even when she saw Emily's body floating."

"She would have deserved her own series on ye olde true crime channel," Josh said, cringing.

"Rose dashed home as soon as she realized Emmett was coming up the path," Mina said. "Emmett found Emily's body, and was, of course, crushed. He went to the magistrate, raised a big stink, but butter wouldn't melt in Rose's dirty lying mouth. She just reminded everybody of how 'accommodating' Emily was to customers, free with her favors. She had a lot of admirers. And of course, all of her teatime harpies backed up her story. They suddenly remembered Emily flirting with their husbands, too, because Rose *helped* them remember. They supposed that she must have met some other man and she 'got what she deserved'—which was freaking awful. If Emily's ghost was lurking nearby, I hate that she might have overheard that. And everybody believed that Rose was too weak and sick to hurt anyone, but her husband was questioned by the magistrate pretty closely. Rose enjoyed that part.

"And weirdly, even after basically showing me how she murdered someone, this was the point in the 'memory' where Rose really started trying to change how I saw things. But she couldn't hide the fact that she continued poisoning herself, just a little bit at a time.

She enjoyed the sympathy she got when she was sick. And it only added to the 'proof,' reminding everybody that Emily must have been poisoning her, because 'look at the long-lasting effects it's had,' et cetera. In fact, she insisted they change the name of the bar to The Wilted Rose, to remind everyone of poor victimized Rose. She let the family think it was their idea, of course, but it was her," Mina said.

"She *was* the worst." Caroline's lip curled back. It turned out she *was* descended from a murderer, but definitely not how she thought. "OK, so, why didn't you tell us any of this before? Because this is a wealth of valuable information that we could have used a couple of hours ago."

"Because you cut me off!" Mina cried. "You said you didn't want me involved in any of this and gave me a big lecture about ghost safety. You treated me like a little kid."

"OK, I can see now, that was a mistake," Caroline said. "I'm sorry."

"It's OK, after I got mad—a couple of days after—I realized it was nice to have someone who's not Dad worry about me," Mina said. Ben smiled at her, his chest tightening in a coiling fashion. Caroline cared about his children, and they felt that. He hoped they never lost it.

"But you withheld information because you were butt-hurt," Josh added.

"I don't get butt-hurt," Mina replied primly.

Josh arched an eyebrow. "Mina."

"OK, maybe a little bit," Mina conceded. "But I didn't know it was going to be important information, OK? The last bit—which, again, I don't think Rose meant to tell me. Eventually, all that poison caught up with her, and she died. I think people just chalked it up to all the health problems that she was always talking about, plus, you know, poison."

"What does any of this mean?" Caroline asked.

Mina shook her head. "No idea. But I think part of the reason she was able to smack you three around so easily—"

"Hey," Riley interjected.

"Was because Josh and I weren't there," Mina continued. "For some reason, Rose has a harder time manipulating me. Maybe because I don't have a blood connection to her or because I'm already used to being manipulated by my own mom, and she's a lot better at it than Rose. It's like I'm vaccinated against it, or something."

Ben shot a curious glance at Josh, to see if he would contradict his sister.

Josh merely shrugged. "A triangle is great, but a pentagon is a lot harder to break."

"I concede your point. No more leaving you out," Riley said. "Sorry, guys."

"So, Emily clearly isn't the source of the curse because she doesn't have a grudge against the Wilton family. I could feel her grief and loss out on that cliff, and she didn't have room in her heart for the kind of hate involved in what was done to your family...killing your relatives... So, I can't believe I'm saying this but...could it be Rose?" Alice suggested.

"Oh, my god, really?" Mina asked, her eyes going wide. "I mean, she's awful, but how could she do that to her own family?"

It was a brief balm to Ben's mind, that as bad as Mina's

relationship was with her mother, Mina's young mind couldn't comprehend the idea of a mother hurting her own family in that way. It was a small comfort, but it was something.

"Rose liked to control people, you said," Riley noted. "Maybe she saw her family leaving the island as the ultimate loss of that control. She couldn't stand it. I mean, look at how she responded when Emily wanted to leave, and she didn't even like Emily. So maybe she found a way to punish your family members who tried to leave that control."

"Oh, man, Caroline, I'm sorry. I should have said something earlier," Mina said, looking stricken.

"I'm not sure I would have believed you, before I saw the things we've seen," Caroline said, putting her arm around Mina.

"OK, but how does it work?" Josh asked. "How do we get them to move on?"

"Well, that I don't know, dammit," Riley sighed. "We know what happened, but what good does that do?"

"When Emily was possessing Caroline, she said she wanted to be buried properly," Ben said. "She's attached to her shoe buckles, so her spirit's been trapped all alone at Vixen's Fall all these years. And Rose has been keeping her silent. So maybe she wants justice of some kind too, since she's never been able to tell her story."

"So, we bury human remains without telling anybody?" Alice mused, "Caroline, what does the Michigan legal code have to say about that one?"

"I mean, she was murdered, but it's not like we can bring Rose to justice," Caroline said, frowning. "Other than maybe finding Rose's attachment object and sticking it in a box with, like, really smelly cheese and dirty sweat socks. Can ghosts smell? I'm a little ashamed I've never asked Plover."

"I could write a journal article in a historical publication that trashes the hell out of her," Edison offered.

"Aw, that's sweet," Caroline told him, patting his hand. "But I think that would probably upset my remaining family members. But also, fuck Rose, so do what you will."

"If we did contact the authorities, we would have to answer all sorts of questions about how we 'found' her, without sounding completely suspicious. Digging near the edge of Vixen's Fall isn't exactly a fun weekend activity," Riley added. "I think this is a 'discretion is the better part of valor' situation. We dig up Emily's remains under cover of night and bury her somewhere inconspicuous near the church with as much dignity as we can provide. That's all she wanted."

A moment of silence passed as the group sort of sank back into their seats.

"That was a lot for one night," Caroline mused as she leaned into Ben's side.

Ben nodded, glancing around at the assembled group. He knew these people cared for his kids, cared for Caroline. He'd made the right decision, bringing his children to Starfall. They were thriving. Hell, they were blooming. They had *magic* and purpose here. They had people who would nurture them and protect them, but at the same time, they were so young. They were supposed to be worried about SAT scores and fender benders, not magical battles with murderous ghosts.

But what could he do?

He had offers for other jobs. They came into his email account regularly as medical head-hunting firms attempted to find physicians for open spots in hospitals across the country. But could he really uproot them from the most stable environment they'd known in years? *Should* he do that, before they were "locked in" to the island, like Caroline? And what about Caroline? They had something real and true that he wanted to hold on to. Even if he wanted to leave Starfall, how could he risk losing her again?

He scrubbed a hand across his face. It was late, and this was too much to deal with all at once.

"Anybody want to binge-watch ghost-hunting shows?" Mina asked.

"No!" the others chorused.

Mina scoffed. "Well, you wake me up at two in the morning and give me coffee, what do you expect?"

Chapter 14
Caroline

FRESH FROM EMILY'S UNOFFICIAL, PREDAWN funeral, Caroline walked—slowly—along the shoreline near her family's home, pondering the new, disturbing knowledge they'd gleaned from their night on Vixen's Fall.

Could a member of her own family be the cause of all their heartache? Could one woman's need for control echo so far that she would hurt any member of her family who unknowingly defied her?

From what she had seen of that ghost—the malevolent, smirking presence in The Wilted Rose—yeah, Caroline could believe that. She'd seen it for herself, the callousness, the speed with which Rose had pushed Emily off Vixen's Fall—not one moment's hesitation. But *how* was she able to do it? That was the question. What was Rose's attachment item? If it was the portrait, they were screwed, because they still hadn't located it, and she wasn't sure how to feel about it. The coven didn't believe the portrait was her attachment object. And yet, it was important enough for someone to take it. Why would someone do that? There had been so many strangers through the barroom during construction. Maybe one of them thought it was valuable? A couple of vintage beer taps had come up missing, too, so it was possible. But it was also possible that her brothers had just put the taps in the wrong place. Then again, it was also possible that her brothers had thrown the portrait into a dumpster, because it was easier than carrying it to the storage area.

After they'd taken a day to recover from Caroline's sleepwalking theatrics, they'd returned to the cliff. It had taken surprisingly little digging to recover Emily's skeletal remains. As they gently laid the bones (and Emily's shoe buckles) in a lovely rosewood box Riley purchased from Alice's shop, they sang songs they hoped Emily would enjoy. The academic in Edison was in an emotional fetal position, changing historical space this undocumented way, but he silently supported them as they carried Emily's remains to the churchyard.

Mina and Josh had been included in the effort—under Ben's uneasy supervision—and Caroline didn't think it was a coincidence that Rose didn't try to stop them. Mina probably had a good point about being immune to Rose. Caroline's ancestor wouldn't like that. How they'd all managed to bury the remains under some ivy growing near the building's historical marker, Caroline had no idea. Emily *had* shown up at the churchyard gate, smiling.

"Right at the *cornerstone*? Oh, I like you." Emily had chuckled as Ben took the kids home. Riley, Edison, and Alice wanted to stay, but there were things that Caroline wanted to say to Emily in private.

"I'm sorry it was my family that did this to you," Caroline said. "I really didn't know."

"I understand that," Emily said. "But did I enjoy that it was

Rose's own blood that would give me what I wanted? Yes, I did. It all worked out for the good."

"I'm assuming that you and Rose aren't on speaking terms," Caroline said, making Emily snort. That was something Caroline didn't even know the dead could do. "But I think maybe Rose cursed her descendants, so that we couldn't leave the island. I don't want to believe it…but from what I've seen… How, how could she do that?"

"Rose would rather tear something valuable to the ground than allow someone to defy her, to think they'd won." Emily reached out to pat Caroline's arm, sending a shiver down Caroline's spine. "The woman wanted to run her own little kingdom, where she was queen—unquestioned, unchallenged. And she met any opposition like most mad monarchs do."

"Swift violence and unrelenting bat-shittery," Caroline nodded. "Got it."

"That's an interesting word," Emily mused. "'Bat-shittery.' I like it. It's almost enough to make me want to stay, to learn more. But, a bargain is a bargain. And I have nothing left to hold me here. I want to move on to what's next, to see if I can find Emmett in whatever's beyond."

"Good luck to you," Caroline told her. "And thank you. I'm not sure we would have learned what we did about Rose without you, well, provoking her."

Emily grinned. "You're a good woman, Caroline Wilton. Better than she ever was. Just…don't let Rose lie to you. She's good at that, and you, being an honest person, won't see what she's planning for you."

"I appreciate the wisdom," Caroline said.

Emily's smile began to fade as *she* faded, gently transitioning from this plane to the next until she was just a tiny speck of light in the early morning shadows. It was always easier, almost beautiful, when the ghosts moved along voluntarily.

So now, Caroline found herself shuffling through the silty shores, close to the Wilton family home. The old house rose in the distance. Overlooking the water, the shabby Dutch colonial with peeling blue siding and white trim that hadn't been painted since… since Chris. The bushes, once so tidy and trimmed, were wild and overgrown. Her mother didn't have time to tend to them, much less replant the flowers that had once bloomed in the window boxes on the first floor. While Caroline didn't have flowers planted either, her own little cottage was at least recently painted a sunny yellow. Her mother had hated it, calling it the color of a "half-rotten egg yolk."

She wondered when her family had moved to the old house. She'd never thought much about it. The house had always just been there. Surely, they'd moved there after Rose had died. Maybe it was because Rose's ghost was making them uncomfortable, living in the bar?

The lights were off upstairs, but there was a lamp burning golden in the little den her father had claimed as his own a few years before. He'd insisted that it was so he didn't wake her mother with the TV when insomnia woke him in the middle of the night. But she and her brothers knew that he simply waited for her mom to drift off—usually before nine—and crept down the creaky stairs to sleep in his drooping mustard-colored recliner.

She could just go home, she told herself. She'd had a long day, and the sun was barely rising. She could shower and drink some coffee and catch an hour of sleep or so before she returned to Riley's for a team meeting.

She sighed, staring at the lonely light in the window.

Shit.

Instead of the much more comfortable option of walking to her cottage, Caroline climbed the creaking porch steps. Her parents still didn't bother locking their doors, something she could not understand in the age of *Dateline*.

The house smelled as it always did, of old cooking and older paper. Her father's paperbacks were stacked on every available surface in the den, but somehow, their smell permeated throughout the room, reminding Caroline where she'd gotten her love of the written word. She followed the sound of the TV playing some seventies cop show involving a lot of car chases and screeching tires.

Denny Wilton was sprawled in his easy chair, his green terry-cloth robe open over his worn pajamas. Caroline stilled, tilting her head against the doorframe as she watched her father doze. When Chris died, her dad hadn't turned to gambling or alcohol, which Caroline would have almost understood, given the family's vocation. He'd turned to grief. It was his whole day, sitting in this dark room, thinking about Chris. And part of it made her angry. He had three children left. What about them? Why couldn't they be enough reason to carry on?

Caroline wasn't being fair. She knew that. The death of a child and the devastation that followed wasn't an algebraic equation that ended in all sides being equal. But it didn't stop her from feeling this way.

The pajamas and robe were normal attire for Denny before

about three p.m. After three, Mom got home from work, and she'd fuss if she found him in his pajamas. But at this time of day, she was probably upstairs getting dressed for work.

His brown eyes fluttered open, and he smiled when he looked up and realized she was there. "Hey there, apple dumpling."

The corner of Caroline's mouth lifted. "Hey, Dad."

"You're up and about early," he said as she sat on the drooping goldenrod-colored couch beside him. "Your mom said you're just about ready to go back to work."

"Yep." She nodded. "No crutches, no brace."

"Well, that's good, dumpling. I know your mom needs your help. Get back out there and give 'em hell." He reached out and patted her knee.

Caroline nodded. She could let it go. It was early. She'd already been through the emotional wringer—for the day, for the week, for the year. But...she might never have this opportunity—or the nerve—again.

She took a deep breath and thought of Emily—who had to work every day for someone who tried to convince the whole town she was a murderous, poisoning husband-seducer. By comparison, having an emotionally difficult conversation with her own relatively harmless father wasn't so scary.

"Well, I'm glad that's your attitude, because I'm here to give you the same advice."

Her dad practically did a double take. "What? What are you talking about?"

"I love you. I'm saying this because I love you," she said, fighting back the sour, wet heat gathering over her eyes. "Chris's death was…awful, just freaking awful, but it's been years. And while I understand you needed us to support you and take care of the things that you couldn't for a while, it's time for you to give a little of that support back. Mom has carried the weight of the family and the bar and everything for so long that I don't think she remembers what it was like not having everything on her."

"That's not fair," he shot back.

"No, you're right. It's not fair that we lost Chris. It really, really sucks. But you're not being fair *to Mom*," she told him. "She needs you. She needs her partner back. Even if it's just small stuff like covering a shift at the bar or cleaning the house or having dinner ready when she gets home. She needs you to do more than sit in the dark and stare."

He stood up and turned on her. "You don't know what it's like to lose a child."

"Again, you are right, I don't know what that's like, but I know what it's like to lose a brother. And I know what it's like to lose a father to grief. And I know what it's like to lose a mother to work and regret and stress. I'm not saying you have to 'get over it,' because that's not how it works. Ever. But you have to *try* more," Caroline said.

"Well, if you're so worried about your mother, why don't you help more?" he asked testily.

"When?" Caroline asked. "I'm working my shifts. And then when the boys don't show up for their shifts, I work those."

"So ask the boys to show up for their shifts," he said. She stared at him for a long, silent moment, before he added, "OK. That was a stupid thing to say."

"Asking us to do more is not a more reasonable solution than you leaving this house and getting involved in our business and our lives," Caroline told him.

Her father seemed to sink in on himself, becoming even smaller. "It's my fault. It's my blood that got Chris killed. Nobody else on the island has had this happen to them. Maybe your mom should have married some other man, so you would have been safe."

An anger rose in her, a burning, acidic fury that she didn't know she was capable of—and then the frustration that she couldn't explain about Rose or her insanity because...her dad would never believe her. For most of her life, he'd been a "brick and mortar" man. Unless he could see it and touch it with his big, scarred hands, he refused to believe it existed. Until Chris died, he'd called the curse "superstitious bullshit." She wasn't entirely sure he believed it now, but he needed to blame his son's death on *something*—even if it was himself. And even if she showed him what the coven could do, acknowledging the existence of magic and hateful ghost grudges could be too much for him.

Caroline felt the temperature in the room change, like she was drawing the heat into herself for some sort of magical storm. She could feel it in her hands, gathering, and she didn't know what was going to happen. Riley could move haunted objects with her mind, but she didn't think there were any of those objects in this room. And if this energy had nowhere to go, would it hurt her dad? She took several slow breaths, focusing on letting that magic drain away into the air around her.

"Chris dying—Was it because of anything you did? A choice you made?" she asked him.

"No!" Denny exclaimed.

She swallowed heavily. "And if Chris had died of a heart defect or a tumor or anything else he could have inherited from your genes, would you have blamed yourself like this?"

Her dad nodded. "Maybe."

"Would you have processed it a little quicker?" she asked.

"Maybe," he sighed.

"Dad, I'm not saying you have to work through it right this second. I know that's not how it happens, but you have to start trying, OK?" Caroline asked.

He whispered, his eyes welling with tears. "I don't know if I can."

She wrapped her hands around his. He clung to them like a lifeline, as if she could pull him out of this undertow of despair that had him trapped. She cleared her throat. "Are you going to make me give you the Batman advice?"

He groaned, lowering his head until it was almost touching their joined hands. "No."

Denny looked up at her. For the first time in years, her dad's smile was genuine, a shadow of its former self, but there and sincere. It was such a promising first step that she couldn't help but take the next step and the step after it. She nudged him with her shoulder. "It always worked on me."

"I don't need the Batman advice," he huffed. "And for the record, I gave some version of that advice, even before the movie came out!"

She grinned. Once she had Denny Wilton indignant, she had him.

"It's not even Batman speaking," Denny sighed.

"And yet, we call it the Batman advice," Caroline said, throwing up her hands. "And what advice is that?"

"It doesn't matter that we fall down, it's about how we get back up," he said. "Or something like that."

"It's time to get back up, Dad," she told him. "Or at least, prop yourself into a sitting position."

Her dad nodded. "I'll get there."

She stood and kissed his forehead. "That's all I ask."

Days later, Caroline sat at Ben's breakfast bar, sipping from her mug. She wasn't really sure how to feel about any part of it.

It felt weird to be sitting "unchaperoned" in Ben's kitchen while he slept upstairs. She wasn't sure she'd ever been left alone in this house, even when they were kids. It felt weird to have her own mug at Ben's house, but the kids had simply ordered a copy of her *I could be reading* mug and put it next to her breakfast plate one morning. It still felt weird, sleeping in the same house as his kids, not that she and Ben engaged in "adult activities" with the kids there because that seemed super inappropriate. But still, the kids had greeted her in the mornings, asked if she wanted jelly or cream cheese on her bagel. They didn't make a big deal out of it, so she was choosing not to, either.

The weird cherry on top of this weird sundae was that…it felt so normal. She'd felt like she was a part of the family unit—not quite a parent, but not "the houseguest that won't go away," either.

And at that moment, she wanted to wallow in the normalcy, in having something in her life that mattered, and yet had nothing to do with ghosts or the bar or her family. It was her own, to make or break.

And yet...

She loved these kids. Seeing her father barely climbing out of his very real trauma after all these years was a reminder that the danger the kids faced was very real. And beyond her personal stake—of adoring those kids and fearing for their safety down to her soul—the very idea of Ben facing that sort of loss, the pain of it—it was just intolerable.

The question was, what could she do about it? *Could* she do anything about it?

The clatter of the side door opening and the *clonk* of boots in the mudroom caught her attention and made her lips tilt. How was it that teenagers could never get from point A to point B quietly? And how was it that she could so easily determine the sound of Mina's footsteps from Josh's?

Well, OK, Josh's size-twelve foot probably had something to do with it.

"I have secured for you the very last of Iggy's cherry rugalach," Mina said, solemnly setting the blue-and-white Starfall Grounds box on the counter in front of Caroline. "I had to fistfight a tourist from Missouri to get it."

"You did not," she huffed, opening the box. She paused. "You didn't, right?"

"You may never know," Mina snickered.

Caroline laughed and poured a coffee for Mina. "You were out late last night."

"Your mom asked me to drop by to finish up some inventory in the basement," Mina said.

When Caroline opened her mouth to protest, Mina added quickly, "Just the section under the stairs. I was only there for an hour or so. And I didn't see Rose once. I think she's learned not to mess with me. Which means I win."

"Or she's saving her strength to shove *you* off a cliff," Caroline muttered.

"I think you should be more worried about the fact that you have cocktail sauce down there," Mina countered.

"What's so bad about cocktail sauce?" Caroline asked.

Mina winced. "I asked your mom, and you haven't served anything with cocktail sauce since the 1980s."

Caroline grimaced. "Ew."

"So, yeah, we're gonna need to call some sort of hazmat team, because I don't think I'm qualified for moving it or disposing of it," Mina said.

"No, you are not," Caroline agreed, shaking her head. "OK, so you were only at the bar for an hour or so. Where were you the rest of the night? And I'm asking not in a supervisory adult way, but as someone who knows that there's a psycho ghost with a grudge against your coven roaming free on the island."

"Good point, and um, I snuck down to the beach to hang out with some kids," Mina said, blushing slightly. "There was a bonfire, the obligatory guitar played by a guy who only knew three chords, some beer—which I didn't drink because I don't want my dad to have an actual cardiac event."

"I'm sure he appreciates that," Caroline grinned. "Any particular kids?"

Mina began toying with the string that kept the bakery box closed. "Just this one guy, Derek Branner. His dad runs the Starshine ferry line."

Caroline searched her memory for a Derek, but the Branner family were Seventh-day Adventists and never came into the bar. She could remember a chubby-cheeked little boy who'd wiped out his bicycle in front of the Rose about twelve years ago. He'd been pretty brave about the whole thing, but Caroline didn't know if that was enough of a recommendation to date Ben's daughter.

"I don't know. I like him. He's really smart and funny and nice—and not the fake 'nice to your face while he's texting his buddies about how fast he thinks he can get your bra undone' kind—but the real sort of nice. He's *kind*. But he's pretty set on staying here and helping his dad run the family business, and I'm gonna be leaving for school next year..." Mina said.

Caroline again attempted to do the mental math on the bike kid. How much older was he than Mina? Oh god, she was not capable of doing this math. Ben should be doing this math. But she was sure he would freak out completely at the idea of his daughter dating a college boy. Mina needed a mother figure right now, and Caroline was struck with a sensation eerily similar to her dream of being shoved from Vixen's Fall. She was not qualified for it, but she was all Mina had. She wracked her brain for what she wished someone would have told her before Ben left.

Mina looked at her, her shoulders nearly to her ears. "I don't know. Everything feels temporary. And I get that's sort of normal, but...I don't want to get in some weird long-distance relationship."

"I think you might be overthinking it, a little bit," Caroline suggested. "I mean, I'm sure this boy is nice, and kind, but he's just a boy, you know? One of dozens of boys you're going to know over your lifetime. I wouldn't worry about it so much."

"I'm a teenager. Worrying about boys is my job right now."

"Understood. But remember that you're going to like the next boy," Caroline promised. "And the one after that. Look, you're a smart girl—to the point that you scare me a little bit. You're Mina freaking Hoult. You can go anywhere in the world and do anything. So go out and do it."

Caroline sincerely hoped that was still true and that magic wouldn't keep Mina bound to the island. But that wasn't knowable yet, so Caroline decided to take her own advice and try not to worry.

She heard creaking behind her, as if through glass, but she was on a roll and continued panic-talking. "So don't let some boy determine how and when and where you're going to do anything. You don't want to spend your college years tied to a long-distance relationship, afraid that you're going to outgrow the other person, hurt them, when you're supposed to be out living your life."

The words almost burned as they came out of her mouth, voicing what she wanted for Mina, even when Ben doing exactly that had hurt her so badly. But Mina was a different person, her own person. She had to make her own way.

"Enjoy it. You don't want to spend your time pining after one guy. You're going to be a completely different person by the time you're grown up—according to your dad, that's literally on a cellular level. Don't hold yourself back because you're afraid you're going to miss out. Go meet new people. A lot of new people. Find out what the world has to offer."

Mina was chewing her lip thoughtfully. "You're making good points—Dad?"

Caroline turned to see Ben standing behind them, all sleep-rumpled and grumpy. The panic subsided just a little bit. Ben would be able to help Caroline convince Mina she was right. "You want some coffee?"

"No," he said, his tone cold enough to make Mina's chin draw back a bit. "Mina, honey, could you go to Petra's and get me a bear claw?"

"But I got a whole box of pastries right here," Mina said, frowning.

"Go get me a different pastry, please," Ben said, taking his wallet off the counter and handing her some cash.

Oh, so Ben wasn't "just out of bed" grumpy. Ben was mad. And given the rigid set of his shoulders and the red in his cheeks, he was really mad.

Shit.

"OK..." Mina said, sharing a confused look with Caroline as she left the kitchen.

"Is everything OK?" Caroline asked, even though, obviously, it wasn't.

"No," Ben said, turning on her. "I'm really trying to stay calm here, but...what the hell are you doing, telling Mina that if she likes a boy, it doesn't matter? That she should enjoy as many of them as she can?"

"OK, that's not exactly what I said," Caroline protested. "And I would think you would want me to tell your teenage daughter not to prioritize boys when she should be studying and enjoying college!"

"I don't want her to treat people like they're disposable!" Ben insisted. "She's already seen enough of that from her mother."

"I never *told* her to treat people like they're disposable! Where is this coming from? Wait, is this about you and me? I thought we'd talked this through, Ben," Caroline said.

"Well, it turns out, I'm still a little mad about it," Ben cried, throwing up his hands. "And for the record, we didn't tie ourselves to a long-distance relationship because that's not what *you* wanted. You told me to go, so I went."

"Yes, because that's what was best for *you!*" she cried. "Also, *you* walked away from *me!* Do you think I wanted to be left alone? With *my family?* I wanted to be with you, but you needed to be somewhere else and even though it hurt, I let go."

"Well, no one asked you to do that. I didn't want a martyr, I wanted you!" Ben told her. "But you...how did you act like I never existed? I would come back to visit, and you would just pretend I wasn't even there! How are you even capable of that?"

"Because I was trying to make things *easier for you,*" Caroline insisted. "And yeah, maybe for me a little bit, too. Do you have any idea how hard it was for me, watching you come back to the island all content and successful and being happy *for you,* but dying a little bit inside every time I saw it? Do you think if I thought of people as disposable, I would still be anywhere near my family? Do you know how easy it would be to walk away from people who treat me like I'm a convenience? A tool? I might as well be a fucking can opener for all the family affection I get. I stick around because I have no choice. Where else am I going to live? Work? Move? And pardon the *fuck* out of me if I want Mina to have more than that. I want her to have the whole world. I'm terrified she's going to be stuck here, not just because of some boy, but because of her magic, too. It's the same life I have to live, and I want her to do better."

"But what if it ends up being what *she* wants? I thought we were doing pretty great together, this time around." Ben scowled. "I'm sorry you're stuck here with me now. I didn't realize you've had such a miserable life and that, since you're trapped and can't do any better, I'm your disappointing consolation prize."

"I'm not saying that!" Caroline cried. "Where is this even coming from?"

"Look, I think there's some old stuff coming up here," Ben said, shaking his head. "The Mina conversation is obviously bringing up hurt feelings that are very clearly still left over from when we were kids."

"Well, that's on you," Caroline said, her voice so hard and cold that she barely recognized it. "If you're going to freaking ambush me like this, when I was just trying to help your daughter, throwing around historical bullshit you haven't bothered to bring up until now, I don't know if this is going to work."

Ben deflated. She didn't know if it was the glacial flint in her tone or the fact that she'd already picked up her purse and her shoes. But there was a finality to what had just happened. She wasn't sure exactly at what point she'd lost control, but it felt like there was no coming back from it.

"It probably won't," Ben said, nodding.

"So we should probably just stop now before we do something that means we can't speak again," Caroline said, swallowing thickly. "I'm gonna go."

"Caroline, please—"

But she was already out the door.

––––––––––

Caroline did the only thing she could think to do, being this upset. Riley's house was right there, next door, and she ran to it like a sanctuary. How had it gone so wrong so fast? Ten minutes before, she had been quietly contemplating her life with the kids, and then she and Ben had a relationship-wrecking fight and tore it all down.

Maybe this was better. If it could fall apart so easily, maybe they shouldn't have tried at all. Ben could go back to raising his kids, finding someone better, someone who knew what they were doing with adult relationships and healthy connections with teenagers. And she could go back to her casual weekend relationships. They didn't hurt.

Shaddow House's front door swung open before she'd even reached the porch.

"Thanks," she muttered, though she still wasn't sure to whom. Riley was waiting at the bottom of the stairs, in her robe, looking very confused. Mina was pacing and wringing her hands. Plover seemed to be hovering behind her by two steps, looking equally distressed. Around them, various haunted objets d'art were rocketing around the room.

"I'm so sorry," Mina said, her cheeks streaked with tears. "Dad doesn't *get* mad like that. And he never sent us out of the house with my mom, even when it was really bad—"

"No, no," Caroline said, putting her hands around Mina's arms. "Honey, there is nothing for you to apologize for. This is a conversation that probably needed to happen a while ago, OK? It's adult stuff—old, wet, unstable conversational TNT. It wasn't caused by you. You just happened to be in the room when it went off."

Mina sniffled and buried her face in Caroline's shoulder. The haunted bric-a-brac settled onto their various shelves and surfaces with a clatter. Plover was not pleased—emphatically.

"Explain this, Miss Caroline," he demanded. "What has upset Miss Mina so thoroughly?"

"Ben and I had what people of our generation would call a…" Caroline said.

"Epic 'burn it down to the ground' fight?" Mina suggested, wiping at her eyes.

"You weren't even there," Caroline reminded her.

"I listened at the door," Mina said, her mouth drawing back at the corners.

Caroline gaped at her. "Mina!"

Mina flung out her arms. "He sent me after bear claws! What was I supposed to do?"

"Is that a modern euphemism?" Plover turned to Riley. "Miss, I request that you take my mail tray next door to Gray Fern Cottage so I might have a *discussion* with Dr. Hoult."

Riley chuckled. "Plover, you know that wouldn't work. The locks keep you in place here."

"Well, we didn't think the children were going to be granted magic before, did we?" Plover exclaimed. "We haven't tried taking my object out of the house!"

Caroline smiled sadly at him. "It's sweet that you're worried, but I can handle this myself."

Plover grumbled to himself in a distinctly British tone. "I'm not worried. I am…*put out* with the doctor."

"My dad never got this mad when he fought with my mom,"

Mina said. "Because he'd given up on her a long time ago. So, if I were you, I would consider that a good sign?"

"Grown-up business, Mina," Caroline told her.

"Fiiiine," she sighed.

Now that Mina's emotions were somewhat contained, Caroline finally noticed the papers and notebooks spread across the parlor's coffee table. Riley had been taking some pretty serious notes on her family tree, and...

"Um, Riley, when did you have time to test my DNA?" Caroline asked, pointing to the reports on the table.

"Did you know you drool in your sleep?" Riley asked. "Especially when you're on pain meds?"

"Rude," Caroline gasped. But even in her distress, she was grateful to have something to focus on besides her mess with Ben. She would grasp on to anything at this point, even ill-gotten genetic infographics.

"I used a private lab. I was checking for any sort of genetic markers that were unusual—good news, there weren't any. There's not a single marker for any sort of cancer or any gene-based disease. And I started thinking—isn't that in itself, weird? So I did some digging on genealogical sites, and no one on your father's side of the family dies of disease. If they don't leave the island, they live a long, long life. The people who marry into the family? Completely normal life spans and incidence of disease compared to their demographic. And that includes accidents. But any offspring they have with your father's side seems to pass along the disease-proof gene," Riley said.

"I'd never thought about it," Caroline conceded. "But yeah, I guess that's weird. Also, I'm assuming Edison helped you with this."

Riley looked offended. "*That's* rude."

"Sweetie, there are charts involved," Caroline said, giving her a sympathetic look.

"Fine," Riley huffed. "But I was thinking, it's extremely odd for Rose's ghost to be so intertwined with different family members. So, what if the attachment object isn't an object...it's you?"

Caroline frowned. "Sorry?"

"What if Rose is so attached to her family that the attachment object is your blood, literally? She can go off the island with you because she's attached *to you*. She'll protect and nurture you as long as you stay in her good graces. But if you break her rules, she can...I don't know, mess with your nervous system. When you think about it, human bodies are this awkward engineering wonder that shouldn't work, in terms of physics and physiology. So much can go wrong with every step we take. All it would take is a split second of her messing with your inner ear, preventing your optic nerve from communicating the right information with your brain—hell, making you place your foot wrong when you put it down, and bam—you step out in front of a bus or step off a ferry gangplank. Bottom line, she makes you pay dearly."

"That's sick," Caroline breathed.

"Does Rose strike you as a particularly well-adjusted person?" Mina asked.

"Good point," Caroline said. "So...why hasn't she hurt me in the last few months, now that she knows I'm aware of her?"

"You're pissing her off, but you're not violating the terms of her 'user agreement,'" Mina said. "Rose strikes me as a stickler for the rules."

"So, how do we get rid of the attachment object when *I'm* the attachment object?" Caroline mused.

"Very carefully?" Riley guessed.

There was a long moment of silence.

"Do you want to go back to talking about your fight with my dad?" Mina asked.

"Double nope," Caroline told her.

———————

It took a few hours before Caroline felt comfortable that Mina's magic was under control enough for her to go back home. As mad as she might be, Caroline did not want anyone or anything in Ben's house to be subject to magical teenage tornados.

Regular teenage tornados were bad enough.

Caroline promised Riley she was going to retreat to her cottage and drown her sorrows in ice cream—a strategy Plover did not support, but Riley contributed a pint of Regina's Rocky Road Trip. She'd changed into some real pants and a T-shirt she wouldn't miss in case of an ice cream mishap when her phone beeped. Sticking her spoon in her tub of ice cream, she checked her screen. Will's girlfriend had texted her.

That was...weird.

Tabby never texted her. Because they didn't need to talk to each other really, and there was no point in it when she could just text Will. Plus, Tabby lost her phone so often that there was maybe a forty percent chance she would see any phone communications.

The text read, Will says the Rose is finally ready for inspection! Come by ASAP. Your mom is so excited.

Tabby had attached a photo of Will and her mom, talking in the barroom at the Rose. Will's hand was raised, and his head tilted toward her as if he was trying to explain something. Her mother was looking into the camera with a stern expression.

Tabby added a second text that read, As excited as your mom gets.

Caroline laughed for what felt like the first time all day and tucked her phone into her back pocket. This was what she needed. Distraction. She rushed out of the kitchen, realizing about halfway to town that she'd left a perfectly good tub of Regina's ice cream on the counter.

Oof, she could never tell Regina, who would revoke Caroline's sprinkle privileges.

At least one thing was looking up, she supposed as she wove through the early evening crowds. If the Rose was ready for inspection, they might actually be ready to open by Labor Day and recoup some of their summer losses. She would have something to focus on, besides her hideous fight with Ben and the wreckage of…whatever they'd been on their way to becoming.

Just outside of the Rose, Caroline overheard tourists griping about the construction fencing, how they liked "that old place" and it wasn't a summer without a visit to the Rose. She smiled to herself, careful to slip through the mesh fence when she was relatively sure no one was looking. She didn't want someone to follow her through.

She used her keys to open the front door, locking it carefully behind her. The barroom was completely dark, and it was a weird feeling. She'd only ever seen it with at least ten neon signs lighting it.

Even in the dark, she could make out that the walls were lighter, a sort of pale blue or gray, maybe, which was nice. The space seemed more open, but she supposed that would look different when they brought in the tables. But it smelled pleasantly of new paint and freshly sawed wood, and that was a good change.

"Hello?" she called, setting her purse on the floor near the bar. "Mom? Will?"

Tabby had sent her a photo of her mom in the dining room. Where was she?

A shadow moved in the corner. The light color of the walls made it a little harder to see her, but Rose was there, smirking at her. Like she knew something that Caroline didn't. Which, she supposed, was fair.

Wait.

Now that she thought about it, the background of the photo had wood paneling. These walls were painted, so the photo couldn't have been taken that day.

Was this some *Parent Trap* thing from the kids? Could they have recruited Cole to get Caroline and Ben into the same place?

"Mina? Josh?" she called. "If this is you, kids, I appreciate it—and I'm sort of impressed that you got Tabby involved, but…"

The floorboards behind her squeaked and she thought, *This doesn't feel right.*

Stars exploded behind her eyes. The pain of being hit by a tiny motorbike was nothing compared to the agony at the base of her skull as she dropped to her knees. She couldn't even feel her feet, it hurt so bad. But she could feel her face when she flopped forward, and her cheek made contact with the floor. *What the hell did Rose hit her with?*

Her eyelids drooped as she heard footsteps behind her.

Wait, Rose couldn't make footstep sounds. And she was still hovering in front of her. As Caroline's eyes drifted shut and the sight of heavy boots seemed imprinted on the back of the retinas, she thought, *How many times can you be knocked out in a year?*

Chapter 15
Ben

HOW WAS IT POSSIBLE TO hurt this much without an actual physical injury?

There was a hollow ache in his chest that made it hard to breathe. He'd checked his blood pressure twice to make sure he wasn't having some sort of cardiac event. He never knew it was possible for the human heart to actually break, but here he was drinking at a bar, listening to the sad indie rock of his youth.

Granted, he was at his own kitchen bar, and he was drinking cold-pressed juice, but still...

Nope, it was sad, no matter how you sliced it.

Caroline wasn't answering his calls or his texts. In the old days, she would have at least told him to go fuck himself and then explained in graphic detail how and with what he could follow those directions. And she would have said it to his face. But this silence? It was unnerving. It was wrong. It told Ben exactly how badly he'd messed up.

He'd called in sick to the office for the first time in...he didn't know how long. He knew it was going to be a letdown to Dr. Toller, taking on all Ben's appointments for the day. But so much had happened and…he just didn't know how he'd messed things up so bad, so quickly.

The things he said, the stupid, horrible things he'd said. He didn't even know where they came from. He didn't realize those old feelings were still festering there, so close to the surface. But then he'd heard Caroline telling Mina to repeat their mistakes, acting as if it hadn't nearly destroyed them both. She'd spoken of avoiding Ben as if it hadn't hurt, as if she was doing him some sort of favor. As if that made it easier for him to leave her.

He thought he'd moved past it. He was wrong. And now, it was almost a day later and he hadn't heard from Caroline, and he was sinking back into that old feeling of having lost her. It was a familiar feeling that made acid rise into his throat.

He couldn't wallow in it. The kids needed him. He would need to keep this grief private. He would need to keep it together, even as the kids needed to interact with Caroline and the coven for guidance and safety and to keep Mina from becoming some sort of magical supervillain. He would need to…make Josh breakfast, because Bigfoot himself was lumbering into the kitchen.

Ben cleared his throat. "Morning."

Josh sat next to him at the kitchen bar. "So, you're a little mopey this morning."

"Your eyes are barely open," Ben noted. "And I'm fine."

"Dad, you're brooding like the lead in a '90s WB drama. All you need is artfully messy hair and a rain-splattered window to stare through."

Ben scoffed. "How do you know about WB dramas?"

"Streaming wars, Dad. Streaming wars." Josh crossed to the fridge and grabbed a bubbly water. He poured his dad a glass and slid it across the kitchen bar. "So, tell me your troubles."

It was possible his kids were spending too much time at the Rose.

"I don't want to drag you guys into my problems," Ben told him.

Josh snorted, sounding far too much like Caroline. "Well, that's the dumbest thing I've ever heard you say. And I once saw you try to order a *pizza* at that Burger Barn in Indiana."

"Their menu is confusing. And I was really tired, son."

Josh huffed, "Dad, we live with you. We know when you're having problems. And it actually scares us more when you try to hide them than when you just admit that it's happening."

When Ben could only stare at him, Josh rolled his eyes. "We *knew* when you and Mom were fighting. We know you tried to keep it away from us, and we appreciated it, but we heard, no matter how loud you turned up the TV. We knew you and Mom weren't OK. Some people just aren't meant to be married to each other. But knowing how hard you're trying to make a life for us, to make things easier on us, it makes up for a lot, Dad. We appreciate it. We appreciate you. And we know how weird it's been, how much life has changed since we got here. Your job. The house. Your daughter having secret ghost magic. Hell, your son getting to talk to ghosts as a friend of the coven is probably still pretty weird."

Ben snorted. "I'm sensing a 'but' coming."

"But pull your head out of your ass," Josh told him. "And go fix what you messed up with Caroline."

The lack of even an ounce of sympathy or remorse had Ben sputtering. "Wha—?"

"Mina told me about Pastry-gate," Josh said. "For some reason, you adults seem to think we don't hear things or talk to each other. It was an unfair fight, Dad. What was the point of all that therapy if you aren't willing to apply it real life? You brought up old stuff without warning, like it was something you just talked about. You told Mina and me that's a crappy way to fight and outlawed it as part of the Dubstep-Screamo Conversational Conflict Decrees."

Ben snorted at the memory of hashing out appropriate strategies to handle disagreements over music choices during their road trip.

"You brought Caroline into our lives," Josh said. "Of course, she's going to have advice for us. Hell, there are few people around here more qualified to give us advice, living here her whole life, having magic. And if her advice to Mina hurt your feelings, well, get over it. It's not necessarily about you. Caroline is right. Mina is way too young to be settling her whole future right now, even if this boy is dreamy and noncreepy. You and Caroline were too young to plan your whole lives out when you left for school. You both had a lot of growing up to do. And if Caroline sounded a little too…vehement? Is 'vehement' the right word?—forceful, emphatic, whatever other vocabulary list word that means 'making her point too hard'—in her advice to Mina, well, that should tell you how much it hurt to give you up. If it poked at a bruise in you, you need to process that in a way that doesn't wreck your whole relationship, life, and ability to be a morning person."

It was a humbling thing, to realize your kids were smarter than you. Ben reached up and fluffed Josh's hair as his son leaned his head against Ben's shoulder. Josh had to lean *down* to do it, which was even more of a blow to Ben's ego, but he would process that later.

"It's not wrong to want something for yourself," Josh told him. "And if that happens to be Caroline, who is really cool and can tolerate you *and* your kids? And your kids like her? A lot? Well, that works out, doesn't it?"

"I don't know if things are that simple, Josh," Ben admitted.

"Dad, is it possible that you're just being an incredible doofus?"

"Anything is possible, son."

———————

Ben wasn't proud of how long it took him to work up the nerve to leave the house. He'd been wrong. He wasn't too proud to admit that. But still, apologizing was going to be hard, even with the clear apology guidelines set forth in the Dubstep-Screamo Conversational Conflict Decrees.

He said goodbye to Josh and jogged down the stairs of Gray Fern. He stopped at the sidewalk between his gate and Riley's. He realized he didn't know where to look for Caroline. When they were kids, it would have been one place—the Rose. But now, she also could be at Shaddow House or her own house or Alice's shop or even Petra's bakery. He was happy for her, that she had so many options now, people to turn to—including his own children, whom he was starting to suspect would side with her in any future disputes.

That wasn't going to save him any time or shoe leather, as his father would have said.

Plover didn't answer the door, not that he would have been able to, Ben supposed. But the ghostly house father did stand behind the glass of the door and give Ben a silent, disapproving stare, which communicated all Plover needed to, Ben supposed. Searching the bakery, the cottage, and Alice's shop yielded similar nonresults. The Rose was locked up and everything inside was covered with drop cloths.

He didn't even see Cole inside, looking like the cover for a romance novel about a smoldering handyman werewolf.

Dick.

Calls to Gert, Alice, and Mina went unanswered. Finally, he had some luck, finding Riley and Alice outside of the courthouse-slash-police-department-slash-jail, talking to one of the locals, Dutch Hastings.

Maybe it wasn't luck. He knew the moment he saw the set of Riley's shoulders that something was wrong.

"I'm sure it's OK, Riley," Dutch was assuring her. "And you can't talk to Trooper Celia like that."

"I didn't call her names," Riley insisted. "I just reminded her that the first twenty-four hours after someone goes missing are the most important."

"And then you threw the F word at her," Alice reminded her gently.

"I did tell her to 'fucking Google it,' which was rude," Riley admitted, scrubbing a hand over her face. "I lost my temper, and I will apologize. Look, Dutch, I'm worried. It's not like Caroline not to answer her phone. Her mom hasn't heard from her since yesterday, and there was a carton of ice cream melting on the counter in her cottage. Caroline Wilton does not waste ice cream, period."

"I don't know if that's enough to build a missing persons case on, sweetheart," Dutch told her.

"What do you mean, 'missing'?" Ben barked.

Dutch jumped, turning to find Ben staring at him. He blushed under his salt-and-pepper scruff. "Ben, I'm sure that's not what's going on. You know Caroline's been at loose ends since the accident..."

Ben blanched. Alice looked panicked.

"No," Riley snapped. "Caroline wouldn't just disappear. She's not picking up her phone. She's not with Ben, or her parents, or her brothers."

"I'm sorry we didn't answer your calls, but we were inside talking to Celia. Riley's really worried, Ben. We can't feel her," Alice said quietly, glancing at Dutch. "Her...energy. It's like it's not on the island, and that's not good."

Dutch gave Riley an indulgent smile. "It's nice that you girls are so close. Caroline's gone a long time without good friends."

Edison jogged up the sidewalk to greet them. "Any word yet?"

Riley and Alice shook their heads. Edison put his arms around Riley. "It's going to be OK. No need to panic just yet."

"Oh, we are well past that," Alice told him, grimacing.

"Just give me a minute," Ben said. He opened his phone and texted Mina, asking her to dial Caroline's number. When Mina responded with a series of question marks, he added: She's not picking up for the rest of us, but she'll probably pick up for you.

A few minutes later, Mina texted back: No pickup. Should I worry?

Ben looked up to Riley. "No luck."

Riley shook her head. "If she's not picking up for the kids, she's not picking up for anybody."

"Oh no, now I feel bad taking up Celia's time with my stupid boat thing, especially when she's so busy with all the tourist nonsense going on this weekend," Dutch said, frowning. "It is a little weird that Caroline is MIA at the same time someone takes off with my boat," Dutch mused. He turned to Ben. "I just put it in the water for the summer and was heading over this morning to tune it up. Damned thing was missing."

A little line formed between Riley's eyebrows, something Ben had come to recognize as her "wheels turning" expression. "Does that happen a lot here? People stealing boats?"

"Not necessarily," Dutch said. "Sometimes it's just kids being stupid. Sometimes it's tourists being stupid. A lot of it is stupidity. I have a GPS tracker installed on it. Once Celia reports it to the mainlander police, they should be able to track it pretty easy."

"Really?" Riley marveled. "Can you tell when the boat was moved?"

"Oh, yeah," Dutch pulled out his cell phone and his reading glasses, perching them at the end of his nose while he peered down at the screen. He opened an app on his phone showing a map of Lake Huron. "It was part of the package when I bought it. Never thought I would have to use it. Says here, it moved last night around eleven o'clock, and it's stayed in the same place all day. Smart-ass kids left it near a campground, I bet. I just hope it's in one piece when Celia sends the state troopers out for it."

Ben watched as Dutch dragged his finger across the screen to an area across the lake, a state park known for picturesque but isolated campground sites.

"Thanks, Dutch," Riley said, standing on her tippy-toes and kissing his beard-roughened cheek. "Let me know if you hear anything from Caroline, OK?"

"Sure, Riley. Don't worry. It's not like she left the island," Dutch scoffed.

Suddenly, Ben was angry. As if there was no way Caroline could get hurt just because she was on the island. The whole island just took her for granted because she couldn't go anywhere. Why did they just accept that?

Riley's phone beeped with a text. She sighed in relief. "Caroline texted me."

"Oh, good," Dutch said, patting Riley's shoulder. "Well, I'm gonna go home and wait for my boat, like a runaway horse." Dutch ambled off.

Riley's expression darkened as she flipped through the screen on her phone. She turned the screen to Edison, Alice, and Ben. It was a photo of Caroline, her bound hands close to her face. She was bleeding from the back of her head. And she appeared to be unconscious, or at least, asleep.

The text accompanying it read: Do you miss me? If you ever want to see me again, pack up the locks and get ready to trade. Location to follow. Call the police, I'm dead. He will know. You're being watched right now. You have everything to lose, he doesn't.

"What the fuck?" Riley panted.

"Breathe," Alice told her, taking her hands. Meanwhile, Ben's knees seemed to crumple from under him. Edison caught his elbow and held him up.

Someone had taken Caroline. Someone had hit her over the head and tied her up and was threatening to kill her. How had this happened? After everything, he'd lost her. And the last words they'd said to each other were angry.

"We've got you," Edison murmured, even as his voice shook. "You're not alone. The girls are gonna fix this. OK? You're not going to lose Caroline."

Edison didn't sound sure of himself, but Ben appreciated that he was trying.

"Why didn't we feel her?" Riley demanded, glancing around at the tourists milling around them. "You've felt me panic before, when Edison tried to break up with me."

"Maybe she didn't have time," Alice whispered. "Maybe whoever has her knocked her out before she had a chance to be afraid and she's still unconscious."

"I don't know if that's a good thing or not," Riley replied.

"It's gotta be Clark," Edison said. "I walked past his office earlier and there was a sign on the door that said the firm was closed. Clark never closes the office."

"I don't know if that's proof," Alice said, frowning. "Who do you think *he* has watching us? Do you think we're dealing with a bunch of Welling heirs? People working for them? What if they've been watching us this whole time?"

"It doesn't matter. It doesn't matter who has her. All that matters is that we get to Caroline as quickly as possible," Riley insisted. "And we have the advantage of knowing where she is."

"So do we call the cops?" Ben asked. "I think we should call the cops."

"No, somebody *might* be watching us," Alice said. "We don't want to give him a reason to hurt Caroline."

"The person who took her thinks we have to wait until he gives us the location," Riley said. "He's not counting on us showing up off-schedule. So we just have to find a way to get across the lake unnoticed."

"Across the lake?" Ben asked.

"Some place called Starfall Views Camp-Inn Resort," Riley said. "Dutch showed me on his phone."

"It sounds like something Clark would do," Edison said. "He knows we would never look for him at a campground. It's sort of brilliant, in terms of camouflage."

"Well, it's not like we can take the ferry," Riley said. "If we *are* being watched, everybody's going to notice us leaving together. And if Edison goes anywhere near it, it will be island-wide news."

"I'm willing to swim it," Ben growled. "This guy is dangerous, and we need to get to Caroline as quickly as we can. I won't have her hurt."

"I don't think we'll have to swim." Edison scraped a hand over the back of his neck. "I have an idea."

Chapter 16
Caroline

CAROLINE'S HEAD HURT. AND NOT just in the "experimenting with cheap tequila" way. It felt like someone had whacked her over the head with a hammer.

Oh, shit, she was pretty sure someone had whacked her over the head with a hammer. Or a bottle. Or a boat oar. Why did she live around so many things that could be used to give her a concussion?

Ow.

She smelled…Funyuns? And exhaust fumes.

Was she being held hostage in a gas station?

She'd only visited a handful of gas stations in her lifetime, but they definitely had a memorable olfactory signature—like one of Nell's unsellable air fresheners. She forced her eyes to open and winced at the intrusion of light.

She was in some sort of vehicle. Her head was swimming so much that she couldn't tell if it was moving. Her nose was nearly bumping against beige-and-mauve rippled upholstery. She turned—or at least tried to—before she realized her feet were bound. Her sneakers scrabbled uselessly against the long bench seat she was lying on. Her hands were duct-taped in front of her. At least her mouth wasn't taped, because she was pretty sure she was going to throw up.

Breathe, she told herself, even as tears burned at her eyes. *Deep breaths; don't panic.*

She'd always told herself that she would stay calm if she'd ever found herself in this sort of situation—though she'd allowed that living on a tiny island where she knew pretty much everybody, her risk of kidnapping was pretty low. And she wasn't about to lose precious time freaking out.

She glanced around, seeing that she was inside some sort of camper—a really messy camper. In addition to dirty men's clothes and soiled towels, it was chock-full of hastily stacked canned food and camping supplies. The carpet was littered with bits of paper and mystery stains and... Was that Cheetos dust? Something about it smelled familiar, like clovey cologne and sawdust. Paint thinner.

Her stomach rolled up into her throat, even as she tried to place it. Where had she smelled that before?

And oddest of all, the missing portrait, the purple-lady ghost in her younger phase, was tacked to the far wall of the camper— perfectly straight and smooth.

"What the shit?" With considerable effort, Caroline rolled on her side and concentrated on not throwing up. Distantly, she could hear voices from the front of the camper—the "vehicle" part of the RV?

It took her a few seconds to focus enough to make out the words being said—though she wasn't sure whether it was the concussive head-ringing or the wall separating her and the truck cab. "Look, I don't know what your problem is. But she's right in there, just do your voodoo, or whatever, and finish her off so we can get this thing going."

Another voice, whisper-hissing, like a nest of snakes writhing against each other. "You're ransoming her. Isn't the point to keep her alive?"

"Not necessarily. The point is to scare Riley, throw her off her game," the man's voice replied. "Take away her resources and force her into cooperating. We can't get into Shaddow House without her. And if we take Caroline out of the equation, something I know you'll enjoy—I can slow Riley down enough that…"

He sounded familiar, but she couldn't quite place him. Ugh, she could think a lot faster if she just threw up already, she was sure of it. But then she'd be stuck in what amounted to a roomy car trunk with her own sick.

"I find I don't like this," the hissing voice answered. "It doesn't seem sporting, killing my descendant when they haven't left the island of their own choice. Standards are meant to be maintained."

Rose.

That had to be Rose. It was different from the strident screams she'd heard before, the steel-wool whispers. Mina had described her voice as cold, like icy nails rippling down her spine. Yeah, that was about right.

"You didn't have a problem with the previous, what was it, twenty-six?" the man asked.

Rose preened. "Twenty-seven. And each of them left the island, trying to leave me. So a price had to be paid."

"They don't even know you exist," the man protested.

"That doesn't change anything. I need to see them, to know they are holding up my family name. If it wasn't for me, they wouldn't even exist. I have the right to see everything they say and do. To leave me behind is an insult." Rose seethed. "How dare they? Walk away from me as if they had the right to live just as *they* see fit. I am the head of this family!"

The man snorted. "That wasn't true, not even when you were alive."

"Without me, the family would have been nothing, had nothing," Rose scoffed. "Their purpose was to stay where we had wealth and influence, to fulfill my vision. It was only when they didn't follow my instructions that there were problems. And the generations after? There was no way to communicate with them, so I was forced into more drastic measures."

Caroline blinked. How could Rose sound so...bored, as she was describing the murder of her own flesh and blood?

"The point of the matter is, I don't see how this helps you accomplish your goal," Rose rasped. "Even if that foolish Denton girl brings you these...whatever they are, she only has a handful of them. It doesn't get you the full collection."

"Yes, but it will slow her down, set her back. It will give me enough time to figure out another plan." The man sounded desperate, and not entirely bright. "Riley's been fucking up my plans since the minute she stepped onto the island, ordering me around, telling me where to go, keeping me from looking for the locks as ordered. But you, you were like a gift, when you reached out to me, like the universe was just *handing* me a new way of getting Riley to do my work for me."

"Oh, I see," Rose said when he finally stopped talking. "Yes, how clever of you."

Whoever this was, it felt like Rose was fucking with him. She was just toying with him so he would keep talking, give her more to work with. Wow, her great-great-however-many-great-grandmother was sort of a gangster. Caroline might have respected her for it if she wasn't so damned awful.

OK, first step, sitting up. You can't fight evil from a prone position.

It took a few tries, but Caroline used a combination of wriggling and mental cursing to force herself up.

Oh, jeez, that was a mistake.

Caroline leaned her head back against the window. Sunlight poured through the glass, warming the back of her neck and head. *Oh, that was nice.* How could she appreciate something as mundane as sunshine on her John Denver-less shoulders when she was being abducted by her dead relative and a mystery guest?

Focus. *Focus.* She'd read something online once about how women should yank their hands down against their hips if they ever found their hands bound with duct tape. But, at the moment, it felt like high-handed advice written by people who had never been hit in the head with a hammer-slash-possibly-a-boat-oar.

She took several deep breaths and stood, bracing herself against the cluttered counter when her brain protested mightily. She raised her hands, groaning quietly, and slammed her joined wrists against her hips. She hissed in pain but did it again. And again, harder and harder, until she could fully swing her hands behind her, and the duct tape finally gave way with a *riiiip*.

"Oh, thank you," Caroline panted, nearly crying at the relief of being able to rub her hands together.

And it was in that moment that she realized that she hadn't heard Rose or the mystery asshole talk for several minutes.

And her ankles were still bound.

Shit.

The door to the RV swung open. Caroline spotted a small cast-iron frying pan on the counter and slung it toward the movement.

Cole ducked just in time, letting the frying pan fly out the camper's open door.

It was all she could do not to flop face-first onto the disgusting RV carpet. It hurt knowing she'd been fooled, that she'd let this man into her bar, into space shared with her mother, with Mina. But Caroline supposed she should just be grateful that Cole hadn't taken one of them.

He'd played all of them with his *aw-shucks-I'm-just-here-to-help* schtick, and they'd underestimated him. Had he been colluding with Rose all this time? Why had she reached out to him? Had he known she was there before he arrived on the island?

The coven was so used to looking for clever, underhanded miscreants, like Kyle, like Rose. They'd forgotten that sometimes, you had to watch for who seemed harmless.

Was her coven safe? Riley? Alice? The kids? Would her friends come for her, or was she on her own? Maybe it was better that way. Ben could find some other woman, better suited for him, for his kids. Yes, the loss would hurt Riley and Alice, but Josh and Mina would be there for them.

And her family? Oh god, her parents. Maybe her dad would

take her advice, since it was the last conversation they'd had…and not sink into another guilt-fueled spiral. Maybe her brothers would step up and help… Yeah, that didn't seem likely.

"Oh, Caroline, does that mean we're not going to stay friends?" Cole simpered at her in mock sympathy.

"Asshole," Caroline sniped at him, even as she wobbled on her feet.

She picked up a can of soup from the table and whipped it toward him, hitting him square in the chest. He yelped. "Bitch!"

"I don't miss twice, and your sloppy ass left me in here with a camper full of projectiles," Caroline said.

He rolled his eyes and reached forward with his massive paws. Ducking out of her swinging range, he yanked at her taped ankles, making her flail backward as he pulled her out of the RV. She supposed she should be happy she didn't smack her head against the counter on her way down.

He left her splayed in the dirt, with Rose standing over her, peering at her with curiosity. Oh, great. "I gotta tell you, in terms of grandparents, you *suck*," Caroline spat. "And I've seen Alice dealing with her grandparents, so the bar for sucking is pretty high."

"How hard did you hit her on the head?" Rose asked Cole.

She wasn't anyplace she knew on Starfall. She could hear lapping in the distance, and could smell the exhaust from a highway somewhere nearby.

Oh, no.

Caroline sat up, finally losing the war with her nausea and throwing up into the dirt. At least she wasn't trapped inside with it.

"Classy," Cole said, smirking at her. Caroline grabbed the frying pan from where it had landed and brought it crashing down on Cole's foot. He howled, and she took aim at his knees. He kicked it out of her hands and slapped her, making her cheekbone feel like it had buckled under his huge hands.

"All of you think you're so smart, you witches—hell, you Wiltons," Cole huffed. "You know your family forgot I was around after a week or so? They acted like I wasn't even in the room when they were talking. Giving me all sorts of information about where you were, what you were doing. That bimbo Tabby left her phone on the bar half the times she was there. It was only a matter of time before I got into it."

Cole pulled the bright-pink glitter-covered cell phone from his pocket and waggled it at her.

"Dammit, Tabby," she grumbled. She looked around what seemed to be a campsite. They were the only vehicle parked in a fairly secluded section of an RV park. Cole had parked broadside, facing the water. A rusted tan-and-white sign to her right stated it was the Starfall Views Camp-Inn Resort. She'd heard of it—a past-its-prime campground where tourists made reservations when they had no other options. No wonder there were no other RVs nearby.

Oh, shit. She was definitely off-island. How long had she been gone? Did it count when Rose took her off Starfall herself?

She needed some sort of guidebook for hereditary magic curse rules.

"Look, it's nothing personal," Cole insisted, crouching next to her. "You have something the Wellings want—the locks. The

Wellings have something I want—money. And I just happened to have put myself in the position where I can get access to both."

He reached into his back pocket and pulled out one of the locks. It looked...different than the others they'd found, worn and dulled by age. It looked like it had been handled quite a bit by hands that were...well, the sort of hands that were OK with living in a Cheetos dust–covered RV.

Caroline could feel the cold, angry energy emanating from the metal loops. It sent a shudder down her spine, being this close to a lock without her coven.

"I found this one in the flue of the kitchen fireplace, when I was doing Riley's aunt's remodel," he said. "Didn't tell the Wellings, though. It was a bit too early in our relationship to know how much I should show them, how gullible they were."

"The Wellings sure did love hiding those in fireplaces," she muttered. She had to get that lock back from Cole. Poor freaking Riley was back on Starfall, looking for locks that weren't even in the house.

"Well, they had to work within the original footprint of the house," Cole said. "Honestly, the Wellings are lucky that the Dentons haven't found more of these over the years. When you think about it, it's fascinating that the original shape of the house hasn't changed much, given all of the altera—"

"Is that the only one you found?" Caroline asked.

"You have no appreciation for historical architecture." Cole sighed.

"I care a little bit more about my throbbing freaking head than listening to you waffle on about old buildings," Caroline seethed at him. "Can we just skip to the part of the supervillain speech where you tell me your big plans? How do you even know about the locks in the first place?"

"Oh, anybody who can see ghosts knows about the Wellings, how the Dentons crushed them, sent them scurrying underground," Cole laughed. "And families like mine? We don't have pedigree, but we see enough to recognize an opportunity. The locks control ghosts? I want as many of them as I can get. I don't care about catching them all. I just want to catch enough, enough to run my own agenda. The Wellings were dumb enough to stake me while I sent them bullshit progress reports, and that's on them for not watching me closely enough."

"There's a whole underground communication system for families who can see ghosts? Like 'Spiritualist Facebook'?" Caroline asked, her hand creeping across the ground toward the frying pan. Cole stomped on it, making her cry out in pain.

"Word of mouth has been around a lot longer than social media," Cole said blithely, as if he hadn't just broken one of her fingers.

"That's quite enough," Rose intoned from her standing position. Cole's head jerked upward, as if he'd forgotten she was there. "I won't allow you to injure my descendant's person any more than necessary."

"Necessary?" Caroline scoffed, cradling her injured hand against her chest. "Also, can I just ask, what the hell is going on with the portrait? It's not your attachment object, so...why so obsessed with it?"

"Just because my spirit isn't permanently joined to the canvas doesn't mean I don't enjoy looking upon it, remembering the best days of my life," Rose said, smiling through the open door at her own face. "Proper deference for my portrait was how young Cole here first gained my attention. But now..." She turned to Cole. "I mentioned before, how I ran my family, making sure they did as they were told. I made sure they were useful. You're no longer useful."

Cole's dark eyes narrowed. "What are you saying?"

"I believe the expression is, 'I'll take things from here,'" Rose said, her smile thin. She leaned over him, the smoke of her form enveloping him.

Cole held out the lock, balancing it on his palm. "Stay back!"

Caroline arched a brow, "Really? It's not a 'cross versus vampire' situation. I thought your family had experience with this."

"Well, how does it work?" Cole practically shrieked, shaking the lock like a blinking flashlight. "How do I make the lock control her?"

"You don't know?" Caroline marveled. "You don't have magic?"

"It's not about magic, it's about the locks!" Cole insisted.

"Oh, buddy, you just peed on an electric fence, and you don't even realize it," Caroline sighed, shaking her head. "I would almost feel bad for you, if you hadn't hit me over the head with a hammer and broke my finger."

"It was a bottle," Cole told her.

"Still rude," Caroline grumbled.

"I'm bored," Rose sighed, dragging the misty tips of her fingers down Cole's cheek. "And you're becoming more of a nuisance than you're worth."

"But you can only hurt members of your own family!" Cole yelled.

Rose's smile was downright feral. "My dear boy, where on Earth did you get that impression?"

The corners of her mouth drew back into an impossible, manic smile as she plunged her hand into his chest. Cole screamed, clutching at his heart. He looked to Caroline as if she could help him, but she wasn't even sure she could work magic with her hand mangled. She didn't know what Rose was doing and had no idea how to counteract it. Cole's face went pasty gray, and he slumped to the ground. His breathing was labored, and he seemed to have to work to draw in the oxygen that fueled the next breath.

Rose patted his cheek. "Now, be quiet while I talk to my, well, let's just say 'granddaughter.'"

Caroline scrambled back against the RV, tugging at the tape on her ankles as Rose loomed closer. She searched the ground for something sharp, something to cut at her bindings. Instead, her hand closed over the lock Cole had lost in his death throes.

"Now, what to do with you," Rose murmured, tilting her head this way and that, staring at Caroline like she was a specimen on a pin. "I must admit, your little branch of the family has vexed me the most. The amount of whining from the lot of you was just intolerable, and your father, staying away from the inn. The audacity."

"It's a bar," Caroline replied.

"It's an *inn*. I am not a barkeeper. And your father is the least appreciative of the lot, for the legacy I've given him."

"You killed his *son*," Caroline reminded her, her good hand searching the ground for a rock or a stick or...something to tear at the duct tape.

"Because he was straying from the path I made for the family! Your father should have *thanked me*. Even he told your brother not to leave the island, to stay on Starfall where it was safe! And your stubborn, disobedient brother refused to listen—so proud, always thought he knew better! Sharper than a serpent's tooth are the objections of a willful, disobedient child!"

"That is not the quote," Caroline said.

Rose carried on as if she hadn't even spoken. "All your brother had to do was stay where he was told, to follow my instructions, but he had to go see that *girl*, that *strumpet*, writing so freely to a man. She was no fit woman to marry a *Wilton*. And I wouldn't have it. He had to serve as a lesson to the rest of you. And you, my Caroline..."

"Don't ever call me that," Caroline snapped.

"Don't interrupt me, it's rude," Rose sniffed. "You were one of the few bright spots in a dismal generation. You were always obedient, always aware of the consequences for moving away from me. It pains me to do this, but clearly, your family needs another reminder of the consequences of rebellion."

Keep her talking. Caroline sucked in a deep breath while her brain tried to process the potential outcomes of this situation. *She loves the sound of her own voice, loves being in control. Keep her talking until the others can show up or you can figure out a plan.*

"So...what?" Caroline asked. "You're just going to keep killing us off until there are no more of us left to disappoint you? There's only a handful of us left at this point."

"I'd rather you be dead than a poor reflection on me," Rose said primly.

"No one knows you *exist*," Caroline said.

"Perhaps I should save myself the trouble," Rose mused with that clinical detachment. "I could take you all in one final act of mercy. The constables are eager to find a plausible reason for the unexplainable, even in this age of electricity and technology."

"You might get me," Caroline said, remotely registering the sound of buzzing in the distance, a low hum echoing over the water. "But it's not going to have the effect on my coven that you think it will. I don't think you'll ever be able to go home. They'll put wards on the Rose, so you can never go back in. Hell, they might even re-create the locks, so they can banish you from the island. You overplayed your hand, like most tyrants do, because you think you're never going to run into someone meaner and crazier than you."

The buzzing noise got louder and louder. And out of the corner of her eye, Caroline saw an object flying toward her. It was bright red and coming at her with a dizzying rate of speed.

"Caroline, cover your eyes!" Josh thundered over a bullhorn. Caroline shrieked and threw her hands over her head. She grunted at the pain in her hand as something struck the RV over her head. Salt and herbs rained down around her.

Rose screamed, half-insult, half-rage, as she sizzled away.

When the "sprinkling sound" stopped, Caroline looked around to see herself surrounded in a not-quite-perfect circle of damp rock salt. Remnants of red latex laid scattered among rose petals and herbs. This had a certain teenage girl's brilliantly spiteful fingerprints all over it.

Caroline cackled as Rose's damaged form lumbered away into the woods. "You forgot about magic. You forgot about how much people could love each other. And you forgot about Mina freaking Hoult."

Swiping wet salt from her cheeks, she looked toward the water to see Ben, Riley, and Alice waving at her from a little speedboat. Caroline huffed out a joyous cry as they beached it. She was so glad to see Ben, as well as the kids, who were zooming up beside the boat on a neon-green Jet Ski...and Ben seemed really surprised to see them.

Which was weird.

Mina was holding some sort of balloon slingshot thing. Josh was driving, which seemed to be the thing that was making Ben nervous. That was reasonable, considering Josh was operating a bull-horn with one hand while steering with the other. Caroline wasn't a parent, but that seemed really, really unsafe.

The sight of Riley helping Edison flop over the stern of the boat made Caroline's chest go warm with affection. Edison got in a boat. For her. Her heart was touched.

All of them spilled out of their watercrafts, Riley supporting Edison as he kissed the silty shore. Alice sprinted up the beach, pocketknife at the ready to cut Caroline's feet loose.

"Was that a water balloon full of rock salt?" Caroline asked, grinning at her.

Alice threw her arms around Caroline, kissing her cheeks, her brow, and then spitting out the grains of rock salt clinging to her lips.

Mina was next, hovering at Caroline's side and sobbing against her chest. Josh carefully patted Caroline's shoulder. She covered his big hand with her uninjured fingers.

"The trick was only adding the water at the last minute so the salt didn't dissolve, and filling it partially with air to keep the latex at tension—it only worked because the ride across the lake was pretty short," Josh said. "And of course, the water-balloon catapult that we stole from a kid on the beach."

"It doesn't strike me as the sort of thing a child should have, really," Caroline mused. She had to keep talking about this nonsense, or she would bawl. She would lose all control of herself and sob out her hysterical relief.

Nope, *nope*, too late. Ben baseball-slid in front of her and wrapped her and Josh and Mina in his arms. Caroline was sobbing anyway. Mina and Josh gracefully exited from the group hug and let Alice and Riley hug them while Ben checked Caroline's injuries between fierce hugs.

"I'm so sorry," Ben said, holding Caroline. "I said stupid, asinine, useless things because I was hurt and I was scared. I *am* so scared to lose you again. I don't think I could survive that."

"I said stupid, asinine, useless things too," she said. "Because I'm scared that I'm not enough and I won't ever be. And you need more and the kids deserve more and…"

Ben stopped her mouth, kissing her. "Bullshit, I need *you*. I think my kids deserve *you*. And you deserve my kids, and I mean that in a nice way, not in a vindictive way."

"Thanks, Dad," Josh huffed, stripping out of his life vest.

Caroline laughed, kissing Ben. The kids, to their credit, uttered not one single "ew."

"It's going to take us a while to figure this whole thing out, but we're going to do it, because it's important. You're important. I love you. I've always loved you. I will always love you," he swore.

"I love you, too," she said, kissing him.

"This is all very sweet, but I'm kind of feeling the gathering energy of a certain bitch-faced hag-ghost," Riley huffed, helping a pale, shaken Edison sit down next to Caroline. An angry hiss sounded in the trees. "Yeah, I said it, you hateful old wench!"

"Thank you, Edison," Caroline said, patting his knee with her good hand. "I know what that cost you."

"You're family," Edison panted. "And somebody has to be here to post your bail."

"Well, the good news is, I'm alive," Caroline said, nodding to Cole's body. "But Cole is not. Rose killed him."

"Well, now I see that bail joke was mistimed," Edison muttered.

"Dang." Riley blanched as Ben moved toward Cole's body, feeling for a pulse. He shook his head.

"I knew she was capable of it," Alice mused. "All ghosts are capable of it, really." She paused to shudder. "It's just so awful."

"She is awful," Caroline agreed. "And we really need to banish her before she takes out my entire family."

"How did you even get here," Ben asked his kids, moving Caroline to his lap as he examined her injured hand. "The last I saw you, you were under Plover's supervision. Reading."

"We stole a Jet Ski!" Mina cried, her cheeks red but drying. She laughed at her father's expression.

"We're going to talk about that later," Ben promised them. "You don't know how to run a Jet Ski."

"Video games," Josh said, shrugging. "They're very educational. And Mina's kidding. We told Dutch we were willing to go look for his boat, to confirm the location, and he said we could borrow the Jet Ski if we gassed it up before we brought it back."

"And I'm going to have to talk to Dutch about *that* later," Ben sighed.

Mina rolled her shoulders, uncomfortable under some invisible strain. "Rose is here, and she's gathering herself. She's...not happy."

"But she's smug," Josh said, a shiver running down his spine. "She thinks she's won something. Caroline, how long have you been off the island?"

"No clue, but hey, look, a ghost lock," Caroline said, holding up the lock.

"You found one!" Riley cried, grinning.

"Technically, Cole did when he was remodeling the kitchen for your aunt," Caroline said. "So...pretty sure we're gonna need to search this hell pit on wheels before we call the authorities."

"Good note, after we push Rose out of this dimension," Alice said.

"We brought some of the locks with us," Mina said, pulling a tote bag over her shoulder. "Maybe they will help."

Riley frowned. "You did what?"

"Plover told us where they were hidden in your office, so we brought them. You took one outside before without destabilizing the house, so we thought it would be OK. I figured we might need them if we found Caroline and the ghost," Josh said. "Which, given your expression, is something else we're going to have to talk about later."

"Yes, yes, we will." Riley nodded, clearly trying to maintain her cool. "All of us, plus Plover, will have a conversation about coven safety and operational security and doors that only respond to my retinal scan."

The kids looked chastened, but Mina insisted. "But we helped, right? If one lock opens a pinhole portal, several locks could open a portal big enough to shove Rose through."

Riley agreed. "I will validate your choices, once my terror runs out."

"OK!" Mina said brightly. "But she's gathering right outside the salt circle, coming back like ghost herpes."

Ben scowled.

"You're the one who insisted on a thorough health education!" Mina reminded him as Josh helped Caroline to her feet. "Now, Dad and Edison and...Cole's body just sit there and try not to get hurt."

"Josh, get in the circle, just in case," Riley said. "I'm not taking the chance of failing because we needed our 'listener' involved."

"Got it." Josh handed a lock to each member of the coven.

"We're going to have to move outside the salt's protection," Alice said. "Remember, Rose is manipulative and cruel. And she's on the verge of losing, which is when manipulative and cruel people do their worst."

"Oh, little Alice," Rose crooned, materializing just outside the salt range. "You would know more about manipulative people than anyone, wouldn't you?"

Alice paled slightly. Caroline touched her hand. "Sorry, I said something to her about your grandparents."

Alice nodded, and the coven surrounded Rose's re-formed mist.

Rose turned on Riley, grinning, a mad glint in her eyes. "I knew your ancestors. Snobbish wastrels that they were, thought they were too good to mix with my family."

"Nah, it was probably just your personality," Riley told her.

"Those little toys won't work for you two, because you're not Dentons," Rose told the kids, smirking. "You're just castoffs, so unlovable, your mother didn't even want you."

Mina and Josh smirked right back. "Yeah, yeah, change the playlist, because you're on repeat, you half-assed mean girl."

"And they're Dentons if my magic says they're Dentons," Riley said. "And my magic says they are, so suck it!"

On opposite sides, Riley and Caroline passed their locks around the circle. Each person followed, drawing a magical line from their lock to the next person's, creating a circle of energy around Rose.

"You wouldn't do this to your own blood," Rose insisted, her voice wheedling. "You, the best girl, the sweet girl who does all she can to take care of her family. You wouldn't do this to a Wilton. What would your poor father say?"

"Oh, that was the wrong card to play," Josh scoffed. "Mentioning her father. You just don't understand actual human emotions, do you?"

Riley and Caroline, holding their locks again, pushed them forward until the circle pressed in toward Rose and opened over her head. Wincing, Caroline used her good hand to draw Alice's pocketknife across her injured hand's palm, blood welling over the loops of her lock. Cole's lock, which in its own way made sense. Blood would bind the magic, bind Rose, break the hold this woman had over them, generation after generation. She was afraid to look up, to see what was on the other side of that circle, but she did it, because she wanted to know that wherever Rose was going, it was a fit punishment for what she'd put their family through.

The void was formless. Rolling black nothing, cold and empty and silent. And somehow, all the more terrifying for its emptiness. There was no comfort. There was no peace. There was a void. That was what Rose deserved.

"We'll go on, long after you've forgotten your own name in that sea of nothing," Caroline told her. "I'll never mention you again. I'll never tell my family what you did or who you are. I'll go through the histories and remove any trace of your name. I'll talk to my father about renaming the bar. We're going to be happy. And you'll be nothing."

"You don't know what you're doing," Rose insisted. "You need me, the family needs me, to keep them in line. You're going to find out just how small you are."

"Shut. Up!" Caroline shouted, clenching her fist and raising it, pressing Rose up through the portal. Then she and Riley drew their locks back, and the portal closed. All five of them repeated the motion, breaking the circle of light.

In unison, they sank to their knees and dropped their locks into the center of the circle. They breathed together, each not quite sure what to say about what they'd just done. Caroline glanced over her shoulder, where Ben and Edison sat against the RV, wide-eyed.

"Is anybody hungry?" Josh asked, breaking the silence. "I could really go for some pizza. Does doing magic make you hungry? Is this how it feels?"

"You're always hungry," Mina said. "And you seem unaware

that there are food groups other than pizza. And Pop-Pies. My Pop-Pies. My *illicitly obtained* Pop-Pies."

"Don't start with the Breakfast Food Streaming Service Peace Accords," Alice said, laughing.

"I'm not sure they brought about any sort of real peace," Riley added, shaking her head.

"It's a fragile peace," Caroline said. "As flaky and insubstantial as a Pop-Pie crust itself."

"Seriously, I'm hungry now," Josh complained. "Shoving mean old ladies through interdimensional portals to a possible hell is *exhausting*."

Edison snickered. "I'm willing to cover the pizza, and to test out Caroline's newfound possibly-not-cursed-ness."

"I don't think I appreciate the casual nature of your tone, sir," Caroline replied. "And you're just trying to avoid getting back on the boat."

"Yes." Edison nodded. "Yes, I am."

Chapter 17
Caroline

SEVERAL POP-PIE NEGOTIATIONS LATER...

IT WAS WEIRD FOR CAROLINE to walk from Gray Fern Cottage to her parents' house. She'd trudged the same path back and forth from her cottage to The Wilted Rose, over and over, for so long, it had become a muscle memory. How long had she stayed in that unhealthy pattern, just because it was safe? But she supposed, after all, it wasn't safe, because Rose had basically been keeping them hostage on the island under the threat of death for generations—even if they didn't realize it.

At least, that was what Caroline told herself, when she found herself standing in front of the bar. It felt like some strange alien world that she was afraid to enter now. The last time she'd walked through that door, she'd been ambushed. She'd nearly died. It wasn't the center of her world anymore, the thing she had to fight for, and she wasn't sure when that changed. It was probably the moment that Riley stepped off the ferry.

She'd spent so much time being afraid of what could happen if she left the island, she never considered the threats that could come from it. But now the world had opened up to her with a speed and breadth that left her dizzy. And she hadn't decided what to do with it just yet. She'd never considered the possibilities of her life, and everything felt like too much too soon, and yet not enough.

She opened the door and found her family polishing glasses, resetting the taps. The family tchotchkes, minus Rose's painting, had been replaced in the alcove over the bar. Wally looked miserable, but no more so than Will, who—according to Mina—was coming up on his fifth consecutive day of work without being able to get out of it. Her mother had actually gone to Will and Tabby's place to roust him off his couch and march him into work. Caroline cleared her throat to keep the laugh contained.

"Hey there, apple dumpling," Denny called from the swinging kitchen door. He carried a crate of carefully plastic-wrapped liquor bottles to the bar top and set it down.

The kitchen was largely unchanged, other than a coat of fresh paint, and as a historical piece, the bar was also treated to a new varnish face. But the ceiling was whole again, and snowy white. The wood paneling had been painted the color of fading sea mist. The outside windows had been replaced with a french door added so the barroom opened out onto a properly braced and refurbished deck. The ancient floor had been stripped and refinished to a high shine. Hell, Caroline was pretty sure that Cole rebuilt all the booths on the exterior wall.

The new color, the new shiny finishes, the lack of "spilled beer smell" made the barroom seem like an entirely different place. It was open and clean and free from the regrets that weighed the very grain of the wood down for centuries.

Cole might have been a treacherous, murdery psycho, but he did a nice job with carpentry.

Gert sidled up to Caroline, carrying another crate of booze. Caroline hissed, taking the crate out of her hands. "Oh, Mom! Your shoulder's not up to that just yet."

"Well, consider it physical therapy," Gert grunted.

"Dad's here?" Caroline asked.

Gert's brows rose. "Well, apparently, he gave some thought to what you said about us needing him. And he decided you were right, it was time to sit up, or something."

Caroline smiled. Across the room, her dad winked at her.

"I don't remember asking you to talk to your father on my behalf," Gert drawled.

"Well, somebody had to," Caroline said. "And we don't count on Wally and Will for things."

Gert pressed her lips together, trying to suppress a smile. "Caroline."

"I know, I know," Caroline snickered, feeling a bit more confident in poking at the bruise of her brothers' previously coddled state. "They help in their own ways."

Gert nodded. "Exactly."

"Unless those ways involve lifting," Caroline added.

Gert snorted. "Caroline."

Caroline's lips twitched. "Or cleaning."

"Sweetheart," Gert said.

"Or unpleasant tasks, of any kind," Caroline said, shaking her head.

"Caroline Anne!" Gert laughed.

"That was the last one," Caroline promised before lifting her hands and crying, "Oh, or saying no to Tabby!"

Caroline felt a light tap on her butt, courtesy of her mom's left foot. She snickered.

Her father wasn't going to just magically "get over" Chris's death—if there was such a thing as getting over a death—but there was a better chance for him to heal, now that he was out in the world. Her family didn't know about the mess with the ghosts or their selfish ancestor or the number of times Caroline had almost died in the past year. And they didn't need to know, because they were safe now...as safe as one could be in today's world.

Nope, no gloomy thoughts now. Today was a day for new beginnings and hope and all that shit.

Wally huffed and puffed across the room, slinging a cleaning rag over his shoulder. He did not take the case out of Caroline's hands, but she didn't expect him to, really.

"Oh, Caroline, thank God you're back," he said as Will approached from behind. "I think I'm done for the day. I've been at this for, oh, three-four hours?"

"Yeah, I've got to get back home," Will said, stacking a couple of glasses on top of Caroline's case. "Tabby needs me to empty the dishwasher."

"No."

Will blinked at her. "What do you mean, 'no'?"

Caroline rolled her eyes and handed her burden to Will, glasses and all. "I mean, no, I'm not here to work. I came by to officially give you this."

She took a carefully folded piece of paper out of her back pocket and smacked it, open, against Wally's chest. He frowned at it while he read it. "What's this?"

"It's my official notification of vacation days I plan on taking over the next month. There will be fourteen of them, starting with today."

"What?" Will scoffed. "What do you mean?"

"Vacation days, which I'm allowed as part of my employment at the Rose," Caroline said. "It's less than a tenth of what I'm owed, in terms of back-vacation days. Back-cation? I'm not sure what you'd call it, but Mom and Dad wrote the policy so they'd accumulate year to year, so if you don't like it—or the fact that I'm going to be taking quite a few of them over the next year or two—go talk to them."

"Well, I'm just gonna take my vacation days, then," Wally said. "I don't want to be here while you're off. That's not fair."

"You don't have any accrued vacation days, Wally. Every time you called in 'I don't feel like it,' that was a vacation day," Caroline said.

"You don't know that," Wally told her.

"Who do you think handled the office and all the employment paperwork?" Caroline asked, shaking her head.

Will laughed, but Caroline asked, "What the hell are you laughing at? You're in the hole two vacation days."

"That's not what a vacation day is!" Will cried.

"You took the paycheck, didn't you?" Caroline sighed. "Boys, for a long time, you've let Mom and I carry the weight of the bar. It's not fair, and it's not OK, and I'm not doing it anymore."

"But it's just easier to let you handle all this stuff," Wally said, tossing her vacation paper aside.

"For you, yes, I'm sure it is easier. But I am planning to have a life in the near future. So I need you two to get your shit together and put in an effort here. I'm not even talking about an extraordinary effort, just the bare-minimum effort, like showing up for shifts that you're scheduled for...when you're scheduled for them. Now, if you'll excuse me, Ben and I need to pack up the kids. We're taking them to Ann Arbor for the weekend. Mina's thinking about U of M," Caroline said.

"Wait, what?" Gert dropped what she was doing and turned to Caroline. "What do you mean 'for the weekend?' You can't do that."

Caroline opened her mouth to explain, but Gert interrupted her. "Not because we need you at work, but it's not *safe*, Caroline, you know why. You can't leave the island for more than a day. None of you can. You know that."

Will and Wally looked uncomfortable, and for once, Caroline felt sorry for them. They didn't talk about the curse, out in the open. It was like they thought speaking about it would make it real. They couldn't pretend it away if they talked about it.

She closed her eyes. "Look, I can't explain why I know, but the problem that has, let's say, haunted our family for generations? It's not going to be a problem anymore."

"What problem?" Will asked, glancing at his parents.

"Does this have anything to do with all that time you've been spending at Shaddow House?" Gert asked.

"Yes, I can't explain what that is, but we've been working on resolving that problem for our family. And I have every reason to believe that we don't have to worry from now on. We can leave the island, come and go freely."

"Oh, Caroline, you haven't done anything...silly, have you?" Denny asked.

For once, Wally looked truly concerned. "Like signed any weird-looking documents in blood or anything?"

"No. There have been no Faustian bargains, I promise," Caroline said, laughing. "It has to do with the Shaddows. And our family, and how long we've lived here. And something that happened a long time ago that wasn't our fault. And we don't have to pay for that something anymore."

"That sounds crazy," Will told her.

"Yeah, I know," Caroline conceded.

Denny shook his head, his face pale. "Honey, I'd love to believe you, but it's always been this way for us."

"I know," Caroline conceded. "And I know that it's hard to believe, and I'm not giving you a lot of details. Just trust me."

"And what, you think you need to just take a weekend away to test the theory?" Gert asked. "That's just stupid, and you are not a stupid girl."

"I don't need to test it," Caroline replied. "I already did. Ben and I took the kids to Traverse City last week. We rented a house for the weekend. It was great."

She smiled at the memory. It had been a heady experience. Colors seemed brighter. Food tasted better. Music sounded sweeter. She'd practically stuck her head out the car window while rolling down the highway.

Wally gaped at her. "You did what?"

"OK." Caroline clapped her hands together once. "This was fun; see you in a while. Enjoy the move-in. Bye."

Denny cleared his throat. "Caroline."

Caroline called, "I was gone for three days. It was fine."

Gert found her voice to yell. "Caroline Anne Wilton!"

But Caroline was already out the door. Behind her, the Rose loomed, unhaunted.

The door of Shaddow House opened to her as if she was a Denton born. She walked in, smiling to herself. Her family was here. Ben was sitting by the fire, going over patient files. Josh and Mina were seated at the coffee table, squaring off against a lovely blown-glass chess set haunted by Nicholas, a child prodigy who died in the 1980s. Nicholas was very patient with their novice moves, grateful to hang out with people his age—sort of. Edison and Riley were lounging on the couch, quietly enjoying the scene.

Caroline wondered, did they get lonely, sometimes, in their house on the hill? How long would it be before they changed the picture with new children or marriage? How long could this little family hold like this? They had seven of the locks now. And that was incredible progress in very little time. But would they manage to find the remaining locks, or would that burden be passed along to Mina and Josh after her lifetime? Had she set up her own generational obligation, after all her efforts to get out from under the Rose?

Caroline shook her head. Better to focus on the task at hand and enjoy this time while it lasted.

Her attention was turned to where Alice was sitting off by herself, in the atrium, handling an enamel vase covered in a pattern of crisscrossing rue leaves. Alice looked pale, like she hadn't slept well. Caroline wasn't sure what was going on with her. Yes, Rose had been a little more sinister than their usual ghost, but Caroline hadn't lost any sleep over banishing her.

Or maybe it was that she was lonely? It had to be hard, with Riley and Caroline paired off, and Alice...well, Alice had never shown much interest in anybody.

Maybe it was more cumulative stress?

Caroline stroked Ben's arm as she passed. He smiled up at her, content, but stayed in his seat as she sat next to Alice on her chaise. "You all right, sweetie? You seem a little off."

"My grandparents are coming back to town early," Alice said, her voice shaking. Caroline put her arm around Alice's narrow shoulders. Alice sank against her, leaning her head against Caroline's.

"I guess they called some of their old acquaintances here on the island and heard that I was spending too much time out of the shop. They've come to 'question my judgment and commitment to the family business.' So they're coming back to review my performance."

Caroline scoffed. "Like you're some employee?"

"I am technically their employee," Alice reminded her.

"They still suck," Caroline said. Alice made a noncommittal noise. "Come on."

Caroline dragged Alice into the parlor, where they joined their family in front of the darkened fireplace. Alice offered Mina a wan smile as she perched near her on the floor and moved a knight into a more advantageous position. While Josh offered her a grin, Nicholas grumbled openly.

Caroline took some papers out of her pocket.

"Well, I have news. I'm going to take some classes at State to finish out my biology degree," she said. "And then I'm going to apply to a folklore program at a regional university in western Kentucky. They offer a low-residency master's degree, so I'll only have to go to the campus for a week every six months or so."

Edison gasped. "That sounds amazing! Do you think I could…"

Riley held up a finger. "No."

"Oh, come on," Edison huffed. "It fits perfectly with my history background."

"You already have all of the degrees," Riley told him. "Leave some for somebody else."

Edison pouted. "Fine."

"We have more than enough on our plate," Riley said, kissing him. "We have enough challenges, enough friends, enough love."

He sighed against her mouth, "You're right."

"Would you two mind not pawing at each other in the presence of the children?" Plover huffed, appearing behind the couch.

"Thank you, Plover," Mina told him sweetly. "Someone had to say it."

"Is that so?" Ben's smile turned predatory as he pulled Caroline into his lap and kissed her soundly.

"Oh, Dad, no!" Mina gagged.

"There's nothing grosser than parental figure–level PDA," Josh said, shaking his head.

Caroline tried not to let her heart skip, telling herself that Josh probably wasn't referring to her as a "parent," just his dad. But it warmed her soul just the same. They'd accepted her. They loved her and were invested enough in her to be grossed out by PDA involving her.

Aww.

"This is like when Grandpa used to sing Grandma that 'Sexual Healing' song when he thought no one was around," Josh said, shuddering. Caroline cackled as Ben trailed kisses along her neck. Alice and Riley giggled uproariously.

"No!" Plover cried. "This is really too much! Dr. Hoult! This is beyond the pale! Have some common decency, sir! There are ladies present!"

"I'm sorry, Plover, I have a lot of time to make up for, and I'm going to have to claim all the kisses I can, while I can," Ben replied.

Plover's eyes narrowed at Ben. "I'm getting my tray."

Epilogue
Clark

CLARK SAT AT HIS DESK, shrouded in midnight darkness. He contemplated the glass of bourbon in his hand, watching the color shift by the solitary light of his green desk lamp. His burner phone was going to ring at any second, he was sure of it. And he was going to savor this moment.

Despite all the public trappings of "island contentment," it had been a year of silent, seething frustration for Clark. In the aftermath of his "failure" in utilizing Kyle, Clark had been shut out, humiliated. He'd had several of the Wellings' locks *in his grasp*, and they'd just slipped away, with no mistake on Clark's part but putting his faith in the wrong person. He'd thought Kyle to be the perfect tool—malleable, desperate enough to take terrible risks, not savvy enough to take countermeasures against Clark. To find out that he'd been betrayed by Kyle postmortem…?

Well, Clark was glad the little shit was dead, even if it wasn't by Clark's own hand.

Every development since Riley Denton had stepped on the island had been a disappointment. Hell, he'd even lost his vantage point to spy on Shaddow House when Clifford Martin's incompetence went from helpful (making Gray Fern Cottage unrentable and therefore available for Clark's exclusive spying use) to obstructive (pissing Ben off so badly that he'd returned to the island). He'd thought he was managing the Wellings' expectations, even after Kyle's misstep. But then, they'd shut him out of their operations, ignored him, insulted him, hired an outsider to operate independently of him, and expected Clark not to object. And yes, Clark had been pleased that Cole had been found dead off-island in what he could only assume was some *girl-power* triumph for Riley and her coven. That could only work in Clark's favor, making his employers more frantic, putting *them* at the disadvantage.

Yes, it would make his job more difficult in the long run. But the problem with Cole had been resolved without dirtying Clark's hands. In the big picture, he considered that a zero-sum balance. Clark was all about the big picture, when the big picture looked like dollar signs.

The silence of his office was broken by the buzzing of his burner phone.

Clark smirked and held his hand over the phone. He let it ring four times. When he finally picked up, he drawled, "Imagine my surprise, to receive this call, when you've made it clear that my services were no longer required."

"Don't get smart now, Graves. It doesn't suit you," the voice on the other end of the line rasped.

Clark snorted. "I can do anything I like. I'm not the one who is losing to a bunch of girls, nerds, and dead people."

"You seem to forget the leverage we hold over you," his

employer seethed. "Being disbarred would be the *least* of your concerns if we decide to apply that leverage."

Clark frowned, even if he was sure that was a bluff. He was ninety percent sure. "I don't see why our relationship has to become adversarial now after so many years of working together. You've done some things you regret. I have made errors in judgment. There's no reason why we both can't salvage the situation."

"I'm assuming your inside connection is still in place?" the voice asked.

Clark smirked. "Absolutely."

"And you're prepared to apply the necessary pressure?"

And even though there was a tiny, almost imperceptible pang of something like conscience in his gut, Clark answered, "Without hesitation."

"Redeem yourself, Clark, and we can give you what you want. Fail us and, well, you won't have anything to worry about. Ever."

The connection closed with an electronic beep. Clark rolled his eyes and stared into the darkness.

Time to get to work.

Acknowledgments

As always, thank you to my patient friends and family, who listen with grace when I complain and fret. I would like to thank Jenn Mason, whose expertise was essential in answering the question, "What happens when you hit a person with a moped?" Jessica Roux's *Floriography* provided obscure and helpful information about the meaning of flowers. Thank you to my wonder-agent, Natanya Wheeler of Nancy Yost Literary Agency, who brings so many amazing things to my life. To Rose Hilliard, thank you for giving me the creative freedom to write without limits—even if those limits would probably be sensible. And finally, thank you, Jocelyn Travis, for all of your help and encouragement as we got this story ready for print!

About the Author

Molly Harper is the author of more than forty paranormal romance, contemporary romance, women's fiction, and young adult titles. A lifelong romance reader, she graduated with a Master of Fine Arts degree from Seton Hill University, focusing on writing popular fiction. She lived in Kentucky for most of her life before recently moving to Michigan with her family…and she's still figuring out how to choose outerwear and play complicated winter card games.

Website: mollyharper.com
Instagram: @mollyharperauth